LOVERS

Judith Krantz
LOVERS

CROWN PUBLISHERS, INC.   NEW YORK

Published by Crown Publishers, Inc., 201 East 50th Street, New York,
New York 10022. Member of the Crown Publishing Group.

Random House, Inc. New York, Toronto, London, Sydney, Auckland

CROWN is a trademark of Crown Publishers, Inc.

Manufactured in the United States of America

Design by June Bennett-Tantillo

Library of Congress Cataloging-in-Publication Data
Krantz, Judith.
Lovers / by Judith Krantz.—1st ed.
p.   cm.
1. Man-woman relationships—California—Los Angeles—Fiction.
2. Women in the advertising industry—Fiction.
3. Los Angeles (Calif.)—Fiction.   I. Title.
PS3561.R264L68   1994
813'.54—dc20   93-44175
                                                            CIP

ISBN 0-517-59333-5

10 9 8 7 6 5 4 3 2 1

First Edition

For Steve, with all my deep continuing love. As yet another professional football season begins and my husband becomes, if not hard to find, all but impossible to interrupt, there is no one else to whom I would dream of dedicating this novel. When the games are over, I know he's always there to read a fresh chapter and become that indispensable, honest, clear thinking, often inspired and inspiring sounding board all writers need—and only a lucky few can find in their own home.

Acknowledgments

As always, I've depended on the kindness of top professionals to give me inside knowledge of the workings of their worlds, and as has happened so often in the past, I've met nothing but generosity and warmth and welcome. I couldn't have written *Lovers* without these people.

Warren Titus, Chairman of the Seabourn Line and one of the leaders of the world's cruise industry, who gave me invaluable amounts of his time, information, and a distillation of his long experience.

Adrienne Hall, a dear longtime friend and one of the top creative women in the world of advertising, the Vice Chairman of Eisamen, Johns & Laws. Adrienne gave me extraordinary perspective on the advertising scene in Los Angeles and New York over the decades.

Russ Collins, the brilliant and charming President and Creative Director of Fattal & Collins, the Los Angeles advertising agency on which I did not, in any way, model Frost/Rourke/Bernheim in this novel. Had either my imaginary Archie Rourke or Byron Bernheim been like Russ, my heroine would have married him as quickly as possible and this novel would have been a very short story with an instantly predictable ending.

Eric Hirshberg, Vice President/Art Director of Fattal & Collins, a delightful and multitalented young man who turns into a demon basketball player when he's not creating extraordinary graphics.

Buzz Kaplan, Executive Vice President of Fattal & Collins, who is the spark plug as well as the glue holding all the talents of the agency together with his kindness. If this is a mixed metaphor, it's because Buzz isn't easily described.

Colleen Mackay, Assistant Account Executive of Fattal & Collins, a woman who operates beautifully and calmly in what is still somewhat of a male-dominated world.

LOVERS

1

In Los Angeles there is no driver who isn't prudently wary of the peppery band who pilot tiny Volkswagens. They are known to be a race of aggressive, intrepid free spirits who make it a point of pride to dart pugnaciously in front of any Rolls or Mercedes ever built; who automatically and outrageously take precedence at four-way crossroads and zoom unapologetically into parking spaces that have clearly been staked out by more impressive and less quickly maneuverable vehicles.

Gigi Orsini bought herself a flat-out flaming scarlet Volkswagen convertible when she decided to accept the copywriting job at Frost/Rourke/Bernheim, the advertising agency that had been wooing her for months.

For years she'd dutifully driven a worthy but dull Volvo, a gift from Billy Ikehorn, her stepmother, but now, during the three-day weekend she allotted herself between leaving one job and starting another, Gigi plunked down a bundle of slowly accumulated cash for a car she could relate to. She put its top down and caressed its gleaming flanks; this mad machine, frisky and lighthearted, was exactly right for her new maturity, her new career, her new status. It was a nimble, merry car that suited Gigi's optimism in this year of 1983, a year in which Barbra Streisand had the film industry poised to judge *Yentl*, the first film she dared to star in and direct as well as produce; a year in which L.A. got ready to host the Summer Olympics; a year during which Queen Elizabeth, game under her headscarf, visited President Reagan's mountaintop ranch in the middle of a violent storm; a year that saw Kareem Abdul-Jabbar, in his prime, sign an unprecedented contract that paid him a million and a half dollars a season; a year in which the finality of the last episode of "M*A*S*H" struck a notable note of sadness in the otherwise prosperous lives of millions of Americans.

Now, on an optimistically promising late fall morning in this optimistic year early in the optimistic 1980s, Gigi Orsini, electric with nerves, teeth grinding with caution and apprehension, feeling none of the arrogant insouciance a VW owner deserved, slowly cruised the parking lot behind the old-fashioned, vaguely Spanish-style office building on Sunset Boulevard near La Cienega where Frost/Rourke/Bernheim was located. It was the first day of her new job and she hadn't felt so shy since beginning high school, when she'd been as bashful as she had ever been in her normally unself-conscious life.

If only she didn't have a built-in need to disturb the status quo of her life, to upset the applecart, if only, Gigi jittered to herself, she'd been able to remain happily in the safe and wildly booming bosom of Scruples Two, the fashion catalog that she'd come to think of as the family business, she wouldn't now be looking for a parking space in a state of gibbering fidgets, about to take her first steps in advertising.

Archie Rourke, copywriter, and Byron Berenson Bernheim III, art director, were two of the three partners in the agency that had set up shop in Los Angeles six months ago, arriving fresh from New York. As Gigi pulled in gingerly next to a sleek Porsche, she reminded herself of the words that Archie had used while he was trying to persuade her to come to work for them.

"Advertising is the *major* art form of the second half of the twentieth century," he'd said. "Three hundred years from now, when a museum curator is putting together a show to make our era live again, the material will be drawn primarily from television commercials and magazine ads." She hadn't made her decision based on the content of his words, but she'd noted the absolute sense of conviction with which he delivered them, as if the worlds of the theatrical arts, writing, music, and photography existed only to be incorporated in great advertising. They'd aroused Gigi's sense of adventure and given birth to a curiosity that had eventually led to this paralyzing moment.

Gigi punched the car-alarm code absently and smoothed down her skirt with hands that trembled slightly. At least she was appropriately dressed. Each time she'd had lunch with Byron and Archie, they had worn the California version of East Coast high dignity, sporting Armani suits with fine, striped dress shirts and superior ties. Advertising, she understood, both from Archie's words and the way he and Byron put themselves together in the heartland of casual, was a business that took itself seriously. Both of them looked as if they could be agents, and agents were the most rigidly well-tailored men in California.

Certainly Archie was as smooth-talking and persuasive as any agent she'd ever met, a man she could only describe to herself with an inward giggle as a handsome brute, as if his rakish, devil-may-care brooding looks, with the unbeatable combination of black-Irish curly hair and policeman-blue eyes had been assembled for viewing through the pages of a Regency romance.

Rusty-haired Byron was a contrast to Archie, a tall, elegant man with a mild and slightly awkward manner at the corners of which lurked an interesting edge of mockery. His world, Gigi thought as she walked through rows of cars, seemed to be filled with private jokes, and his gray eyes often widened and flashed with humor as he sketched his striking graphic ideas on tablecloths. She was amused at the way the two men interacted. They'd been a team for so long that sometimes they sounded like two sides of the same fairly irresistible person.

What was bothering her as much as anything, Gigi realized as she threaded her way reluctantly across the parking lot toward Sunset Boulevard and the entrance of the building, was that damn magazine article she'd read last night. What evil hazard had thrust it in her path, that helpful article in that caring woman's magazine, an article that told her everything she needed to know about the first day on a new job?

She hoped gloomily that she wasn't going to be driven to volunteering for the company's annual blood drive, one of the recommended ways in which to get to know your fellow workers. Perhaps she could get away with inconspicuously observing the local atmosphere before she made an active move in what the writer had called "workplace politics." The article warned sternly against getting involved with the first friendly people you met, since they were bound to be the "office losers"; it instructed her to be upbeat without being overly bubbly, for bubbly would seem desperate; to smile in a way that indicated warmth but not unprofessional pushiness; to make a seating chart of her co-workers in order to memorize their names and to prove herself quietly over a period of months as she waited patiently, without a touch of fatal overeagerness, to make an impression in the company's "collective corporate subconscious," a concept that the writer of the article had assured her was rock-firm even if unacknowledged.

"I will be good," Gigi murmured firmly in the immortal words of Queen Victoria when she discovered that she was about to succeed to the throne.

"Oy!" Gigi halted suddenly as she walked past a delivery truck. Goosy, twitching with nerves, overloaded with all the information she'd absorbed, she suddenly needed to make a final inspection. She wore her one gray flannel suit, a recent gift from Prince, the great New York designer, cut with classic perfection. Its hemline, demure but not dowdy, bisected the middle of her knee; under the jacket she wore an immaculate white cotton blouse. She was five feet four inches tall but looked taller as she stood in perfectly plain black high-heeled pumps worn with opaque black panty hose. Her only jewelry was a pair of simple pearl earrings and the Cartier "Bathtub" watch with an alligator band that Billy had given her as a good-bye present at her going-away party when she left Scruples Two, a watch as expensive as it was discreet.

Was anyone ever so absolutely right, Gigi wondered, could anyone make a better first impression? But being absolutely right went against her grain. Her own inclination was always toward the offbeat, the riotously unexpected, and although this leap into advertising demanded a new wardrobe, an old impulse had led her to pull her favorite hat down over her hair, streaked by her own hand in all the reddish-orangy-yellowy-golds of a cluster of variegated marigolds.

It was a deep-crowned late-Edwardian hat made from a beautifully faded floral linen. The hatband was a double width of heavy crimson taffeta, trimmed in front with two red cherries, a large red velvet rose, and several appliquéd green velvet leaves. The wide brim was pulled up at the front and anchored to the band by the rose.

This was a hat that a girl had worn when she'd seen her fiancé off to the Great War, Gigi thought, a brave, frivolous hat that had made her face bright. She knew that the fiancé had come back from the war, otherwise why had the hat's owner kept it so carefully stuffed and wrapped with tissue, in the box bearing the name of a London milliner that Gigi had discovered as she searched for antique lingerie? Until today, Gigi had kept the hat on a stand as a decoration for her bedroom, but now it transformed the severity of her costume with an aura of missing charm. She adjusted it carefully. The eighty-year-old hat felt as right as everything else she had on felt foreign and constricting.

Gigi pulled back her shoulders, tilted her chin, and marched out from the protection of the delivery truck, picking up speed and snap as she rounded the corner, entered the building, and, with a hint of her usual insubordinately dancing Jazz Baby walk, rapidly mounted the flight of steps that led to the offices of Frost/Rourke/ Bernheim.

"Mr. Rourke said to tell you he felt terrible about it, but he and Mr. Bernheim have had to go over to a client's for an emergency meeting," the receptionist said as Gigi announced herself. "He just couldn't be sure when they'd get back."

"Oh." Gigi looked at her blankly.

"I'm Polly. He left instructions to give you a temporary office while you waited." The receptionist scrutinized her with wide eyes, looking as dubious as Gigi felt. Gigi had been asked to come in after the working day was under way, at ten-thirty, so that Archie or Byron would be able to take her around the office, introduce her around, and get her settled.

"Whatever you say," Gigi responded, pulling her hat even more firmly down over her forehead so that it covered her bangs and pointed eyebrows, her curiosity high to see the offices in which Archie and Byron worked. She followed Polly into a maze of corridors with glimpses of large, high-ceilinged rooms in which a small number of people were hard at work, looking oddly scattered in their underfurnished quarters. The offices of Scruples Two were decidedly short on elbow room compared to FRB, Gigi observed. A few of the workers looked up incuriously as she passed and then turned back to their typewriters, word processors, or drawing boards, immediately identifying her pulled-together, elegant self as not germane to their tasks.

It was like being a visitor on a film set, Gigi thought as her eyes darted from left to right under the brim of her hat without catching a single interested glance. They recognized her instantly as neither potential cast nor crew and, without prejudice, dismissed her as unworthy of interest. Advertising might well be the art form of the second half of the twentieth century, she observed, but those few of its practitioners she observed seemed to be passionately scruffy and as carelessly dressed as ballet dancers in their oldest, drabbest rehearsal clothes. One or two of them sported bright plumage in odd colors and unusual shapes. There was too much of a contrast in this for it not to mean something, she realized, but what?

"Here we are," the receptionist said, gesturing as they finally entered a tiny room where fluorescent tubes hung down from a high ceiling and cast an uninviting light. "It's too small for two people, so nobody ever uses it."

"Doesn't anybody have his own office?" Gigi asked.

"No way. They don't like to be alone, it makes them nervous. Miss Frost is the only one with a private office. The creative teams are joined at the hip . . . you'll see. Can I get you some coffee?"

"No, thanks," Gigi answered. "I'll be fine here, Polly." She gave the retreating receptionist a close-mouthed smile that she hoped was warm yet not desperate, neither overeager nor unprofessional. The little room contained nothing more than a nondescript desk covered with towering piles of hundreds of magazines: *Vogues* and *Bazaars* from all countries, years of back copies of *Elle*, *Town and Country*, and some ultra-high-fashion magazines from France and Italy that she barely recognized. She prowled around the desk, closed the door to the office firmly, and sank into a surprisingly comfortable, battered old armchair that she found hidden behind the desk.

Well, she knew Polly and she knew where Polly sat. That was a beginning. She could, of course, start leafing through the magazines she assumed had been dumped there for her inspiration, but the idea wasn't remotely tempting, following on the heels of the shock of this non-welcome. There was a phone on the desk, but the only number that came to mind was 911.

Somehow, Gigi told herself, as she took deep breaths to conquer her hyperventilating, she'd made a grave mistake about the corporate subconscious. There was no chance she would let herself be introduced to those people out there in her overdressed state. Why hadn't Archie or Byron warned her? Why had they entrapped her by their own attire? At least when she'd started high school she'd known exactly what all the other kids would be wearing, and that knowledge had enabled her to get through the first awful day before she made human contact. Of course, if she were truly, deeply self-confident, it wouldn't matter—she'd have the basic inner assurance to meet anyone dressed in anything, assaulting the corporate norm without a second thought. She'd be Anna Magnani, she'd be Lauren Hutton, she'd be Martha Graham. No, Bella Abzug. Better yet, Barbara Jordan. How could her hands and feet be icy while sweat was forming on her forehead? How could she, Graziella Giovanna Orsini, be reduced to acting like such a wimp just because she hadn't known the dress code? On the other hand, even Ralph Waldo Emerson had admitted to submitting with admiration to a lady who had told him that the sense of being perfectly well-dressed gives a feeling of inward tranquillity that religion is powerless to bestow.

As she arrived at this reflection, the door opened without a knock, and someone stuck a head into the room.

"Where are you?" an unknown man's voice asked.

"I'm working," Gigi muttered, hunching farther down until only the top of her hat could be seen as she buried her face behind a magazine. Emerson's presence had vanished.

"Jeez. Already? I thought we could destroy a few bagels and trade life stories," he said, stepping into the room.

"Maybe later," Gigi said testily, not raising her eyes, "much later. I'm getting into this."

"I'm David," he said. She had the impression of someone trying to peer down at her from a great height.

"Gigi," she admitted, shifting her chair closer to the highest pile of magazines and pressing herself into the lee of the desk, the shield of the magazine almost touching her nose.

"Polly told me you were here. Sure you don't want a bagel? I just got 'em fresh. Or there's some terrific Chinese stuff from yesterday. We pulled an all-nighter and there's lots left. I could stick it in the microwave. I've got a box of Fig Newtons in my office, and an espresso machine. Come on, I'll make you a cappuccino." His voice was eager and full of curiosity as he advanced, about to edge around the desk, obviously trying to get a look at her.

"No! Absolutely not! Nothing!" Gigi turned herself into the smallest possible surface, bringing her knees up to her chin and planting her shoes on the seat of the chair. Only shoes, hat, hands, legs, and the smallest slivers of gray flannel on either side of her hips and shoulders were visible as she menaced him with her voice.

"Nothing?" he repeated incredulously.

"Food is the last thing on my mind," Gigi said as coldly and dismissively as possible, cowering in her chair. "I told you I was busy. Close the door when you leave."

"Sure," he said in disappointment. "I'll catch you later. Maybe we can lunch? *Great* hat."

In less than a minute he had rematerialized as a large hand holding an apple. "Got it! You're into organic food. This is Mrs. Gooch's guaranteed best. Now, what's your sign? I'm a Leo. I'm not convinced about astrology, but you can't rule it out. Tell me about the first time you went to bed with a guy. How much of a disappointment was it? Did you cheat a lot in school? How much credit card debt do you feel comfortable with? Are you married, single, divorced, or—"

"OUT!" Gigi screeched, batting the apple to the floor.

My first office loser, she thought, as she heard the door shut. He was worse than those warned about in the magazine. They'd said that losers would be suspiciously overfriendly because they had no one else to talk to. They hadn't mentioned maniacal personal questions. The article had emphasized that you had to watch out for the office outcasts who clung to every newcomer. It was fatal to let them link themselves to you. You'd be known by the company you kept, and it was better to lunch alone than to lunch with the wrong people. Her sign, indeed!

Getting rid of that leech had made her feel more in control. Her mind was working again, Gigi realized. She leapt up and, with first one shoulder and then the other firmly pressed to the office door so that no one else could come in, she hastily snaked out of her skirt and jacket. Next she adjusted the plain white shirt, which fell below mid-thigh. She rolled the sleeves up above her elbows, undid the buttons so that it fell open just above her small, high, upstanding breasts, unconfined by any bra, and flipped up the collar so that it reached her ears. She could leave the fine white material hanging loose like a smock, but she wasn't your basic smock person. Remorsefully but without hesitation, she took off her hat and attacked the hatband. Once removed from the hat, it wrapped twice around her waist, a snug, wide cummerbund. Opaque panty hose could easily pass for tights, she assured herself, fingering her earrings. Pearls wouldn't do. She put them in her bag, hung the two joined cherries over one almost-pointed ear, and thrust the red velvet rose firmly into the front of the cummerbund. Damn, she wished she had a mirror, Gigi thought, grinning as she fluffed out the swinging silken bell of her hair. She folded her skirt and jacket carefully and hid them in one of the empty desk drawers, along with what was left of the hat.

Now, ready for anything, she leafed rapidly through a copy of Italian *Vogue*. FRB had been invited to pitch for the account of Indigo Seas, an established, San Francisco–based manufacturer of swimsuits designed especially for the oversized woman, and the pitch was to be the first campaign Gigi would work on. As she turned the pages, so much more outrageously avant-garde than those of American *Vogue*, she saw nothing but tiny two-piece suits on girls with bodies no mature woman would want to contemplate in her worst daydream. Hell, brooded Gigi, she didn't need to look

9

at magazines that had nothing to do with reality, she needed to be alone in a room with a word processor and her imagination, or else in a big department store, communicating with living humans, suffering women engaged in the winter ordeal of shopping for swimsuits for resort wear or the following summer. What's more, she was starving. Chinese food . . . noodles, spareribs, spicy spring rolls, sweet and sour squab . . . if only someone else but an office outcast had made that offer, she thought longingly. Funny how reheated take-out was so much better than the first time around, and she'd been too nervous to have breakfast. Why was it that when that intrusive lunatic had mentioned Chinese food, she'd started to crave it?

Impatiently she slammed the magazine down and started pacing around the room. Not only was this like being kept in after class, but it was unbelievably rude. Archie and Byron had come after her hungrily, courting her with lunches, phone calls, visionary words, and promises of a fabulous future in advertising. She'd said no to them many times before she'd finally said yes, yet now here she was, seduced and abandoned, in an office she'd never visited before, stuck in a cell adorned only by windows that offered her a small, grimy view of a parking lot, with no idea of how to escape and no information about their return. What if their meeting lasted all day? She peeked quickly into the dauntingly confusing length of empty corridor outside the office and realized that even if she could find someone to direct her back to Polly's desk, she didn't have the inclination to attempt it.

Gigi returned to the armchair, slumped back into the worn-out cushions, put her legs up on the desk, and lost herself in morose contemplation of her new shoes. She had to admit in all modesty that she had truly marvelous legs, she decided, relaxing and lowering the lovely smooth shells of her eyelids so that the long lashes on which she used three layers of black mascara set up a bristling hedge in front of the pupils of her eyes, which were the green of a Granny Smith apple. Perfectly divine legs . . . legs to conjure with . . . legs to cause an empire to topple . . . legs . . . legs . . .

Gigi was sleeping deeply an hour later when Archie and Byron burst into the office, uttering apologies to the empty room.

"Shit! She's gone!" Byron shouted.

"Calm down," Archie said. "Where could she go?"

"Back to Scruples Two . . . wait, see those shoes?"

"More to the point," Archie crooned as he walked around the desk, "see those legs!"

The two men gazed down at Gigi, delighted to find the butterfly they had been chasing for many months at last captured in their net. She was a rare prize, a collector's item, and God knows they needed her desperately. The powers that be at Indigo Seas had been enchanted by Gigi's copy for Scruples Two, and she could be the key to capturing a vital piece of business. Not only that, but the two of them specialized in food accounts, they hadn't yet been able to find a truly talented fashion copywriter, and the acquisition of Gigi would open doors to a new set of potential clients.

"You just going to stand there and admire her?" Byron inquired.

Startled, yanked back to reality, Archie broke out of his contemplation and growled in his best Papa Bear imitation. "Who's been sleeping in my chair?"

"You jerk, you'll frighten her," Byron hissed.

"Well, you try, then."

"Gigi? Ah, Gigi . . . are you awake?" Archie whispered loudly. "Come on, wake up."

Gigi slept on.

"Maybe we should just let her sleep," Byron suggested. "Maybe she's tired."

"She started on the payroll this morning," Archie said firmly. "And everybody's always tired in this business. If they aren't, they're not working hard enough." With a quick gesture he snatched Gigi's shoes off her feet and beat a tattoo with their heels on the desktop.

Gigi's eyes flew open. "What's going on? . . . Give those back!"

"See," Archie said, pleased with himself, "it works every time. Women have a deeply rooted protectiveness about their items of adornment. Now, a man might have slept through it, but—"

"Say, hello, Gigi, we're sorry we're late," Byron interrupted him, punching him in the shoulder.

"Where are my manners?" Archie asked the heavens. "Gigi!

The house of Frost, Rourke and Bernheim is thrilled and delighted to welcome you to its collective heart. On behalf of my partners and myself I wish to extend our most sincere apologies for not being here to greet you this morning, but alas . . ."

"My shoes," Gigi demanded, swinging her legs off the desk.

He gave them back to her with a bow. Gigi put them on and jumped up, feeling an immediate boost as she moved to the vertical plane.

"I was expecting the turnkey with my bread and water any minute now," she said severely. "It's like Devil's Island in here, without the ocean view."

"Didn't anyone offer you coffee or a bagel?" Archie asked.

"I came in here two and a half hours ago," she replied, forgetting her weird visitor and looking at her watch. "It seems to be lunchtime and, as I remember, you guys intend to take me out for lunch today. It was billed as a little welcome party."

"Damn! Wrong. Sorry, Gigi, unavoidable change of plans," Archie said.

"We have to postpone that lunch," Byron explained, embarrassed. "As of right now, we're on deadline for a totally new campaign for Bugattini Pasta. The account guy came back from Italy last night and he's changed his mind about the stuff he approved before he left."

This sort of abrupt switch was normal in the agency business, although it couldn't have come at a worse time, he gloomed to himself. The client's demands always came first, especially since Bugattini was the most considerable of the few clients they had. They'd just have to leave her to her magazines for a few hours while they tore into the new plans.

"Wait a minute, Byron," Gigi said indignantly, "forget the lunch. I can find my own way to the nearest tuna sandwich. But you and Archie promised to take me around the office and introduce me to everybody, and spend the afternoon settling me in. I'm not spending one more minute in this room! I feel as if I've been shanghaied and put on a boat to Macao. This is not starting well, and when a fish stinks, it starts at the head. So far you've been nothing but lunches, promises, and no delivery. You two came chasing after *me*, remember? I never dreamed of a job in advertising until you guys talked me into it. My old job is waiting for me with open arms, and I'm returning to it."

She glared at them in righteous outrage, her fists on her hips, her almost-turned-up little nose as accusing as the bright spots of anger that had suddenly appeared on her cheeks. Gigi Orsini aroused was a splendid combination of her fire-eating ancestral stock, totally Irish on her mother's side and Florentine Italian on her father's. She shook her head vigorously in thorough disapproval of the two men, her long wispy bangs flew up from her pointed eyebrows, and every wrathful curve of her perfectly formed oval head managed to express the feeling of affront she had been experiencing since her arrival.

"But, Gigi . . ."

"Gigi, we've got no choice . . ."

"*We're* the creative team on Bugattini, the two of us, it's our biggest new account . . ."

"Be reasonable . . ."

"Fuck reasonable. I'm out of here," Gigi said with dignity, picking up her handbag.

"So *this* is what you look like," a familiar voice said from the door.

"David, where the hell were you?" Byron shouted.

"This is all your fault, David," Archie accused him. "Now Gigi's trying to leave because you didn't take care of her the way we told you to."

"This continues to stink," Gigi said in disdain, moving purposefully toward the door. On top of neglect, they had actually *planned* to fob her off on the office loser, she thought grimly, brushing by, without a glance, the lanky man who leaned on the door frame. He put out one long arm, wrapped it around her waist, swiveled her around, and returned her to the room, where he held her firmly in place by standing behind her with his arms tightly around her waist.

"Let go!"

"Nope."

"*Let go!*"

"I will not. You've rejected me enough today. You actually hurt my feelings." He sounded amused—worse, he was totally unimpressed by her words and her vigorous attempts to get out of his grasp.

"David, hands off," Archie commanded, trying vigorously to pry Gigi out of David's hold.

"Both of you, stop it!" Byron joined in the tug-of-war, making it a three-way battle, grabbing Gigi by her shoulders and pulling her toward him.

This wasn't entirely unpleasant, Gigi thought. Scruples Two, with its largely feminine staff, had never made such flattering claims on her body. Nevertheless, these rude, untrustworthy creeps were probably leaving bruises.

"FIRE!" she screamed, as loudly as she could, and was rewarded by her freedom as each of the three men released her and dashed into the corridor. As they milled about, not finding a sign of smoke, she righted her ruffled feathers. These goons expected her to be reasonable, she realized. They *took it for granted*, although the word "reasonable" had never been mentioned in previous discussions of the conditions of her new job. But she'd *been* reasonable for most of her life, and she hadn't made a break with the past to continue in that mode. If she even once allowed them to think of her as reasonable, she'd be stuck with it, and they'd tack on "reliable," and "undemanding" as well, all adding up to an impermissible "predictable." She planted herself on her instincts; it was lunch or good-bye. If the concerns of Bugattini Pasta could be allowed to overshadow her arrival, she was in the wrong place.

By the time the men had returned to the room, Gigi was perched on the desk, her arms crossed, her legs crossed, and her bright head tilted at an ominous angle.

"Where are we eating," Gigi asked Archie, "now that you've worked up an appetite?"

"The Dôme?" Archie sighed, giving up. Another expensive lunch. She'd better be worth it.

"Why not?" Gigi smiled approval.

"David, go get your jacket and tie," Byron told him.

"He's coming too?" Gigi sniffed in disbelief. David paid no attention to her, busy looking for the big horn-rimmed glasses he'd lost in the shuffle and unsuccessfully trying to smooth down his too-long brownish hair that, combined with his beaky nose, gave him the look of an untidy, uncommonly agreeable young eagle.

"Naturally," Archie said.

"He grabbed me. I don't permit that sort of thing."

"I had to," David said lazily, settling his glasses on his nose with relief. "You're my teammate. I had to keep you from making a big mistake. That's one of the things teammates are for."

"Teammate?" she exclaimed, jumping off the desk in a rage. Now they'd really lost her.

"You and David are the new creative team on Indigo Seas," Archie said. "Do you mean he didn't tell you?"

"He's our best art director," Byron added, "after me."

"He never mentioned a word," Gigi said indignantly.

"Sometimes young David Melville has a problem with indirection," Archie agreed indulgently.

"He asked me things I wouldn't dream of telling a stranger," Gigi sputtered.

"Yeah, it's best to get all that personal baggage out of the way right off the bat. We encourage it in creative teams," Byron told her. "Prevents embarrassing surprises and awkward moments."

"I'll get my jacket," David said graciously, "while Gigi gets dressed. We can't take her to the Dôme in just a see-through nighty and panty hose, provocative though it is. 'Tain't fittin'."

"And what have we here?" a woman asked in a cool, clear voice, entering the receptionist's office as Gigi, Archie, Byron, and David, now a festively attired, laughing group, were about to leave on their way to lunch.

"Victoria! We didn't expect you back till tomorrow," Archie said. "Gigi, this is the Frost in FRB. Victoria Frost, Gigi Orsini."

"Why this mass exodus?" Victoria Frost asked Archie, not greeting Gigi.

"Lunch at the Dôme," Archie answered expansively. "Come with us, we're celebrating."

Gigi's smile died as she watched them. Where she came from, people said hello, shook hands when they were introduced, and looked at each other in the process. They even smiled. In fact, they always smiled, for it was all but impossible to greet someone, even at a memorial service, without automatically turning up the corners of your mouth, however faintly. Victoria Frost's severely lovely face remained expressionless except for her dark eyebrows, which indicated surprise.

"Indeed? And just what are you celebrating?" she asked evenly, finally looking down at Gigi as appraisingly as anyone ever had, taking her in with one swift glance and visually dismissing her.

"My first day on my new job here," Gigi said firmly. She had not spent half of her formative years in the home of Billy Ikehorn, who had no peer in the world of well-dressed women, to be intimidated by a look from any woman alive, although she recognized that Victoria Frost, in her pure sweep of espresso-brown wool, had conclusively nailed the too-simple-to-be-anything-but-perfect look as totally as an Olympic gymnast receiving marks of ten from every judge.

"Your what?" Victoria asked in cold astonishment.

"Victoria," Byron broke in, "we probably forgot to tell you, there's been so much else going on while you were out of town, but you must remember that we tried to hire Gigi away from Scruples Two."

"When last I heard, she wasn't interested," Victoria retorted. "What changed her mind, Byron?"

"I doubt that *Byron* knows exactly," Gigi answered. "But *I* have my reasons."

"And I'm sure they're valid. However, that offer was made some time ago, unless I'm mistaken. And turned down several times. Just exactly when did Gigi decide to grace us with her presence?"

Gigi spoke up. "Oh, I believe it was—let me see, exactly, in point of fact, *precisely* at nine-forty-five, last Thursday night, after one too many glasses of wine on an empty stomach. On the other hand, it may possibly have been five minutes later. Or earlier. I didn't check my watch. Why do you ask, Victoria? Isn't the offer still open? Am I unwelcome?"

"Victoria!" Archie said warningly.

"Gigi!" Byron implored at the same second.

Gigi ignored them, addressing herself directly to the tall, slim young woman with severe brown hair and severe brown eyes.

"Because if I'm unwelcome, to anyone, there's still a tuna

sandwich with my name on it waiting back at my desk at Scruples Two."

"I don't mean to sound ungracious . . ."

"You've succeeded remarkably," Gigi interrupted.

"However, my partners and I agreed to consult each other on hiring and firing," Victoria continued, as if Gigi hadn't spoken. "I'm not personally familiar with your work. As far as I understand it, you haven't had any advertising experience, and I wonder if this is the right moment to . . ."

"Victoria, shut the hell up," Archie said, grabbing her by the elbow and marching her quickly down the hall and into another office.

"Well, well, well," Gigi drawled, "I can see why I haven't met Miss Frost before, Byron. She was your horrid little secret. Good-bye forever, Byron. Good-bye, David, oh, and say good-bye to Archie for me." She tucked her handbag under her arm and started out of the door.

"Wait! Come on, Gigi, stop it!" Byron blocked her way. "Victoria has nothing to do with the creative side, Gigi, she's strictly new business and keeping the clients happy. You'll never, *ever* have to work with her, I promise! She's just surprised that this happened while she was gone."

"If this is the way she reacts to surprise, how does she act when she's provoked?" Gigi asked, trying to get around Byron but finding it impossible.

"I've never seen her provoked," Byron answered, moving quickly from side to side. "I've never seen her like this, either. She must have had a terrible trip. Please, Gigi, don't leave," he pleaded. "You know we want you madly, we adore your stuff, and God knows, we're all in love with you. You sleep like an angelic baby and you wake up like a flower."

"All well and good," Gigi said, trying not to be softened by his words, "but the lovely Miss Vicky—"

"Don't *ever* call her Vicky," David said, trying without luck to keep from laughing.

"The lovely, welcoming, easygoing Miss Vicky isn't my cup of tea. Byron, you can't force me to work here, you know, so please get out of my way or I'll be forced to knee you in the groin."

"Knee *me* instead," David said, planting himself in front of Byron, his arms wide apart to show that he wouldn't defend himself. "There's a pecking order around here, and I'm paid to take the pain."

"Oh God." Gigi collapsed in a fit of giggles. "I've never had to cope with so many big silly men in one morning in my entire life. Are we bonding yet?"

"Still there? Good work, Byron, stout fellow, David," Archie said, running back into the reception room. "Victoria is sorry she can't join us for lunch, Gigi, and she begs you to accept her deep apology for the unforgivable way she behaved. She has a terrible migraine, PMS, and a ghastly cold coming on. Allergy attack too, pollen or whatever, something in the air, but she's thrilled that you took the job."

"What a shame she can't join us," Gigi said lightly, knowing that she'd met an enemy. "Perhaps it might help Miss Vicky's symptoms if she took the poker out."

2

L ess than a week before Gigi
joined Frost/Rourke/Bernheim, on a Wednesday morning in November of 1983, she had arrived at Scruples Two determined to
fire her secretary, Sally Lou Evans, who never finished the work
Gigi asked her to do, yet had such a maddeningly unlimited and
imaginative repertoire of excuses that she somehow managed to
squeak by. Pretty Sally Lou was wildly popular with the other
secretaries in the office, always ready to offer her homemade
brownies, a tip on mending broken fingernails, or a flattering opinion on a new haircut. She was an attractive nuisance, an excuse
for gathering and loitering, the office equivalent of a hometown
soda fountain or the best truckers' diner on a long highway. Gigi
had never fired anyone in her life, but when the office manager,
Josie Speilberg, to whom she'd brought her complaints, offered to
do it for her, she'd decided that she should take on the task herself.

"Come on, Gigi, it's tough to fire people. That's what I'm here for," Josie said in her self-appointed role as the most indispensable person in the entire company, relishing the prospect of a task that would be just one more item in her agenda as Vice-President in Charge of Sanity, the official title she had received as the price of turning down L. L. Bean when they'd tried to lure her away from Scruples Two.

"I hired her, I should fire her," Gigi insisted, "it's sort of a rite of passage."

"I always fired people for Mrs. Ikehorn—I mean Mrs. Elliott," Josie said, for she still wasn't used to Billy's new married name after many years of working for her as Ellis Ikehorn's vastly rich widow. During Billy's second marriage, to Gigi's father, Vito Orsini, Josie had called her Mrs. O, which was as far as she was prepared to commit herself at the time. As it turned out, she'd been a visionary, for that marriage had lasted barely a year, leaving Gigi as Billy's only meaningful and lasting legacy. Now Josie embraced the name of Mrs. Elliott, whenever she could remember it, for she took credit for being instrumental in promoting Billy's blissful third marriage.

"Nope, thanks, Josie, but I'm going to be straight with Sally Lou. She's just not getting the job done."

"Can I give you a tip? There's one perfect way to fire people that makes it easier all around. You start out by saying, sympathetically, 'Sally Lou, I can see that you're not happy here.' Then, no matter what she says after that, you just keep repeating, 'No, Sally Lou, I know you love the office, but trust me, you're not happy here. I know you need the job, but you're not happy here. You'd be happier somewhere else.' "

"Josie, she loves it here. She's the office favorite, queen of the sorority. I'll sound like a lunatic."

"That's not important. Just get the firing over with in a friendly way. You're concerned for her, that's the message."

"I'm on my way," Gigi said firmly. "Thanks, Josie. But how will I ever be able to believe anything you tell me again, now that I know how your mind operates?"

"Well, what happened?" Josie asked Gigi when she spotted her in the company cafeteria at lunchtime.

"Sit down and I'll tell you," Gigi invited, looking dazed.

"Hard time, huh? It can be rough, but it'll never be as hard again," Josie sympathized. "It's a trial by fire. Firing must be a gender thing. Men don't have the same problems with it."

"Sally Lou thanked me."

"Say, you must have been good," Josie marveled.

"She thanked me for *noticing* that she wasn't happy. She said she liked me too much to say anything, but she's been miserable working at Scruples Two. She's been trying to make the best of it."

"Why, the little ingrate! What a nerve, after all you've put up with."

"Josie, she was just being honest. She was relieved that she didn't have to quit . . . she has a phobia about quitting."

"I don't get it."

"Sally Lou said, and I quote, sparing you her Bette-Davis-in-a-snit tone of voice, 'This is a boring office. Boring, boring, boring. There isn't a single available man around to flirt with, nobody but a lot of women, nice women, but women.' What's more, she'd expected something glamorous when she came here, because of the reputation of Scruples, the store, but the catalog business is repetitive. She thinks my writing is very nice but after all it's not gripping, like 'Dear Abby,' and there's an opening for a secretary at Creative Artists. Apparently the place is full of men, and who knows what it could lead to? She says her 'people skills' haven't been utilized here. So she kissed me a tearful, grateful good-bye, collected her pay, and left. Now I have to get a new secretary."

"Why didn't you make her stay till you'd found a replacement?" Josie demanded.

"I didn't have the heart to incarcerate her any longer. She wanted to zip right on over to CAA."

"I knew you should have let me do it," Josie said in righteous tones.

"Could you find me a new secretary, Josie, preferably a guy? Maybe he'd find a satisfactory social life here."

That evening, after work, Gigi lingered over a solitary, pre-dinner glass of wine. She'd been living alone for over three weeks while Zach Nevsky was away on location, in preproduction for a film in Montana, and he wasn't due back for another three weeks. A year ago they had rented an old house in the Hollywood Hills, on Laurel Lane, one of the many mysterious, little-known twisting streets that rise high behind the Chateau Marmont, an utterly charming semi-ruin of a more or less Spanish-Italian-French Provençal house that had been built in 1927, with three stories that climbed the steep hill, and a view of Los Angeles from every southwest-facing window.

The house had come furnished with a few basic pieces, and during the last year Gigi had remade its interior with romantic and whimsical finds from flea markets and swap meets, holding her extravagantly disparate choices together by stapling hundreds of yards of various evocative and slightly faded floral fabrics to all the walls, hanging every window in full, floating swags of white dotted swiss, and painting each floorboard in washable green deck paint so that each room had the frothy gaiety and relaxed ambiance of a summer house. She set a round table for herself inside a pair of French doors that led out to a large balcony, where the elaborate wrought iron was wreathed in white jasmine that was just beginning to bloom, scenting the air with richly potent nostalgia. On the other side of Sunset Boulevard, far below her, the lights of Los Angeles performed their traditional magic show with all the promise of city lights seen from a height anywhere in the world, and what's more, the real-estate agent had been right. On a clear day you actually could see Catalina. And so what?

She felt bleakly gloomy, Gigi realized. Heavy-hearted. In fact, utterly depressed. Zach's absence was getting to her, and it was worse every day. The last time he'd returned from a distant location shoot—and that hadn't been so long ago—he'd promised her to try to accept only those jobs that would keep him in L.A., for he was in such demand as a director that he could decide among a multitude of offers. But he had quickly become so deeply fascinated by an offer to direct a movie based on a Pulitzer Prize–winning novel about life a hundred years ago in Kalispell, Montana, that she hadn't had the heart to ask him to turn it down. How could she refuse to marry Zach and yet expect him to reject projects that fulfilled his ambition and vision? If she were ready to leave her job, become a wife, and follow him from one shoot to another, they could be together full-time, Gigi reminded herself, but exactly what kind of a life would that be, besides peripatetic?

She already knew the answer, she admitted. Even when both of them were home, they were rarely alone together. "Full-time" togetherness didn't exist for more than an hour or two. Not for Zach Nevsky, unless he was asleep.

She remembered the days when she and her best friend, Sasha Nevsky, had shared an apartment while they worked in New York. It was then that she'd met Sasha's Off-Broadway director brother and actually been enough of a hero-worshiping patsy to be charmed by the way his life had the shape and sound of an ongoing party. Zach had hundreds of friends in the theater, and sooner or later they all seemed to drop by his place, uninvited, coming almost every night to take a warming, revivifying bask in the glow of his conviction of the importance of actors in the world. They flocked to heal their insecurities by listening to his great, unguarded, confident laugh, to give themselves courage in their professional struggle by sheer contact with him in all his rough power, his longshoreman's height and width, which belied the cleverness, intelligence, and generosity with which he wrestled to the ground the problems they brought him.

Zach was a bloody theatrical institution, Gigi told herself in a gust of sudden rage. A fucking institution, a giant sauna who should be transformed into a large building made of concrete, not flesh and blood. Then all the needy people who demanded a share of him could walk in and shelter themselves in his walls, and she would be spared the illusion that he could be loved like an ordinary man. A girl who was so pig-stupid that she'd fallen in love with The Institution that Walked Like a Man had only herself to blame.

Gigi got up to go into the kitchen and make herself dinner, but stopped with the realization that not only was she not hungry, but she was too furious to be able to swallow. In her state of mind she was afraid to put anything into her mouth without someone around to apply the Heimlich maneuver. Wine was safe, it went down easily, and perhaps wine would soothe, she hoped, pouring

23

another glass and returning to the view that normally made night music, but tonight looked as dull as Sally Lou found Scruples Two. But at least the lights below were shining *now*, unlike the stars and their unsettling intimations of the eons of time starlight traveled before it reached her eyes. What a bummer, knowing that you're looking at the sparkle of a star long dead, Gigi mused, sipping slowly from her glass.

Resolutely, fortified by a touch of meditation on the unsatisfactory nature of the Milky Way and the evanescence of human existence, Gigi made an attempt to replace her anger with Zach with annoyance toward Sally Lou, but she found that all she felt for her former secretary was sympathy. Naturally that girl was bored. It was getting tedious enough for Gigi to do her own work, much less have to deal with it secondhand, as Sally Lou had. Was it only today that she'd realized it? Had she been so preoccupied with avoiding what felt more and more like a doomed and insoluble problem with Zach that she hadn't been aware of a growing disenchantment with her job?

This *was* a night for nasty truths, Gigi thought, opening the French doors and trying to escape from her perceptions as she went out onto the balcony. With luck she'd find a vicious Santa Ana wind or perhaps a werewolf's full moon to explain her thoughts. She scanned the heavens and discovered an innocent crescent moon, clear skies, and a still night. She wished she smoked. She saw herself leaning on the balcony, as if it were the railing of a departing transatlantic liner, exhaling a stream of smoke with a worldly, brave, and resolute air as she turned her back on the past and sailed toward an exciting, daring, romantic future. In her high school days, when she and Mazie Goldsmith watched the classic films in Mazie's father's projection room, the stars in Hollywood acted with their cigarettes. Maybe that was what was wrong with movies now. No cigarettes, and particularly no expressive cigarette holders.

Suddenly shivering in the chill of the autumn air, Gigi had to go back inside, where she curled up on a couch and thought about lighting a fire and listening to some music. But not, for God's sake, Nat King Cole, who would bring tears to her eyes. Or Patsy Cline, who would make her sob out loud. Or anyone else who sang songs of a faraway lover and understood how lonely and miserable she felt.

Well, what *about* Scruples Two? Gigi pushed fruitless personal thoughts from her mind and concentrated on a problem she could do something about. Almost three years ago, when she had first come up with the idea of a catalog named after the world-famous Scruples, the boutique Billy had created, a catalog offering far less expensive clothes than Scruples; a catalog geared toward busy working women, wives and mothers, with neither time nor money to waste, she had asked Billy to let her call it Scruples Two. In all fairness, it had been Spider Elliott who'd finally convinced Billy to agree and to invest money and energy into the launch of the catalog, but Gigi had written the copy that explained the new concept and accompanied each photo. She considered herself as much responsible for its success as was Prince, the designer whose work Billy had commissioned, and as Spider, who'd also invested, and had designed the look of the catalog down to choosing the last model, the last piece of type.

Prince's work was ongoing, constantly presenting him with fresh problems as the catalog expanded and seasons changed. Spider now ran the entire company while Billy stayed home with their twin boys, and he faced new challenges on a daily basis. Aside from the marketing decisions he made with the Jones brothers, he was in charge of keeping the graphics of every issue of the catalog fresh and tempting, particularly since other companies were competing vigorously in the huge market Scruples Two had first defined. The catalog was a solid success, growing bigger by the month, thanks to expert management and brilliant execution. It was part of the American fashion establishment; even *Vogue* used and credited items from it, recognizing that many of their affluent readers also bought by mail order.

Yes, everyone but she had fresh work on hand, Gigi realized clearly. Sasha, now Mrs. Josh Hillman, mother of little Nellie, was back too, after her maternity leave, busily chasing down new things to sell besides the core of Prince's capsule collections, while Gigi was reduced to writing the obligatory copy she could do in her sleep. Now that she'd set the style, any good copywriter could be hired to continue it; they didn't need her. No, damn it, Scruples

Two had stopped being fun sometime in the past, and she hadn't noticed until Sally Lou had brought it to her attention.

"Gigi, I can see you're not happy here." She spoke the words out loud and knew they were true. True and final.

But, unlike the irresolvable fury with Zach, this was a dissatisfaction she could change, Gigi thought, getting up and pacing around the room. She'd never given Archie Rourke and Byron Bernheim the kind of *no* that meant absolutely positively not under any circumstances, good-bye and good luck, don't call me and I won't call you. She'd allowed them to keep trying to persuade her to join their agency, enjoying their blandishments and blarney without intending to take them up on their offer. In fact, she'd given them very little serious thought. Why, when she'd considered herself tucked so snugly into her familiar job, should she hanker to leap into a new field she'd never worked in before, something highly problematic, something so unpredictable and challenging?

"Because I'm bored—fucking bored fucking *bored!*" Gigi announced to the quiet room as she went into the kitchen to find something really fattening to eat.

The next morning Gigi woke after a few hours of broken sleep to find that her recognitions of the evening before had crystallized into an unmistakable determination to change jobs. In the course of one night, Scruples Two had become part of the past, as beloved as ever but clearly an area in which her work was finished. Frost/Rourke/Bernheim now announced itself to her as the alluring, unscripted future. There'd never be a better time than today to make the change and get it over with, she decided as she gulped her breakfast and hurried to dress. All her work on the newest edition of the catalog was completed and last week when she'd spoken to Archie Rourke he'd been as eager as ever to entice her into the advertising business.

Yes, she knew she was right to leave, but there was still the matter of breaking the news to Billy and Spider and Sasha. They were family members to her; she dreaded telling them.

Why had Josie said it was tough to fire people? It was so much worse to quit, Gigi thought as she hesitated outside of Spider's office, remembering the night she'd written the introductory copy for Scruples Two. Until that point the only things she'd written had been cards to go with gifts from her own collection of antique lingerie, cards in which she could riff as much as she liked, take any liberty, please herself without worrying about the public. She'd been so nervous before she'd read that introduction to him that when he'd liked it—no, when he'd loved it—she'd been as proud as she'd ever been in her life. Nothing would ever make her forget the flying thrill of that moment. Taking a deep breath, she opened Spider's office door and went in.

Spider was alone, studying a page of figures, his long, sinewy body contorted in various graceful ways, for no office chair had yet been invented that could accommodate him. As usual, he re-minded Gigi of a great blond pagan who had been somehow trans-formed into a businessman without losing any of his free-spirited, laughing, essentially sensuous charm. She was delighted to find him alone. She couldn't have talked to him in front of anyone else and she hadn't wanted to make an appointment to see him alone, because that would have sounded unnecessarily ominous.

"Hi, got a minute, Spider?" Gigi asked, remembering vividly the day she'd first met him. She'd been sixteen, and she had arrived in California only the night before, seeking refuge with her father after the death of her mother. The very next afternoon she'd found herself transformed, dizzy and giddy with the excitement of Billy's offered friendship compounded by her new haircut and new clothes, walking into an office at Scruples, where Spider and Val-entine were, to Billy's shocked amazement, wrapped in each other's arms. The first word Gigi had said to him was "Congratulations," when he'd explained that he and Valentine had just been married, and the first thing he'd said to her was that she was more sophisti-cated than Billy. He'd been so protective, so interested in her right from the start, this Viking of a man who'd become her hero from the minute she laid dazzled eyes on him, this glorious guy to whom no woman, no matter how much she loved another man, could be indifferent.

"Ah, Spider Elliott, damn it, but I'm really going to miss you," Gigi heard herself blurt out in a voice laced with regret.

"What's the matter with you!" Spider jumped up from his desk in alarm. "Are you sick?"

"No, of course not."

"You're marrying Zach and leaving town?"

"That's not in the cards."

"Then why the fuck did you scare me like that? You sounded exactly like Ali MacGraw in *Love Story*."

"Sorry . . . I . . . I'm . . . oh . . ." Gigi stopped, wordless. The only unspoken sentence that came to her mind was, "Spider, you're not happy here."

"Gigi," Spider said gently, taking her cold hands, "you're not making sense. Sit down right here and tell me all about it. Whatever it is, I'm sure I've heard more lurid tales."

"I'm leaving Scruples Two for a job in an advertising agency." Gigi said the words as quickly as possible.

"The hell you are!" Spider's eyes searched hers and, as always, reached into and understood a woman's mind as rapidly as those of any man alive. "You are. Yep, indeed you are, and there's not a thing I can do about it. I've always thought you were cautious to a fault, Gigi. That'll teach me to take a woman for granted. You've changed without giving me warning. Or else I'm losing my touch."

"I didn't know myself, Spider, until yesterday. I fired Sally Lou and then I fired myself . . ."

"Could you be more specific?" When Spider laughed at her that way, with his sunlit blue eyes almost closed and the deep lines suddenly intensified at their corners, Gigi always felt she heard a clap of giant hands. Relief warmed her as she told him everything that had gone through her mind the night before.

"And this agency, what's-her-name Frost and the guys, you're certain that they're an outfit you can be happy with? After all, there are lots of other agencies in L.A."

"Archie and Byron are a terrific team. *Smart.* I've seen their work and I like them. The way I figure, they can only prosper. They're billing about thirty million a year after a mere six months in L.A., and with the entire economy going wild, advertising's a good place to be. I had Prince's ad manager check them out on Madison Avenue, and he gave Archie and Byron a rave. It makes sense for them to want me for a swimwear account, it plays to my strong point, and after that, well," she said, suddenly feeling shy in her ambitions, "I believe maybe interesting things could happen."

Spider got up and started prowling around his office, looking at Gigi as he walked back and forth, remembering that tremulous, oddball, mysterious little figure who had abruptly popped into their lives, an unknown daughter out of Vito's past, a whim of Billy's turning her into a legal ward and an unofficial stepdaughter. Gigi, without whom none of them would be together today; Gigi, whose talent they had come to count on; Gigi, who had outgrown them. Damn it to hell, he thought, he was the one who was going to do the major part of the missing, more than it would be fair to tell her, more than she knew or should know. She had to be free to make whatever she could of herself. There was no telling how far she could go, this woman who had never realized, on that single night when she'd stopped him from trying to make love to her, that it was almost the only time he'd been rejected in a lifetime of conquest.

"When do you want to leave?" he finally asked reluctantly.

"I think I should . . . leave right away," Gigi answered firmly, "without two weeks' notice. You have more than seven weeks before the next catalog will be due at the printers; that's plenty of time to find and train another copywriter, but Archie needs to put together the Indigo Seas pitch as quickly as possible."

Her voice wasn't apologetic and her words were irrefutable, Spider noted ruefully. Already someone else's needs were coming first with her. Archie! Archie indeed! What kind of name was that? Did he have a butler named Jeeves?

"I thought about it all during breakfast," Gigi continued rapidly, "and since I'm leaving, I should let them know today, leave here . . . tomorrow . . . so I can be there by next Monday."

"Jesus, you're a heartless bitch. What about the big going-away party, the gold watch for two and a half years of faithful service, or would you rather have a silver tea service?"

"I was hoping to avoid exactly that. Please, Spider, no fuss. Josie will slime me with a guilt trip that'll break my heart."

"I could too, if I wanted to. A guilt trip you'd never recover from."

"But I knew you wouldn't. That's why I told you first of anybody. Do I have your blessing?" Gigi's impudent mouth, with its upper lip that curved naturally in a hint of a smile, was frankly laughing at him now, and so were her large, beautifully shaped green eyes that reminded him so much of Valentine's.

"You have my blessing, my wholehearted blessing, combined with my wholehearted wish that you'd stay. But you're not wrong to want to try something else, you've picked your time wisely, and although you can never really be replaced, we'll just have to be good soldiers and carry on without you—I know there's no real room for major career growth in a catalog, Gigi, but an advertising agency's something else."

"Oh, Spider, thank you!"

"Do you want me to tell Billy for you?"

"No, I'll go and see her now, at the house. I'm afraid she won't be as open-minded as you are, but I wouldn't feel right about not telling her in person."

"Brave little Gigi. Still, you never know. Billy took a few risks in her day too, she's grabbed her life in both hands and changed it more than once. Maybe she'll understand, in spite of the fact that she counts on you."

"Maybe," Gigi said doubtfully. Billy, even with the softening influence of marriage to Spider, was still the most demanding woman she'd ever had anything to do with, and Billy had many perfectly valid reasons to feel that she'd singlehandedly invented Gigi. Abandoning Scruples Two would be much less of a trauma if it didn't mean letting Billy down as well.

Spider leaned down, grasping her shoulders, and shook her hard and briskly for a minute, like a friendly lion expressing a number of unutterable and complicated thoughts to a pussycat. Then he took her face tenderly in both of his hands. "Remember what you said when you first met me, way back when?"

"Of course. 'Congratulations.' "

"Congratulations to you," he said, kissing her on the cheek. "And good luck, Gigi darling."

"Mrs. Elliott's in her sitting room, she said to go right up," Burgo O'Sullivan said to Gigi. "Hey, kiddo, you've got that look on your face that you had when I told you a girl couldn't get into my poker game."

"Yeah, well, I was sixteen then, and starting high school, so naturally even your penny-ante weekly game sounded like a better idea than meeting new kids."

"Fresh, still as fresh as ever. So did you wreck the car? Seduce another chef right under my nose, the way you did that poor English fellow?"

"Burgo, when will you start treating me like a adult?" Gigi gave an unconvincing smile to wise Burgo, who filled a multitude of undefined but indispensable jobs at the great house in Holmby Hills.

"I'll give it some thought," he answered, "and let you know. How about a cup of tea? It might steady your shaky nerves. You look the way you used to when I first tried to teach you to make a left in heavy traffic."

"Burgo, you're imagining things. I've got to go talk to Billy."

"It's an emergency, then. You never refuse a chance to visit the kitchen."

"Sort of. I'll come by afterwards and tell you all about it."

"Is that a present for me?" Burgo asked, looking with interest at the white box with a blue satin ribbon on it that Gigi carried.

"No, it's for Billy, for having the babies. It's not fair that people send things to newborn children who don't know the difference, and not to the mother, who did all the work."

"I see, a bribe."

"Burgo, you have an innately suspicious mind, you should be ashamed of yourself. See you later." Why did he always see right through her, Gigi wondered as she left him. The present she had brought, from her precious collection of antique lingerie, might, just possibly, soften Billy's reaction. But a bribe? Never! . . . Or . . . maybe?

In spite of the need to hurry that she had impressed on Burgo, Gigi found herself dragging her steps as she walked through the spacious rooms, which fairly vibrated with color and freshness, and in which every corner offered intriguing places to stop and linger and inspect the fascinating multitude of objects and antiques and flowers that seemed to have been placed there by a happy chance, instead of by Billy's constant rearrangement of her treasures.

Upstairs, at the end of a long corridor, the door to Billy's sitting room was open.

"I'm in here," Billy's voice called faintly. Gigi found her flopped heavily on a couch in an attitude of complete exhaustion, her crop of short, heavy, dark curls drooping messily around her face, the lids falling wearily over her smoky eyes, her skin pale and bare of makeup. She wore one of Spider's old shirts over a pair of baggy jeans, and it was impossible to believe, at the moment, that this wiped-out scrap was the magnificent Billy Ikehorn, the embodiment of the groomed-to-perfection, the exquisitely dressed, the splendidly bejeweled kind of woman of whom the world possesses perhaps several hundred, with only two or three as internationally famous as she.

"Spider didn't say you weren't feeling well," Gigi said in concern. "I wouldn't have come if I'd known I was going to disturb you."

"Whatever are you talking about? I'm perfectly fine," Billy said, too weakly to sound indignant. "I've just finished putting the boys down for their nap, that's all. This is the best possible time to see me. Come sit down here next to the couch."

"Did Nanny Elizabeth leave?" Gigi asked in concern, putting the box down on a table. She hadn't seen Billy at home more than four or five times since the twins, Max and Hal, were born, and then only on the weekends, when they were showing off the babies, with Spider expertly performing fatherly chores, as well as the experienced nanny hovering in the background.

"Of course not, she's around here somewhere, probably doing their laundry."

"I don't get it. I thought that with a great full-time, live-in nanny you wouldn't have to do all the scut work, and just look at you . . . Why don't you get another nanny if she can't handle it?"

"She can, Gigi, she can. Nanny Elizabeth's the best in the West, and I'm afraid I may be driving her crazy because I won't let her do everything. But if I don't feed the boys, and burp them and change them and put them down and get them up, they'll end up thinking she's their mother, not me. This is the most important time of their lives, crucial time, Gigi, and if I miss it I can never get it back. Did you know that if people grew at the same rate as babies do in their first year, we'd all be about a hundred and eighty feet tall? So you see . . ." Billy's voice trailed off at the thought of the immensity and importance of her task.

"But, Billy, twins . . . Aren't you *supposed* to have help with twins?"

"In theory, of course, but the people who decided that never stopped to think that one twin could end up not getting as much maternal attention as the other. I can't risk that. They're four months old, a very impressionable age."

"Personally," Gigi said, prudently suppressing a smile, "I don't remember anything about being four months old."

"You think you don't, but everything that happened made a difference. *Everything,* believe me."

"No doubt, but it's too late now. Listen, Billy, there's something I want to tell you . . ."

"Gigi, it's more important for you to listen to me now. There's something you've really got to understand before you have children yourself."

"I'm not planning any, trust me." Gigi allowed herself a giggle at Billy's new piece of bizarre thinking, since it was directed at her.

"You never know, and unless I make you realize the truth this minute, there's a chance that I might not remember, because people forget the first months of their children's lives the way they forget childbirth . . . having them is already a blur." Billy spoke in a voice that a prophetess might envy. "Now listen carefully. *Babies are a lot smarter than anybody realizes.*"

"Okay, okay, I'm sure they are, especially Hal and Max, but, Billy, I came to . . ."

"Gigi, how do you think babies *control* you?"

"Huh?"

"Control. They can't talk, they can't walk, but they control you. I'll bet you haven't the slightest idea of how they do it."

"You can't leave them alone and you won't let the nanny do it, so you *think* they control you," Gigi said, trying to restore reason.

"Wrong!" Billy sat up. "That's just what everyone says, because they know nothing, nothing!" Her voice lowered to an intensity that made Gigi lean forward in amazement. *"They control you with their eyes, yes, just their eyes!"*

"Sure, Billy," Gigi agreed quickly. Like purple aliens from another planet, spaceship residents visiting in the middle of the night, of course they did. Hal and Max controlled reckless, impulsive, billionairess Billy Ikehorn with their wondering baby eyes. Should she make an immediate excuse to leave the room and phone Spider, she asked herself. Did he not realize how totally obsessive Billy had become—just obsessive, or was it really crazy? Or did her weirdness seem natural to him, since the twins were his first children too?

"I can tell that you don't believe me," Billy said, brushing her hair back in a gesture too tired to be impatient. "Just bring me that blue book over there on my desk, the one that's open."

Gigi hastened to do as she was told.

"Thanks," Billy said, trying to find a particular page in the book, which was entitled *The Interpersonal World of the Infant*. "Now listen. This is about what happens during the first three-to-five month period in a baby's life, and that's exactly where the boys are. Are you paying attention to me?"

"Yes, Billy."

Billy looked at her sharply to make sure. "Okay . . . here it is. 'The infant takes control—over the initiations and terminations of direct visual engagement in social activities . . .' What'd I tell you? There's more, and I'm quoting here, 'The visual-motor system, is . . . virtually mature . . .' Did you hear that, Gigi, *mature*, and then he says that 'when watching the mother and infant during this life period, one is watching two people'—*people*, Gigi—'with almost equal facility and control over the same social behavior.' So! What did I tell you? *Equal facility!* They're four months old and I'm forty and we're equal! And it gets worse," Billy said dolefully, and read on. " 'They can avert their gaze, shut their eyes, stare past, become glassy-eyed. And through the decisive use of such gaze behaviors'—*decisive*, Gigi!—'they can be seen to *reject, distance themselves from, or defend themselves against mother.*' Isn't that terrible! Oh, God help me," Billy cried, sighing deeply, "they can reject me." She took a deep breath and shook her weary head sadly.

"But they don't!" Gigi almost shouted.

"Well, that's up to them, Gigi. Listen," Billy said, reading again. " 'They can also *reinitiate* engagement and contact when they desire, through gazing, smiling, and vocalizing.' That's the only thing that keeps me going, the reinitiation part." Billy fell back on the pillows.

"Who wrote this?" Gigi demanded suspiciously, picking up the book.

"A famous infant psychiatrist, Daniel Stern. It's my bible. I

wish I could understand everything in it, but it gets very complicated. Still, you see I'm right. Hal and Max control me, I can't
help it."

Gigi bent over the page Billy had been reading from. "Wait a
minute, Billy, he says that 'the mothers *give* the infant control'—
you left that out. You don't *have* to give them control."

"Yes you do. You'll see. Try to force a baby to look at you
when he doesn't want to. It absolutely, positively cannot be done.
Or just try to make them look away when they're giving you that
teary, outraged, utterly pitiful glare because they're unhappy. Oh,
I adore them, Gigi, but they're *fiends*, utter fiends . . . ."

Gigi got up, took the book away from Billy, and removed it
to the desk. She spoke in the voice of a psychiatric nurse dealing
with someone who was fractious and disoriented, but who needed
encouragement rather than coddling. "Billy, I'm sure they'll grow
up and be perfectly nice kids. Not fiends. This, as they say, is but
a phase. Meanwhile, on another front, I'm leaving Scruples Two
to work in an advertising agency, writing copy. Tomorrow's my
last day."

"Say that again." Billy raised herself on one elbow.

"Come on. You heard."

"Oh, Gigi, I'm so delighted for you! That's *wonderful*! Give
me a kiss!"

"You're not . . . upset?"

"Of course not! What kind of selfish person do you think I
am? I've been wondering when you were going to spread your
wings, get off this particular branch and fly away. Lord, Gigi, when
I was your age I'd spent a year in Paris on my own and lived in
New York and held down an exciting job, I'd had all sorts of lovers
and then I'd married Ellis and I'd been to state dinners at the
White House in my Dior ballgowns and he'd bought me Empress
Josephine's emeralds and the ranch in Brazil and the place in Bar-
bados and I was on the Best Dressed List—heavens, what *hadn't* I
done, years before your age! You've always been a late bloomer,
and Zach is your first real romance. He's wonderful, of course, but
you haven't really . . . well, had a lot of experience, shall we say?"

"Forget about my shortcomings, Billy," Gigi pounced. "Let's
talk about your lovers—you've never mentioned that little item
before. Could you be more precise? Some specific details?"

"They've passed into history," Billy laughed. "You heard it once, but from now on I'll deny it," she added with a renewal of her habitual energy. "I've been worried about you. Zach is away so much, and your job isn't nearly enough for your scope, but you seemed so content to let things go on as they were . . . I didn't want to stir things up in your little love nest. This is great news, just stupendous! What kind of agency? Is it that new place that was trying to recruit you before the babies were born? Frost something?"

"Right, same place. Archie Rourke, Byron Berenson Bernheim the Third, and Victoria Frost."

"Oh yes, I remember, Millicent Caldwell's daughter," Billy said in the voice she used unconsciously when she spoke of those few women she considered her peers. "What's the daughter like?"

"I haven't met her yet. But the guys are wonderful."

"Married?" Billy asked sharply.

"No they're not. God, you're conventional."

"You will be too, when you've been married three times. Just watch out for them. No office romances."

"But weren't you Ellis's secretary?"

"That was the exception." Billy shrugged and blushed faintly. "I still don't recommend it. Does Spider know?"

"Yes, I have his blessing. He understood perfectly, even why I have to leave so quickly."

"But, darling, we can't let you go without a going-away party. Josie can arrange it in an hour."

Gigi growled and complained, but Billy, already at the phone, dialing Josie at the office, paid no attention. As she heard the familiar sound of Billy issuing a long list of detailed instructions, Gigi realized that this was an opportunity to get away before she had to hear anything more about the powers of the fearful, mind-bending twins. She kissed the top of Billy's head, waved, and disappeared down the corridor, closing the door behind her. As she walked toward the staircase she crossed the path of the admirable nanny, carrying a basket of newly washed baby clothes.

"Nanny Elizabeth, may I ask you something?" Gigi said, stopping her. "Is it my imagination, or is Mrs. Elliott overly . . . involved . . . in taking care of the boys?"

"My first-time mothers are always over or under, Gigi. I've never had an even-keeled one yet, not in twenty years," the sturdy

Midwestern woman said, smiling and unsurprised. "Now, Mrs. Elliott's definitely way over—I think it was that book that did it—but there's nothing to worry about, she's as strong as a horse, and I give it another month or two to taper off to normal. When they're underinvolved, I do get concerned. It's not that I mind the extra work, but the mothers themselves miss so much."

"Do you believe that babies actually control adults with their eyes?"

"Well, of course, everybody knows that, Gigi. And if it weren't with their eyes, it would be with something else, count on it, the little devils."

After Gigi left, Billy noticed the box tied with blue satin ribbon. She opened it with immediate curiosity, realizing that Gigi had become too caught up in the discussion about the twins to give it to her. Under layers of tissue she found a peignoir made of gleaming satin in a particularly voluptuous shade of pink. It was elaborately decorated, with deep insets of Valencienne cream lace at the throat. Lace insets, four inches apart, ran vertically down the length of the garment all the way to the hem, where the lace foamed into a wide flounce that trailed on the floor. On the arms of the peignoir, more lace fell from mid-arm to the wrist.

Entranced, Billy carried the peignoir into her bathroom and put it on in front of a full-length mirror, pulling it closely together so that her jeans and shirt were completely hidden. Another woman looked at her from her mirror, a woman with many a seductive secret, a woman she had forgotten she had ever been. She gazed at herself with astonishment and an immediate feeling that she was startled to identify as sexual arousal. Good grief, what was going on here, Billy asked herself, opening the card that Gigi had written to go with her gift.

> Gabrielle, yes, indeed, that Gabrielle, the divine one
> who invented "Le Coucher de Gabrielle," always said that
> this peignoir was her lucky charm, for she wore it for her
> debut at the Folies-Bergère. Her debut took place on a night
> in the springtime, it took place, of course, in Paris, and it
> took place at a time when all women, no matter what their

position in society, wore five layers of undergarments, fastened together by an infernal system of straps and hooks and buttons that had been invented so that it would take a very long time indeed for them to be removed. Women, especially our divine Gabrielle, did not wish to seem as if they could be easily conquered by any man. Every woman knew that men only wanted one thing of them, and this one thing they were determined not to surrender, for their Mamans had told them of the dangers of allowing men to have their way, and their Mamans were wise in the ways of the wicked world. Gabrielle, who lived on very few sous in a tiny attic with a view of the tops of the trees of the Parc Montsouris, was a dreamer by nature, and as she watched the buds on the trees swell in the purple twilight, she thought of all the unmarried men, all over Paris, who were, at this very minute, going home to their empty bachelor apartments. Oh, soft-hearted Gabrielle! These men, dangerous and wicked though they were, she told herself, must be lonely in their empty rooms. She felt pity for them, a pity that grew deeper as a new moon rose and the evening star spoke to her. Wasn't there anything that a charitable girl could do to make them happier, she wondered, without, of course, surrendering that precious thing that was of great price? Night by night Gabrielle meditated until she arrived at an idea that no one in the history of civilization—or at least in France, which is the same thing—had ever had before. What if a woman, a woman as demure and chaste and lovely as Gabrielle herself, were to permit these poor bachelors to watch her undress for bed? What if she were to arrive on the stage of a theater, well-covered, it went without saying, in her pink satin and cream lace peignoir, for which she had saved all her extra sous for three years? What if she were to allow her peignoir to slip to the ground, while a pianist played light classical music to which she would listen, unaware of the eyes upon her? What if, slowly, very slowly, in time to the music, she were to remove, with delicate manipulation of all the fastenings and buttons, the first of the five layers of dainty undergarments that every woman wore? And another and another? And yet another? Of course, she would never

38

remove the last layer, the chemise and the knickers, for that would not only encourage men to have indecent thoughts, but it would bring the gendarmerie to close the theater. There should be a screen on the stage, Gabrielle realized, so that when she took off that last layer and put on her nightdress, a high-necked white nightdress made of heavy starched linen that no woman need fear being seen in, she could do it behind the screen. And there should be a bed on the stage as well, a simple white bed into which she would slip, taking only two quick steps from the screen to the bed. Perhaps an audience could be found for this decent representation of an event from everyday life, Gabrielle told herself, as she made a rendezvous with the director of the Folies-Bergere.

Ah, Gabrielle, the toast of Paris, Gabrielle who invented le strip-tease out of compassion for her fellow men, why did you never allow any of the men who wanted to marry you and share your little white bed to accompany you home? You could have married two kings, twenty-five noblemen, and two hundred stockbrokers, one more handsome than the other. Was it because each night, after you had given the performance of Le Coucher de Gabrielle, you changed into your dove-gray velvet coat and your hat with the gray ostrich feathers and told your coachman, who drove your four gray horses, to hurry to return to your big house that now looked out on the trees of the Parc Monceau? Was it because you were happily eager to go home without a king or even a stockbroker, and watch over the sleep of your little twin boys? Was it, oh, soft-hearted Gabrielle, because you knew only too well what happened to women who listened to men, and surrendered that priceless possession they only possessed if no one else possessed it, for such is fate? To say nothing of biology?

With love from Gigi.

Billy read the card and laughed and cried a little and resolved to wear the peignoir tonight, for she too had listened to a man, and she, like Gabrielle, had no regrets.

As soon as Gigi got back to Scruples Two, she made a lunch date with Sasha, who was free that very day. Sasha Nevsky was the last important person to whom she had to tell her news, except for Zach, who wouldn't care where she worked as long as she was happy.

And her father, of course. Vito Orsini was in Europe for the moment, but as soon as he came home she'd have dinner with him and discuss the whole thing. Their relationship had grown close and warm in the past years, and often, when Gigi was alone, Vito would take her out, always to a different restaurant, and insist that she order the most expensive things on the menu, and talk over all sorts of things, with an intimacy she didn't believe would be possible for a daughter who'd grown up normally in her father's house.

"You look awfully pleased with yourself—did someone just give you a lifetime supply of perfect panty hose?" Sasha asked her closest friend, with whom she'd shared apartments in New York and West Hollywood until, little over a year ago, she'd met Josh Hillman, Billy's lawyer, and agreed to marry him on their first date.

"I'm so excited and relieved I don't know what to do," Gigi admitted gaily. "I was dreading telling Spider and Billy that I'm leaving, but they both think it's a great idea."

"Leaving? Leaving Los Angeles?" Sasha looked bewildered.

"Of course not, leaving Scruples Two."

"What?" Sasha shouted. "You're doing *what?*"

"Stop making that awful noise, for heaven's sake, it's not going to bother you. I've got that job at the ad agency I told you about, isn't that terrific?"

"It's the worst news I've ever heard! How can you do this to me, Gigi? Oh God, I don't—I *won't*—believe it, you're just springing this on me, as if it doesn't matter? What ever happened to you to make you so cruel?"

Two large tears plopped out of Sasha's eyes and dribbled down her cheeks, merely enhancing her Edwardian beauty, that classic Gibson Girl profile, that lavish luster of black hair and black eyes and white skin that, in combination with her marvelous body and irresistible walk, had made her the best lingerie model on Seventh Avenue before she joined Gigi in Scruples Two.

Gigi looked at her in astonishment. Sasha, the famously hard-hearted tormentor of the male sex; Sasha, who had brought Josh

Hillman, the most eligible single man in Beverly Hills, to his knees in one evening; Sasha, the sweepingly tall, the domineering, the possessor of all the answers—weeping? She'd never seen a tear form in those eyes before.

"But, Sasha," Gigi protested, watching more huge tears appear, "it shouldn't make any difference to you. It won't change anything between us, you're always out of the office with your assistants, why in God's name are you crying? Stop it, or at least get out a Kleenex, this is getting embarrassing . . . people are looking at you."

"Let them look," Sasha gulped as a narrow ribbon of tears dripped off her chin and hit the tablecloth. "I'm not ashamed of honest emotion."

"If you'd just explain . . . What emotion, exactly? It can't be that you're going to miss me at Scruples Two, because we hardly catch sight of each other at work anymore, it can't be envy of my new job, because you have a fantastic job of your own . . . What's this all about?" Gigi demanded sternly, handing Sasha a napkin. She hadn't gone through a morning of confronting Spider and Billy to let Sasha, of all people, make her feel like a betrayer.

"It . . . it just won't *be* Scruples Two anymore if you go," Sasha finally said, getting her voice under control, although the tears continued to come.

"Be reasonable! It's a huge business and getting bigger every day. I'm not irreplaceable."

"Sure, someone can copy your writing style, but you and me, oh, Gigi, we *were* Scruples Two before there really was one . . . it was just the two of us, me and my ratty old collection of Christmas catalogs and you and your idea of how to make a better one . . . If you leave, the spirit, the essence goes out of the whole thing."

"Sasha," Gigi said gently, "that spirit was gone ages ago, as soon as Scruples Two became a definitive success and the marketing guys came in and started to make the big-money decisions. You're remembering the start-up time, when Spider and Billy and the two of us were all creating something together and taking a gamble that we were right. It's like people in the third year of a Broadway success wishing they were back rehearsing before the first-night curtain went up."

"*Oh, Gigi, we had so much fun!*" Sasha spoke in a voice of loss and sadness that Gigi thought was strangely unjustified, considering that her friend now had what any woman would consider a perfect life: a husband she adored, a heavenly baby girl, a job she did brilliantly, and all the money anyone could want.

"But aren't we still having fun?" Gigi asked, deeply puzzled.

"No! *We're grown up now.* Grownups don't ever have fun the way we used to, and if you don't know it now, Gigi, you will, just you wait." Sasha seemed full of a strange, inappropriate grief.

"Good Lord, you're twenty-six, you're married and a mother, if you weren't at least a little bit grown-up now you'd be in trouble," Gigi said, trying to ignore her friend's unaccountable misery and bring matters back onto a plane of reality.

"Do you think I don't know all that?" Sasha flashed.

"Well then?" Gigi challenged.

"Oh, it's all right for you," Sasha said. "You're playing house with my loopy genius of a brother—you can flit around and try this and sample that—you're nothing close to a grownup yet and you don't have to live up to . . . to . . . live up to *things.*"

"Are we talking about my quitting or the married condition?" Gigi asked tartly.

"Oh, I don't know," Sasha said in confusion, "whatever you say. You tell me, Gigi," she implored.

"No, you tell me."

"Oh, Gigi," Sasha burst out, "Josh is *such* a grownup. The real, solid, serious, unchangeable thing. The first few months it didn't seem to matter that he's fifty years old, but . . . well, I guess I didn't expect that he'd be so deeply involved in things I don't really care about . . . I thought we'd be like every other newly married couple, just starting out together, but now . . . oh, hell!"

"Look, Sasha, be sensible," Gigi said firmly. "Josh was the senior partner at one of the most important law firms in Los Angeles when you met him, he was a pillar of the community, you knew that going in, didn't you? Did you expect to live in a small cottage by a waterfall as the wife of the most important lawyer at Strassberger, Lipkin and Hillman?"

"How about finding yourself suddenly filling the shoes of the wife of one of the leading fundraisers for the Music Center, Cedars-Sinai Hospital, the County Museum of Art, and at least a half a dozen other worthy organizations? How about getting to know all the top good-works wives in town and having to keep on excellent, lunching terms with them when they have daughters my age and they all know his first wife and adore her? How about black-tie benefit dinners three nights a week, with endless speeches, and you can't sneak out early because your table is too conspicuous or Josh is on the dais? How about he secretly thinks I should be home taking care of Nellie instead of going back to work, because that's the way it is in his world, but he's being understanding about it, very obviously understanding, because he knows that he has to compromise, considering all the things I've compromised about?"

"It sounds worse than awful!"

"Yeah," Sasha sniffed in rebellious resignation.

"Can't Josh stop doing some of those things?"

"He's already disconnected himself from half of the stuff he used to do—I only mentioned the causes he's so committed to that he won't drop them. I can't expect him to eliminate his social conscience . . . one of the things I love about him is that he's such a good man, so genuinely good, so genuinely sweet . . . oh, shit! I wish he weren't. Or rather, I wish he were the way he is, *without* being involved in doing all that stuff . . . does that make sense?"

"Not a hell of a lot."

"Why should it be that the things men do best and that give them so much pleasure aren't the things their wives wish they were doing?"

"Ask your 'loopy genius of a brother,' " Gigi said grimly.

"Not you too?"

"Me too."

"Well, at least I warned you, you can't say I didn't," Sasha reminded Gigi virtuously. "I told you not to get involved with him."

"I remember distinctly. You admitted you were jealous. You said Zach was 'yours.' *And* you called me a slut."

"See? I told you we had fun!"

3

Now, only four days after her lunch with Sasha, Gigi found herself settling down in an office with David Melville, after as hasty a lunch as Le Dôme had ever served. Thanks to the old-fashioned scale of the building, their office was a real room rather than the usual creative team's cubicle. Both of them had their feet up on their desks and their shoes off.

"Let's share your thoughts about swimwear," David said invitingly.

"The whole subject is sheer bloody hell for anyone over eleven," she answered firmly. "What I want to know is more about Victoria Frost. Her name wasn't even mentioned during lunch. You boys put on a terrific flimflam, lots of war stories about the accounts that got away, lots of good jokes you can tell a woman without being sexist, I almost got a contact testosterone high from the proceedings, but the ghost of the highly absent Miss Vicky seemed to be sitting right there at the table with us. Tell me all about her."

"I've only been here six months, and she never seems to be around for more than a week at a time," David said lamely.

"You've got to know something, Davy, my lad—come on, give!"

"I don't have any information on her personal life. Honest. But professionally she's tough and experienced and she's totally about management. She's our official rainmaker, she's perpetually on the hunt for new accounts, and whenever we present our ideas to a prospective client, she's always an essential part of the pitch team. Victoria relates exceptionally well to the client's point of view—the client's 'culture,' as we quaintly put it, as if they were a foreign country."

"What if the client's culture rejects our ideas?"

"Then we come home, to our own little culture, and bang our heads against the walls until we get new ideas or die, whichever comes first."

"She doesn't try to persuade the client that our ideas are good?"

"That's the creatives' job. She reminds us of what we have to do to keep the account. Compromise is what Victoria's all about. Also sucking up to the client, otherwise known as building the kind of personal relationship that keeps them happy."

"So who really runs the agency?"

"Huh?" He looked startled.

"Victoria, or Archie and Byron?"

"The three of them together. They're the principals, they own the agency and split the profits, how I don't know. Arch and By are co–creative directors; Victoria's the executive director and chief account supervisor."

"What happens if they disagree? Do the creative directors prevail, or Miss Vicky?"

"Now you're into stuff I really don't know about," David protested. "I don't go to those meetings."

"Do you have a theory about why she was so pissed off at me right from the start?"

"She's been generally tense lately, and when she gets back from New York she's particularly unpredictable. But I think that it must have been that you don't look like a new-hire creative, in that suit you come off looking like management, and that's an area she's violently territorial about. Management definitely belongs to Ms. Frost."

"But there must be other managers in the agency," Gigi objected, "other account executives, just as there are three other creative teams, besides Archie and Byron."

"They're all guys, and she's their absolute capo. She hired every one of them. Advertising in general is a man's business, and in FRB more than in most. Victoria is the only woman in the place with real clout, and definitely the only one who dresses like management. All the other female creatives wear really casual clothes, except for Ziggy and Joan, both art directors, who're deeply into bizarre. Arch and By still sometimes dress New York, particularly when they pitch, like they've been pitching you. I dressed up today just because of lunch."

"Well, at least I know it wasn't anything personal," Gigi sniffed, unconvinced. No way would she believe that a dress-code infraction on the part of a new hire could provoke such a hostile reaction. "So back to you, Davy, my boy. Are you married, single, or divorced? We still have all that intimate stuff to tell."

"We don't have time for that now," he said, dismissing her friendly question. "Swimsuits are the business of the moment."

"In a perfect world, no woman should have to expose her flesh in a well-lit public place, with the exception of twenty-five females who were born, nay, genetically destined, to model swimsuits for a brief period in their lives," Gigi said judiciously. "Perhaps between the ages of seventeen and nineteen, give or take a few years at the high end."

"Do you or do you not intend to help me sell swimsuits, or what my mother called bathing suits?" David asked, scowling at her. He couldn't possibly be in love with Gigi, he promised himself. Please God, somebody tell him that it hadn't happened as soon as he'd been able to get his first good look at her. He didn't have time to be in love, advertising was a sixteen-hour-a-day calling, not a job, and he'd vowed to put his private life on hold for at least a decade.

"Where's that cappuccino you were so hot to make me this

morning?" Gigi asked longingly, with a tiny wistful sigh that made the hair rise on his nape.

"Swimwear's a vast market, Gigi," David insisted, feeling himself, to his horror, taking incredible secret pleasure in just saying her name. "Lots of magazine ads, lots of editorial support in the magazines, lots of in-store tie-ins. After all, women have to cover their bodies when they swim, and they can't wear the same one suit forever."

"Would that they could. And would that I had the Fig Newtons I remember you pushing earlier. I'm still hungry."

"Research shows," David went on firmly, ignoring his burning desire to bring her, on bended knee, every crumb of food in the office, "that the most common areas women complain about are heavy hips, expanding waists, pot bellies, jiggling bottoms, and other normal, post-puberty, gravity-induced changes. The master designers at Indigo Seas have devised many ways to minimize these problems. Have I lost you already, Gigi? *Gigi!* You may not know it, but two other creative teams, Kerry and Joan and John and Lew, have also been put on the Indigo Seas pitch. We've got heavy internal competition here. They're sitting in their cubbyholes as we speak, trying to come up with something so good that they're going to make us look sick. Will you, for Christ's sake, pay attention?"

"I'm sorry, Davy, I'm in another place," Gigi said without any hint of repentance. "I was just trying to decide if I'm ready to reveal the details of how I lost my virginity, and I discover I am."

He ignored her, his heart pounding. Had he really been naive enough to hope she was still a virgin? "Indigo Seas specializes in suits that give the large woman a shot at looking okay. We've got a clearly defined target customer—the latest Lou Harris poll shows that fifty-eight percent of Americans are overweight—"

"So they claim." Gigi shrugged indifferently. "My sign is Aries, by the way."

"Why the hell did they hire you? That's what I want to know." David took off his glasses, slammed them on the desk, and glared at her. Aries, his fatal love sign. He'd been in love twice in his twenty-eight years, each time with an Aries. Even the cosmos was against him.

"What's that supposed to mean? Do you hate me because I rejected your sinister organic apple?"

"Don't make everything so damn personal, for crying out loud! Victoria spent weeks just getting us invited to make this pitch, and so far you've been one hundred percent negative about the prospective client. But you were hired to manufacture *yearning*, Gigi, you have to make a woman yearn to buy an Indigo Seas suit."

"No woman in her right mind yearns to buy anybody's swimsuit, not Cole, not Gottex, not Sandcastle, and a large woman yearns less than any other," Gigi said stubbornly.

She really wasn't ready to get down to work yet, Gigi thought rebelliously. Archie and Byron still hadn't found the time to introduce her around the office, there were no Indigo Seas suits around to give her an idea of what they looked like, and trying to think copy in a vacuum was something she wasn't used to; she had always written from the inspiration of merchandise, or at least photographs.

"We have to *force them to yearn*," David insisted.

"That's not logical. You can't force yearning, my boy. Yearning is involuntary, look it up in the dictionary."

"Not at FRB, Gigi. That's the crucial difference between thinking catalog and thinking advertising. Here we invent yearning. Better get with the program, Gigi. Let's see a little enthusiasm, damn it!"

Irritated, Gigi stood up and threw him a snappy salute. "But I am enthusiastic, sir! Show me that target again, I'm ready to take off at dawn. Bombs away, *sir!*" He wanted enthusiasm, he'd get enthusiasm.

"Stop kidding around."

"Yes, *sir.*" She saluted again.

"I mean it. We have work to do."

"Certainly, *sir.*"

"If you salute again, I'll tear your arm off."

"Yes, *sir!*"

"Sit the fuck down!"

"Yes, *sir!*"

"If you call me 'sir' again, I'll rip your head off."

"Whatever you say, Davy, my pretty one, my lovely lad,"

Gigi said, sitting down and feeling more like herself. A touch of rebellion, even purely symbolic, refreshed her as it always did.

"It's such a kick having a teammate . . . I've never had one before . . . perhaps I've been carried away by your seniority." Gigi flitted her eyelashes at him and, just for the hell of it, favored him with a shamelessly flirtatious smile, the one she secretly thought of as "old three eyes," irretrievably, irrevocably inescapable. Was David aware that when he took his glasses off he had the most amazingly huge and interesting light brown speckled eyes? Like the girls in the old movies, nearsighted men always had an edge when they took their glasses off.

"Why are you smiling at me like that?" David demanded, wondering how his private life could be put on hold for a decade when the only private life he'd ever want was sitting right there in the office with him.

"Because I'm trying to drive you crazy—sir."

"You don't really give a shit about swimsuits, do you?"

"No team spirit, sir, that's always been my problem."

"It's a seven-million-dollar account, small for some people but major for a boutique like us. And Indigo Seas is a solid company with terrific growth potential."

"Oh, wow!"

"You have the vocabulary of an eight-year-old."

"Seven million, hey, that's almost enough to make a really cheap movie," Gigi teased. The poor benighted guy was just too serious. She owed it to him to make him smile.

"Gigi, we're still wasting time."

"On the contrary, we're getting to know each other, getting the personal stuff out of the way, as Archie suggested. Or was it Byron?"

"I don't want to hear how you lost your virginity, Gigi, I've changed my mind. I *never* want to know."

"Ah, gee, that hurts my feelings. If you won't listen now, you'll just have to go through it later. It's not a subject we can skip, like third grade. But okay." She grabbed a yellow pad and a pencil.

"Davy, you keep calling the target customer for this client 'large.' I know and you know that you really want to say 'fat.' We probably agree that 'fat' is not a word that will sell this product. Even 'plump' won't do. So could we think of our customers as 'abundant'? Abundance is a lovable concept, lots of good things to eat and drink, plenty for everybody, joy and comfort all around."

"Sure. I'm just the art director here. Never large, always abundant, as far as I'm concerned."

"At Scruples Two we sell tons and tons of dresses for abundant women. We call them 'Dolly Moons.' "

"How the hell did you manage to use Dolly Moon's name? Her last movie with Dustin Hoffman was the best!" David sat up straight.

"As usual, Dolly was trying to lose weight, so she decided she'd be motivated to diet by wanting to stay *out* of wearing Dolly Moons, and gave us permission to use her name. And she's Billy's best friend, that helped. A lot."

"We obviously can't get her for Indigo Seas."

"No. But my point is that in the catalog we didn't shoot the Dolly Moons on thin models, we used real abundant women. Abundant women know damn well they're abundant. They're deservedly suspicious, and get infuriated when they're being shown size-six models wearing clothes meant for them. There's nothing wrong with being abundant, some women naturally are, some not. In any other century—even early in this century—it was a non-issue. Many men, a surprisingly large group, have no objections at all to abundance. You can *never* underestimate the charms of abundant women. But when they buy swimsuits they're gritting their teeth and hating the idea, so they put it off as long as possible. In order to merely get them into the stores we have to make swimsuits at least a somewhat *desirable* purchase—but yearning is out of the question."

"I'm listening."

"The Nina Blanchard Agency has a whole list of former models who grew too abundant to work. That's where we found them for Scruples Two. Why don't we show the product on the most proudly abundant and prettiest model we can find? Make her our Indigo Seas poster girl?"

"Well . . . yeah . . . maybe," David said slowly. "It's never been done, but that doesn't mean it can't be."

"Maybe a guy with her?" Gigi wondered.

"No, I see her alone in a pool, a lush Venus in lush turquoise water . . . she's . . . she's not floating . . . she's bursting up out of the water, straight up from the bottom of the pool, lush sparkles of water flying through in the air all around her, lush shoulders, lush hair slicked back off her face, and a lush smile, terrific teeth —all you see of the product is where it's doing a sensational job of holding up a lush pair of abundant boobs—big boobs weren't on the list of complaints."

"And the copy line is 'Are You *Woman Enough* for Indigo Seas?' "

"That's all?"

"That's all we need."

" 'Woman enough' . . . don't you want to amplify on that? Do a riff? About the designers who understand what to minimize?"

"No," Gigi said firmly. "Once we get women curious enough about being 'woman enough' to venture into the swimsuit department, they'll find that out for themselves. The hard part is getting them there at all."

"Okay. Here's the look." David used a marking pen on a sheet of special tissue paper and passed the sketch over to her. Gigi looked at it quickly. "You're really good," she told him.

"Yeah. That's why they let me work with you. It's a reward— instead of a raise."

"How many other ideas do we need?"

"How many do you have?"

"I don't know yet. I'm just starting. 'Woman Enough'—that could be 'For the Woman Who's *All* Woman—Indigo Seas.' Or how about using 'abundant' in Italian—*abbondanza!*—a line that asks, 'Have You Got Abbondanza?' and then a checklist of things like—oh, you're learning to tango, you cook in four languages, all the neighborhood kids hang around, you whistle at construction workers, you've won prizes for your barbecue, you have five terrific red dresses, you sing like Dolly Parton, you give great head— and then we say, 'Indigo Seas, the Swimwear for Women With Abbondanza!'—and get Sophia Loren to pose in Indigo Seas. She does eyeglass ads, she's got great cleavage, she's the incarnation of *abbondanza,* why shouldn't we take a shot at getting her?"

" 'Great head'! You can't put that in the copy!"

"Davy, for heaven's sake . . . I think I shocked you. You're blushing!" Gigi rolled her eyes in wicked delight. "I was just making sure that you were paying attention."

"I was." He must have gotten an unfocused look, David thought, while he was visualizing Gigi taking off a tiny little shrunken Indigo Seas suit.

"I'm trying for a sort of what-the-hell, let's-not-get-too-serious-about-swimsuits kind of mood. Women love to take checklist tests, I always do when I see one anywhere. Damn! I just realized I don't have *abbondanza*. I never whistle at construction workers."

"Don't change the subject just when you're cooking," David begged. "We need at least four ideas that we think really work, plus others we don't have as much confidence in, for Arch and By to shoot down. Not only that, but when we get to the pitch meeting we have to show we've tried a lot of different approaches, explored various alternatives. But not too many, never confuse the client."

"I see what you mean about banging our heads against the wall. If I weren't a woman and didn't know Dolly Moon and how she feels about her body, I might be wondering where to go next," Gigi said thoughtfully. She stood up with sudden determination.

"We've got to take a look at some real, live swimsuits, Davy. Come on, let's go to Nordstrom's sports department for some on-site, in-depth research. And then let's drop in at the Department of Motor Vehicles and talk to the ladies waiting in line for their eye tests. My old dad always told me they make the best focus groups. You don't have to pay them, and they love to talk."

"Listen, Gigi, I'm sorry that I said you weren't serious, that you didn't give a shit about swimsuits."

"You know the Chiat/Day motto, 'Don't take your work seriously, but take it passionately'? That's what I'm striving for, step by step. Hey, Davy, stop! Don't you dare look for your keys. I'm driving you in my new little red wagon."

"Did you know I had a cousin who's a shopping-mall almost-billionaire?" Billy asked Spider, as they sat having drinks in front of the fire before dinner, alone now that the twins were finally stowed in their cribs.

"Nope. What's his name?"

"Winthrop, Ben Winthrop. In fact, Benjamin Warren Saltonstall Winthrop, no less. Ring any bells?"

"Loud and clear. He's one of most aggressive of the businessmen of the eighties, according to *Forbes*, although they're more polite about their terminology. I didn't know you were related. He operates out of New York, not Boston."

"Maybe, but he's also one of the awful tribe of evil cousins who persecuted me when I was growing up in Boston. There were dozens of them, all beastly. I don't remember anyone named Ben, but he called this afternoon and identified himself convincingly. The Warrens are part of the family tree that came over on the *Mayflower*."

"It sounds to me as if his blood hasn't thinned out too much, in spite of all that genealogy."

"He said he was out here on business and would love to come calling. I haven't been back to Boston since Ellis was alive, and I haven't seen any of my cousins since Aunt Cornelia's funeral, when I was twenty-four. I certainly don't remember a Ben Winthrop back then."

"Did you invite him over?"

"Of course, sweetheart. Would I miss a chance to show you off to any of that snobbish, clubby, self-satisfied gang that made my life a misery when I was a poor little poor girl? Would I pass up an opportunity to show off the twins?"

"I think you've reversed the order of your areas of pride," Spider said, temporarily willing to come second.

"Not by much. Anyway, he's coming to dinner tomorrow. Let's ask Gigi, she's all alone and I'm dying to hear about her new job."

"She's only been there two days."

"True, but what about the importance of first impressions? You decided I was a frosty bitch the minute we met."

"Weren't you?"

"Damn right I was. And I'm proud of it. At least I have that period of my life on my résumé, now that I'm brainwashed, barefoot, tied to the kitchen stove, and pregnant."

"Again?" he asked mildly.

"Just an expression."

"That's a relief."

"Don't you want more children?" Billy asked piteously. "No little girl?"

"Of course I do, but not right yet, darling, not until Max and Hal stop controlling you with their eyes and start verbal interaction in which you might be able to get the better of them."

Did his cousin Billy Winthrop also take a pair of bodyguards with her wherever she went, Ben Winthrop asked himself in mild surprise as he leaned out of his car to give his name to the guard at the gatehouse that stood squarely at the driveway entrance to Billy's estate in Holmby Hills. This was almost like Houston, that great boomtown, he thought, where one of his richest friends had built a watchtower on top of his house, manned round-the-clock by men with machine guns. Hugely rich people in Boston and New York, including people who had as much money—well, almost as much—as Billy Ikehorn, were known to walk the streets, take taxis, even subways. Surely this was excessive? Or perhaps not? He still knew little, after all, about the intricate local rituals of Los Angeles wealth, although he intended to become a quick expert on the subject.

Los Angeles had fascinated Benjamin Winthrop for years. It was the last American frontier before Hawaii in his plan to pinpoint certain privileged parts of the world with his malls. Now thirty-five, he had entered his teen years in the 1960s, a fact that might have sidetracked a boy with less focused ambition, but Ben had zoomed right through those tempting, throbbing years without feeling the slightest temptation to drop out, tune in, turn on, or acquire flower power. He'd homed in young on real estate, the way millions of his generation had homed in on rock 'n' roll, and singlemindedly he had started to acquire mall sites while he was a freshman at Harvard, by borrowing against the funds he could expect to come into at twenty-one.

Most un-Bostonian, his father had considered it, disapproving of something that deviated so far from what he considered a proper use of a sound business mind. "You should plan to go into the family trusts, many of them eventually your own, Benjamin, instead of trying to cover good land with ugly parking lots and hid-

54

eous shopfronts," he'd said dryly, as he sat in the library of his Bulfinch mansion on Mount Vernon Street. "Brains like yours should be used for the conservation and growth of family capital and the protection of the public institutions that depend on our support. Certainly not on something as essentially vulgar and aesthetically immoral as those repulsive malls. That's why I've decided not to invest with you."

Clearly his father was not the stuff of which clipper ship captains were made, Ben told himself, no matter how many such rip-snorting, rough-and-ready pistoleros had founded the family's fortune. So much the worse for the old fellow. He'd been obligated to give his own father a chance to get in on the ground floor, but now that he'd missed his shot, there wouldn't be another.

Ben Winthrop took his father's refusal as final proof that his own plan to base his future operation in New York was sound. The Boston financial decision-making climate was frequently influenced by moral judgments. Ben considered himself warned by Lewis Carroll in *Alice in Wonderland*. "Tut, tut, child," said the Duchess. "Everything's got a moral if only you can find it."

Early in his life, at the age when people were still giving him children's books, he'd decided that he didn't have a minute to waste and morality didn't intrigue him. No man ever made a fortune by seeking moral opportunities, and in the course of the last decade and a half, Ben Winthrop had become a millionaire eight hundred times over, both from his malls and other investments he made on the side, particularly in shipping. His eye was always on the alert for opportunity, and the gods of opportunity, so flatteringly courted, rewarded him richly.

Although Ben Winthrop's quick success in business might have indicated that he was an impatient man, such a judgment would have been wrong. He had an innate capacity to judge when patience, a keen and relentless patience, would repay the investment of his interest, and he was disciplined in the art of waiting and watching and coddling a project along until precisely the moment when it reached perfect ripeness. Then he would leap, quickly and thoroughly, and take what he wanted and make it his own. Anything he possessed, he insisted on possessing in its entirety. The concept of sharing was foreign to him, and profoundly distasteful.

He treated women he coveted in the same way as he treated pieces of property, cultivating them with a deliberately lulling patience until exactly the propitious moment. He was more than enough of a self-observer to understand the advantage of his somewhat academic exterior that gave no clues to his inner and predatory self. He had graduated from Harvard summa cum laude, with a genuine interest in literature and history, and a genuine love of beauty in all its forms. His greatest pleasures were making money, loving women, and observing beautiful objects. When a woman or an object struck him as exceptionally worthy, he would stop at nothing to acquire her or it.

Ben Winthrop had no idea of the extent of his pride. He would have been astonished if anyone had called him immoral. He was amoral, he occasionally told himself with an inward smile, a man to whom petty moral judgments could not apply since he was outside the narrow world of morality, elevated by his own efforts to the rational sphere of nonmorality where the sensible and rich existed, envied by those who were unable to leap as high.

Ben Winthrop had always been keenly interested in the big clan's other outstanding rebel, Billy Ikehorn, whose doings had gradually become the stuff of family legend. He had been a kid when she left Boston and just seventeen when, at twenty-one, she'd married Ikehorn, but he still remembered how the women of the family had discussed the subject of Josiah Winthrop's daughter quietly among themselves at Sunday lunch, in tones that were the Boston equivalent of scandalized gossip. He'd read about her building of Scruples with the approval he reserved for absolutely anything that showed a spirit of enterprise, short of unsuccessful bank robbery.

As he let Burgo take his car, Ben Winthrop looked over the vast house and its acres of surrounding gardens, softly illuminated by night, with quick appraisal. An expert on every kind of real estate, he still got a thrill out of recognizing the ultimate, no matter if you couldn't build a mall on it. He was shown in by a maid, and advanced to meet Billy with his characteristic quick and long stride, that of a man who was always in a hurry.

"Welcome, Cousin Ben," Billy said, scrutinizing his face. "I certainly can't say that you look familiar."

"That's probably because we've never met. I was part of another wave of cousins. Your bunch never fraternized much with mine until we got older."

"My bunch never fraternized with *me*," she said in the matter-of-fact way people learn to deal with the deepest wounds of childhood.

Ben Winthrop was a man with presence, Billy decided as she introduced him to Spider. He had a lean, hard face, a lean, hard body, a lean, hard handshake and a slow, thoroughly convincing smile that had, even in the moment of greeting, something thoughtful about it, as if it weren't prompted by an automatic response but by a genuine inner decision.

Nanny Elizabeth came downstairs and presented Max and Hal. Billy watched as her new cousin looked them over closely, knowing enough not to offer them a stranger's finger, covered with a stranger's germs, to touch and, God forbid, then put in their mouths. Instead he stroked the soles of their feet with more than the normal degree of appreciation she would have expected from a bachelor.

"I don't have children, but that indescribably wonderful way they smell has a powerful impact on me," he said as the nanny carried the sleepy pair away. "I get to inspect a lot of them, my friends are all reproducing like mad, but your two have more powerful stares than any I've encountered. I feel as if they've scanned my brain and judged it passable, just barely. Am I wrong, or are they particularly fine examples of their species?"

"Nah, they're mutts," Spider said.

"In that case, I stand corrected."

He was a clever boy, Billy thought, this Ben Winthrop, or rather a clever man. She looked at him with renewed interest. He had a high and lightly furrowed forehead that gave him an almost intellectual air, lots of independent-minded brown hair that grew in several directions at once in spite of a good haircut, a biggish, long, bumpy, idiosyncratic nose, highly strokable like that of an intelligent dog, a firmly cut mouth, long and thin, and a good chin. His eyes were the indeterminate deep gray blue of a changeable winter sea, and the way they were set under his brows gave him a look of being trustworthy and open, although she doubted that a mall tycoon would possess those attributes. He must be at least three inches shorter than Spider, perhaps barely six feet tall, and he moved well, in possession of the space around him. There was something slightly professorial about him, Oxford donnish, Billy thought, which most probably was due to the lingering influence of growing up in Boston.

What would his cock look like when he was aroused, she wondered. *Good God!* How had that popped into her mind? She who was so totally ga-ga about Spider that other men didn't exist. How on earth could she have had such an outrageously inappropriate thought?

Deeply shocked at herself, Billy quietly sipped a glass of champagne while Spider talked to Ben. Finally she decided that her question only proved that old habits died hard, sterling wife and noble mother though she was. Or did it mean that Ben Winthrop had the kind of sex appeal that made every woman he met entertain such speculations? She preferred the latter explanation, although the days when she'd had similar thoughts about every attractive man she saw lay not that far behind her.

"Anybody home?" Gigi's lighthearted voice rang with the assurance of a certain welcome as she came into the brightness of the house, bringing with her that perceptible, all-but-visible suggestion of a creature who should, by all rights, be spending her life dancing the Charleston, a creature whose personal attitude toward reality, a shimmying, swaying, tantalizing, ain't-we-got-fun attitude, came out of a decade long past.

"Everybody, darling," Billy called. "We're in here."

Gigi entered the room wearing slim brown velvet jeans tucked into her favorite pair of soft brown suede boots, which came up over her knees and ended in a wide cuff. Her pale green woven tunic was belted with thick gold cording, and there was a ruff of Irish lace at her neck. Gigi's small breasts were visibly held up by nothing except youth and sheer Irish nerve. With her bangs and bell of orangy hair, she looked like a figure in a tapestry, a pageboy, a minstrel, a young prince, or a girl disguised as a boy for a masque.

After Gigi had kissed Billy and Spider, she turned to Ben Winthrop with her usual directness, offering her hand with open curiosity widening her eyes.

"Gigi, this is my cousin Ben Winthrop. Ben, this is Graziella Giovanna Orsini, my stepdaughter."

"So formal? Is that because Ben is my stepcousin?" Gigi asked. "After all, Billy, you endured a year of my father, but you've kept me more than seven. You and I could even be considered married by common law, if one of us were a man, stepdaughter or not. So why shouldn't your cousin be my cousin? I don't have a single one of my own, and I've been deprived long enough. I *claim* this cousin."

"There's a certain rough justice to that," Spider said, enjoying Billy's perplexed look. "Ben's my cousin by marriage, now that I think about it. Why don't you just consider him a cousin-once-removed, Gigi, whatever that means?"

"Do I have a vote?" Ben Winthrop wondered, taking an involuntary step toward Gigi in a desire to see exactly what shade of green her eyes actually were, behind that bristling barrier of black lashes.

"This is not a democracy," Gigi informed him, a smile deepening on her smile-shaped lips.

Oh, she's up to no good tonight, Spider thought, surveying her. It's either the new job or Zach being out of town too long, but she's using that potent, private-blend heartbreaker stuff, and we all know that's not playing fair, don't we?

"What is it, then?" Ben asked. "A monarchy?"

"A benign dictatorship," Gigi said. "Hal and Max make the rules, the rest of us live to understand and obey, right, Spider?"

"Too true, kiddo. How's your new gig?"

"Fascinating, crazy, confusing, nerve-racking, intriguing, utterly manipulative, and at the same time curiously innocent. When a product is one of our accounts, it really, truly *is* the best. If it's not, it's beneath contempt—there's no place for gray hats in advertising. I'm what's called a 'new hire,' so everyone is suspicious of me, plus I'm a 'creative,' and creatives are notoriously flighty and childlike in their desire for approval, so for the moment I can do no wrong and no right. It's entirely different from Scruples Two, where we functioned rationally. Advertising is like a lunatic asylum crossed with a kindergarten—I absolutely love it! It's about ten thousand times harder than Scruples Two."

Gigi looked excitingly reckless, Billy thought, like a combatant, a small, vital female fighting cock, living with a strutting glitter, ready to risk, to plunge, to take any chance. How could hawking bathing suits to overweight women cause this particular metamorphosis, or was it due to someone she'd met at work, or merely being out on her own? Gigi was deliciously, visibly full of herself in a complicated way; excited, almost overwhelmed, yet bursting with vitality.

"Who are you working for?" Ben asked.

"A new shop, a boutique called Frost Rourke Bernheim. They used to be with Caldwell in New York. You probably wouldn't have heard of them."

Gigi didn't know much about the recent history of advertising Ben Winthrop thought in amusement. So she'd joined the notorious account-nappers and found them curiously innocent. His new cousin-once-removed was clipper-ship-worthy for sure.

The evening ended early because Billy had to get up at dawn to give the twins their bottles. Gigi, her mood restless and much too keyed up to consider going home, accepted when Ben Winthrop asked if she'd like a nightcap.

"Where would you like to go?" he asked. "Silly that we have to take both cars. I feel ungallant."

"This isn't neighborhood-bar territory . . . no corner pub for miles. The nearest place is the Bel Air Hotel, but you'd never be able to find it by yourself," she said, superior in her local expertise. "The few little signs to the hotel are easy to miss. Follow me." Gigi lifted a grandiose arm, pointed forward, and hopped proudly into her VW.

Soon, after driving through the dark, winding roads of Bel Air, unlit, it seemed, deliberately, so that only residents could find their way about, they settled in a far corner of the little-used but spacious bar of that smallest and most elegant of Los Angeles hotels, a bar where a wood fire glowed under the mantelpiece even in the summer, a bar lined with dark wood paneling, where the banquettes were covered in tapestry and the green leather chairs studded with nailheads, a bar designed to look like a man's retreat in a British castle.

"Where do you live?" Ben asked Gigi, who had curled up in the corner of the banquette, her boots tucked under her, elaborately tasseled pillows tucked behind her back, as if she were in her own living room.

"In the Hollywood Hills."

"An apartment?"

"A tiny house," she answered, purposefully brief. Gigi had no intention of broadcasting the exact circumstances of her private life to any man, particularly one she had just met. "Are you here to violate our lovely state? Pave it over with manicure salons and quick-copy stores and croissant bakeries, because if you are, it's being done already."

"I don't do mini-malls," he laughed. "I do the real thing, branches of department stores, multiplex movie houses, chain grocery stores, high-end speciality shops, restaurants—"

"Rape *and* pillage."

"Exactly."

"On the theory that if you don't, someone else will."

"Absolutely. Except I insist on getting there first."

"It's so refreshing to meet an honest man," Gigi said in mock admiration.

"Honesty is my middle name, after Saltonstall. Don't you want to know more about me?"

"Or, as David would say, 'Let's get the personal stuff over with.' "

"Who's David?"

"An art director. We're a creative team, the two of us. Can you imagine a business that puts two strangers into one room all day long and expects them to work up a winning ad campaign together in the week we have before the pitch?"

"And will you?"

"They're betting on it. I have a feeling it could—might— maybe—just happen. Stranger things have come to pass in the ad business, or game . . . at least I think they used to call it a game."

"It sounds a hell of a lot more fun than solving my latest problem."

Ben Winthrop looked at Gigi closely. During dinner he had been too caught up in general conversation to pay close attention to her, but he had not, for a second, been unaware of her presence. He was a man who, rightly, considered women one of his areas of expertise. He had had many of the loveliest in the country for the period during which they interested him. Gigi did not fall, neatly or otherwise, into any category he recognized.

Women, in Ben Winthrop's opinion, all played games, and she hadn't revealed the nature of her game, although she must have one. He knew he was a cynic, but any man who wasn't a cynic about women was something worse, a fool. She wasn't getting by on charm, although she easily could have; she wasn't using her looks more than other women of equal visual delight; she didn't seem to have an agenda in his regard. That, of course, could be an agenda in itself, but she was probably too young and inexperienced for such a subtle nuance.

"And what's your latest problem?" Gigi asked.

"I'm going to have to foreclose on my first tenants, the Muller family. My company is a landlord as well as a builder, and sometimes the landlord part gets painful. Kids' Paradise is a chain of toy stores that is about to be put out of business by the spread of Toys "Я" Us—they can't match Toys' rock-bottom discount prices, and the merchandise is basically identical. I have a Kids' Paradise in almost every one of my malls and I'm friends with their management, but they haven't been able to pay the rent, not for months."

"How many Paradises does that make?"

"A hundred and two. I own seventy-three malls, and they have stores that aren't in malls as well."

"Seventy-three! The mall-master!"

"I cover the country—and it's a lot of country. I make it a point to build as close as I can to highly prosperous areas so that our tenants do upscale business and I get upscale rents."

"Where are you building in L.A.?" Gigi asked. Ben Winthrop's eyes seemed frank and undefended. Nevertheless, they revealed nothing he didn't intend them to show, she thought. He reminded her of basketball coaches in TV close-ups during the playoffs. When their "game faces" were firmly in place, the camera couldn't get the slightest hint from the coaches of how upset or pleased they were with the performance of their teams, not even after the game was over. They had to make themselves into charlatans in order to remain authentic.

"Right now we're in construction in Santa Monica, Culver

City, and Encino. Then I'll spread up north and down south, on land I've already bought."

"It sounds like an invasion," Gigi said with a low whistle. "Did you bring the pods with you? Are you friendly to us natives, or are we merely a species you plan on observing from afar, the playthings of the gods?"

"It all depends on the status of your credit cards."

"You come from Planet Visa?"

"Precisely."

"How crass!"

"And I thought you were in advertising."

"Only for the last two days," she protested. "I haven't learned to be a hard-hearted businessman like you. Foreclosing on something called Kids' Paradise, and you actually admit it!"

"Told you I was honest. Business is business, eventually, no matter how you hate to do certain things. Look, you should see the renderings of the elevations of my mall in Santa Monica—it's truly beautiful. The city gave me permission to buy the land and the permits to build because it's architecturally outstanding. Let me show them to you, let me redeem my reputation."

"I couldn't make time tomorrow to look at a long-lost folio of da Vinci drawings—it's back to Indigo Seas and the abundant woman, all day, all night, if necessary."

"It'll just take ten minutes, now, not tomorrow. I have them in my suite . . . here."

"Well, why the hell did you let me think you didn't know how to get to the hotel?" Gigi asked indignantly. "You want to redeem your reputation, you claim to be an honest man, and you didn't tell me you were staying here? Ha!"

"You looked as if you were leading a cavalry charge into the wilderness—I simply enjoyed watching you, I like your style, I admire a spirited female, is that a crime?"

"Yeah, yeah," she muttered, unimpressed.

"Please?"

"Oh, all right. But only because I claimed you as cousin-once-removed. I was overly impulsive, I see that clearly now, but I owe you the benefit of the doubt."

"I'm honestly impressed," Gigi said, after she'd taken a long look at the architect's drawings. "As malls go, this must be as good as it gets. But I guess there won't be a toy store in it."

"It looks that way, unless Toys "Я" Us moves in, and with our high rents that's not likely."

Gigi got up from her seat near the coffee table and began to pace slowly around the large sitting room of Ben's suite, a room that breathed luxury in twenty-five shades of terra-cotta.

"Did Kids' Paradise ever advertise?" she asked.

"Locally, but not much."

"Hmm. Listen, Ben, I had to go to five baby showers in the last six months—one of them for Billy, one for Sasha, three for Spider's sisters. The guests were all women with money, from comfortable to rich, the kind who live near your malls. And I have *never* in my life seen such presents!"

As she spoke, she walked faster and faster, shaking her head at the memory of the excessive baby showers.

"I didn't know such absolutely gorgeous baby clothes existed, and all the equally special outfits for when the baby stuff is outgrown—then there was a slew of really expensive toys and things that are more for the mother to enjoy than for kids to use or play with, like antique crib quilts, antique children's chairs, music boxes, old doll's tea sets."

Gigi stopped walking and turned to him.

"Ben, listen, here's my point. After the presents are opened, the guests invariably start comparing notes on how impossible it is to find something special for these showers, how much harder it is than finding things for a bridal shower. These occasions are more and more frequent with so many women having babies and lots of them having them later in life."

"Why do I have the feeling you're leading me into a trap?"

"Because I am. Just listen. Baby-shower guests are feeling the pressure to one-up each other with everyone watching as the guest of honor opens each gift. It's obscene! Take me, for example. Once I spent hours looking for something really great to give Sasha. I was desperate. Finally I found a bookstore in the Valley that specializes in old children's books . . . I bought out their stock, every Oz book, every Beatrix Potter, every Hardy Boy, every Nancy

Drew . . . I gave Sasha a first edition of *Glinda the Good,* and now I'm set for years of parties and I'm keeping my source a secret so that no one copies me."

"Gigi, your altruistic impulses are impressive. But could you get to the point here?"

"Have I got your attention? Good. Okay, I realize I live in a community where everything is bigger than life, but doesn't it make sense that this baby-present mania has spread to *all* the expensive suburbs, in a less dramatic way no doubt, but you know that trends start here first. Shaker Heights? Oak Forest? Brookline? La Jolla? The Main Line? You know. Doesn't that mean that there's a need for a store that sells *nothing but* upscale children's things, *especially to grandparents?*" Gigi had stopped pacing and was standing in the middle of the room, her hands spread eloquently.

"Grandparents?"

"God, you're such a dumb bachelor, Ben! Grandparents give the world's most ridiculously expensive presents, because they had to hold back and try not to spoil their own kids, but now all bets are off. Plus one set of grandparents is always viciously competitive with the other set."

"I still don't see it," he said skeptically, drawing her out. Bachelor or not, Ben Winthrop spent many thousands of dollars every year on suitably impressive presents to the newborn babes his cousins were producing at a constant rate, as well as on presents to the many godchildren who had been foisted on him by his Harvard classmates. Birthdays seemed to come around on an almost weekly basis, and Christmas was a nightmare. One of his secretaries was permanently detailed to keep on top of the children's gift situation and she complained about its difficulty.

"I want to change Kids' Paradise, make it into a Scruples for kids' gifts. Call it, oh . . . oh . . . The Enchanted Attic, yeah, that's it!—*The Enchanted Attic*—redecorate to fit the name, turn their entire merchandising policy upside down, bring in a line of fabulous gift wrappings—the right wrapping is essential, the box has to be a signature box—make it *the* place to find the best, most exciting, and original presents, the Tiffany of toy stores, plus kids' antiques and clothing the department stores don't have, and a great line of specially designed smaller gifts, like Tiffany's baby teething rings, for example, for people who want to spend less and still buy status and—"

"Oh, I don't know," Ben said expressionlessly. He did know, he'd known from the minute she'd said "Scruples for kids" that this idea was a natural, a potential gold mine, his kind of investment, for his malls were located in precisely the communities where such shops would flourish.

"Why the hell not?" Gigi put her hands on her hips and looked at him challengingly. "Give me one good reason. Aren't you supposed to be a visionary?"

"You talk fast, lady, but making it happen would take a major infusion of capital."

"I think capital is less of a problem than location. If you let the Kids' Paradise people, the Mullers, stay put until they change over, they won't go belly-up and—"

"What's in it for you?" he demanded.

"But isn't that obvious? They'd absolutely *have* to advertise. That would be an essential part of the deal. The Enchanted Attic would have to become a client of FRB and I'd bring in a piece of new business."

"That's all you want? You're sure?"

"I never want to go back to retailing, thank you very much, but I just bet Billy—it's right down her alley—might be—"

Ben pounced before she could complete that thought. "Stop right there, Gigi, I never work with partners."

"Say that again."

"I never work with partners. I enjoy gambling now and then, so I'll put up the capital myself, refrain from foreclosing, defer the rent for as long as necessary, and hire a retailing expert to work with the Kids' Paradise people."

"Oh, oh, oh . . . !"

"Why are you wailing like that?"

"You're going too fast! Wait just one hell of a little minute here! You didn't say anything about an advertising budget. No advertising, no Enchanted Attic."

"What sort of budget did you have in mind?" If he hadn't had a lifetime of practice in keeping a straight face, he'd have had to smile at her naiveté.

"Well. Hmmmm . . . we're pitching a seven-million-dollar account just to try to sell one brand of swimsuits to one type of woman, not all of whom swim . . . and here we're talking an *explosion* of kids . . . upper-income kids, right up to preteen, all of whom have birthdays and Christmas . . . let me think . . . to make a dent with a chain of a hundred and two stores . . . I'd imagine," Gigi said, guessing wildly, "you'd need lots more than that for print advertising to establish the client's identity. After all, Indigo Seas already has an identity, and The Enchanted Attic doesn't. Oh, absolutely *more*. You'd want national print in the glossy magazines and local print in the city magazines and then you couldn't possibly leave out the parents' magazines or the women's magazines . . . I'm not even thinking about TV . . . say twelve million the first year." She held her breath.

"I'd say . . . eight. Until the metamorphosis is complete, the ads will be less than full-throttle."

"But, Ben, it pays to advertise."

"At the end of the year, I'll reevaluate."

"I don't know," said Gigi, and stopped.

"Go on, say what's on your mind," he urged, laughing. "It's not as if you won't eventually."

"I don't know, as the saying goes, whether to shit or go blind. *YIPPEE!*" She collapsed on the sofa, hugging herself in delight waving her boots in the air. "Wait a minute," she said in the middle of her transports. "You won't change your mind, will you? Is this a done deal or isn't it? Shake hands on it," she demanded.

"It's a deal, here, let's shake." She might still ask for a percentage of the profit, since it was her idea, even after they shook on the deal, Ben Winthrop thought, or Billy or Spider might advise her to ask for it, and he'd be obligated to go along. But why worry now? After all, he could be wrong and The Enchanted Attic might not pan out. Worst case, he'd have a loss against his pre-tax profits.

"Let's have a drink to celebrate," he suggested.

"Oh. No, I really have to get home. I had no idea it was so late."

"I'll walk you to the valet parker."

Ben's suite was at a good distance from the entrance to the hotel, and they walked through dimly lit pathways bordered by the lavish displays of flowers for which the hotel was famous, which linked a series of mysterious dark courtyards in which fountains played. As they entered the last courtyard, both lost in thought, Ben stopped and drew Gigi close to him. She looked up in surprise and saw him smiling down at her.

"Sweet cousin-once-removed, you're quite a revelation," he said, and bent over and kissed her hard, his long mouth, even in that quick moment, quickly possessive, his lips pressing hers with an unmistakable potential for passion. Gigi's entire body stiffened in instant resistance. He released her immediately so that she didn't need to draw away. *Mistake*, he thought, furious at himself, *big mistake*. What had come over him to make such an obviously premature misjudgment? She had entranced him tonight, but that was no excuse for his stupidity. He never jumped the gun, damn it! It wouldn't happen again, he promised himself in a cold rage of pride.

"I'd like to see the agency," Ben said, in an impersonal tone, as if nothing had happened. "When's a good time?"

"I'll have to tell them first." Gigi matched his cool. "I haven't thought that far ahead."

"Will you call tomorrow and let me know? I'll be back here by six."

"Absolutely," she said, moving as quickly as she could toward the lobby lights, where the darkness of the pathways of the hotel disappeared.

As Gigi drove off, Ben walked slowly back to his suite, still thinking about Gigi's reaction to his kiss. Yes, of course he had chosen an inappropriate moment, but her reaction seemed excessive. Was she gun-shy? Was she taken? One thing he was sure of, there was nothing specifically personal about it. He was sure she liked him, or he would never have touched her. She was a puzzle, Miss Gigi Orsini, and one day he would solve that puzzle, he promised himself. But he would do it with such patience, with such cunning, with such invisible planning, that she would come to him of her own accord. He owed himself that for her resistance, for her stiffening at the touch of his mouth. No woman had ever reacted in that way before.

One kiss, Gigi thought, as she drove home, just one perfectly natural kiss, from a man who knows nothing about Zach, and you act like a teenager. Why did she feel so . . . shaken . . . guilty

. . . no, as if she'd just escaped . . . *danger?* Well, that was totally ridiculous. She wouldn't allow herself to be irrational. As she ran up the stairs to her bedroom she decided on the perfect antidote to her lingering feeling of confusion. She'd phone Davy and tell him the incredible news. Even though it was late, even if he was asleep, he was her teammate and should be the first to know.

4

Oh, Gigi, sweetheart, this is no way to live." Zach Nevsky's voice contained the wholehearted power of persuasion that freed actors to attain heights they never imagined they could reach. His love for her added an irresistible weight to the deep emotion of his words, his voice roughened at the edges by insistence.

Gigi felt an unwelcome wariness spike suddenly into her mind as they lay entangled on their bed. She had been inhaling, her nose buried in his chest, whiffing up the complicated infusion, the utterly satisfactory soup of masculinity that was particular to Zach after they made love, so blissfully content that she felt as if she were floating weightlessly, expanding cell by cell into an aromatic heaven, until his words broke the spell.

She had heard similar words before, she had heard that tone of voice before, she had let Zach lure her up to the top of a high mountain when she barely knew how to ski, because of his ability to talk her into following him anywhere. She had been brought down from that mountain in tears and terror, lucky only to have broken a leg, and if anyone in the world was immune to the tenacious persistence, the dogged conviction, the great-hearted bossiness of Zach Nevsky, who believed so deeply that he knew better than you did what was right for you, she was.

"Zach, darling," she answered, trying to summon her reason as well as she could while lying captured in his arms, relaxed, grateful, deliciously sore, possessed from head to toe. "I've barely started at FRB . . . it's only been three days. How can I possibly take any time off? Unless . . . well, I suppose I could leave Friday after work and come back Sunday night—now that's a possibility, if the flights are right."

Zach had unexpectedly come back to Los Angeles in the late afternoon of the day following her dinner at Billy's, and she'd found him arriving home just as she returned from the office. In this preproduction phase of his Kalispell epic, major budget problems had declared themselves and Zach had flown in with certain of his co-workers to confer with the studio chiefs before things got out of hand. Tomorrow, after a full day of meetings, he intended to fly back to Montana with the problems solved and saddlebags stuffed with an infusion of fresh money.

"I'm not talking about a weekend, Gigi—I can't stand my life when we're apart," Zach told her. "When you walked in tonight and I saw your little face, I knew right down to the core that you *had* to quit this new job and marry me and *be* with me, the two of us together, with none of this ridiculous wait-and-see stuff. It's a question of *survival*, Gigi. We're doing something criminally insane, darling, we're wasting all the time we should be having together, we're losing something *irreplaceable.*"

As she lay unmoving on the bed, he bent over her face intently, with all the massive maleness he commanded. Gigi looked up at him, at the dominating way in which his head sat on his strong neck, at the arrogance of his reckless, prominent nose with its broken ridge that was matched by the determination of his demanding mouth, and she mentally dug in her heels.

"Zach, we've had this conversation before," she said. "What's changed in our circumstances?"

"Look, when I left for Montana I was so full of this new picture and its possibilities that I blanked on the amount of time I'd committed to, I put the fourteen-week shooting schedule out of my mind, I didn't admit to myself that we'd be apart again for months and months—but now—hell, being away from you is taking half the fun out of making this picture."

"You should have thought of that before you made your decision. The shooting schedule hasn't changed, and God knows, we talked it over for hours." Gigi tried not to let her irritation show in her voice as she moved away from him and drew the sheet over her legs.

"I know we did, darling, and it's all my fault. Totally, absolutely my fault." He was so utterly contrite that Gigi grew more annoyed. It wasn't fair of him to insist on having his own way, no matter what mistakes he made and admitted to.

"Your last two pictures were made on location in New York and Texas," she said evenly, "and I couldn't go along. We met on weekends when it was possible, which was next to never, because you mostly had to work straight through. Next you had your choice of directing three films right here in Hollywood, but you were determined to do this one."

"Why the hell didn't *you insist* that I turn it down?"

"God damn you, Zach! Now you're blaming me because you went ahead and did what you were dying to do!" Gigi disentangled herself completely and propped herself up on one elbow.

"You're right to be mad at me. I'm mad at me! Mad as hell, darling. But we could have it all if you'd only marry me, don't you see, isn't it evident?"

"What I see is that you could have it all, Zach, and I'd turn into a kind of privileged camp-follower. Whenever your job left you time for me, I'd be there for you . . . if I hadn't gone raving mad in the meanwhile."

"Come on, angel, don't talk dumb. There's a whole life there for you—it's the most beautiful country that ever was—you could be hanging out, making friends, the producer's wife is a nice woman, she'll be around, and you'd meet people in the town—you could come to dailies, in fact there just might be a chance I could wangle you a job in wardrobe, even though you're not in the union —there must be ways to get around—"

72

"Shut the fuck up, Zach Nevsky!" She sat up so quickly that he jumped back to avoid her head striking his chin. "Those are insulting suggestions and you should know it! Hanging out, as if I were in high school. It's amazing how you can overlook the fact that I have a job right here."

"Oh, sure, advertising. Big deal!" Zach sat on the edge of the bed, speaking with a clear contempt he didn't bother to hide. "Great line of work. You know as well as I do that advertising is a legalized form of fraud. My God, nobody *needs* most of the stuff that's advertised, they could perfectly well keep their car five more years, drink the well scotch instead of Cutty Sark, use the supermarket brand of toilet paper, eat the cheaper brand of TV dinners —they all taste equally lousy—and give me a break, does one kind of battery really last longer than any other kind?"

"You sound like a bright twelve-year-old who's just discovered Marxism," Gigi said firmly. She didn't want this fight, she hadn't picked it, but she wouldn't let him bulldoze her.

"Three days in advertising and by God you're a convert, you're actually defending it," he said, grinning at the sight of her stubborn face. "This Archie character had the incredible chutzpah to tell you it was an art form, and you didn't pack him off to a good movie?" Zach mocked her from Olympus, secure in his belief that film and theater were the only lasting art forms of the twentieth century. "You should have told him what George Orwell said— 'Advertising is the rattling of a stick inside a swill bucket.' "

"Look, Zach, let's not get into that art-form discussion right now," Gigi said, sitting hard on her temper. She still hadn't had a second to tell him about Indigo Seas or The Enchanted Attic, for they had fallen into bed with a monster hunger the moment they found themselves together. "Look at the time. Five people will be ringing our bell in a few minutes, and neither one of us can answer the door naked. Art is long and life is short, so get your pants on, darling."

"Actually the words are 'Life is short, the art long, opportunity fleeting, experience treacherous, judgment difficult, so get your pants on, darling.' " Zach grinned. "Bet you don't know who said that."

"You win," Gigi responded, thinking that if you didn't love Zach, it might be quite possible to learn to dislike him. A man with a phenomenal memory could always find a way to prove him-self right.

"Hippocrates. From a Greek pageant I directed in high school."

" 'Judgment difficult,' huh? I'll remember that. What should I wear? Where are we all eating?"

"Well . . . here, actually."

"You didn't," she gasped, incredulous.

"Sweetheart . . . it's only a couple of people and we need to talk privately . . . a restaurant isn't a good idea . . . some sim-ple pasta—you know it won't take five minutes the way you work . . ."

"Zach, you walk in here unexpectedly, throw me in bed for an hour, make love to me two or three times, start a major discus-sion about our future, and now you want me to start cooking pasta for a crowd . . . Have I left out anything?"

"It was only twice, actually," Zach said hastily, "but you're right, we'll go out. I'm sorry, sweetheart, it's just that cooking's so easy for you . . . and . . . never mind, where should we go?"

Gigi gazed at him, shaking her head. Zach truly looked crest-fallen, his big, beautifully muscled, naked body slumped on the edge of the bed. Oh, what the hell, she thought, why not? A little pasta, a glass of wine . . . she adored feeding people and she hadn't cooked for anyone but herself for much too long. Zach had to have a tight war plan for tomorrow. He'd assembled his team—his producer, his agent, his chief assistant on the picture, the script writer, and the film editor. Tonight was an emergency council before they went to fight with the studio, and unquestionably the troops had to be fed.

"I'll make something," she told him, "it's okay, I don't mind, in fact it's fun."

She had ten minutes to shower and jump into some pants and a T-shirt before the doorbell rang, Gigi figured. As she toweled herself dry, she excitedly planned a meal for seven people with the stores she kept in the house for herself, and by the time she put a bucket of ice cubes and an array of bottles and glasses on the coffee table in the living room, she had invented an angel-hair pasta served with a sauce derived from vitello tonnato, made of of puréed canned tuna fish, tiny defrosted green peas, capers, anchovies, olive oil, chicken stock, chopped parsley, and chives. There was always a hunk of aged Romano cheese in the house to grate over everything, there were loaves of Italian bread and containers of ice cream in the freezer, there were plenty of greens for a big salad. Probably not her finest hour, Gigi thought happily, as her experienced hands flew over the chopping board and deftly operated the can opener that defeated Zach's always clumsy kitchen efforts, but it would fill seven stomachs.

"Toots, could you pass more pasta?"
"Sweetie, is there some more sauce down near you?"
"Hon, where'd the other loaf of bread go?"
"Darling, do you have a little garlic in the kitchen?"
"Kiddo, where'd you put the cheese?"
"I'm allergic to anchovies. Do you have a can of tomato sauce?"
"Kiddo, could you bring out another bottle of that red?"
"Anybody see any chocolate sauce?"
"Mind if I check out the fridge for strawberry ice cream?"
"Pasta, toots! We need more pasta down at this end!"
"Hon, is there more salad left anywhere?"
"I could use a clean plate here, sweetie."
"Anybody see any chocolate sauce?"
"Wasn't there any strawberry ice cream?"
"Darling, would you get out the brandy? And some glasses?"

"Thank you, Gigi, it was a really lovely dinner, even if you forgot the garlic, even if there wasn't any strawberry ice cream. It was lovely of you to fetch and carry and pour and serve while we talked our excited grownup talk that was too complicated for you to be expected to understand it. It was lovely of you not to mind being treated like an incompetent waitress and a thoughtless hostess. It was lovely of you not to notice that nobody was sure of your name, toots, hon, sweetie. It was lovely of you not to care that we were too busy with our important business to bother to say 'please' or 'thank you,' " Gigi muttered to herself while she busily moved from the living room to the kitchen, beginning to restore order.

"You talking to me?" Zach asked, as he strode back and forth, wide awake and too charged up by the excitement of being on the eve of battle to stop moving.

"No, just keeping myself company."

"God, what a great group of people! Didn't you think they were great?" His expression was radiant with enthusiasm; his dark, excited eyes, his full mouth, and his taut, tanned skin all reflected his bursting energy.

"Great," she assented.

"It won't be like this all the time, darling, we won't have to waste time worrying about money problems, although you can never ignore them, but that great *mood* everybody had, that essential spirit of a bunch of people all working together, all passionate about it, *gaudy with passion,* that's what you'll adore!"

Gigi stopped with a stack of dirty plates and turned to look at him.

"Where exactly am I going to adore it?"

"Come on, sweetheart," Zach said impatiently, "in Montana. You know you're coming back with me, why are you being so fucking pig-headed? You can be a little stupid sometimes for a smart chick, did you know that?"

"You haven't even given me a chance to tell you what's happening in my job," Gigi said, still holding the plates.

"Okay, what?" He heaved a sigh of resignation.

"Forget it. I don't need you to listen at gunpoint."

"It's not that I'm not interested," Zach protested. "I'm sure that whatever you're doing in—excuse the expression—advertising, you're doing it brilliantly, but Gigi, darling Gigi, that can't make the difference here, don't you see? Oh, baby, it's glaringly clear that you'll be happier being with me, the way I'm happier with you," he said in his most guileful and persuasive voice. "Look, sweetheart, wasn't tonight just a bitch of an eye-opener? It could be like that all the time, you'd be able to *watch me work,* you could be on the set with me every day, every minute that you wanted to be, you could be in on every discussion, just like tonight, you could see how I get things done—"

"Could I . . . sit at your feet?" Gigi's voice was quiet, her question asked with a calmness that fell just short of being overstated.

"Well . . . actually . . . you'd have be on the sidelines most of the time, there's a sort of zone of concentration around the director and the actors, but I'll try to give you as much total access—"

"Sit down."

"I can't, I'm too restless," Zach protested, striding about like a warrior, a prince, a patron, a potentate, so vivid with his sense of his own potential that he didn't notice the unusual colorlessness of her voice.

Gigi opened her hands and let the stack of plates drop with a crash on the tiled floor. *"Sit down!"*

"Jesus, what a mess! Here, let me help."

"Sit the fuck down, Zach Nevsky, leave the fucking pasta, leave the fucking sauce, leave the fucking *plates!*"

"Gigi, poor baby, you're overtired," he said, as loftily amused as he was concerned. "Come on, sweetheart, I'm going to put you to bed where you belong." He picked her up easily and carried her, screeching, into the bedroom, ignoring her kicking and elbowing as she struggled to make him release her, ferocious but ignored. He laid her on the bed, where, unwilling and determined, she thrashed about as hard as she could in his massive arms. He kissed her protesting mouth, not letting her lips form a single word, although she tried, frantically and ineffectually, to turn her head away from him. Totally outmatched as they fought, Gigi felt Zach quickly and adroitly ripping off her jeans and her panties as she kicked him in a rising arc of fury, her broken words still smothered by his kisses. One of Zach's arms held her tightly down on the bed and with his other hand he covered one of her breasts, caressing it with a rhythmic squeeze, as if to quiet down an excited small animal, his breath coming faster as he felt the shape of her flesh under the thin T-shirt. Gigi struggled harder, frantically trying to twist her breast away, but Zach, in swiftly rising excitement, slipped his fingers under the fabric and captured her breast more tightly than before, his grasp becoming firmer and more purposeful as he found her silky nipple. He moaned, stabbed by desire, and lifted himself up so that he lay heavily over her bucking body. He ground his penis relentlessly into her thigh, and she felt the quick movement of his hand away from her nipple as he opened his zipper. She tried to scream as he entered her, but his tongue filled her mouth.

Gigi bit Zach's tongue as hard as she could.

"Shit! That hurt!" he shouted in surprise and rage, rearing back, a bit of blood showing at the corner of his mouth, still holding her down on the bed.

"*Get off me!*" Gigi screamed.

"Why did you bite me?" he cried angrily.

"Because you're raping me, you lousy bastard!" She was panting with outrage.

"Rape? Don't kid yourself—you want it bad! You're dying for it! You need another good fucking to get rid of the rotten mood you're in! You just want my *attention.* Do you think I don't know why you had a buzzard up your ass all night? I had to hold this meeting, but you begrudged me every single second of it." He let her go and stood up, glaring at her.

"My God, you really, truly don't know me at all," Gigi said violently as she saw the total of her long-deferred adding-up of unconscious computation, a total that included less surprise than grief and pain and a deep anger. "All you can see is yourself, as big as the sun and twice as bright. Everything is a function of Zach Nevsky, from what interests me to how I feel. All I can *be,* everything I *am,* is in the reflection of your glory."

"That's not true! We love each other, *that's* what's important!"

"It *was* important," Gigi said, almost to herself. There was a low thunder in her voice, and her lids were half closed over eyes that held a commotion of lightning. "I tried to make it the most important thing in my life, and I could for a while . . . and I did for a while . . . but that's . . . not possible anymore. My life can't be only *about you,* don't you see? I *will not* let that happen to me. The longer we're together, the worse it gets. I've finally understood how totally impossible we are together. What you just tried to do, what you said—no, Zach, you ruined it."

"You're being melodramatic, for God's sake, Gigi," Zach said as a look of fear spread over his face. "You're taking one little thing, one bad evening, and making it into a big deal. Look, what do you want me to do? Just tell me . . . I'll stop asking you to quit your damn job . . . I'll take it seriously, so help me God, even if it kills me . . . I'll pay attention to your needs . . . I'll be sensitive and caring and aware, all that shit, Gigi, I swear I will. I'll change!"

"I don't believe you. I don't trust you. Not even to be a liar or a hypocrite, which is all you're offering." Gigi got off the bed and went to the closet. "I want you out of here and I don't want you to come back, not ever," she said tightly, in a dead but resolute voice, as she threw him the sweater and heavy jacket he'd hung up earlier. "Don't bother taking your keys, I'm going to change the locks." She left the bedroom, crossed the living room, and stopped at the head of the stairs, waiting for him to leave.

"Don't be a total asshole Gigi, we haven't finished talking," Zach shouted at her.

She turned and fixed him with a look so steady that it was like a metal bar between them. "You don't live here anymore," she said in a strong voice.

"You stupid little idiot . . . how can you be so stupid . . ." he groaned out loud as he hesitated at the stairs. "Just because you had to cook one lousy little dinner . . ."

"Get out. Get out before you make it worse."

"It can't get worse," he begged, letting her see his all-but-abject yearning.

"Just go. Go!" Only after he left did the savage, rending tears come, but not once did she change the decision he'd forced her to make.

Josh Hillman's legal business took him to New York infrequently, so whenever he was in Manhattan he made it a point to lunch with other lawyers with whom he did long-distance business, at least one lunch to reinforce months of communication by phone and letter.

Today, the day on which Gigi and David were presenting their Indigo Seas ideas to Archie, Byron, and Victoria, the day on which Zach Nevsky was trying to pry more money out of the reluctant studio heads, the day on which Sasha Hillman was going to a lingerie shower for the newly engaged daughter of one of his partners, Josh Hillman sat in the private dining room of the firm of Westcott, Rosenthal, Kelly and King. A few of the younger partners had been invited to lunch, men Josh had suggested to Bill Westcott that he should meet, since he might find himself dealing with them in the future.

The conversation was deliberately low-key and relaxed, Josh drawing out the younger lawyers, not taking measure of their legal minds—for if their brains were not exceptional, these young men would never have found themselves in this grand, high, paneled room—but of their characters. In the years to come he would need a rough working knowledge of how decent a fellow each one was.

The talk ranged from fly-fishing to tropical islands, from Ronald Reagan to the slow construction of Trump Tower, from the breeding of puppies to the raising of children, from the state of the stock market to the state of the younger men's romantic lives. Josh took a lively part in the conversation without revealing anything more personal than his fondness for full-grown Skye terriers. He was here to cull, listen, absorb, and learn.

Kent Rosenthal and Bill Westcott congratulated one of the younger men, Tom Unger, an evident favorite, on his recent engagement.

"We were convinced that Tom would never marry," Kent said to Josh.

"I tried to introduce him to my wife's niece, but he wasn't interested, said his heart was broken," Mike Kelly remarked ruefully. "Then he goes out and finds Helen."

"It *was* broken, seriously damaged anyway," Tom Unger protested. "I didn't see anyone for almost a year after Sasha disappeared."

"And that's what you call constancy?" Kent Rosenthal asked.

"It was the longest I've ever spent without a date since tenth grade."

"Tom is our official hopeless romantic," Bill Westcott added with a grin. "Every law firm needs one. But only one."

"Sasha who?" Josh asked. His heart, with a quickened throb of alertness, pounded heavily.

"Sasha Nevsky." Unger shook his head sadly. "Helen, my fiancée, is a fantastic girl and she'll be a wonderful wife, but I'll be the first to admit she's no Sasha. Sasha was unique."

"How so?" Josh queried casually.

"Well . . . it's not important, it's ancient history. Really."

"Come on, Tom, we've all heard about the unique Sasha, girl in a million. You can tell Josh," Mike Kelly said, laughing at Tom's reluctance. "He lives in Hollywood, he's unshockable."

"Oh, okay, it seems impossible now that I've met Helen, but this gorgeous creature, Sasha, had me completely under her spell," Tom said. "The problem was that there were always two other guys in her life at the same time, right along with me, and she never hid it. Never even tried to. She called herself the Great Slut—she came right out with it, proudly too, I'm not kidding, she just laughed at your expression and dared you to object. There was almost something . . . pure . . . about it—that honesty."

"And you didn't object?" Josh asked, his expression curious.

"Sure I did, I hated it, but I went along. The others did too. Sasha had a way of making men forget about their territorial rights. And the way she claimed that kind of liberty—the same as a man would—made you unable to argue that she shouldn't have it. God knows, I tried without success. I guess I could plead temporary insanity. On the other hand, I still wonder if maybe she was right, maybe an unattached woman *should* have total freedom. The guys here are all too chauvinistic to give me an argument."

"Tom's our point man on civil liberties," Mike Kelly said, laughing heartily.

"You didn't want to marry her?" Josh probed.

"She wasn't interested in marriage . . . which, as it turns out, was for the best, now that I have Helen."

"So what happened to her?"

"That's the strangest thing. One day she disappeared and that's the last I ever heard of her. No letter, no good-bye. I hope she's happy, wherever she is. She was . . . utterly remarkable."

"Told you he was a hopeless romantic," Bill Westcott said. "Want a brandy, Josh?"

"No thanks. In fact, gentlemen, I'd better be getting back uptown, pleasant as this has been."

"Gigi, you look like you pulled three all-nighters in a row. Are you sure you're okay for the presentation?" David Melville worried as he looked at her, dressed in a black turtleneck sweater tucked any old way into a pair of black corduroy pants, both of them obviously as old as her battered black leather boots. She looked like some sort of eighteenth-century orphan who'd been apprenticed to a chimney sweep, he thought, except for her contemporary pair of enormous sunglasses. Her face was pale, she'd made no effort with her hair, which floated around her weary features as if she hadn't bothered to brush it this morning, and she wasn't even carrying her usual bagel from Bagel Central, the help-yourself food counter in the central corridor where the agency employees congregated at all times of the day, often picking up some of their best ideas as they stood around chatting and gossiping over sticky buns or fresh fruit.

"I had a bad bad night, must have been something I ate. I'm tired is all."

"It's nerves, you just won't admit it. We've had too much time to anticipate and worry. If only we'd been able to make our presentation yesterday, when it was hot off the drawing board, but no, they were all too busy working with other creatives. Damn!"

"I'm not worried," Gigi said drearily. "I couldn't care less, if they like it, fine, if they don't, fine too. Life goes on."

"Oh, wonderful! So you're the kind who takes refuge in 'I couldn't care less' when you're nervous as hell." His voice was gently accusatory. "So much for Miss True Grit of 1983."

"Have it your own way."

"Would a Valium help?"

"What would it do for me?"

"Take the edge off your anxiety, for crying out loud!" he said, running his fingers through his already rumpled dark hair until it stood on end.

"You take it, Davy. You need it." She smoothed his hair idly.

"I've had one already. Come on, Gigi, they should be in the conference room in a minute—you're not going to keep those sunglasses on for the presentation, are you?"

"I have some sort of weird eye infection. I look awful."

"Ah, you poor kid, tension goes to your eyes, huh? I get hives —listen, even if they don't like our Indigo Seas stuff, which is impossible, they'll be jumping up and down about The Enchanted Attic."

"Yeah, yeah," she said drearily.

"On your feet, march!" he ordered, in a military bark.

"Okay."

"Damn, I'd feel better if you'd only throw me a salute."

"Okay." She saluted limply and muttered "sir," as an after-thought.

"You make me wish I hadn't asked."

"You kids have hit it!" Archie jumped to his feet in excitement the second that Gigi and David came to the end of a half-dozen Indigo Seas ideas, illustrated by the sketches David had comped up.

"If this stuff doesn't get us the account, nothing will," Byron agreed, thoroughly enthusiastic. "Congratulations!"

"I hate to rain on your little parade," Victoria Frost said coldly, "but in your desire to con fat women into thinking there's something glamorous about obesity, you've managed to totally ig-nore the client's chief selling points, the reasons why these women buy their suits: their famous power-net panels, their patented bra cut, their industrial-strength stretch fabrics, and their huge range of sizes—that's what they're selling at Indigo Seas, not a cheap imitation of Sophia Loren."

What an overtouted, brassy showboat their little Miss Orsini had turned out to be, Victoria thought with sour, vindictive dis-dain. Archie and Byron had set their hearts on hiring someone who was totally unsuitable, as she'd known the minute she'd laid eyes on her. She had nothing against attractive female creatives, but there was something she instinctively sensed and detested in Gigi from the first, something aroused by her cocksure attitude, her lack of awe for Victoria's power and position, her unearned self-confidence based on nothing but insolent youth—that whole and still-untarnished youth with its idiotic illusions that the whole world lay before her. She'd learn better, but meanwhile she had to be dealt with. It didn't help that Gigi was clever enough to operate with the perfect awareness that all three of those fools, Byron, Archie, and David, were at least a little bit in love with her.

"We know all that, Victoria," David said, interrupting the brief silence that had fallen after Victoria's remarks. "But we're looking to do something different here, to light a fire under women so they go into the stores with their minds *open and curious*, turned on enough by the ads to look out for the big Indigo Seas shoulder identification tag—the tag itself would contain all that technical information. We didn't want to do text-heavy ads for a fashion product."

"You're mistaken, David," Victoria said. "You were letting yourself be carried away by a chance to do pretty pictures, trying to sell the sizzle instead of the steak. Indigo Seas suits are hardly 'fashion,' they're more like girdles to swim in. This work cannot be shown at the pitch meeting. Indigo Seas is looking for a new marketing partner, not a Francis Ford Coppola."

"Excuse me," Gigi said, "but all the points you've mentioned are right there in the ads they're currently running, Victoria. Why is Indigo Seas looking for another agency if they're satisfied?"

"When you've been in the business as long as I have, Gigi, you learn never to ask a client *why* they've put an account up for review. It's often a reason that has absolutely nothing to do with the current campaign, some sort of internal company matter, private politics. But you do *try* to use some basic common sense when you pitch. You don't *deliberately fail* to mention their strong points."

"Victoria," Archie said, "this stuff of David and Gigi's is so fresh and yummy, it's so tasty you can bite into it, for Pete's sake, why not give it a chance?"

"It's different, Victoria, it's newsy, it'll grab attention, Indigo Sea's been around for years, everybody's sick of the power-net panels, those words alone are enough to turn you off," Byron said indignantly. "This stuff is *juicy!*"

"Swimwear for fat women *cannot* be 'juicy,' Byron," Victoria informed him with a small, belittling twitch of her mouth. "Nor can fat women be 'lush.' "

"Where is that written?" Gigi demanded, jumping up in a rage, a boiling, rattling, welcome rage that finally took her mind off her tattered soul and the fact that someone named Zach Nevsky existed. "Where the fuck is that written!"

"Really, Gigi," Victoria chided her in icy scornfulness, "this is a presentation, not a streetcorner brawl."

"Don't 'really, Gigi' me! You keep on talking about 'fat' women when we use the word 'abundant,' you're so damn condescending that I know that in your heart of hearts you don't think they should be allowed to go swimming, and if that isn't bad enough, you want to play it safe and give the client what you think it wants—if this is advertising, I'm in the wrong business!"

"I daresay you are," Victoria drawled. "Perhaps we should go back and review the stuff Kerry and Joan did, as well as the work John and Lew produced. A lot of it wasn't bad at all. We were too hasty to reject it, in my opinion. Or an FRB gang-bang may be in order, if Gigi and David can't see their way clear to fixing their work."

"Victoria!" Byron looked at her incredulously. "We hired Gigi for exactly the kind of work she and David have turned out here—what's wrong with you?"

"Why don't we have this little discussion in private, Byron? I think we can ask Gigi and David to excuse themselves." Victoria remained calmly seated, fishing about in her purse, withdrawing her attention from Gigi and David.

"I'm not finished," Gigi said, standing foursquare in her boots. "And I'm not a child you can excuse from the table."

"Gigi—" Archie began.

"I'm not leaving, Archie. Davy and I will make the necessary changes to the Indigo Seas ads."

"You will?" Archie asked, amazed at her quick surrender.

"No big deal," Gigi responded, shrugging as she reined herself in. Some battles would keep, and whatever a gang-bang was at FRB, she didn't like the sound of it. "There's another thing before we've finished here. Two days ago I solicited new business from Ben Winthrop, the mall developer. I got him to promise me an eight-million-dollar account for an image-creating campaign for a chain of up-market toy stores called The Enchanted Attic."

"You solicited new business?" Victoria asked, drawing an incredulous breath and turning white. "Just who gave you the authority to do that, may I ask?"

"I gave it to myself, Miss Vicky."

David's jaw dropped. Archie and Byron froze at Gigi's impudent and aggressive tone.

"And, Miss Vicky, if that's a problem for you," Gigi continued, "I'll take the eight-million-dollar Enchanted Attic account away with me in my little pocket and find an agency that wants it and that appreciates my work. It's my account, I developed it, and it goes where I go."

"Oh, indeed. How enterprising of you. I wonder why I've never heard of this chain of stores," Victoria asked the stunned atoms of air in the room. "Could it possibly be something you invented on the spur of the moment?"

"As a matter of fact, I did," Gigi said, her hands on her hips.

Jesus, David wondered, how'd she turn from a chimney sweep into a pirate in a split second?

"You've never heard of it," Gigi continued, "because it doesn't exist except as a hundred and twenty-two bankrupt stores called Kids' Paradise, most of them located in Ben Winthrop's malls. He's going to invest in their business, retain their locations, totally reposition their marketing, redecorate from top to bottom, and advertise them as the equivalent of Scruples crossed with Tiffany's for kids' gifts—places to find the ultimate in toys and clothes for babies through pre-teens."

"So there actually *is no* Enchanted Attic account, is there?" Victoria pounced. "Much less an eight-million-dollar account. It's all on the if-come, isn't it? Before they have any reason to advertise, they have to totally reorganize, rebuild, restock, invest a fortune, and you have no guarantee that it'll be done, do you? Even if it does happen, it's many months down the road, a year, maybe longer. That's not what anyone with experience would announce as new business."

"I have Ben Winthrop's agreement." Gigi sounded more sure of herself than ever.

"And just exactly what would that be worth? Can we take it to a bank?"

"If it isn't solid enough for you, just say so," Gigi flared. "I'm satisfied."

"Ben Winthrop," Victoria drawled. "He's related to your stepmother, isn't he? You have pure nepotism to thank for this opportunity, if that's what it turns out to be, which I somehow doubt."

"I'm sure you know infinitely more about nepotism than I do," Gigi answered, "or at least that's what Ben told me when he filled me in on your background, Ms. Frost." Gigi felt as deeply refreshed as if she'd had an excellent night's sleep.

"I hate to interrupt your heart-to-heart here, ladies, but don't you think that you could wait for another time? Don't we all have work to do?" Archie asked desperately.

"I'm finished for now," Gigi said, impervious to the consternation in the room. "Come on, Davy, I'll buy you lunch."

"How long will we have?" Gigi asked David several days later, as they left his car with the valet parker at the Beverly Wilshire. Indigo Seas had taken two meeting rooms at the hotel for the occasion, one for the pitches themselves and one in which their executives could confer privately. The senior members of the pitch team, Victoria, Archie, and Byron, pulled in behind them.

"Indigo Seas said an hour and a half maximum. But we're going right after lunch. That means they've heard two pitches this morning, eaten lunch, and haven't had time to get tired yet. It's ideal timing."

"So they'll hear four pitches in all, one after us?"

"Don't know. They might have asked four more agencies to pitch tomorrow. Or yesterday. Or they might have scheduled three for this afternoon . . . they never say."

"Is this like being rushed for a fraternity?" Gigi was fastening on the details of this new experience, unlike any other she'd ever had, in an effort to quiet her stage fright.

"Do I look like someone who'd try to join a fraternity?"

"No. Do I look like someone who'd get into a sorority?" Gigi had adopted an outfit that she hoped would convey creative punch with a proper awareness of the client's importance—indeed, the importance of the entire swimwear industry. She'd put together some of Prince's pieces from various Scruples Two catalogs, a slender green wool skirt that flared out at the hem, a finely striped green and white blouse with poet's sleeves, silver buttons, and a collar that hinted at the Tyrol, worn with a small red velvet vest hanging casually unbuttoned over her antique chunky silver Santa Fe belt. At the last minute, that morning, she'd added a pair of dashing red lizard cowboy boots that made her look taller.

"You look like something out of *The Sound of Music* crossed with *Shane*."

"My God, I never thought of that," Gigi said, horrified.

"No, no, that's good. Great! Everybody loved *The Sound of Music*. It's infinitely reassuring. A subliminal coup. Even Victoria didn't say anything against it when you wore it for the rehearsal. Do you think my one and only suit's okay?"

"You look like Gregory Peck in *Roman Holiday*. You're absolutely beautiful."

"So are you, Gigi, darling, beautiful." Good God, David thought, he'd even go to a pitch every day in the week if it gave him a legitimate opportunity to tell her she was beautiful and call her "darling" without making her diabolic pointed eyebrows jump with surprise.

"When will they let us know?" Gigi demanded for the tenth time that week.

"That's another thing we can't project, Gigi darling," he responded as he had ten times before, knowing that she was too distracted to notice the second endearment. "They'll let it be known who gets the account in their own good time. Today, tomorrow, or two weeks from now. Whoever gets it, the news will travel with the speed of light."

"There's something profoundly sinister about all this," she said.

"Nobody pitches a seven-million-dollar account without suffering, that's the price of getting into the game. It's sadistic, but I bet every industry has these little cruel rituals."

"Not at Scruples Two."

"But that was family."

"Do you think we should pray?"

"I'm a Congregationalist, we don't pray for business success. Or at least I don't think we do."

"What's a Congregationalist?"

"A mild, liberal sort of universal Protestant, we love everybody, Gigi, especially you," David said fervently.

"Does this elevator not run or what?" Gigi asked impatiently as Archie, Byron, and Victoria joined them in the lobby, Archie and Byron natty in full-throttle Armani, Victoria more chastely businesslike than ever in a perfectly plain navy suit that could have been cut by Balenciaga with his own hands if he hadn't elected, at his peak, to stop making clothes because the few women he deemed worthy of his talents no longer existed.

The pitch team, not bothering to pretend to make conversation, found the third-floor meeting room in which they were to set up. Victoria was greeted at the door by a dignified middle-aged woman who introduced herself as Jane Fairbrother, executive secretary to the president of Indigo Seas, George Collins.

"Make yourselves comfortable," Jane Fairbrother said with a pleasant and utterly impersonal smile. "The bosses are running a little late. Can I get you coffee or tea? No? There are pitchers of water at your table, let me know if you run out."

Gigi surveyed the room. At one end was a group of chairs for the audience, at the other end a simple table with five chairs behind it and an easel at each side.

"Just sip the water," Archie hissed in her ear. "It doesn't help cotton-mouth, no matter how much you drink, and you don't want to have to pee in the middle of this."

Victoria sat down in the center chair, flanked by Archie and Byron, while Gigi and David, carrying the large leather portfolios filled with their carefully arranged mock-up ads, sat at each end.

After a short wait, a group of people entered from the connecting room. Victoria rose to make the introductions.

First came the three Collins brothers, who owned Indigo Seas: Henry, John, and George, who was the senior brother and clearly the most important of the three. Then came the marketing director and his male assistant and the advertising director with his male assistant. As the three brothers took their seats in the second row, three soberly dressed, dumpy older women sat down in the last row. They must be the brothers' secretaries, for each of them held a steno pad and a pencil. Victoria nodded graciously at them, but obviously she had never met them before, and no Collins brother introduced them to the FRB team.

The Collins brothers, Gigi thought, either hired their secretaries for their efficiency, or their wives hired them for their safety. As far as she could judge, the brothers were all in their early to middle thirties, and each of them, in spite of a strong family resemblance to each other, was a different variety of dark and handsome. And impassive. She had never seen such a lack of expression, neither friendly nor unfriendly, neither bored nor anticipatory, but empty of everything except the steady, almost unblinking attention of their dark eyes under their dark brows.

Their faces remained blank as Victoria went through her paces, explaining how Frost/Rourke/Bernheim, with its clever researchers and state-of-the-art media buying department, was uniquely qualified to determine and position the ads for Indigo Seas, how closely FRB would work with the San Francisco–based swimwear company, how any one of them was ready to get on a plane at a moment's notice to work out even the smallest detail, how perfect a match FRB was for a company like Indigo Seas.

She was impressive, on target, strong and smooth, Gigi thought. She'd never seen this particular Victoria Frost, and she wanted to applaud when Victoria sat down. George Collins thanked her with the briefest of words.

Archie and Byron spoke second and third, presenting other aspects of the FRB story, including their own years of experience in New York, the youth and strength of the agency, its innovative handling of the accounts it had won in the last year, and their availability to the Collins brothers in their personal creative capacities. They mentioned Gigi's work in creating the Scruples Two catalog and David's three Belding Bowl Awards for artwork. Each of them was as convincing as Victoria had been, their different personalities meshing into such a desirable unit that Gigi found herself amazed that she hadn't joined the agency the first time they asked. Obviously they had pitched her at a lower level of intensity than they reserved for potential clients.

As she heard Byron winding up, Gigi took a slow sip of water, wishing desperately for an ice cube to suck on. Her lips were glued together and she had no spit in her mouth. If only she and Davy had been seated side by side, he could have held her sweating hand under the table.

Gigi tried to focus only on the clients, looking at the brothers for some signal, something at all that would reveal that they were a tiny bit impressed, not just exceptionally polite speechless, expressionless mimes, but found nothing except dignity, solemnity, unmoving attention, and a level of grooming that far outdid Arch and By. Their suits, their shirts, their ties, their shoes, their haircuts, even their fingernails were all beyond perfection, if there was such a thing—beyond, Gigi thought, even the distinction and elegance cultivated by her own father, Vito Orsini.

Bella figura. As the words popped into her mind, she knew instantly that the Collins brothers were Italians by heritage. No American businessman without Italian blood would lavish the time, money, and attention that were necessary to look the way they did. To present a *bella figura* to the world, no matter what was going on inside, was an Italian tradition that reached from the nobility to the peasants. She'd seen her father maintain his *bella figura* when he was the laughingstock of all Hollywood, when he owed money everywhere and was barely scraping by on credit . . . Archie gave her an elbow in the ribs, and she realized that Byron had just said, "Now Gigi Orsini and David Melville, our creative team, will show you the ads we've prepared."

Gigi got up, feeling as light as an arrow speeding from a bow. David was going to lift the heavy pieces of cardboard and she was going to talk the clients through them, since he was art and she was copy. But first, she thought, tingling, a little native pride. These brothers were three young Vito Orsinis and they didn't scare her one little bit. Not one *piccolo* bit.

"My name," she said, slowly and proudly, looking George Collins straight in the eye, "is Graziella Giovanna Orsini." George Collins blinked. John Collins blinked. Henry Collins blinked. Even the secretaries, Gigi saw, exchanged a quick glance. David gave her a look of astonishment, but what would a Congregationalist know about the importance of being Italian?

In the next fifteen minutes she showed them a dozen ads, designed to incorporate all the copy points that Victoria had demanded, written in Gigi's own intimate, one-on-one prose, and accompanied by David's sketches of a woman who, although not actually bone-thin, could not have been more than ten pounds above a model's ideal weight, a gently rounded woman, attractive, highly idealized, and acceptable to Victoria Frost.

They were good ads, but not great ads. Gigi knew it and David knew it. They were a great deal better than what Indigo Seas had been running, but they didn't zoom. As she finished she watched the Collins brothers and saw George's shoulders lift an all-but-imperceptible shrug. "Eh!" she could hear him thinking, dismissively. Gigi could read Italian body language instantly, and she knew he had judged the ads and found them far from exceptional. Not bad, just not exciting.

Gigi looked at David and gave him the wink they had agreed on. He turned and zipped open another portfolio. One by one, Gigi showed the audience the ads she and David had first created, never turning to look at the table behind her, where the rest of the pitch team was seated.

Each of the ads had been photographed on a beautiful former model who had developed more liberal *abbondanza* than either of them had originally imagined. She was . . . unquestionably overweight . . . even very overweight by the standards of every woman, but somehow on her the pounds looked good—firm and shapely and mysteriously right. *Abundant.* The last two ads were new. One showed the big, happy, luscious model halfway out of the swimming pool, grabbing the arm of a handsome, fully clad, and obviously fascinated cowboy. The copy line said, "Come on in —the water's Abbondanza!" In the final ad, the model and the cowboy were immersed in the water up to their shoulders, hugging and laughing into each other's eyes, and the copy line asked, "Are you happy to see me—or is it just my Abbondanza?"

A hush fell over the meeting room as Gigi finished. George Collins thanked her.

"Will you excuse us while we adjourn?" he added, addressing Gigi.

"*Prego,*" Gigi said. *Prego,* one of the few words of Italian her father had taught her, that most useful word you can never misuse under any circumstances, the word that means everything from "please be my guest" to "of course" to "excuse me" to "would you mind if I walked in front of you" to "by all means."

Behind her she felt, rather than saw, Victoria beaming death rays at her head.

"We'll wait to talk about this someplace else," Archie said with a strangled sound. Archie, Byron, and Victoria sat in total silence. Gigi and David made an unnecessarily lengthy and neat production of putting the cardboards back into their portfolios, not daring to glance at each other for fear of falling into a fit of crazy laughter, since they had nothing left to lose.

The connecting door opened, and everyone from Indigo Seas

returned to the room and settled in their seats, except for one of the secretaries, who sat down next to George Collins.

With a big smile, George Collins indicated the secretary. "I wish to present my mother, the Signora Eleonora Colonna," he announced. "We all work for her. Mama?"

"I like your work," Signora Colonna said with grave approval, standing up and sweeping her eyes over the FRB team. As soon as she spoke, her great personal power was evident. "My two younger sisters like your work," she said, turning to indicate the two women who were still seated in the back. "My sons like your work. I am the originator and patent holder of the bra cup and the power-net panel, and you are the only agency to understand that no thin woman would wear them. There is no need to wait to tell you that you have the account. Welcome to Indigo Seas."

"*Grazia mille*," Gigi said, since everyone else seemed to have lost their voices. They were two of the other words she knew in Italian.

"*Prego*, Graziella Giovanna," the older woman said, giving her a very personal smile. "You knew we were Italian? Your famous research department, perhaps?"

"Not until I recognized the *bella figura* of your sons," Gigi answered.

"Then why did you dress in the colors of the Italian flag, Graziella Giovanna?"

"I'm . . . superstitious," Gigi said, improvising wildly. "My father, Vito Orsini, always said they were lucky colors."

"And your mother? She is Italian also?"

"No, Irish. Also a green and white flag, but with orange."

"Ah—so that explains your hair."

"No, Signora Colonna. Peroxide."

"You'll come up to San Francisco. There are too many men in the office. I have good boys—Giorgio, Enrico, and Gianni—all wonderful boys, but I should have had a daughter. My sisters and I will show you our new designs, pick your brains. You have style. No *abbondanza*, but a great deal of style."

"*Grazia*, Signora Colonna. With pleasure, Signora Colonna."

"*Prego*, Graziella Giovanna." She took Gigi's hand in hers. "I look forward to your visit. I'll call you tomorrow and we'll set the date. Perhaps you will spend the night and meet my grandchildren. Also all boys—eh, what can one do?"

Around them the Indigo Seas people were shaking hands with Archie, Byron, Victoria, and Davy, laughing and talking in an explosion of the tension they had all been under, but around Signora Colonna and Gigi there was the circle of respect everyone instinctively accorded to the head of the clan and the person she had clearly singled out of all the group from Frost/Rourke/Bernheim.

5

On Gigi's first day at FRB, Victoria Frost sat in her office, not even attempting to eat the fruit salad Polly had brought her, still enraged at the thought of Archie, Byron, Gigi, and the expensive lunch they were unquestionably consuming at that very minute. How dare they hire a new copywriter whom she hadn't stamped with her approval? How dare they take her out to lunch as if advertising were one big party and there was no urgent work to be done?

She'd told Archie, after two creative teams had come close to burning out on the Indigo Seas pitch, that he should take time off from everything, especially his exhausting social life, dig in, and work on the job himself—no one had ever decreed that swimwear copy had to be written by a woman. But he'd wriggled out of a job he didn't feel qualified to tackle just long enough for Gigi to come along. She wasn't even a woman, she was nothing but a twit, a full-of-herself brat who thought that because she'd had a certain little lucky success in the catalog business, she could make the switch to advertising with no knowledge or background. Her partners had clearly lost their judgment.

The girl had the brand of cuteness that she personally most disapproved of and men, those predictable fools, found enticing. Couldn't they see that it was all manufactured by obviously dyed red hair, deliberately overdone mascara, a sexy little body, and animal high spirits? The only thing she didn't dislike about Gigi Orsini was her suit. You could always recognize Prince's cut and the quality of his fabric, but they were wasted on this flamboyant creature who'd undoubtedly feel more at home in rhinestones. It was almost incredible that she'd been more or less brought up by Billy Ikehorn, who, if she had nothing else, had taste. When she'd still lived in New York, Victoria remembered, and the branch of Scruples had been open, she'd been able to find exactly her sort of clothes there, as had her mother, whose type was so different from her own, yet just as discriminating.

Yes, she and her mother, Millicent Frost Caldwell, were entirely unalike, but no one could say that either one of them was easy to please.

Although the very last thing in the world she wanted was a child, Millicent Frost, at twenty-one, was already far too much of a bred-in-the-bone copywriter to give her daughter anything but a name that possessed the desirable note of regal and historic resonance that her own mother had neglected in naming her after a favorite aunt. She called her baby Victoria with the indifferent agreement of her husband, Dan Frost, to whom an infant was as much of an inconvenience as it was to her.

The Frosts had married far too quickly, as people did in the conservative climate of 1951, and Victoria was born aggravatingly soon, a mere year later, forcing her irritated mother to take ten days off from her job at a good-sized agency, Jack Abbott & Partners, where she was already regarded as the most interesting and original young mind in the shop. She was clearly a golden girl and she wore with effortless ease a charisma that was composed of pure kinetic energy and innate charm, carefully covering what Millicent was clever enough to know was an unseemly amount of ambition. She was a tiny, vivacious blonde, pretty in a delicate way, and possessed the priceless gift of striking both men and women as nonthreatening. Millicent Frost remained charismatic up till the moment of childbirth, charismatic even in her annoyance at spending time interviewing potential nurses, and doubly charismatic as she returned triumphantly to work, leaving Victoria in the care of a strong-minded, dependable young woman from Zurich, named Lori Shaefer.

Lori brought Victoria up to be a neat, obedient, healthy child who did her nurse credit when her parents looked in on her for a few minutes each evening before they hurried out to cocktails or dinner. Dan Frost was a junior account executive at a large agency, and his job description included a great deal of socializing.

The Frosts were divorced by the time Victoria was two. Dan drifted off to Chicago, and then to Milwaukee, his child-support checks tapering off until they stopped entirely and Millicent found herself financially responsible for her daughter. Fortunately, at twenty-four, her rapid rise at Abbott, where she was now vice-president in charge of the entire copy group, enabled her to continue to afford Lori as well as a part-time cleaning woman, a private nursery school for Victoria, and weekly trips to get her hair done at Saks.

Lori remained with Millicent Frost while Millicent's success increased month by month. One day, when Millicent was thirty-one, astounding her employer almost as much as herself, Lori took her sizable nest egg out of the bank and returned to Switzerland to shop for the husband she had most certainly earned.

"You're going to love boarding school, sweetie," Millicent assured Victoria, who still couldn't believe that Lori had actually left her.

"Why can't I stay here?" the girl asked imploringly. "I love my school." She was tall for ten, almost as tall as her trim mother, and skinny, with regular features and long, dark brown hair. Not pretty, Millicent knew, but certainly not homely. Neither cute nor interesting looking, just an ordinary, well-behaved ten-year-old—although perhaps she had a certain unusual dignity—with the normal possibilities any ten-year-old has, possibilities it was her duty to maximize.

"Victoria, you'll never make the right friends here, you can't learn to ride, you can't learn French properly, Central Park hasn't been a decent place to play for years, your weekends aren't organized the way they were when Lori was with us, there's no one to supervise you—oh, for heaven's sake, Victoria—you can't do yourself justice unless you go away to a first-class school."

"Justice?"

"Sweetie, you're going to have a wonderful time. I wish I'd had your chances," Millicent Frost said unyieldingly.

Victoria was going to go to the expensive New England boarding school Millicent had had so much trouble getting her into, whether she understood why or not. The girl was decidedly too old to be cared for by another governess, for that was what Lori had virtually become over the years, and yet too young to be entrusted to a live-in, full-time housekeeper, even if such a person could be found now that the supply of young European women had dried up.

Millicent worked long, demanding hours. She left Abbott when Victoria was six for Doyle, Dane, Bernbach, the hottest agency in the business, where she was one of a number of vice-presidents. Her nonstop social life was largely client-related and absolutely necessary in her position. Her time simply was not elastic enough to include helping a child with homework or arranging for sleep-overs or worrying if her daughter had clean clothes for school the next day. To Millicent such a possibility had become utterly grotesque.

Victoria Frost was sent to the boarding school, which was near Boston, and to the very best summer camp in Maine. During school holidays and in the weeks between the end of the school year and the beginning of camp, if Victoria was not invited to stay with a friend, Millicent found a series of pleasant young female graduate students who needed part-time jobs, to keep her daughter occupied and entertained.

Millicent Frost was careful always to attend parents' weekend at school and camp, she never missed instructing her secretary to send wonderful presents to school for Victoria's birthday, and she became famous for the catered Thanksgiving and Christmas feasts to which she invited all of her unattached friends from the office, parties at which her daughter was pleasantly, if quietly, in evidence. Other women at Doyle, Dane wished they were as good at combining motherhood and career as Millicent Frost obviously was, judging from the composure of tall young Victoria, who had learned to conceal her hatred of her mother so well that no one was aware of it but she herself.

Until Lori went back to Switzerland, Victoria had been content enough in her closeness to her governess to accept without too much question the cult of her "wonderful mother" that Lori enthusiastically espoused, seeing how hard pretty little Mrs. Frost worked without a man to take care of her. For a while Victoria was too busy adjusting to the life of her well-run school to think about her mother, but soon she became aware of the amount of attention her new friends received from their mothers, the loving letters and the long phone calls.

Occasionally she too received a brief, brisk letter her mother had dictated to her secretary, responding to the two weekly letters the school obliged its students to write home, but, as she visited her school friends and observed their family lives through hungry eyes, she realized painfully that although no other girl she knew was as thoroughly and carefully supervised as she, year in and year out, she was almost entirely neglected by the one person who could not be paid to spend time with her.

There was absolutely no one with whom Victoria shared this observation. She absorbed it slowly, incorporating it into her essence as she passed through puberty and entered her teens. Her mother was the source of everything she possessed, every expensive party dress and school uniform, every ticket to the ballet and the theater, every sailing lesson, every hour on horseback, every ruffled pink-and-green plaid pillow in her recently redecorated bedroom. Each costly detail of her privileged upbringing had been paid for by her mother's brilliant achievements.

Of course, she knew that it was not enough. Without an expression of maternal love, without her mother's desire to spend time with her, it could never be enough. It was unforgivable, utterly unforgivable, now and forever.

During the fall of 1968, soon after Victoria's sixteenth birthday, while she was in her sophomore year of high school, Millicent Frost, who looked no older at thirty-seven than she had a decade before, surprised herself and everyone who knew her by falling deeply in love with a man nine years younger than she, Angus Caldwell, a rising star at BBD&O. At twenty-eight, Angus was known as the most seductive account supervisor in a business in which no man, much less one who dealt with clients, could survive without possessing some strong aspect of seduction. Angus Caldwell was a man of great and undeniable charm, a tall, graceful man, the son of generation after generation of sheep-raising Scots who had moved easily over their acres, altogether a sandy man with rather rough, freckled skin and sandy, silky hair that fell forward over his forehead, a man whose dark gray eyes had an appeal he didn't seem to realize, whose charm lay partly in a hesitant smile that was both shy and slightly melancholy, and partly in his look of an overgrown schoolboy. Yet Angus Caldwell was fully as ambitious as Millicent Frost, a self-made man whose heritage had been nothing more than a decent mind, a love of books, and the ability to inspire trust in everyone who met him. Millicent's love was returned, the difference in their ages was of no importance, and although they had only known each other for a few months, they made plans to get married as quickly as possible.

Millicent would have preferred to keep Victoria away at school for the wedding. In her judgment the girl had grown up to be respectably good-looking, even what was often called "handsome" in an earlier day, because of her fine height, her upright figure, the unblemished clarity of her pale skin, which was creamy, not sallow, the gloss of her thick brown hair, and the clarity of her well-placed brown eyes with their surprisingly long, dark lashes under dark brows. The money she'd spent on Victoria showed, Millicent congratulated herself. She'd produced an aristocrat.

But she was an unsettlingly mature sixteen, and that dignity which had been charming in a child of ten made her daughter seem too mature for Millicent Frost's liking at this particularly romantic moment in her life. Victoria hadn't looked like a genuinely young girl for years, leaping past the awkward age in one bound, never needing braces or slouching or evidencing any of the normal and adorable awkwardness that one looked for in a teenager. Nor, to her mother's critical eyes, was she particularly endearing. Coupled with her height, she had developed a cool and withholding presence, a self-possession that entirely lacked the sweet youthfulness that Millicent felt she had every right to expect from such an expensively cultivated bloom. Aristocrat or not, Victoria simply had no charm, Millicent told herself, and she reflected, with a sigh of disappointment, that all the good skin and hair in the world couldn't match the value of a touch of charm. She didn't even use the gift of her amazing lashes, but preferred to look at people as unblinkingly as possible.

Still and all, Victoria had to be brought down from school, even in the middle of her midterm exams, or people would wonder why she wasn't at her mother's side at the church ceremony that had been hastily but carefully planned to include everyone of importance on Madison Avenue. Fortunately, among Victoria's party dresses bought for prep-school dances, there was one that would be entirely suitable, a forest-green velvet minidress with its own short, flaring jacket.

Victoria had an exam on Saturday morning, which would just give her time to change, make the plane from Boston, and get to New York in time for the ceremony. Millicent arranged for her to be met at the airport by a chauffeur and driven to the St. Bartholomew's on Park Avenue so that she could meet Angus before the wedding started.

The plane was a half hour late and Victoria arrived, flustered and apologetic, only just in time to walk down the aisle in front of her mother, who had held up the wedding as long as she could. Angus Caldwell waited for them calmly, his longish sandy hair well brushed, his dark gray eyes gentle, yet full of anticipation. He turned to Victoria, bending down toward her, and took her nervously shaking fingers in both of his big, warm hands. He held them tightly, looking into her startled eyes with kind concentration, lifted an eyebrow in appreciation, grinned shyly, and gave her the smallest of winks. Then he turned to his bride. During the ceremony Victoria was unable to look away even once from Angus Caldwell's face. She had fallen instantly and utterly in love with him, her first love, her only love, a love that she knew, with all her lonely soul, would endure for a lifetime.

Angus and Millicent Frost Caldwell resigned from their respective agencies as soon as they returned from a brief honeymoon, and formed their own agency, Caldwell & Caldwell. Within a day of the announcement of their partnership, Angus received a phone call from an old friend, Joe Devane, owner of Oak Hill Foods, a medium-sized company he had started ten years earlier. Until then, Oak Hill had been considered safe at Ogilvy & Mather, but now that Angus was in business for himself, Devane intended to move his account, with Angus's word that he would always handle it himself no matter how big Caldwell & Caldwell got.

From that first day on, Millicent and Angus climbed, almost effortlessly, it seemed, from success to success. An astonishing number of creative people from every giant agency flooded them with portfolios containing their best work in the race to become an early part of the Caldwell team. Large accounts fell in over their transom without solicitation, flooding them with challenging problems that their joint ambitions and talents were superbly prepared to meet. It was a stampede that only the success of Wells, Rich, Green several years earlier had equaled.

When Victoria graduated from boarding school, a year and a half later, Caldwell was doing seventy million dollars a year in billings, and employed more than a hundred people. Victoria applied to three respectable colleges, and was accepted by two of them. As a graduation present, Millicent Caldwell planned to give her a summer traveling in Italy, but she refused to leave New York.

"The only thing I want is a summer job at the agency."

"But that's not a present, Victoria. The kids we give those jobs to are prepared to work hard as hell all summer long—weekends too, if necessary."

"So am I. Please try me, Mother. I've never wanted anything so much."

"Absolutely not. It wouldn't be fair to someone who really needs a job."

"What about next summer?" Victoria begged.

"Look, sweetie, it's commendable of you to want to work, but you've had a busy senior year and now it's time for you to have some fun. When I was your age, I would have given anything for the kind of summer you're going to have. For girls like you, summertime should be spent enriching your life, socially and culturally. Not only that, but I'd be accused of favoritism if I gave you a job, and I can't have that."

Nor, thought Millicent Caldwell, could she have an eighteen-year-old daughter camping in the apartment for three months, right on top of Angus and her. Good Lord, they were practically newlyweds! Had Victoria no sensitivity to the possibility that her mother might enjoy being alone with her husband, without a hulking teenager around to spoil things? No, of course not, children, no matter how old, never allowed themselves even to touch on such thoughts about a parent.

The next summer Victoria was sent to a riding family in the English countryside, and the following summer she spent in Greece. After that, Millicent sent her to France for her junior year abroad at the Sorbonne, and made sure that she spent that summer touring Italy. She never spent more than two or three nights in a row under her mother's roof. Christmas and Thanksgiving brought her home to New York, but the other college vacations took her to the homes of friends, where the welcome was warmer than at her mother's.

When Victoria graduated from college, she managed to get a summer internship at Hill Associates, a small advertising agency, where her relationship to Caldwell & Caldwell was regarded as a glamorous plus.

At Hill Associates, Victoria ran errands, made coffee, and delivered mail; she watched, she listened, she absorbed and remembered every detail she was able to observe of how their business was conducted. She talked as much as possible to the people who had time to talk to her. It was not surprising how many of them there were, and how long and informatively they were willing to chat, when they found out whose daughter she was, a detail she mentioned in the most unassuming way possible. At the end of the summer she again asked her mother for a job.

"Victoria, don't be utterly absurd," Millicent Frost Caldwell said. "You have no special artistic gifts, and you've never shown a genuine flair for writing. You were a good all-around student, but advertising—well, it takes a certain touch, a special feeling, a unique something. If you had it, even at Hill, you would have somehow popped up and been noticed. They would have offered you a permanent job when the summer was over."

"They're not big enough to need me. Look, Mother, I know I'm never going to write copy or be an art director. I'm aware of my inadequacies."

"Well, that's a relief. Then what is it you want to do here?"

"I know I can become an account executive, given time."

"Indeed? Do you really?"

"I have the necessary abilities," Victoria said with the kind of self-confidence that is so strong that it needs no emphasis of tone, no coloration of persuasion. "I'm not creative, but I get along with creative people. I appreciate what they do, and I respect it."

"But, Victoria—"

"No, please don't interrupt me, Mother, hear me out. Anybody who understands creative people can *learn* to be an account executive. It takes a person who is good at listening to the clients' concerns, analyzing them intelligently, and communicating them clearly to the creative people. At the same time, you can't allow the creative people to get upset when their favorite ideas are rejected."

Her mother lifted her curly blond head in surprise. Victoria was dead right about account executives.

"It boils down," Victoria continued, "to being a reliable, organized, detail-oriented go-between with whom everybody gets along. I'll need training and seasoning, but I know it's what I want to do, and that's half of it. I'm young, but I don't look particularly youthful and eventually—soon—I'll be ready to start as account executive on something small. You always say that advertising is a young person's business—you were writing copy and having a baby at my age. In fact, since I'm twenty-two, you were already supporting me with your work! All my life I've been doing what you want, Mother, now you have an *obligation* to give me a chance. I want to make my own living, have my own apartment, live my own life."

"How on earth can a job as an account executive be what you aspire to, Victoria?" Millicent was filled with disappointment and dismay at her daughter's determination. "My God! Just look at the education I've given you, look at the marvelous places you've been to, your travels, your wonderful summers! Look at all the ideas you've been exposed to, all the people you've met—why, Victoria, why?"

"Oh, it's your inspiration, Mother, what else could it have been?" Victoria said, giving Millicent an unusually generous smile that made her, for the moment, astonishingly beautiful. She knew she had won, as she had to, after all these dutiful years of learning and travel during which she had never once wavered in her perfectly hidden, endlessly growing love for Angus Caldwell.

Victoria Frost had never felt any real interest in any of the young men she'd met, a number of whom had been attracted to her interestingly unusual seriousness and her soundly reliable good looks, the quietly glossy radiance that her health and vitality gave her. Victoria Frost was so profoundly unavailable that many of them had pursued her, piqued and fascinated, unable to believe that their advantages, their wealth, their family backgrounds, their indisputable eligibility, could be overlooked by a girl who wasn't, after all, when you came right down to it, a raving beauty. Oh, she had a good body, an excellent body, but she didn't have a hint of a sexy attitude, which was more alluring than mere flesh, of which there was so much around. Still, Victoria was oddly . . . aristocratic, yes, aristocratic was the right word for her. She had the confidence to be exactly what she was, so utterly *present*, without using any of the female tricks of the trade, she belonged to herself in an infuriating way, as if she were better than you were. Victoria made you want to make an impression on her, make her sit up and take notice of you, make her change something about herself to please you, but even those minor hopes were doomed. She'd been known to let a boy kiss her, of course, but as far as anyone knew, that was Victoria's limit in the 1970s, when there weren't supposed to be limits, and girls from the best families everywhere experimented with everything.

By 1978, Victoria was twenty-six. Only four years out of college, she had recently been made an account supervisor at Caldwell & Caldwell, where she was responsible for the four account executives who worked on the various Oak Hill Foods divisions. The food company had grown mightily in the ten years since it had become Angus Caldwell's first client, and it now billed almost a hundred million dollars a year, a sizable chunk of the almost billion dollars a year that the giant agency did worldwide.

"I'm not happy with Victoria," her mother said to her husband.

"Why? She's doing a spectacular job. Joe Devane thinks the world of her."

"How dense can you be, Angus? There are other things in life besides work. Victoria doesn't date anyone in particular, she's always being introduced to somebody new by all those girls she went to school with, every one of them married by now and some divorced and remarried—yet my daughter, as far as I know, is . . . *celibate,* for Christ's sake! If that isn't enough to worry me, what is?"

"First of all, you don't have any proof, it's just a hunch of yours," Angus said, raising an eyebrow at his frowning wife. "Not that Victoria would necessarily tell you if she were having a romance. Absolutely to the contrary, I expect. The two of you hardly ever see each other, much less talk about anything intimate. I rarely remember that you're mother and daughter. Second, I don't get that feeling about her at all, if by 'celibate' you mean asexual. In my opinion, Victoria's merely exceptionally discreet—she always has been . . . an enigma, hasn't she? But I've felt that there is a kind of—oh, a deep, glowing warmth there, an unexpressed emotional side to her, something very private, very personal, very positive. I'm sure it's a question of her finding the right man. She's almost an old-fashioned girl, Millicent, and part of that is because of the way you brought her up."

"I gave her all the things I yearned for and never had," Millicent Caldwell said defensively.

"I didn't mean that in an invidious way. Victoria has standards, she has a sense of self-worth, she's focused in a way no other girls of her age are, at least none I've met. She's far more mature than her age."

Angus Caldwell looked wearily at his wife, off on yet another of her frequent and silly frets. Millicent was almost forty-eight now, and ever since she'd entered an early menopause, six years ago, she'd become increasingly irritable, argumentative, cranky, and difficult to live with, although it hadn't affected her work. Millicent's mother and aunt had both died of breast cancer, and therefore, to her bitter disappointment, the doctors wouldn't give her estrogen therapy.

Millicent had had a facelift when she was forty-five, but that hadn't changed the fact that the woman he'd married when he was barely twenty-eight and she could still claim to be in her thirty-seventh year, had changed more than he would have believed. She was, as people said, "pushing fifty" now, and he was a man still in his thirties, at the height of his powers. The nine-year difference in their ages, once so insignificant, was often on his mind.

Millicent was still, God knows, very blond and still pretty—he knew to the minute exactly what she went through every day to remain so—and she was more vivacious than ever. Yet, in her exquisitely feminine clothes and the monstrously valuable jewelry she always wore, making her collection of gems a trademark of her style and a sign of her success, she seemed to have become a brightly painted little bird, flying about with forced energy, twinkling and glittering and growing drier and more artificial every minute as she attempted to maintain that alluring golden aura she'd once inhabited so easily. A hummingbird, he thought broodingly, seemingly unable to stop flying and settle anywhere, a hummingbird always in motion, a tiny, decked-out, but curiously unconvincing hummingbird.

It almost, Angus told himself grimly, came down to a matter of skin. Millicent had lost whatever essential juice that once kept her delicate skin so appetizing. A web of fine wrinkles surrounded her eyes; the skin under her chin was slightly lax, so that tendons showed clearly under its surface; she had too many frown lines between her eyes. Not even the most skillful surgeon could eliminate every sign of aging. Although Millicent clung fiercely to the slim outlines of her figure by dint of an hour's daily exercise, although she could still wear a size six, there was an absence of firmness, a lack of freshness when he touched her, something he wanted to do less and less often.

The press was ever more fascinated by her, as the agency grew larger every year. Millicent Frost Caldwell was a major star of the establishment now, someone quoted as an authority, an elder of the advertising community. Angus was equally establishment, but as a woman Millicent attracted more attention than he, particularly since she had systematically created herself as if she were a product for which she was making a market. She never wearied of the work involved in choosing and wearing the most elaborate examples of American high fashion. She was responsible for buying and supervising the decoration of the three lavish, fully staffed estates they maintained in Southampton, Jamaica, and Cap Ferrat, and for their often-photographed Fifth Avenue duplex.

Both Caldwells traveled often, visiting the offices they had established in Canada, London, Japan, and Germany. Frequently they traveled separately, not wanting to leave the agency without one of them in charge. From the beginning of their partnership, one account, Oak Hill, had clearly "belonged" to Angus, and a cosmetics account had equally declared itself in Millicent's domain, but otherwise much of their vast success rested on the fact that their largest accounts liked the fact that with Caldwell they could count on the brains of both a top man and a top woman working together. Many large advertisers had finally accepted the fact that women made the majority of buying decisions in families, but the companies were almost always run by men who felt secure in Angus's attention.

In the course of the past ten years, the Caldwells had become thoroughly woven into the texture of the life of the East Coast's business and cultural elite. They cannily chose to turn their clients into personal friends, and they devoted almost every weekday night to their social life. Angus joined town clubs in Chicago, Detroit, and New York to which his clients belonged, he sailed at the New York Yacht Club with them, golfed and played tennis with them, and joined the Cavendish Club, where bridge reigned. Millicent and he invited clients and their families to stay at their various country places, where she brilliantly created an easy but worldly agenda, mixing clients with friends from international society. The wives of all their largest clients were utterly devoted to generous, hospitable Millicent, Millicent who was a great and powerful magnet in their lives. "The Caldwells" formed a glamorous couple whose private life, social life, and business success were inextricably intertwined.

Angus Caldwell had been sporadically unfaithful to Millicent for the past five years, yet he was too clever to get involved with any woman who might make a claim on him. His affairs were carefully anonymous; they always took place in cities other than New York and were conducted from the beginning as encounters that could never have a sequel. There was a certain sordid erotic excitement in their secretiveness, he admitted to himself, but they were unsatisfactory except for the physical relief they offered. A business partnership with his wife, Angus reflected, kept the money in the family, but it also obliged him to behave like a male version of Caesar's unfortunate wife, who must be "not so much as suspected" of infidelity, for as Millicent grew older and her queenly status increased, so did her discontent, her constant watchfulness, and her jealousy of the younger women in the business.

No romances for him, Angus told himself sternly, and felt, in increasingly frequent moments, that he had lost out forever on an experience that he had enjoyed but once in a lifetime, with a woman who no longer appealed to him, an experience he would renew if it were only possible, if it did not certainly mean the destruction of all he had built in his entire career.

As soon as Victoria got her first assignment as an account executive, less than a year after she joined Caldwell, she spent many hours searching for an empty apartment to move to from her furnished studio. She knew exactly what she needed and found it on a side street between Third and Second, on East Eighty-fifth Street. The building was old, the lobby was far from elegant, the elevators had been inexpensively modernized to eliminate the need for an elevator man, and the management of the building was offering the apartment "as is" without any allowance for its dilapidation.

However, the building possessed the quality of solidity she sought above all else, and it promised privacy, in a neighborhood too far east and too far uptown for her friends to frequent. Victoria bribed the superintendent with three thousand dollars in cash to get her name on the lease. Although the three rooms and kitchen hadn't been touched in twenty-five years, she saw that the walls were thick, the ceilings were of a fine height and the good-sized rooms had pleasant dimensions.

From the moment she stood alone in this space of peeling walls and dirty windows, Victoria visualized it as it could be, as she would create it, guided by passion and instinct, until it became precisely the place in which Angus Caldwell would feel most happy. She knew, without ever having been told, that he would prefer a far simpler decor than any place she could remember her mother considering fit for habitation.

As she supervised the transformation of her apartment, every choice was made with Angus in mind, every change was made for a tall, active man, imparting a kind of subtle, resolutely invisible comfort that few women would be concerned with for themselves alone. The living room was lined with bookcases from floor to ceiling; throughout the apartment the woodwork was painted in a warm terra-cotta, with more brown in it than pink; all the windows were framed in heavily lined, full-length draperies in a slightly deeper terra-cotta linen. The floors were stripped and stained in a dark honey tone; the deep chairs and couches were large, simply designed, and upholstered in mellow brown leather and solid fabrics in shades of deep red and rusts, with one or two touches of green and soft yellow, so that it seemed that early autumn had just arrived throughout the apartment. The wooden tables Victoria chose were country antiques, with a fine patina, the table lamps were plain and thoughtfully placed, and there were a few faded but beautiful rugs on the shining floors.

On her Saturdays she slowly filled the bookcases with cannily chosen volumes, books she knew Angus owned, found in secondhand stores throughout the city. An old mahogany library ladder stood in a place of pride in the living room. Victoria spent nothing on art and little on objects, keeping the rooms uncontrived and uncluttered. Here and there she placed a few creamware bowls that she kept filled with apples and nuts, and there were always several sturdy, well-tended green plants near the windows. The dismal kitchen was repainted a glossy white and given a Mexican tile floor and new working surfaces. Each piece of tableware was old blue-and-white china or pottery in an artfully careless mixture of patterns. Victoria found usable, if battered, copper pots and pans and treated herself to a first-class set of cooking equipment, for in spite of her education she had made herself into an excellent plain cook. There was a large, worn, well-scrubbed, painted kitchen table with unmatched country chairs sitting on a rag rug above which a painted tin chandelier cast a cozy light.

It was as homey an apartment as any man could want.

Within less than a year, Victoria began working exclusively on the many-faceted Oak Hill account. She had been studying the food industry since her sophomore year in college, and by now there wasn't an outstanding campaign for food advertising in the history of advertising with which she wasn't familiar, or a food industry magazine she hadn't read for years, never mentioning this interest to anyone.

When Millicent was out of town on business, if Angus happened to be in New York, it became quite natural for Victoria to invite him over for dinner from time to time. She cooked for herself, she told him, as a rule, and there was always enough for two. What was more simple, it seemed, than for her to put another plate on the kitchen table, open a bottle of wine, and spend a casual evening talking shop, talking books, talking politics and art and any other topic that two intelligent people would discuss if they worked together?

Victoria didn't allow herself to reveal the slightest hint of emotion other than impersonal friendship during these evenings. She made half a glass of wine last her all night, so that she was in total command of herself at all times. She was never caught watching him with too long a look, or using any of the recognized feminine flirtation techniques, not even subliminally. She couldn't make herself into anything other than a female, but it was not as a female that she presented herself to Angus, or as connected in any way at all to his wife. Millicent Frost Caldwell ceased to exist as her daughter spun a complicated, age-old spell in which she became almost completely an interested listener and an interesting talker, someone to whom the life of the mind was deeply important.

During these long evenings, Victoria always sat at a distance from Angus that encouraged conversation yet was just too far away to permit any deeper proximity to be established. When it became time for him to leave, she managed to be busy with something in the living room that had just caught her eye, so that she could wave him impersonally out of her front door. Even when he was sitting at the kitchen table and they were ready to eat, she kept an impassable space between them, scrupulously handing him a bowl or platter or jug across the large table, never bending over to serve him or fill his glass. He had never been invited to take a look at her bedroom in the usual way people show off their apartments in New York, and gradually he realized that he never would be.

Victoria always changed before she expected Angus for dinner. She took off the dark, austere, almost too-old-for-her clothes she had adopted for the office right from the beginning of her job and put on casual garb—old, well-washed, rather oversized jeans, and equally well-worn T-shirts or sweaters. She chose these in colors like apricot or old rose, pastels that weren't fussy but that reflected their warmth on her skin. She always wore a bra under these tops so that her full, thrusting breasts were held firmly in place, but she never wore panties, since it made an important difference to her to be able to feel the rough denim rubbing so intimately on her body, warning her constantly of the role she had to play. She let her hair fall down to the middle of her back, well brushed and loose, she put no makeup on her perfect skin and no makeup on her clear eyes. She looked incredibly young and careless and innocent.

Young, indeed, she was, and infinitely careful and utterly without innocence except for the merely physical. Victoria Frost knew very well that, over the course of time, she was driving Angus Caldwell slowly insane with desire, but she made no move, no sign, gave no word. Everything, she vowed to herself repeatedly, must come from him. She would do nothing to encourage him, nothing to allow him to think that she craved him with every inch of her skin, every cell of her brain. Her victory must be total.

Gradually, even when there was an opportunity for him to possess a woman in a way that would leave no trace, no attachment, Angus Caldwell found himself unwilling to plunge into an unknown body attached to an unknown mind. What he had thought of as a necessary release, a short adventure, began to seem merely shabby when the thought of Victoria came into his mind. He could see her so vividly in the enchanted quiet of her apartment, like a clearing in the woods in its restful colors, with her particular glowing calm, her lovely but impersonal smile, her ready understanding of his ideas, her attentive ear, her interesting opinions.

There was, Angus thought, as he began to look forward more and more eagerly to his dinners with Victoria, only one odd note. Neither he nor she had ever mentioned to Millicent that they met when she was away. They had never discussed this omission. It had been mutually and wordlessly understood from the very first time he had visited her apartment that Millicent would not find acceptable these few hours they spent so harmlessly together. Was this another example of Victoria's tact, that tact she employed so successfully in dealing with clients, or was it because he was, after all, her boss, or was it some sort of reaction to the undercurrent of edgy discomfort he always felt running so strongly between mother and daughter when they were, so infrequently, together? It was far too late to ask Victoria a question about this matter, and in any case he blessed the silence, for Millicent's watchful, growing jealousy included all of the many dozens of women he worked with, and wouldn't have stopped at her daughter, in spite of the fact that Victoria gave her no cause.

No cause. Victoria gave him no cause to think of her with an almost uncontainable, growing lust, yet lust was precisely what was consuming him. He burned, day and night, with lust for a girl who had just turned twenty-seven, a girl who wanted nothing from him but a quiet evening from time to time, a girl who didn't even bother to put on makeup for him, who never came close to him, who never offered any personal information about her life that might have fed his imagination, a girl who had taken him into her life as a friend, nothing more.

In the office, when Angus saw Victoria in a meeting, dressed in the almost monastic black she favored, her hair so severely tamed, her attitude so cool, so competent, so in control that she could pass for a woman in her mid-thirties, all he could think of was how she looked when he had dinner with her alone. Then, when finally a chance of timing made it possible for him to be with her in her apartment, he could only think of how she would look spread out naked on a bed, stripped of those damn jeans and baggy sweaters, naked, her legs open, her eyes closed, naked, waiting for him, ready for him, crying out for him . . . Christ! He had to stop this, Angus Caldwell thought as he dressed for another black-tie benefit at the Costume Institute of the Metropolitan Museum of Art.

And what did Victoria think of when she thought of him, Angus wondered as he leaned forward and examined himself in the mirror of his dressing room. Or did she think of him at all? Did she perhaps dream of one or another of the two young men she had recently lured away from the Grey Agency and with whom she now spent so much time in the office? Archie Rourke and Byron Bernheim, a highly coveted creative team, had been hired to work on the three low-calorie products Oak Hill was planning on introducing. Both of them were Victoria's age, and before Grey they had spent three years at BBD&O, establishing a resonating reputation.

Rourke was a type any young female would find unsettlingly attractive, Angus realized grimly. Black-Irish handsome, so predictably rakehell, whiz-bang handsome it was almost laughable, with that Irish white skin and Irish blue eyes and thick black hair growing in curls too far down his neck, and that Irish way with women. If the talented bastard weren't in advertising, he could run for any public office he coveted, and probably win on the women's vote alone, Angus thought wrathfully. Yes, tough Archie Rourke, whose mother taught English in a public high school outside of Chicago, whose father coached the football team; cocky, blunt Archie Rourke, whose way with words was as lively as his ambition, might make any girl think about him twice.

As for Byron Berenson Bernheim the Third, the art director of the two, he was more likely to be Victoria's type, Angus reflected, his speculations making him more frantic by the minute. Bernheim was the product of a San Francisco family, a highly cultivated clan, with an intellectual mother who supported every cultural institution of the city and a banker father whose art collection was well known even in New York. He was taller than Archie, and leaner, with reddish hair, elegantly put together with none of the bulk that was visible under Archie's jackets; he had a lively, interesting face and he looked as if he could handle himself well in any fight.

Damn them both to hell! And damn all the other men Victoria worked with and the unknown men she must go out with, although she never mentioned anyone's name, and damn the museum only three blocks away from his home to which he and Millicent could easily have walked tonight if she weren't wearing a dark blue Scassi gown that covered her bare arms with a cunning double layer of chiffon that hid the sagging flesh on her skinny frame, for no amount of exercise could overcome the effects of gravity. The dress had also been designed to display her three million dollars' worth of diamonds. Millicent, so charmingly coiffed and made up by an expert who had arrived two hours ago, literally didn't dare to walk any farther than from the lobby of their apartment house to the waiting door of their limousine, for fear of being mugged, even on Fifth Avenue.

6

A few weeks later, Millicent Frost Caldwell suddenly took herself, her jewel case, three suitcases, and her personal maid off to London on the Concorde for several days of countering the raid she had just discovered Saatchi and Saatchi was going to make on their British airlines account. Angus proposed himself to Victoria for dinner.

"Tonight or tomorrow?" she wondered.

"Tonight would be better," he answered casually, "if it isn't too much trouble?"

"How much trouble can it be to warm up leftover stew?" Victoria smiled, and walked quickly down the corridor to her own office to tell her secretary to cancel her date for that night.

"I brought you a Vivaldi tape you don't have," he said as she opened the door.

"Vivaldi and beef stew . . . are they compatible companions?" she asked on a laugh.

"Better save the music for after dinner," Angus suggested. He often brought her new tapes simply because she listened to music attentively, with her eyes closed, and that gave him a chance to look at her for a mercifully long, unmercifully torturing time, without her being aware of his gaze.

Tonight, as they finished dinner and put on the tape, Angus sat back with his legs relaxed, in one of the leather armchairs, his eyelids hooding his eyes as Victoria leaned back on a russet linen couch. Her white jeans were so old that they hung comfortably at her waist without needing a belt, and her long hair drifted in soft strands over the dark peach of a sweater that had rubbed thin at the elbows. She looked as tousled and languid as a girl on a sailboat; she was so full of heedless, bursting youth that his heart reeled. He imagined painfully what it would be like to stroke her creamy cheek with his fingers, to kiss her at the base of her smooth, long throat. It seemed to him that the air in the room must be dense and smoky with his feverish longing to touch her, but no such awareness appeared to disturb her concentration on the music.

As the Vivaldi filled the room, Victoria peered through her amazing eyelashes at Angus, knowing from practice in the mirror that she could do so and still seem to have her eyes closed. His face revealed nothing, she thought in a sharp ache of need to touch his rough countryman's skin, to touch his sandy, silky hair with her lips. She stirred restlessly on the couch. A few seconds after she changed her position, she saw him suddenly, with an almost angry expression, cross one leg over the other in a way that wasn't characteristic of him. She took a deep breath, waited a minute, and then moved again, stretching her arms over her head as if she had a kink in her back. Still watching him through her lashes, she saw him bite down on his bottom lip and press his legs together more tightly than they had been before. Oh yes, she thought, yes, it has to come now, this moment she had been dreaming of and plotting toward for years, it was time, more than time, high time, and if something didn't happen now, tonight, when she had finally seen his excitement and measured the extent of his control, it might never happen, he might never come to dinner again. But still the Vivaldi continued and Angus remained seated.

The volume of space she had established between them, never violated, seemed solid and impenetrable to her. The two of them were frozen by the habits she had so carefully, stealthily nurtured, year after year, Victoria realized. He would never make the first move. Suddenly she couldn't endure the measured formality of the music for another instant.

An agony of impatience, a snapping of her inhuman determination, a shrugging-off of years of self-government possessed her as she rose from the couch, murmuring something about another tape, and mounted to the third step of the library ladder that stood next to the nearest bookcase. She rummaged there with her back to Angus, tears of anger and frustration filling her eyes. She heard his footsteps, and suddenly his arms clasped her waist. She went utterly immobile as she felt him fumbling at the zipper on her jeans. She didn't move or speak when she felt his warm, shaking fingers moving down her bare stomach to the very edge of the springy hair between her legs, but only braced herself against the railing of the ladder so that she wouldn't fall. Let him do what he would, she thought, oh, please, let him do what he would, and when he turned her around and buried his thirsty mouth in the dark bounty that was so marvelously bared to his warm, warm lips, her silence spoke for her.

They stood there for long minutes, too overcome even to groan, as he pressed his head into her belly and explored her with his avid, parched lips and his piercing tongue, her voiceless assent more powerful than any words could have been. He kept at her relentlessly, even when her hands tore at his hair and she ground herself against him, until he became afraid that she would escape him into a bliss he couldn't share. He picked her up and carried her into the bedroom he'd never seen and laid her down on the bed he'd imagined so often and covered her face and mouth with mad, wild, hasty kisses as he tore off his clothes and pulled off her sweater and released her breasts from their bra, as swiftly and hungrily as a criminal. He handled her roughly and ruthlessly, lost to all tenderness, and she responded with a raw willingness that made her as brutal as he was. His last thought was that later there would be time to caress, to speak, to kiss, as he grabbed the club of his penis in his hand and jammed it into her with a violence he had not known he was capable of. Again and again he shoved, his teeth grinding, clumsy, urgent, savage, falling on her like a starving animal on a piece of meat until he was entirely enclosed by her tightness and warmth.

"Yes!" It was the first word she had spoken, and it was all it took to make him buck into the most severely exquisite orgasm of his life. When it was finally finished, he flung himself back, his heart pounding, almost unconscious with relief, until, after a long while, he returned to his senses and realized that Victoria was lying motionless beside him, still panting with a fierce, unrelieved tension.

"You didn't . . ."

"No," she whispered, and Angus bent over her with his lips open to suck her quickly into the climax she had almost achieved in the living room. As he parted her legs, more gently now, he saw the bloodstains on the sheet below her. "I've hurt you!" he exclaimed, suddenly aware of his savagery, his selfish relentlessness.

"I wanted it." She sounded vulnerable, wounded and deliriously alive, utterly made flesh.

"You're bleeding."

"Yes."

"You . . . it was the first time." He was blankly incredulous.

"Of course."

"Victoria, you couldn't have, you couldn't have waited!"

"I touched myself . . . and thought of you."

She laughed low in her throat, a purely female laugh, and he was gripped by a wave of emotions—unutterable gratification, violent flattery, amazed love, and unbearable curiosity—emotions primitive and deep and almost too much to endure, so that he wanted to bite her until she bled, to hit her until she cried out, to kiss her until her lips were raw, to bind her to the bed, to mate with her, blindly, until they were both reduced to husks. *I touched myself and thought of you.* He was hard again, he realized, and now he guided his penis with delicious, careful slowness into her wanting, waiting, welcoming body, feeling with his fingers, which were suddenly delicately sensitive, the folds and concavities of her

118

lower lips, which had been swollen by an onrush of readiness for the past hour. He filled her with a steady, stern penis, hard in that second hardness which lasts so much longer than the first, and he kept it there, motionless, plugging her full of him, while he played with the plump, burning, hesitating rosette of flesh that was the key to her satisfaction. Whenever he sensed that she was about to come, he took his fingers away, only putting them back when she had forced herself to lie quiet again, impaled on his penis, her mouth open in an unuttered plea. She had waited for him. Now she must wait until he chose to release her. Never had he known a woman who understood his demands without words, never had he had anyone so at his mercy, never had he wanted to kill as he came, kill in a carnal ecstasy of total possession, and when he finally burst into her again it was only after finally, almost unwillingly, permitting her the splendid fruit of satisfaction, the terrible, triumphant satisfaction she had waited for so long.

During the four business days that Millicent was in London, they met in Victoria's apartment as early as possible every night, leaving their offices separately, taking separate taxis, using separate keys, and, once they arrived, going directly to Victoria's bedroom and falling upon each other in a thunderclap of such intense passion that it never lessened, never allowed them time to pull apart, stop, and take account of the situation. They were too euphoric to think or plan, too anesthetized by the growing discoveries of each other's bodies, to spare time in talk.

Eventually, Angus had to drag himself off to his home to sleep a few hours, shave, shower, dress, and eat breakfast as if nothing were out of order in his routine. Their days passed in a feverish dream as they attended the usual round of meetings and presentations, surrounded by their unseeing co-workers. Victoria's body was camouflaged in the reliably hard chic of her clothes, and if anyone had inspected her flushed face closely, the only conclusion they might have drawn was that she'd had a good night's sleep or had somehow managed to get some sun. Angus found he could run the company on autopilot for a few days. When they both happened to be in the same meeting, they never dared to look directly at each other; when they had to lunch with a group of Oak Hill executives, they barely managed to swallow, although not one of the men around the table noticed that Angus Caldwell and Victoria Frost were any different from their usual efficient, businesslike, good-humored selves.

"What's going to happen now?" Victoria made herself ask, the night before her mother's return.

"The only thing I can think about is how we can be together. We can't . . . sit around and *wait* till she goes out of town—that's out of the question."

"But the two of you have social obligations almost every night, there are no excuses you can make."

"I just don't know what to do." He sat up in bed and buried his face in his hands.

As she had expected and feared, Angus wasn't ready yet to tear his life apart, Victoria reflected. He hadn't allowed himself to realize that of course it all must come tumbling down before it could be built up again with her. It was too soon for him to face the reality that he had to turn his back on everything he'd taken for granted, too soon for him to acknowledge that she must replace her mother, her unloving, ungiving, unnatural mother, whose punishment had been too long in coming. But Angus was still only thirty-nine, he had as much time ahead of him as they needed, and she would wait. Wait and wait. Now that she was sure of him, how much easier it would be. Hadn't she waited since she was sixteen for him, held herself out for endless, arid years with nothing but her will and her love to keep her going? She couldn't risk a wrong move now that she had achieved the victory that had never seemed impossible. She had always known that she must eventually win Angus away from her mother. He had belonged to her from the minute she had first seen him.

"We could get a place near the office," Victoria said hesitantly, as if she hadn't meditated long on the question. "We could meet there now and then . . . at lunch or right at the end of the afternoon, before you have to be home—you could be out having an early drink with a client or playing bridge—we could manage an hour here and there."

"Oh God, darling!" He buried his face in her shoulder. "An hour! An hour's nothing!"

"But what's the alternative?" she asked.

"None," he groaned, "none."

Within a few days, Angus had rented a well-furnished studio apartment that was only a five-minute taxi ride from the offices of Caldwell & Caldwell, and had arranged for regular maid service. They met there whenever they could, sometimes by rigorous planning, jointly managing to avoid their business lunches, and sometimes at five in the afternoon. However, their busy schedules, which depended on fulfilling the demands of so many other people, made their times together few, short, and maddeningly unpredictable. The weekends, which the Caldwells usually spent in Southampton from the spring through the fall, were especially difficult to endure, and Millicent Frost Caldwell's brief trips out of town still remained their only periods of genuine freedom.

Almost a year passed, and their ravening desire for each other became stronger with every unexpected postponement of a meeting, every time they had to tear themselves from an hour in their warm bed and put on their public faces. Unslaked desire, desire that grew stronger with its infrequent release, possessed them whenever they were not together, a gnawing undercurrent of permanent hunger, a confirmed addiction, an addiction they welcomed in all its manifestations.

"I can't touch Millicent," Angus confessed late in that year. "I haven't touched her since our first time."

"Has she said anything?" Victoria asked, screaming in her head for him to tell her, for God's sake, tell her mother the truth.

"No, she's let it go. Clearly she's decided to blind herself, she obviously doesn't want to know," Angus said, and Victoria heard the clear relief in his voice with cold dread.

Not long afterwards, in early winter of 1981, soon after she had been promoted to senior account supervisor on all the Oak Hill accounts, Victoria faced the fact that it was too comfortable for Angus to have a lover who worked so closely with him, a lover who would do anything to be with him whenever he had a scrap of time for her, and a wife who was determined to ask no questions. Perhaps she could provoke some sort of showdown.

"Mother, I was thinking of coming to Jamaica for a week at Christmas this year . . . that is if you have room for me?"

"We'd love it," Millicent said, hiding her surprise. "But I assume you'd like to bring a beau?"

"I hadn't thought of that, but yes, as a matter of fact, I would. He's no one special, at least not yet, don't get your hopes up, but he'll be an addition to the party. Thank you, Mother."

She couldn't believe she hadn't thought of playing that hand herself, Victoria thought, as she made a telephone call. Count on Millicent Frost to know how to sell a product, dead or alive.

In order to keep busy during her many empty evenings, she had never stopped seeing several of the increasingly eligible men who continued to present themselves to her, only to go away eventually, disappointed in their failure to interest this somehow mysterious young woman who seemed to have escaped even a touch of the neediness they sensed in most of the other unmarried career women they knew. Victoria Frost had a monster job, she got more uncannily attractive every year, she'd never been serious about anyone . . . how could she not be anxious, at almost twenty-nine, to find the right man and take her rightful position in the world? Why did she seem so snugly settled in that mysteriously comfortable little place of hers that wasn't even on a good street? There was no way she could be destined for the permanently unmarried life, happy as she seemed with the arrangement; such a life simply didn't happen to girls like her, smart as hell, rich as hell, and yes, beautiful, for Victoria Frost had become a beauty in the last year or so. People agreed that she'd finally grown into her looks.

Victoria chose the most attractive of her many aspirants, Amory Hopkins, a thirty-five-year-old divorced stockbroker, decisively rich, unencumbered by children, tall, good-looking, well mannered, and possessed of a pleasant, quiet sense of humor. He had the necessary skills at sports, he danced acceptably well, he dressed most acceptably well, and he certainly looked as if he could fuck more than acceptably well, Victoria thought, as he accepted her invitation with deep pleasure. Her mother would be secretly salivating over him. Angus . . . the more agony Angus felt the better.

During the week at the estate near Montego Bay, Victoria deployed every weapon she possessed. Garden-variety flirtation was not among them—it was an art she had never practiced—but as she sat listening intently to Amory Hopkins, during the long conversations she instigated as they sat somewhat apart from the rest of the house party, she cut raw wounds into Angus that no amount of coquettishness could have made. Whenever her low assenting laugh was heard, whenever she grew animated and leaned toward Amory to emphasize a point, running her fingers through her hanging tangled hair, Angus quivered with jealousy. Victoria cast aside her usual style and wore thin cotton sun dresses with nothing under them to restrain her full, swinging breasts, bikinis that revealed the disciplined richness of her thighs and the firm, tight line of her waist, short summer evening dresses that turned her flashing long legs into a scissors thrust to his heart.

Victoria was nicely charming to her mother. She was nicely charming to all the other houseguests. She was particularly nicely charming to Angus, as charming as if he were the elderly stepfather with whom she had a history of years of grateful affection. Whenever she found herself alone in her room, she congratulated herself on that training as an account executive which had made nice charm an automatic part of her repertoire, like a second skin. No un-nice, un-charming account executive survived, either at the top or the bottom of the agency business.

Amory Hopkins would have thought Victoria even more charming than he did if she'd let him make love to her, but she wouldn't, implore though he would. She let him kiss her, she let him touch her neck and her arms, and once, when they were out by the swimming pool with everyone else, she let him rub her with suntan oil wherever he could reach, but she insisted that in her mother's house, it was only decent that she sleep alone.

Once, just once, she contrived to meet Angus alone in the pool house late in the afternoon. He was waiting for her as she entered, grown painfully erect in the few minutes he'd been standing there planning how he would kiss her until she trembled, how he would lead her into one of the changing rooms, lock the door, lift up the skirt of her sun dress, and take her without the slightest regard for her own satisfaction. He owed her that for the way she'd been tormenting him. He knew she'd be so lubricated from the thought of this meeting that he could stick his cock into her without the slightest preliminary. He promised himself to use her so quickly, selfishly, and remorselessly that she wouldn't have time to achieve an orgasm, and then pull out and go away, leaving her lying there mad from humiliating desire. Let her suffer, Angus told himself, let her feel the same tormented arousal he'd felt all week and been unable to satisfy. Let her touch herself and think of him, as she used to, he thought, grinding his teeth in a rapture of anticipation.

Victoria entered the pool house and flew into his arms. He had only kissed her once before she thrust both of her hands into the fly of his swimming trunks, grasped his hard penis, and started to use her fingers in the way he adored the most, cupping and squeezing his balls with one hand while the other manipulated the shaft with a sure up-and-down motion of firmly increasing pressure and swiftness. Angus stood frozen, panting, with the beginning of the certainty that he was about to come, unable to carry out his plan. Suddenly Victoria jumped, startled, as if she'd heard someone at the door of the pool house. She snatched her hands out of his trunks, turned on her heel, and ran out of the pool house as quickly as she had entered.

Oh, she knew how much he was suffering, Victoria thought, as she walked lightly up to the house, for she was suffering just as much. She would give almost anything to have him inside her, anything but the victory she had just achieved.

"Do you think I don't know that you did that on purpose?" Angus raged at her the first time they met again at the New York apartment near the office, shortly after the New Year's Eve that ushered in 1982. "You were obscene!"

"*You* have a life. I don't," Victoria said quietly, unaffected by his anger.

"*We have* a life!"

"It's not enough. I refuse to accept this little." She spoke in a conversational tone.

"Good Christ, we have as much as we can, you must understand that."

"No." She shook her head with an air of finality, sitting on the edge of a chair, her gloves in her hand, like a lady waiting for a cup of tea. He had expected her to be as avid as he was, but she had never looked so removed from thoughts of sex. She was still playing with him, he thought as he walked over to her, bent down, and pulled her up to him, kissing her lips, pulling out the pins that held up her hair, undoing the buttons of her suit and blouse, and then bending to suck hard, hard on her nipples in the way that excited her the most. She allowed everything, she allowed him to push her back on the couch, to undress her, to make her as wet as he wanted to with his tongue, to part her legs, to push into her, but she responded not at all. He took her with a more intense excitement than he had ever known. The more she held herself in check, the more frenzied he became.

When it was over, she asked only, "Was that enough for you?"

"Shit, no! Was it enough for you?"

"It's as much as I can give you," she said implacably. "I have to leave. There's the Lighthouse Ball tonight, and I have to go home and get ready."

Unable to move, unable even to think with any coherence, Angus watched Victoria gather her clothes together and dress rapidly. It was only five-thirty in the evening, there was no need for her to be in a hurry, they still had an hour, even an hour and a half. How could she leave him, aroused and unfulfilled as she was, this girl who lived for his fucking, when it had been weeks and weeks since she'd had an orgasm? At least so far as he knew. He despised himself as he asked, shaking with jealousy, "Who's taking you to the ball?"

"Not Amory. No one you know." And she was gone, leaving him in incredulous despair.

He sat for a long time on the couch, unable to dress, wrapped only in his overcoat, shivering in the warm room, trying to make sense out of what had happened, torn between jealousy of some man who would dance with her tonight and look into her eyes and receive her smile, and the fact that he was again violently thirsty for her body, so ready that it hurt, so ready that now, this minute he would give anything to take her again.

"*You* have a life," she'd said to him. Indeed he did. He had a life that was filled from waking to sleeping; a life in which he was responsible for the fortunes of a huge company; a life in which he had to portion out every minute to meet the demands of his clients, each one of whom expected individual hand-holding, no matter how good the account supervisors were who worked with them; a life in which these same supervisors and their account executives and their creative teams looked to him and Millicent for final approval of the campaigns they planned to present to the clients; a life that included playing hard at the sports through which men like him consolidated their business relationships; a life that demanded that he entertain and be entertained on an increasingly grand scale, that he travel to touch base with his international branches and clients in other cities . . . a life that was crammed full to bursting with obligations that went with his position and achievements as one of the most important men in advertising.

The small spaces of time he'd been able to steal for Victoria could not, reasonably, be added to by more than a few hours at wide intervals, Angus Caldwell realized. What more could he give her?

Imagine, he said to himself, imagine that you got a divorce from Millicent. Imagine that the agency was thrown into confusion and its smooth functioning went to hell for a while, imagine a full-scale uproar, as bad as it could get. Nevertheless, a cadre of clients and creative people would most certainly stick it out with you, and you could start up all over again, on a smaller scale, with your own new agency, and be content with that and whatever growth came in time. Yes, that scenario *was* entirely possible. A number of agencies, headed by two or more partners, endured when those people agreed to go their own ways, creating other agencies as they split.

He certainly had the right to divorce his wife, brilliant, popular Millicent, and marry any other woman, even a twenty-year old, and risk no more than the loss of some of his business and many of his friends. He would probably seem heartless, considering Millicent's age and her role in his success, but people always assumed that they never knew the truth of the inside of a marriage and made allowances. They hated to take sides.

But imagine instead that after you divorce Millicent, you marry *Victoria*. Angus now realized, finally, in hideous clarity, that Victoria's agenda was marriage. How could he ever have been stupid enough to hope that she would be content with the arrangement they had?

Yes, just imagine that you marry your former wife's one and only daughter, a young woman the people you know best have considered to be your stepdaughter for thirteen years, ever since so many of them had seen her as a flushed, tall, beautiful teenager in an emerald green minidress, walking in nervous dignity down the aisle of a church at your wedding, your wife's only attendant.

No! Never! He, Angus Caldwell, knew it wasn't incest. Victoria and he shared no ties of blood. He had never adopted her, never even considered it. He knew she'd been a grown-up sixteen when he'd first laid eyes on her. He knew they hadn't spent a night in the same house in her formative years, except for a few occasions when she was between trains or planes. He knew how distant she had always been from her mother, how rarely he'd even seen her in those six years before her graduation from college. He knew he hadn't touched her until she was twenty-seven. He knew he had never, in those eleven years, considered her in the position of a stepdaughter. Not once, during those innocent dinners at her apartment, those dinners during which they had never touched each other, had he spared the time to remind himself who her mother was. And afterwards . . . no, never. Particularly not afterwards.

Oh, he knew all this, and none of it mattered. Not one single fact. None of it could be explained away as he had just so convincingly explained it to himself. The facts were irrelevant. None of it—*none*—would be weighed in evidence when the scandal came to light, when people heard about it and started the storm of speculation that would never stop, even after his death. Everyone he knew in the world, every man in every club, every client who had confidence in him, every one of the hundreds of people who worked for him, would think of him as a man who had committed a crime against nature. A man who had fucked his stepdaughter. *A man who had fucked her for God knows how long. A* man who had betrayed his wife in the vilest way. A man who should be thrust outside of society. A man to be shunned by any decent person.

He had to give Victoria up, Angus saw in a jolt of clear reason. He had to get out of the fearful danger he had been too muddleheaded and blinded by sex to think through until today. He had trapped himself into the biggest mistake of his life. But he had to ease out of it cautiously, with infinite care, so that no one, *no one*, would ever know. Victoria had it in her power to destroy his life, to lay waste to everything that was important to him. She could be his ruin.

During the next months, whenever they met, Angus Caldwell forced himself to raise the question of their future together. He realized she couldn't go on like this, he told Victoria, he realized how selfish he'd been, he couldn't live this way either, it was against all natural human feeling for them not to be together openly, for them not to marry when they loved each other so. But, my God, they had to be patient a while longer, she must understand that, they had to find a way to have their lives together and still make as little mess as possible, she saw that, didn't she, his intelligent darling? No, he understood that she had to go out with other men, it would look peculiar if she didn't, but he couldn't help being jealous even though he knew she didn't sleep with them, she had to forgive him his jealousy, she had to promise him, promise him that they never touched her, never touched his darling.

Yes, of course he trusted her, he knew how long she'd waited for him, and all he asked was that she make it easy for him while he found the best way to get his freedom, all he asked was that she never deny him her love, her kisses, her own satisfaction . . . he couldn't endure that again. Of course he knew it was taking an eternity, but he couldn't lay the groundwork for their future in weeks or even months. Yes, he realized that she'd be twenty-nine on her next birthday, but he promised that by then he'd have a plan, a workable plan. No, she couldn't get up and leave now, not now, not when he was so ready again, no, she had to let him take her one more time, that was all he asked.

Angus bought almost another year while he searched for the way out.

"Los Angeles! You can't be serious! Why do you want me to go there?" Victoria cried out.

"I want *us* to go there—"

"But—"

"Darling, shut up and let me talk. L.A. is the answer, I just don't know why I didn't see it sooner. It's a chance to start fresh, to build a new life, to have each other and our work and—"

"But why do I have to go first, alone, without you?"

"Because something as big as this has to be done in steps. Listen to me carefully, Victoria. As long as you're employed by Caldwell & Caldwell, you're a prisoner of the company. But if you open your own shop, if you declare your independence, as soon as the divorce is over, I'll join you."

"You actually think I'd be willing to start a little one-woman agency in a city I hardly know, three thousand miles away from the center of the action? Angus, it's out of the question."

"What if your agency opened with some twenty million dollars in billing? Wouldn't a jump-start like that enable you to lure a few top creative people to come with you? And you'd be top dog in your own shop. What if you knew that when I joined you I'd be bringing many millions in billing with me? That we'd become a powerhouse? Wouldn't that be better than staying in the same city as Millicent?"

"*Twenty million?* Where would I get twenty million?"

"You have to leave that part up to me. I know how to make it work. Without it, you don't go anywhere, my darling, and I'll start work on Plan B."

The next day, Angus Caldwell made a lunch date with his old loyal friend and first client, Joe Devane, who owed him so much for the success of Oak Hill Foods.

"Joe, I need a big favor."

"It's yours."

"No, don't say that so quickly. I'll understand if you can't help me out, but Victoria and her mother are having a lot of serious problems."

"Now that's too bad, Angus. I'm sorry to hear it."

"They've never been close, Joe. I've tried and tried to repair the relationship, but when I married Millicent it must have been too late to solve their trouble, whatever it was."

"That's too bad, Angus, a real shame. I've never realized."

"We've hoped to keep it in the family, but now, well,

you're the first to know, but Victoria is determined to leave the agency."

"Damn! Now that's really *rotten* news! You know how I count on that girl. She's tops in my book! It's a crying shame that she's leaving, a crying shame! But what can I do about it? Do you want me to talk to her? Damn it, Angus, if you can't keep her, how can I?"

"That's exactly what I want to talk to you about, Joe. When Victoria leaves Caldwell, she intends to move out to L.A. I know she's planning to take a few of our very best creative people with her and open up her own shop. And we can't do a thing to stop her."

"Shit! What a situation! I don't envy you, but I'm sorry as hell for me, let me tell you. I *need* that girl, we've won a lot of Clios on advertising she's supervised, sold a lot of food too."

"Don't think I don't know it. Here's the favor, Joe. Would you give her some of your business? I was thinking of the three low-cal accounts."

"Take my business away from you? You're asking me to take away twenty million dollars of billing as a *favor* to you and give it to a new agency? Are you crazy, Angus?"

"On the contrary. When Victoria walks away, it's just a question of time before she'll make a bid for your business anyway, *all of it*. It's a logical step for her to take. She's been working exclusively on your accounts since she started at the agency almost eight years ago, she's grown into the job wonderfully, and now your marketing and advertising guys make a perfect fit with her."

"Yeah, more's the pity."

"Joe, there's a chance that you'd want to make the move anyway, but you'd feel too much loyalty to me ever to do it."

"Damn right I wouldn't. We must be billing a hundred million with you now, Angus."

"Something like that, Joe, something very close. But my hunch is that if Victoria can make a clean break, taking a few accounts she unquestionably feels she's earned the right to take, the accounts she's been involved in most intimately, like the low-cal accounts, she may well feel that she's being compensated for the years she's worked so hard. I'm hoping that she won't be as bitter as she is now, and in the end there will be a lot less of a family feud going on between her and Millicent."

"The hell you say! Interesting, Angus, very interesting thinking. Sort of a preemptive strike?"

"Exactly."

"Millicent agree with you?"

"If Millicent ever knew it was my idea . . . forget it, Joe, my life wouldn't be worth spit. Things are really tense at home. In fact, my wife and Victoria aren't talking to each other. I'm the one who's trying to keep the situation workable. I'm counting on you, Joe, whatever you decide, never to mention this."

"Hell, you know me better than that. Look, Angus, let me think this over for a day or two. It's a lot to digest, but, hell, right off the bat, there doesn't seem to be any reason that it wouldn't work. We'd keep Victoria and we'd still have Caldwell. Still, give me a chance to think. Are you absolutely sure you're not going to have second thoughts about this? Twenty million is a big bite, even for a giant agency."

"I've thought about nothing else for months."

"It's been as bad as that, huh?"

"Worse, Joe, worse."

"Just how much do you think we know about Victoria Frost, Archie, besides the fact that she's a dynamite account supervisor and she's the heiress apparent at C&C?" Byron asked.

"How much more do you need to know?"

"Well, I'd be interested to find out why she seems so damned *invulnerable*," Byron said. "She's only about thirty, same as us, but the longer I know the woman, the more she's like a fortress to me. It's not natural. This is not chick behavior."

"This is not a chick, Byron. This is the opposite of chick."

"How come she doesn't have a love life? If she did, with the gossip around this place, we'd know. That still bothers me, although I'd never admit it to anyone but you."

"Maybe she's a lesbian. Isn't that what guys always think when a woman isn't showing any interest in them? One thing I'm sure of, nobody is asexual when you get right down to it." Archie pondered the question further. "Asexual means an absence of sex, like a flowerless plant that can reproduce all by itself . . . Victoria couldn't be asexual."

"Maybe it's all a smoke screen. Maybe she leads a double life as a prostitute in a bordello, like Catherine Deneuve in *Belle du Jour?*" Byron sounded hopeful.

"Byron, I've told you to stop seeing those French movies."

"They say that after four Buñuel flicks you start to grow hair on your palms," Byron brooded.

"Four!" Archie exclaimed. "Obviously you don't pay attention to that great warning, 'Once a philosopher, twice a pervert.' "

"Who said that?"

"Jean Cocteau," Archie answered quickly, counting on Byron not to check the facts. "But look at it this way. Our superior, Victoria Frost, never, ever called Vicky, deals with a great many men in positions of authority, especially at Oak Hill. Maybe her surface is self-protective, merely a smoke screen, a device? One of the many ways legions of women are learning to cope with men in business?"

"Nope. There's more to it than that, Arch," Byron said, who, after several years of working closely with her, still felt personally put off by Victoria's manner that was as poised, polished, and professional as that of a distinguished career diplomat in his posting before retirement, the final posting which is always, by tradition, his most prestigious.

In the course of the last few years, not only had Victoria's outward behavior become seamlessly, almost disconcertingly smooth, but she had perfected her early leanings toward the severely avant-garde, faultless, expensively unadorned exterior of a fashion nun. If she abandoned her blacks and browns and went so far as to wear taupe or white, they appeared as startling as magenta and orange would on another woman. No softening wisp escaped her French twist, and she confined the color on the pure cream of her skin to a clear red lipstick. Her features were both classic and mysterious, for they couldn't hide, to perceptive men's eyes, the fact that something important was being deliberatively left unexpressed. This gave her a fascinating quality that was more than beauty, and made her the object of endless speculation among those who worked with her.

There was passion there, Archie and Byron had long sensed it, but a passion concealed behind a barrier that prevented them from even guessing what it might be.

One day in the late summer of 1982, just before her thirtieth birthday, Victoria Frost invited both men to dine with her at home, the first time they had been so honored, although, in the course of the last two years, she usually accepted the invitations they tendered to the large, informal parties they sometimes joined forces to give, arriving and leaving alone, without the slightest embarrassment.

They were astonished by her apartment and the exceptional ease with which the room embraced them. Still, as they both knew, such invisible victories never came cheap, although the neighborhood was not at all what they'd expected.

Byron and Archie exchanged amazed glances when they were greeted by Victoria, wearing snug red suede trousers, an oversized pink silk shirt cut like a man's, and a pair of magnificent carved-jade earrings. She had undone her hair and brushed it away from her face. It wasn't just that she looked a decade younger, but that she had become a different person from the woman they knew from the office, relaxed and easily approachable, one quality she had never achieved for all her consummate professionalism.

Throughout drinks and dinner served by a maid in the small, candlelit dining room that departed in no way from the atmosphere of the living room, the three of them exchanged nothing more significant than business gossip. They returned to the living room for coffee and brandy. With the brandy, Victoria told them quietly that she had decided to leave the Caldwell agency and open up on her own.

"Don't ask me to explain why I'm doing this," she said, her fine-boned face intent and her precise, clear voice suddenly fierce. "Obviously, both of you have to know that it could only have to do with deep-seated, insoluble problems with my mother, but I just can't give you any details, not now, and probably never. I'm taking three of the Oak Hill accounts with me when I go. You two created those campaigns. You know that I consider you the most talented team in the agency, and I'd like you to join me."

She paused for an instant to look at their faces, stiff in astonishment. She resumed speaking on a slightly gentler note. "Look, guys, if you turn me down, I'll be very disappointed, since Joe Devane really respects the two of you, but he's already agreed to accept another creative team if I can't persuade you. In other words, this move doesn't depend on the two of you, much as I want you to come. *It's going to happen anyway*, with you or without you. I can pick anyone, any creative team I want, from any agency in town, so long as they're willing to take the chance and become my partners. Not incidentally, those three accounts bill twenty million dollars. If you say yes, the three of us would become equal partners in the new agency."

"Wait a minute, Victoria," Byron said, as stunned by her proposition as by the vistas it presented. "Leaving an agency and starting another is one thing, taking Caldwell accounts with you is another. Especially since you're family. Jesus!"

"But things like this have been done from time to time, as you must be aware. Of course it's not considered quite cricket, I know that, but some of the biggest agencies in the business started out that way. Think about that. It's historic fact."

"It's true, it's happened before," Archie said slowly. "But *you* know why you're doing this, and we don't. Can't you at least give us some details of *why* Joe Devane has decided to go along with you on this? Caldwell has handled his business forever. If it weren't for Caldwell, he might just be another food manufacturer."

"No, Archie, I can't. Not even if you decide to come with me. But I can tell you that I would never ask you to leave your jobs unless I was absolutely sure that the situation was going to work out. I'm leaving my own job, abandoning my future . . . what better guarantee do you have than that?"

"Can you tell us *how* it would happen? That's a minimum to ask," Byron said. He and Archie had long dreamed of having their own agency, but they'd never envisioned such a bandit's scenario.

"Very simply and quickly," Victoria said, "the three of us would resign together and form a new agency, Frost, Rourke, and Bernheim, or Frost, Bernheim, and Rourke—the back end's up to you, as long as my name comes first . . . after all, it's my idea. Within a week or so of our departure, Oak Hill will put three products up for review: Answer Soups, Lean and Mean Breads, and

Thinline Desserts, the whole nine yards. Y&R, Ogilvy & Mather, and of course the incumbent, Caldwell, will be invited to bid for them. So will our new agency. After the normal competition we'll be awarded the three accounts. It's a transparent device that fools nobody, but it isn't illegal."

"Victoria, Byron and I have to talk about this," Archie said.

"Of course," she answered, rising. "But I need your answer in twenty-four hours. Yes or no, I'll still always think you two guys are the best."

They'd come, Victoria thought, as she got undressed, they couldn't resist. First, let them give her their assent. Then she'd tell those two unattached bachelors about the move to the Coast. Frost, Rourke, and Bernheim—Frost, Bernheim, and Rourke? What difference did it make, when "Caldwell Frost" was the way people would end up referring to the new agency before the year was over?

"She has so much more to lose than to gain," Byron said.

"Yeah, but she's going to leave Caldwell anyway."

"We hardly know the Caldwells, they couldn't pick us out of a police lineup," Byron pointed out. "I haven't even seen them since the last Christmas party."

"Still, it *is* a question of integrity."

"Victoria has more right to our loyalty than the Caldwells do. She's the one we work for, the person we've been reporting to."

"Byron, you're stretching it."

"She said her problems were insoluble."

"We don't have problems with them," Archie countered.

"We're not partners in their agency, either. This is the chance of a lifetime."

"Damn right it is," Archie said through his teeth. "What price being Mr. Clean?"

"Too high to pay. You want to sit around and see another creative team take over the accounts we launched? Three years of our life and some of the best ideas we'll ever have went into those campaigns."

"So you want to do it?" Archie questioned.

"Are you asking me or telling me?"

"We *are* a team," Archie pointed out.

"You're asking *and* you're telling. You're dying to do it."

"So are you," Archie said quickly.

"We both want to do it and we both think it's wrong," Byron groaned.

"But it's going to happen, with us or without us. We can't stop it, so why shouldn't we be in on it?"

"I can't think of a single reason, beyond ethical ones."

"If we'd been that deeply into splitting ethical hairs, we should have gone into religion instead of advertising," Archie decided, and settled the question.

Everything happened exactly as Victoria told them it would, although Archie and Byron weren't prepared for the amount of attention they got in *Adweek, Advertising Age,* and *The Wall Street Journal,* as well as in the advertising sections of the business pages across the country. The change of three food accounts from one agency to another would not normally have been seen as more than a small news item, except for the mother-daughter angle. Dozens of journalists were fascinated by the rift in what had seemed to be a dynastic family relationship. The split between mother and daughter, about which, maddeningly, not a single detail emerged, was the subject of enormous amounts of newsprint.

"I don't mind all the speculation in the trades," Archie commented to Byron, "but I expected Victoria to be a little bit less of Our Lady of the Perfect French Twist with us after that dinner at her place."

"Do you think that outfit was all part of a come-on? A one-time-only event? An offer never to be repeated?"

"It could well have been, tight red pants and all. But it's not about clothes, it's about her manner. She's reverted to her usual impenetrable self. Even though we're partners, she's still subtly behaving as if she's our immediate superior. That burns my ass."

"Sounds like you were nursing a little thing for her."

" 'Little thing,' Byron? No wonder you can't put words on paper. No wonder you're just an art director."

"The hots, a yen, the urge to stick it to her—"

"Listen, Archie, I admit I wouldn't mind sticking it to her

and neither would you, only I'm smart enough to worry that once she got it, she'd never give it back."

"She's honestly not my type, By, but I want to be treated as an equal, that's the deal we signed on for."

"You agreed to move the agency to L.A.," Byron reminded him.

"That makes sense. You agreed to call it Frost Rourke Bernheim or FRB, depending on how fast you're talking, does that make you a patsy?"

"Nah, it sounded better, came more trippingly off the tongue. Anyway, people'll call it FRB, it's still an unwieldy name. And L.A. makes sense to me too. There's nothing here I need to hang around for, and my folks are in San Francisco . . . new start, new coast."

Soon after the move to California, FRB picked up a number of smallish new accounts: an excellent vineyard in the Napa Valley, Bugattini Gourmet Pasta, the Association of California Artichoke Growers, a Bay Area herbal tea company, an importer of expensive balsamic vinegar and olive oil, and several others—all, frustratingly, in the food business. They had started as a packaged-goods agency, and they seemed destined to stay there unless they could manage to break out of that mold. Their new accounts, in total, billed ten million dollars, just enough to make them feel that they were making progress, but it was less than brilliant progress for people used to the excitement of a large agency and huge accounts.

FRB spent a few cramped months in sublet quarters. Soon, in determined anticipation of additional growth and to accommodate the new people they had hired, Victoria took a long-term lease on offices that were larger than they actually needed, and hired a decorator to renovate and redecorate on a scale that would impress future clients. Although she continued to function as account supervisor on the Oak Hill accounts, Victoria spent most of her time traveling, scouting accounts for the agency, the noncreative area of "new business coordinator" she had staked out firmly and entirely for herself, leaving Byron and Archie to concentrate on what they did best.

Even with all her travel, Victoria managed to see Angus far

less than she had counted on. Millicent was making things difficult, he explained, more difficult than he had expected, and if he rushed her, she would dig in her heels and make things impossible for them. They had already accomplished so much that they only needed a little more patience, a little more time . . .

More time, Victoria thought grimly as she pushed aside the fruit salad Polly had put on her desk. More patience. As if she hadn't given Angus more patience and yet more patience, until she thought she'd die from hemorrhaging patience. They hadn't been able to manage a minute together on her trip to New York, not one single meeting. He'd been unable to see her, and her heart and body felt lacerated, flayed, raw with hatred of her mother and disgust with Angus for his inability to extricate himself from his endless obligations.

And when she'd returned, what had she found? Archie and Byron, the only people she could count on, the only two people who knew who she *was*, who knew her before her lonely California exile had started, were off to frolic and feast and waste time with Gigi Orsini, who was entirely too well dressed and obviously knew nothing, nothing at all, about the advertising business. A girl who, for some reason that she couldn't identify, reminded her of her mother when she'd been young.

7

I met a man named Tom Unger while I was in New York," Josh suddenly remarked to Sasha, shortly after a silent and tense dinner during which Sasha tried unsuccessfully to convince herself that he was merely preoccupied with a difficult case. He'd cut short their usual pilgrimage to watch Nellie sleep in her crib and had led her into the library.

"Well, thank the Lord!" Sasha exclaimed, in relief mixed with anger. "So that's it! Don't you ever do this to me again, Josh Hillman—I thought you'd discovered that you had some terminal disease and were trying to decide how to break the news. You have no idea what you've looked like since you came back from New York yesterday—doom piled on gloom. I've been frantic with worry . . . but I didn't dare ask because I was too afraid of the answer."

"Tom . . . used to be your lover." Josh pronounced the words heavily, with a weighty sigh he couldn't conceal.

"Well, of course he was," she responded immediately, tossing her long black hair in annoyance. "Is that what you're so upset about? The thing I find disgusting is that Tom actually told you about me when he knew we were married. What a lowlife he turned out to be! And you've put me through hell because of your silly retrospective jealousy. Men! You all make me sick!"

She got up from the chair in which she'd been sitting and flounced furiously around the room, scrutinizing Josh as if she'd never really seen him before. His clever mouth, his Slavic cheekbones, his distinguished skull covered with short gray hair, his height and the sardonic yet kindly lines of his face suddenly seemed unfamiliar to her, made strange by the tormented expression in his eyes.

"Do you mean to sit there and tell me that you expected me to be a virgin when we got married?" Sasha finally burst out, since he didn't utter another word. "Did you think that a woman of almost twenty-four had spent her whole life locked in a chastity belt, waiting for you to come along?"

"No. I assumed you'd had romances just as I'd had romances . . . love affairs, relationships, whatever you want to call them. I assumed that, and then I put it out of my mind."

"Then why bring up Tom Unger now? Am I supposed to apologize? And what the hell did you say to him when he dropped this charming little bit of ancient kiss-and-tell? Did you turn on your heel in dignity, or did you pop the guy?"

"He didn't know we were married."

"*What?* You mean Tom Unger is just going around gratuitously dropping my name as one of his ex-conquests? 'Oh, by the way, I had an affair with Sasha Nevsky?' I'm going to call him up, that filthy, slimy bastard, and give him such hell that he'll forget his own name, much less that he ever knew mine. He's as sick as he's cheap! And to think I once really liked him."

"That wasn't the way it happened."

"You'd better tell me the way it happened, Josh, and right now, every word. I won't put up with this shit. I won't let you sit there accusing me of God knows what with every pore in your body. Having a romance with Tom Unger isn't a crime—even if he's joined the criminal classes."

Painstakingly, in deliberate detail, Josh told her everything that had happened during his downtown lunch in New York, not leaving out a single of the damning words he had been listening to in his mind since the minute he left the offices of Westcott, Rosenthal, Kelly and King.

When he had finished, Sasha sat looking at the carpet, rubbing the cord of her sash between her fingers, but otherwise motionless. The silence lengthened between them. Finally she raised her head and looked at him with compassion.

"I'm sorry, darling. Of course you're upset. I can never tell you how sorry I am that I never told you myself. If I'd ever dreamed you'd hear it in such an awful public way . . . oh, I should have known, I should have told you—"

"You're sorry because of *how* I learned that you used to have three lovers at one time? You think that the *way* I heard about that —the *manner* in which I was enlightened—is what's important?"

"Isn't it?" She rose to her feet, pacing the carpet, measuring him up and down with her eyes, as if he were a bedraggled stranger who had knocked on her door and asked to come in to use the phone. "Isn't it?" she repeated with a sharp edge to her voice.

"No, by Christ, it's not!"

"Then what is? Just what is more important, Josh?"

"*You, for God's sake, you!* You did this . . . *thing!* You never even tried to hide it. Unger said each man knew about the others, you thought it was your right, you still do," he cried in a passion of anguish.

"Oh no. I do not." Sasha stopped and looked at him with deep seriousness. She brought her hands together, thumbs and fingertips touching and then opened them, like a blossoming flower, her noble wide brow clear and untroubled.

"I always knew," she said quietly, "from the day I first slept with a man, that when I got married that part of my life would be over. Absolutely over. I have a double standard for sex. Don't you? Don't other men? Don't most people keep a double standard in their hearts about something important, if it isn't sex? I believe that what is perfectly acceptable for an unmarried girl is never acceptable for a happily married woman. It can destroy a marriage."

"Oh God, why can't I make you understand? Three men—three lovers—three men having the right to . . . do . . . things to you—and you, like a juggler keeping three oranges in the air, no more meaningful than that? One on one day, another the next . . . oh, Christ . . ." He buried his head in his hands.

"That's the way it was, Josh, I'll never apologize for that. I had the right to dispose of myself as I wished. If you're waiting for me to feel ashamed, you'll have to wait forever." Sasha was not defiant, simply conscious of the plain propriety of her actions as she saw them, of her fidelity to her own beliefs.

"You really *don't* see," he realized in utter despair. "You just don't want to see."

"I see that I was a Great Slut, as I used to call it, and what of it? I hurt no one. I'll never regret using my freedom for as long as it belonged to me. I never slept with a man I didn't genuinely like. I never slept with a man to get anything out of it but pleasure. I never deceived them. Exclusivity was exactly what I was avoiding. I'd still be doing it if I hadn't met you and fallen in love."

She paused, waiting for him to look at her, wanting to see his expression, but he sat hiding his face, rigid in his chair.

"Try to give me one good reason, Josh, why I shouldn't have lived as I did?" Sasha persisted, determined to get through to him. "What has it taken away from you, what has it taken away from the way I love you? I'm the same person you fell in love with, the same human being you married. My days as a Great Slut are definitively over, never to be repeated, but otherwise I'm me, I'm Sasha. Tell me why you think you have a right to blame me *now*."

"How . . . how many . . . were there?" He spoke as if the words had been dragged out of him with tongs thrust into his entrails.

"I don't know." Sasha's voice rang out indignantly. "I didn't count. Now you're trying to degrade me, but you're only degrading yourself. You should be *disgusted* to ask a question like that. It's beneath you."

"But it wasn't beneath you to go from man to man to man?" he shouted.

"*No, it was not.* I was true to myself."

Sasha's simplicity took his breath away. Josh shook his head, hunching over even further, trying to clear his mind, attempting to see something—anything—from her perspective, but it was as if they lived on opposite sides of a wide chasm and were trying to scream delicate, nuanced subtleties across to each other in a high wind.

"Josh, for heaven's sake, stop sitting there like Job. Get your head out of your hands! This has nothing to do with us *in the present*. It's ridiculous."

He lifted his head and she saw his contorted face, his eyes, which couldn't bring themselves to meet hers. With a terrible lurch of her heart, Sasha saw how far it was from ridiculous. Into her heart flew the knowledge that no matter how strong an intimacy is, it can be overturned by facts that are meaningful to only one of the two people involved.

"Josh!" she cried. "Josh!" Her world could not be ruined, she promised herself as she flew to him and tried to cradle his head. All she needed was time. A just man *must* be able to understand, and Josh was just.

"Oh, Davy, we did it, we really did it!" Gigi exulted over and over in the living room of her house, where she had carried him off with the intention of having a drink to celebrate before going out to dinner. She was in a rapture of euphoria, flying higher and higher in the glory of having won, a clean win, a soaring win, a huge— no, a *gigantic*—win, a full-out Barnum-and-Bailey win that settled forever any unacknowledged doubts that she was meant for the advertising business.

After they'd left the pitch, she and David had decided that it would be unthinkably anticlimactic to return to the office, particularly since one of the senior partners would not be anxious to have them hanging around gloating.

"You did it," he grinned, watching her tumbling around on the couch, unable to sit still in her excitement.

"We did it, and don't start throwing me all the credit again or I'll hit you, Davy Melville. Cheers!" She raised her glass to him. "Down with the ruling classes, knees up, Mother Brown, chin-chin, and anything else you want to toast to. Did you hear Victoria say, 'We'll all get to work on the details on Monday,' did you think she was going to strangle on her words?"

"I thought she was going to faint, not strangle."

David had trouble responding in kind to Gigi's abandon. He was at least half as happy as she was about getting the account, but in advertising as in every other field, no triumph thrills as much as the first one. David still remembered when he'd made his first winning pitch, some five years before, for a half-million-dollar account. He hadn't touched the ground again for three days and nights.

This winter afternoon his pleasure was considerably tempered. He knew it was essentially and fundamentally all Gigi's achievement, but a team lost and won as a unit, so he had won too, and it couldn't have been done with words alone; his inspired photos had been important. But David discovered that he was constricted in any free expression of joy by a stronger emotion, his realization that as Gigi kicked off her boots, threw off her vest, unbuttoned the top buttons of her blouse, and snuggled, with an irrepressible series of bounces, into the pillows of her wide chintz couch, he was growing more and more alarmingly disturbed by her proximity.

This was the first time David had ever been really alone with Gigi. He had had no way to anticipate how different Gigi now seemed to him in her own place, how confiding, how casual, how heartlessly free and easy. If she had designed every move she made to force him to imagine her naked, she couldn't have succeeded as well as her unselfconscious familiarity did. When she bent over to pour them drinks, he thought he saw her breasts fall forward under her blouse. When she brought him the drink, he could have sworn that he could hear her thighs brush together under her skirt. When she raised her glass with a flourish, he clearly envisioned her arms lifting to clasp him around the neck and draw his head down to her throat.

He was going fucking nuts.

"How come you've got such a big place?" David asked. Since Gigi had rushed in and taken only enough time to turn on the two lamps by the couch, the room seemed enormous as the winter twilight fell quickly.

"Just luck. It's a rental . . . one of those things. Oh, Davy, isn't Signora Eleonora Colonna heaven?"

"Heaven. So you rattle around in here all alone?"

"It's amazing how you can get used to more space than you need. Giorgio . . . Gianni . . . Enrico . . . I love them! Are they a world-class act or what?"

"Top-notch. Listen, Gigi, are you seeing anyone? I mean, is somebody going to walk in here and say, 'Who's this strange guy sitting on my couch and drinking with my lady?' "

"I'm not 'seeing anyone,' as you quaintly put it," Gigi yawned, beginning to feel the fatigue of an adrenalin letdown. "I'm nobody's 'lady,' thank you very much. My own woman, Davy my lad, and don't call me a lady ever again. I hate that expression. Woman, female, girl, gal, even chick, but not lady."

"I didn't. I was imagining someone else saying it."

"No one would dare," she said, and with those words she realized that her liberty was real, as real as the empty house she inhabited, as real as the empty bed she slept in, as real as the solitary dinners she ate, as real as the lack of a man's touch on her skin. Only the excitement and pace of preparing for the Indigo Seas pitch had enabled her to thrust aside thoughts of Zach, only brutally hard work had allowed the fact that she was no longer waiting for him to come back home to sink deeply and meaningfully into her mind.

Gigi stretched hugely, her arms high over her head, clasping her right wrist in her left hand and pulling as high as she could, then repeating the stretch with the other hand, trying to ease away some of the tension of the day. She groaned with the relief of it. What she really needed was to have her back rubbed, she thought lazily. "Davy," she commanded, "come over here—you're too far away. Now, take off your glasses."

"If I take off my glasses, I won't be able to see."

"I don't care, I want to look into your eyes," Gigi insisted, determined to have her own way, for, as she quieted down and lost the energy that had been entirely concentrated in Indigo Seas, she found her attention eager to turn to David Melville, who had lived through every minute of the process with her. There was something mysteriously and pleasantly comfortable about sitting here with him. Cozy, chummy, warming.

But what was it about him *exactly*, she wondered with an unexpected rising of a tide of acute curiosity. Suddenly it seemed to her that although she thought she knew Davy, she didn't *know* him, not really. And such ignorance, such almost-taking-for-granted, surely wasn't proper between creative teammates, was it? Maybe, if she knew him better, she would ask him to rub her back, Gigi told herself.

It was getting so dark in the room that she had to lean forward to inspect him closely. "Hmmm—as I thought, the irises of your eyes are the most unusual kind of speckled brown, just like those brown eggs that are so hard to get, your hair is precisely the deep, dark brown of Godiva chocolates, there's not a single light streak in it, and your skin could easily pass for heavy whipping cream. Why, Davy," she said, her eyes wide and deliciously mocking as she stared intently at him, "I could make a chocolate soufflé out of you!"

"And I could make an entire meal out of you," he answered, grabbing her with his long arms, goaded beyond endurance. "I am going to eat you up, Gigi Orsini, until there is nothing left but some bits of red hair and an empty tube of mascara!"

"Davy!"

"It's your own damn fault," he moaned, and kissed her with all the growing passion and love he'd been suppressing since the day they'd met.

"Davy, what the hell are you doing?" Gigi asked, trying to sound astonished. Was a mere backrub all she had in mind, she asked herself with what remained of her honesty. My, what very tasty strong lips he had. Nothing like a soufflé at all.

"Just shut up and pay attention." He kept right on kissing her, and Gigi felt herself growing interestingly languid. Davy was such an absolute darling, but who would have dreamed that he'd be such a good kisser? Who would have expected that he would know exactly how closely she liked to be hugged and held? Who would have realized that lying down next to her—how had that happened?—this lanky Davy creature would feel as reassuringly solid and lovely as a rock that had baked in the sun? Who would have believed that you could work in the same room with a man for weeks and not understand that the beautiful shape of his mouth made it impossible not to kiss him back with the same intensity with which he kissed you? Who would have anticipated that if this man swept your hair up from your neck and kissed you very slowly and deliberately right up and down your bare nape, taking little nibbles as he progressed, you would become violently excited?

As those questions drifted through her mind like a fresh breeze, Gigi knew she was the biggest humbug alive. She wasn't surprised, not at all at all at all.

"Oh, Davy . . ." She stirred in his arms, pressing closer to this heavenly, hesitant man.

"Please, darling Gigi, please give me a chance. I'm so much in love with you that I'm nearly insane . . ."

"*Prego* . . ." she whispered.

"You mean . . ." David hadn't been totally sure what *prego* meant, and he didn't want to make a false move now that he finally held his treasure in his arms and had told her his love.

"*Prego* means do . . . by all means . . . whatever . . ."

"Would that include this?" he asked, trying to unbutton her blouse with his clever artist's fingers, which had started to tremble so much that they were clumsy.

"Whatever . . ." she murmured, closing her eyes so that she could better feel the first touch of his lips on her breasts. When it finally came, she stirred under it as a glade of trees stirs under the first raindrops. "Oh, yes, definitely *that* . . ."

Davy rolled off the couch so that he could kneel on the floor and take both of her breasts in his crafty, sensitive fingertips. He caressed them with wonder, by lamplight, marveling at the vivid pinkness of her fragile nipples, which rose and became plumply erect as he looked at them, marveling at the flushing of her white skin, which created a color so rare that it became an ornament, transfixed by the firmness, the unexpected resilience of her young flesh, each of her breasts a promise that could break his heart. In reverent silence he traced her skin toward the edge of each nipple, until he saw her lift herself upward toward him and her lips shape unuttered assent. Thirsty, trembling, awestruck, he drew close to the tenderly swollen buds made of hot honey and tight silk and gently took each of them, one by one, deeply into his mouth.

Kneeling there, drunk on the taste of Gigi's flesh, David hardly breathed, held in the sweet surge of a thousand daydreams come true. As she grew dense with longing, Gigi gave great ragged sighs and gradually worked her way out of her clothes while he barely lifted his mouth from its deliberate work. Now he was wily,

147

now demanding, now artful, now avid, always cosseting her, always regaling himself.

He remained on his knees, intoxicated and rapt, until he felt her hands plunge deeply into his hair, communicating an unmistakable change of pace that was half question, half invitation. At that he took off all his clothes, each movement punctuated by a kiss as his tongue penetrated her open, fragrant mouth. Gigi dexterously discovered his naked flesh limb by limb. At the hollow at the base of his throat, where the collarbones met, she found skin as tender as the softest glove leather, a pulse beating like the surf of a warm sea. In the glow of lamplight she saw that the joints of his shoulders and elbows and wrists were as beautifully shaped as his mouth, that the fine hair on his chest and arms was as dark as a fall of feathers against the luxurious smoothness of his skin, his muscles well defined, long and solid. As he stood up she said, imperiously and unexpectedly, "Stop . . ."

"Stop?" he cried incredulously.

"Yes . . . I want to see you." Gigi gave a low, playful laugh, allowing full rein to her saucy, erotic spirit. Glorying in her nakedness, she sat up tall on the couch, kneeling on her heels, and took his rearing penis in her hands. He saw the smile fade abruptly from her face as she bit down on her lower lip and drew in her breath with astonishment as she measured his length and bulk with airy, eager fingers, her touch flickering, clasping, unclasping, deliberately maddening. He stood his ground, unmoving, tensing his thighs, thrusting his pelvis forward, his hands forming fists, and willed himself to let her play with him until she had her fill. He adored the teasing punishment she meted out, knowing that it wouldn't be long before the devilish inquisitiveness that had started by making him take off his glasses would get the better of her.

Gigi was torn between the gourmandise of drawing out this moment of fascinated discovery, of prolonging this glorious, sweet frolic of inquisition, and by a growing urgency that could only be relieved by feeling him invade her, fill her, possess her. Her mouth grew dry and her heart pounded impatiently until, unable to make herself hold back a moment longer, she surrendered to the drug of long-deferred desire, fell back on the couch, and offered herself to him as eagerly as the dry land offers itself to the storm.

Now David grew serious, measuring his entrance with the

concentrated precision of an Olympic diver, pleasuring her with knowing measures, meting out, with the hard-won patience of experience, his slowly sliding, deep, full thrusts that went in as far as he could go, and his short, hard, rapid strokes that penetrated only a few inches, holding back his own need in favor of hers, listening to her skin, gauging her sighs, judging her breathing and her sweat, until he wove a veil of pure passion around them, creating a zone of timelessness in which Gigi lost her singleminded rage to reach fulfillment, and let herself exist, aching still but rocked in the moment, exist in his arms and his breath and his heartbeat and the rise and fall of his body above her.

Only after he was certain that they had used that timelessness to begin to learn the uses of their flesh did he permit himself to attend directly to her excitement, to concentrate severely, sternly, on the burning pearl that lay deeply hidden between her legs. Soon she sighed and gasped, her breath finally rising into a series of shameless, uncontrollable shuddering sounds. David smiled for the first time and now plunged freely, over and over, the diver liberated from judgment, immersed himself in the living depths of her until he quickly pounded to his own superb release.

Soon after Victoria Frost moved to California, she rented an apartment in one of a group of gated town houses, vaguely Regency in style, that had recently been built on land once owned by Twentieth Century Fox. The well-guarded complex offered her the advantages of high security and underground parking along with a striking degree of anonymity. She could go straight from her car to an elevator that rose to the fourth and top floor of the building where her apartment was located, one of a group of three other apartments, without seeing anybody or being seen, except by a stray unspeaking neighbor, all of whom were far older than she. Victoria had had all her furniture and books sent out from New York and she had reproduced, in the exceptionally high-ceilinged and well-proportioned rooms, an apartment that was almost identical to the one she had lived in before.

After the Indigo Seas pitch, she spent the rest of the day back at the office, conferring busily with several of the other creative teams, making sure that she didn't get trapped by Archie and

Byron into the usual lovingly detailed and endlessly repetitive reca-pitulation of strategy and triumph that followed a win. She knew she'd made a face-losing tactical mistake, and she didn't want to listen to them try to get her off the hook with all the considerable tact at their command.

As she wrapped a heavy quilted violet silk robe around her waist and made herself a drink, Victoria reflected on the day's events. When she'd taken her position on the campaign Gigi and David had created, she hadn't left herself room to follow the parade if it turned left instead of right, a mistake she'd never made before, an amateur's mistake and a totally unnecessary one.

Ben Winthrop and his Enchanted Attic account still hadn't turned up and become a solid reality, although Gigi had explained that he was in New York for the next few weeks. That excuse would undoubtedly turn out to be as real as the success of the Abbondanza campaign, Victoria thought, unaware that she had tightened her lips and narrowed her eyes in a grimace that made her face turn bleak and forbidding. That little bitch had led a charmed life since she'd appeared at the office, she didn't seem able to put a foot wrong.

Why, Victoria asked herself, did she feel such an instinctive hatred of Gigi? The redheaded tart was doing brilliantly well for the agency, yet somehow Victoria felt that any success for Gigi was a defeat for her. When she'd described Gigi to Angus, he'd said that Gigi sounded like Millicent Frost at the beginning of her career, a diminutive, vivacious charmer, a golden girl sparkling with ideas and energy, but that surely couldn't be reasonable. It made no sense. No one sane would compare a twenty-three-year-old girl with no advertising experience to speak of—who had had exactly one lucky break, with a potential second—to a powerful woman who would soon be sixty and knew more about the agency business than did any other woman in the world. No, that couldn't possibly be it, Victoria decided firmly, Angus's intuitive guess about Gigi was simply wrong, just as wrong as her own first impres-sion, her memory of her mother as a young woman.

As she walked around her living room and turned on the lights, Victoria, grim in her new defeat, asked herself what else Angus could be wrong about. Almost a year had passed since he'd persuaded her to leave Caldwell & Caldwell, and what had she to show for it? One-third of a partnership in a small agency—almost acceptably adequate for the minor, minor leagues, but a blip on a radar screen by Madison Avenue standards—an unwanted exile from the city of her birth, and a forced rupture with all the swains who had swarmed around her in New York. As for Angus and the marriage he promised her—nothing. She could detect no visible signs of real change, in spite of his constant reassurance that she was too far away to be a judge, that he never stopped planning for it, that he was laying the necessary groundwork, but that without their joint patience they stood to lose everything.

His words were like a metal nail file working away under her skin, severing tender nerves, making thin skin bleed; each phone call made her want to scream at him, scream vilely until he did what she wanted, yet he was so entirely convincing, he made so much sense, that she was forced to agree with him and try to beat down her sense of panic.

They'd been together on a total of fourteen occasions during all of last year. On Victoria's visits to New York, Angus had only been able to snatch a few hours for her on nine separate afternoons, coming to her hotel for a few hours before he was expected at home. The other five times they'd been together were here in Los Angeles, in her apartment, during brief visits he'd made to the West Coast.

The long weekends he'd promised her before she left, the trips up the coast to Ventana, the trips down the coast to Laguna, the trips out to the desert—none of them had materialized because there had never been enough time, no chance for him to be out of touch with the office, no reason for him to be in California without a full day of meetings, no excuse for disappearing for a weekend and leaving his wife alone at home.

His secretary and Millicent's secretary had long ago formed a tight alliance, and both of them made sure that they would always know where to find him. They would suffer severe loss of face if he slipped the net for more than a few perfectly explained hours. He might as well be in a maximum-security prison, Victoria thought viciously.

Even phone calls of more than a few minutes were difficult to arrange. She couldn't call him, either at home or at work. The time difference that puts New York three hours ahead of Los

Angeles meant that by the time Angus got to the office where his secretary routinely placed all his calls, it was only 6:30 A.M. in L.A., too early to phone. By 5:30 P.M., when he was free of his secretary's surveillance, it was afternoon in California, just after lunch, a period that was eaten up by business for Victoria. By the time her day ended, Angus was back home or already out for the evening.

In any case, Victoria thought vitriolically, did Angus imagine that a telephone call at three in the afternoon, in a busy office where a stream of other calls kept coming in, could be the equivalent of his kisses? Did he believe that the few times he'd phoned her from his office before his secretary got in, awakening her from her sleep, gave her the equivalent of emotional satisfaction?

No, she'd taken care of herself, thank you very much. And not ineffectively either, Victoria thought, as she settled down in her favorite corner to watch the fruitwood fire she'd lit in the fireplace. Not ineffectively at all.

She'd arrived in Los Angeles with warm letters of introduction to a number of women who were connected to the busy social life she'd left behind in New York. They were women on the highest levels of Los Angeles society, members of The Colleagues, who raised funds for mentally retarded children, members of the boards of the Children's Museum, Planned Parenthood, and the Santa Monica Rape Treatment Center. They worked in the leadership of the Zoo Committee, the Friends of the Joffrey Ballet, St. John's Hospital, the President's Circle of the Los Angeles County Museum of Art, the Downtown Women's Center, and the Host Committee for the Olympics. Victoria had approached each one of these philanthropic and powerful women as if she were a prospective client with a fifty-million-dollar account to award. Victoria had played that irresistible, undetectable customer's game she'd learned how to play better than anyone of her age, and before the first meeting was over she'd mentioned her desire to be useful in her new community. Soon she'd been invited to join in the complicated dance of service to others on which these women spent so much of their time.

And after all, why not? She had everything to offer them, Victoria reflected. It soon became a coup to capture her to work— and so effectively!—for one's favorite cause. Not only was she able to have her agency create and give them the copy and art for their invitations and party programs, but Victoria Frost had all the glamorous allure of someone who had been involved in a famous family rift about which there had been national speculation, but no hint of scandal. She was, as a matter of course, considered the great heiress that every hair on her head proclaimed her to be. Yet she looked unthreateningly sexless in her relentless simplicity, and no hint of her well-leashed carnal cravings escaped as she charmed the women of those groups she quickly penetrated, groups many Los Angeles women had tried to get into for decades without success.

To a small number of her new friends, always the most influential woman in any charity, Victoria confided that she had "an understanding" with a man in London. With a minimum of words she conveyed that he was a titled, landed, but unhappily married man, and that her love was not without hope. It explained, they told each other—for they almost invariably knew each other, joined as they were at the many crossroads of the city's good works —a quality of purity and dignity and slight sorrow that was rare in an eligible young woman who was still unmarried. It explained why she didn't date the still unmarried young men of her age, it explained why Victoria Frost made a perfect extra woman who never flirted with their husbands or their married sons or their sons-in-law, why she was such a welcome addition to their private parties.

They never suspected that she was like a cowboy who rode into a herd of cattle and cut one steer out of the crowd for branding, Victoria thought as the flames of the small fire blazed higher. They never guessed that during the tennis matches at the Los Angeles Country Club, or at the Dinosaur Ball in the Natural History Museum—even on the occasions of her infrequent attendance at the All Saint's Church in Pasadena—Victoria was looking over the possibilities. The man she picked was always a young married man, a very-much-married man with a wife who was one of the darlings of the community, a man who had everything to lose by boasting about Victoria to anyone, by even mentioning her name. They never guessed that when she found a man who appealed to her, a man she chose with the most scrupulous attention to his physical desirability and the shrewdest sizing up of his availability, she waited observantly until she had the perfect opportunity, at a big party, to say a few quiet words into his ear.

"Would you be terribly shocked if I admitted I'm dying to fuck you?" That was all it took. Was it that easy for men with women, she wondered. Would any woman be as enormously flattered and as quickly aroused by a man who said those words as he sat next to her at one of those ubiquitous, convenient round caterer's tables for ten or twelve, at which you couldn't make out clearly what anyone was saying except the one person to whom you were talking? If a man said those words, it would sound like a bad pass, crude and cheap, Victoria mused. Any woman would feel insulted. When a woman said them, a man found it irresistible. God, what complacent, eager fools they were! How simple they were to pluck from their branches!

The arrangements were easy. Their wives weren't Millicent Frost Caldwells. These were young, established businessmen who could get away for afternoon golf games or business lunches without Angus's time constrictions. Victoria herself had only to say she was going to see a client to disappear without questions from FRB.

Many a long lunch, many a long afternoon, Victoria spent with some of the most attractive married men in all of Los Angeles. She used them mercilessly. If they weren't sexually talented, if they came too soon or couldn't get hard more than once in an encounter, she allowed them only a single second chance with her before she sent them back to their wives.

If they proved to be up to her standards, she made them confess their most cherished and powerful secret sexual desires to her, all their special needs, no matter how shameful they believed them to be, all the fantasies that they had never been able to act out with their wives. Just telling her what they wanted, just using the dangerous words while she lay there listening intently, her lips half open, her luscious body covered only by a transparent layer of the sheerest material, her hand—as if she were powerless to stop it —slowly straying between her legs as they spoke, made them wild with lust. After she'd allowed them to play out the forbidden acts with her, Victoria taught them other things their wives would never accept or permit. She made herself into a mistress of erotic practice. There was nothing she wouldn't do except allow herself to be hurt, physically or emotionally. She always took time enough to firmly establish a taste they could never again satisfy, before she dismissed them, enjoying the thought of their future frustrations even more than she had enjoyed their bodies and their credulousness adoration.

Victoria demanded that the men she picked satisfy her before they satisfied themselves, and insisted on their silence as she rode closer and closer to her threshing orgasm, her eyes tightly closed as she imagined Angus filling her body. Her appetite was always for new men, fresh men, the unknown, the pursuit and the capture, rather than for repetition or familiarity. She was never as wild as after she'd seen Angus, after she'd returned to California with her lust for him still alive and unsatisfied and her anger at him making her impatient and hungry, an addict desperate for a fix.

Each man she took, whether only twice or for a period of weeks of frenzied afternoons, was given his leave with the same words, words Victoria knew would keep him friendly and silent for life. "If I weren't so crazy about your adorable wife, I'd never be able to stop seeing you, but I'm terribly afraid of her finding out. She'd divorce you in a minute, you know that, don't you? We must never do anything to hurt her, to hurt your marriage . . . but I'll never forget you, darling. You were simply wonderful . . . oh, yes, so very, very good . . . the best, the very best I've ever known."

Victoria Frost, one year after she left New York, was one of the most sought-after single women in Los Angeles.

A week after the Indigo Seas pitch, Sasha and Gigi met for lunch. They'd been on the phone frequently since Gigi had left Scruples Two, but between their jobs and Sasha's busy social weekends, this was the first time they'd actually managed to set aside enough time to see each other. They'd picked territory halfway between their offices, at the Bistro Gardens in Beverly Hills, where they had a prime seat on the long leather banquette facing the most coveted half of the long room as well as the French doors that opened out to the crowded, flower-filled terrace. There, under space heaters, large tables of elaborately suited and occasionally hat-wearing women were busily ordering chickenburgers with the sauce on the side and celebrating one another's birthdays and anniversaries with piles of smallish, beautifully wrapped gifts.

"What a place for a food fight," Gigi said, looking around at women, some of whose grooming drifted toward taxidermy. "Why do I imagine them throwing great gobs, absolute fistfuls, of caviar from one table to another? And then sloshing buckets of vodka over each other until they're all dripping wet and their hair is ruined?"

"I'd pay cash on the barrelhead to see it," Sasha agreed, her dry voice at variance with her manner of glowing self-confidence.

Gigi turned to inspect her friend. There was something odd about Sasha, she thought, although Gigi was familiar with Sasha's boldest, highest, most lustrous presentation of herself, the gorgeous Lillie Langtry appearance she wore today so glowingly. She was sleek and vivid, her glossy hair swept high above her brow, her lipstick bright, seeming to fly a flag of undimmed success. She confronted the twittering mass of women with friendly indifference, waving here, smiling there, with a sort of benevolent social art that was new to Gigi.

"You look more . . . Edwardian . . . than ever," she ventured.

"And you look more Left Bank."

"Is that a compliment?" Gigi asked suspiciously. The Bistro Gardens was as far from the Left Bank in spirit as the Left Bank was from the Pyramids.

"Absolutely. Is 'Edwardian'?"

"The best. Think about it. When was the last time in history that women were allowed to be utterly female, presented in a framework of glorification? Tiny waists, deep bosoms, glamorous entrances and exits in sweeping skirts, puffed sleeves, lace parasols, marvelous hats loaded with feathers—and then came World War I and skirts got shorter and then came Chanel and chests got flatter and now . . . well, just look around you. Rampant expensive respectability. Everyone's sleek and proper, buttons have replaced ruffles. Women dressing for women. There's nothing sexy about that."

"I don't feel Edwardian," Sasha said, "and I don't feel sexy."

"Neither does Billy . . . it's because you've had babies," Gigi said with the confident expertise of an onlooker and nonparticipant. "Even though you're back at work, there's something about having a new baby at home that kills sexiness . . . but it can't last long, can it, or why would anybody ever have a second child?"

"Beats me," Sasha said, with such a tone of true despair in her voice that Gigi looked at her sharply. As marvelous as Sasha looked, she sounded miserable, and now that Gigi was alerted, there was something . . . unhappy? . . . something wrong? . . . about her eyes.

"Is Nellie all right?" Gigi asked, alarmed.

"Of course she is. I wouldn't be here if she weren't."

"Then what's going on?"

"You're not going to believe this," Sasha said.

"I'll believe anything," Gigi said fervently, thinking of the past week, during which she and Davy had been forcing themselves to work on the myriad details of the actual Indigo Seas ads, their determination detoured by stolen kisses in spite of the office etiquette of leaving their door permanently open, not merely playing with fire but running back and forth through it, until the time came when they could decently leave for the day and rush back to her place.

"Josh found out about my brilliant career as a Great Slut."

"Oh, shit!"

"Worse than that. Remember Tom Unger? The last time Josh was in New York, he met him, and that unutterable dirtball somehow managed to tell the whole story—in front of a group of men who had no idea that Josh and I are married."

"I do *not* fucking believe this!" Never had Gigi so felt the limitation of the basic Anglo-Saxon vocabulary. There must be worse words for such a catastrophe.

"Ladies, today our luncheon specials—"

"NO!"

"GO AWAY!"

"So what did Josh say?" Gigi gasped.

"Well, of course he believed it."

"But after all, it was . . . ah . . . how can I put this? . . . true."

"He had a choice."

"As if there were two Sasha Nevskys?"

"He could have decided not to let it make a difference," Sasha said gravely.

"Taken his knowledge to the grave?"

"Exactly. He didn't have to come running home to me accusingly, as if the world had come to an end. He could have acted as if nothing had been said."

"Look, you know I'm completely and forever on your side in everything, but isn't that unrealistic? Aren't you expecting too much, Sasha?"

"I don't believe so, and I've thought about nothing else since it happened. Look here, Gigi, if I'd been reliably informed that Josh had screwed every last woman in town who had a pulse between his divorce and the time he met me, I would never have brought it up. *Never.* I would have accepted it as something he had every right to do. He's an adult. I'd watch him like a hawk to make sure he wasn't still fooling around, but that would have been that. Over and done with. Part of the past."

"But . . ."

"But what?"

"Sasha, he's a *man.*"

"Oh God, Gigi, you too! Do you realize what you just said? It's okay for him to play around because he's a man, but not okay for me because I'm a woman. Admit you said that."

"I said it," Gigi agreed, shamefaced. "I can't believe I said it, but I did."

"So you have a double standard about sex, yes for men, no for women."

"I—I'm not sure. How could I?"

"But you do," Sasha said inexorably. "You've just never realized it. And that's after all our years of discussion in New York, all the lessons I gave you in how to be a Great Slut . . . you never, ever lost your basic indoctrination in the double standard. You knew exactly what I was doing, but you didn't truly *believe* that I was sleeping with three different men on three successive nights, did you? It was almost a sort of gag, wasn't it?"

"Yes," Gigi said slowly, "I guess it must have been. I never saw them, we kept it out of the apartment by a kind of mutual agreement . . . it was a . . ." She floundered. "Not a gag, no, that's wrong . . . it was a . . . fantasy. I *knew* perfectly well what you were doing, but I *didn't* believe it. Not deep down in my bones, not as if it were real. Knowing something . . . isn't believing. But if I couldn't believe it was true, how can Josh?"

"Oh, he's the opposite. It's completely different for him. He not only believes it, he can't get away from it. He keeps *seeing it happening* in his mind. He goes from scenario to scenario, I can tell, just looking at his face. He's consumed by it, he won't talk to me about it, but I can tell that it's killing him . . . he's one step away from murder or suicide. We try to make conversation about the baby, we try to keep busy with friends so we won't have to be alone together, and when we are, we read or we watch television or he makes business calls—"

"Couldn't you force him to talk about it? Ventilate the whole thing? Wouldn't some fresh air help?" Gigi cried.

"He says that talking about it makes it worse. He simply refuses to discuss it again, he walked out of the room the two times I tried to bring it up. Once I followed him, and he dashed out of the house and didn't come back for hours."

"Oh, Sasha, I'm so desperately sorry! Why didn't you tell me sooner?"

"I thought he might change," she said bleakly. "I thought that if I gave him a little time to absorb what I said, he'd be able to . . . to acknowledge, at least intellectually, that I had every right to live my own life. Now I know that intellect has nothing to do with it. Emotionally he'd prefer it if I'd committed a murder. Josh is twenty-five years older than I am—that's not a question of different generations, it's a question of light years. And it's not just an age or generation thing. It's gender. Would Zach think it was okay?"

"We've never discussed it—he's never known word one about you—but no, I don't think he'd ever be willing to grant a woman that freedom," Gigi admitted reluctantly.

"And you, Gigi, now that *you* know that it wasn't a fantasy, that it was a reality, do you still think it's okay? If you aren't sure, don't say yes to make me feel better, because I'll know you're lying."

"I'm trying to imagine it," Gigi said intently. "Trying to put myself in your shoes."

"Remember, there's *no* Zach in your life, he doesn't exist, you've never even met him, much less fallen in love with him, can you manage that?"

"No problem," Gigi snapped.

"However, there are three men who adore you, three very attractive, unattached men, all crazy about you, and although you're not in love with any of them, you like them very much. They each know about the other two and are willing to go along with your freedom of action. You don't want to choose one among the three, you want all of them, and you give yourself permission to make love to all of them. Can you get *that* into your mind and hold it there?"

Gigi concentrated hard, her eyes almost crossed in concentration. "I've got to make it specific to make it real," she said. "Just for the sake of argument, let's say . . . Archie . . . and Byron . . . and . . . I guess, oh, Ben Winthrop. That would mean Archie on Monday, Byron on Tuesday, Ben on Wednesday, Archie on Thursday, Byron on Friday, Ben on Saturday, Sunday nobody. On Sunday it would be just you and me making dinner, the way it used to be."

Gigi paused and her eyes closed as she surveyed the pictures in her mind. Finally she opened her eyes and nodded her head up and down. "Yep, I can see it. In fact . . . in fact I think I could get to really . . . enjoy it, once I gave myself that permission and got into the rhythm. Oh yes, indeed! *Yummy!* There'd be the fatigue factor—six nights a week sounds like too much—but as long as I wasn't in love with any of them, well, why not?"

"Oh, Gigi, you understand!" Sasha took her hand and clung to it fiercely.

"As soon as I imagined . . . those three particular men . . ." Gigi said, amazed at herself. With Davy there would be four. It wasn't in the cards, not for her, but it was certainly not unimaginable.

"You don't know how much this means to me—especially because you're so far beyond unhip about sex. But, Gigi, don't do it! For heaven's sake, promise me you won't do it! You'll ruin your life!"

"Idiot, of course I promise. But what are you going to do about Josh?"

"Wait. All I can do is keep my head above water and see what happens. He hasn't come near me, he hasn't touched me, he hasn't even kissed me on the lips since I told him . . . and if he keeps on that way, and still won't talk about it, won't go to see a therapist, won't do anything but endure it for the sake of God knows what . . . maybe the baby, maybe because he thinks it's unfair to punish me retroactively or some other crazy idea—I'll leave him. What else can I do? I can't live like this for the rest of my life."

"Oh, Sasha, no!"

"Can you think of an alternative?"

"If he doesn't eventually change back into the old Josh . . . oh, Sasha, I can't give you good advice, it's not my call," Gigi said cautiously. "Do what's right for you. I'm always in your corner."

"Well, enough about me, until further notice. Back to you," Sasha said briskly, changing the subject with relief.

"Me?" Gigi had almost forgotten that she existed in her contemplation of Sasha's problems. "What about me?"

"How come you didn't put Davy in your list of three? What's wrong with him? You tell me what a darling he is every time we speak, and suddenly Ben Winthrop, from left field, is on your list, but not Davy."

"My God, what difference does it make? We were only talking hyp-hypo-hypothetically."

"You're stuttering."

"I am not!"

"*So.*"

"Sasha, you know I can't stand it when you say 'so' like that!"

"You're blushing. Stuttering and blushing. Did you really think you could keep it from me? You and Davy. *Well.* How very interesting," Sasha said, looking suddenly like her old triumphantly superior self. "You're not as unhip as I thought, and just how did this happen?"

"Not until after I'd kicked your revoltingly self-centered, egomaniacal, inconsiderate, hateful beast of a brother out of my house! He doesn't want a real woman in his life, he wants some braindead slave you'd get if you dialed 1-800-WIFE. I was going to tell you—"

"I always wondered how you put up with him. Just because I'm his sister doesn't mean I don't see his faults. Especially when he's never around."

"You sound like the person who says that not only does the restaurant have terrible food but, even worse, they serve such small portions."

"That's the perfect description of Zach. My God, I'm starving. Waiter! Waiter! Where the hell is he—just look, Gigi, this place is almost empty. We never got any lunch. Captain! Could you take our order, please, we're faint from hunger."

8

I was afternoon on Friday in Kalispell, Montana, and when they had lost the light a few minutes ago on this fifteen-degrees-above-zero February afternoon, Zach Nevsky and his producer, Roger Rowan, had immediately repaired to the comfortable, well-heated offices they'd furnished in the Outlaw Inn, the largest motel in town, where headquarters had been established for the duration of the filming of *The Kalispell Chronicles*, now almost seven weeks into its fourteen-week production schedule.

Kalispell, a thriving city of some thirteen thousand people, boasts a number of charming Victorian houses and tree-lined streets, as well as dozens of authentic turn-of-the-century locations, including a twenty-six-room mansion. In 1980, *Heaven's Gate* had been shot there, pumping millions into the friendly community, as well as making Kalispell a byword for budgetary disaster and career ruin. However, the author of *Chronicles* had set his book in Kali-spell, making it the only place where the film could be properly made, in spite of the Cimino curse.

"Who said," Zach asked, sitting down at his desk, " 'Show me a great actor and I'll show you a lousy husband. Show me a great actress and you've seen the devil'?"

"I'd say George Bernard Shaw," Rowan guessed, "except he wouldn't have used the word 'lousy' in that context. Billy Wilder? Hitchcock? No? Okay, I give up, as usual."

"W. C. Fields," Zach said, "and he was long dead before Melanie Adams became the leading female star on the planet Earth. The man was a great prophet."

" 'Prophet'? Hell, no, merely experienced. He worked with many of the greatest actresses of his time—nothing's changed."

"Who cursed us and put her in our picture?"

"You *insisted* on her," Rowan said in patent boredom, "I wanted her, the studio wanted her, the author wanted her, the public worships at her feet, her marquee value alone—"

"Rhetorical question, Rog. It's just that when I think of how hard we had to work to get her, all the thousand and one demands her new agents made now that Wells Cope isn't running her life . . ."

"Look on the bright side, Zach, her work is incredible. You're getting what you hoped for and more."

Directors always bitch about stars, the veteran producer thought wearily, just as if they weren't impossible prima donnas themselves. He hated directors. He hated actors. If only he could make movies without actors and directors, he would be a happy man.

He had hired Zach Nevsky to direct because he was consider-ably less of a megalomaniac than ninety-seven percent of the other top directors working today. Directors, at this time in the history of the business—and Roger Rowan had been producing for over fifteen years—had more sheer power than they'd ever had before, and that power had transformed them into royal tyrants, with all the grandiose self-importance royalty assumes unto itself. Still, Zach Nevsky had earned a reputation, second only to Norman Jewison and Richard Lester, of delivering a film on time and on budget, and that alone made getting him a coup. He wasn't unstable, he wasn't unreasonable, he kept on top of things. If the guy wanted to ask him the source of obscure quotations day and night, it was a small price to pay.

"Would I have fought for an actress if she couldn't deliver?" Zach said, answering Rowan's question about Melanie. "Look, Roger, I'm not an unrealistic fellow. Leaving out a few noble and notable exceptions, I expect an actress as great as Melanie to be deeply and profoundly narcissistic in a way unknown to other women. I expect her to be impossibly stubborn, fiercely greedy, shrewdly and endlessly manipulative, maddeningly unpredictable —if she weren't, I'd wonder if she was a member in good standing of SAG. But this business of her fucking grips—*two* different grips —that's unprofessional! Fucking actors, sure, it's par for the course, especially on location, but wouldn't you expect her to draw the line? Shouldn't there be a question of status involved, if nothing else?"

"My wife says it's perfectly simple."

"What's Norma's take on this?" Zach was curious. Norma Rowan was one of those childless wives who make it a job and a half to accompany their husbands on each and every location shoot, both catering to their every need and making sure they didn't have any unauthorized fun, which almost certainly explained their long marriages.

"Norma says that it's not unusual for an actress to be hot for the blue-collar guys. Unlike actors, members of the crew aren't their own major source of fascination, and since they don't expect the leading lady to deliver for them, they appreciate every bit of snatch they get. Plus they give till it hurts, Zach. Some of them are big, physical guys, used to manual work, as she puts it. Norma can tell you about one of my shoots where the star fucked every grip and gaffer on the set, plus the stuntmen, the cameraman, and four of the drivers—she was an honorary member of the Teamsters Union before her career was over, and it was a long and splendid career. A well-lubricated star isn't necessarily a bad idea, so long as it isn't alcohol that keeps her oiled. So what are you so upset about? Did you have other plans for Melanie?"

"Nevsky's first rule of directing, Rog, never screw the star. Nah, what makes me uneasy is the way she's setting those guys up, one against the other. Allen Henrick's worked for me before, he's a sensible fellow with a wife and kids, he won't let her get to him —he's operating on the half-a-loaf theory—but Sid White's an unknown element . . . he's young, unpredictable, a passionate, intense kind of guy. He's moody, dreamy, maybe a little disturbed. Not your average good-natured grip."

"A grip's replaceable, Zach, but if we send Sid back to L.A., you know Melanie'll hold us responsible and start up, even more blatantly, with someone else," Roger Rowan pointed out. "Anyway, this is Sid's first job, we hired him because Lou Cavona asked us to, and you don't mess with Lou Cavona, grip of grips. He's more than just our Best Boy on this picture, he's a major power in IA, the teamster's union, and if he wants to get his wife's younger brother into the union, that's not just his privilege, it's practically tradition. The Cavonas have been a family of grips since Mack Sennett."

"I don't know," Zach said thoughtfully. "It might be worth getting rid of Sid anyway, no matter how much trouble it is. I've been making it my business to watch him all week—like I have nothing else to do, right? Like I haven't got a picture to make happen?—and he's madly in love with Melanie, true full-blown romantic love, Rog, in love with capital letters. Yeah, Romeo-and-Juliet-style, and don't give me that cynical look, I didn't spend years of my life directing Shakespeare without learning something about passionate love. Sid's jealous of Allen, I mean insanely jealous, and Melanie's not only lapping it up, she's doing everything she can to fan the flames. She's worse than a pyromaniac. So far, only a few of the other grips seem to know what's going on, but that's because it's too bloody cold here for any press to be hovering."

"Zach," Roger said ponderously, "this is just an idea, but what if we tried to get Wells Cope to talk to her? In seven years he must have learned how to handle that woman. I know I'd hate to give him the satisfaction, but isn't it worth a shot?"

"I'd never do that, Rog," Zach replied instantly. "The minute I turn to someone else to tell me how to deal with Melanie is the minute I lose control of the picture. No, I'm going to have it out with her before this goes on a day longer. We shoot tomorrow, and Sunday's her day off, so I'm going to go see her tonight."

"Look, I respect your point of view," Roger persisted, "but

when we decided to shoot in Kalispell, dozens of people asked me how the hell we could go back to the same place where the catastrophe of *Heaven's Gate* occurred. I explained to them that it provided us with a blueprint to know what *not* to do, and so far we've avoided the kind of mess UA had with Cimino. I'm here every second, watching the store, and Cimino didn't have a strong producer aboard. Once work started on the picture, you became captain of the ship and the rest of us, even me, damn it, are passengers, but are you positive you're right? Melanie Adams is accustomed to kid-glove treatment."

"Rog, she's just an actress. The most expensive, most worshiped, most beautiful actress in the world, but still—*an actress.*"

Zach shook his head at the perpetually constipated producer, a worry-wart like all producers, more interested in protecting the production than in making the best possible picture. Rowan was a thoroughly experienced professional, but he'd been born utterly cynical, he had no spark of passion, no iota of vision; to him, film was essentially *product,* just as it was to the studio executives. He, like they, would have been right at home in the pork-belly business. Rowan, who had never produced a picture as important as *Chronicles,* was a favorite of the studio, who had handpicked him. Reason enough to be suspicious. If only a director could get on with his work with the actors, minus the interference of producers and a studio, Zach thought, he'd be a happy man.

"An actress," Zach said, warming to his topic, "is a woman with a certain set of powers and talents and physical equipment that combine to make her employable in bringing other women to life. Call her a virtuoso of personality, illuminated and vitalized from within in a particular way that makes audiences ecstatic, but don't, *do not,* ever let her get the upper hand. I never forget they're essentially *just* women. Controlling actresses is my business. Among many other things, that's what you hired me for. I'm a bloody diva-wrangler, you should know that by now."

"Why didn't you stay in the theater?" Roger asked grumpily. "Stagehands couldn't be as much trouble as grips, too old for one thing. And Off-Broadway actresses have to be easier to control."

"You know, I miss it, actually more than I expected, but it ain't the big time, Rog, it ain't the 'show,' as they say in baseball."

"The 'show.' " Roger was at his most sardonic. "A twenty-five-million-dollar budget, a Pulitzer Prize–winning book that was a huge commercial success, two hundred and fifty locals employed as extras, two of the biggest male stars in the business—and the producer and director are sitting around figuring out what to do about Miss Adams's open-door policy. I wish I could produce a Western with male stars, no love interest except for the bad girls in the local saloon—nobody rooted for them. Ah, shit!"

Did he know anything about Melanie Adams that would give him additional leverage to use on her, Zach Nevsky wondered after Roger left. For if ever an actress was unlikely to be influenced or intimidated by a director, it was this woman, who had become an international superstar seven years ago with her very first film, and he'd be a fool not to use every weapon he could command.

In 1976, when she was nineteen, Melanie Adams had left Louisville for New York, where Spider Elliott had launched her as a model, that much he knew. Very soon afterwards she'd become the protegée of Wells Cope, who produced her first film. His career as a supremely well-financed independent producer had made him one of the most consistently successful men in the entire industry, and once he controlled Melanie Adams, he had taken off into the stratosphere.

Legend, Melanie's second film, had put her to the severe test of acting a part drawn from a character based on the early Hollywood experiences of both Marlene Dietrich and Greta Garbo. She had been up to the challenge, her beauty and talent equal to the enormous demands of the role. Spider's first wife, Valentine O'Neill, had designed the all-important costumes Melanie wore in that movie.

Since then, Melanie Adams had made three more films, each more important and solidly successful than the last, each produced for her by Wells Cope, who was now in his late forties, a cool, witty, profoundly secretive and brilliant man who managed to hold himself apart from the hurly-burly of Hollywood. He worked Hollywood with consummate shrewdness, but by choice he never became a full-fledged member of the filmmaking community.

Cope's exact relationship with Melanie had never been

understood by all the people who made it their life's work to understand such things. No journalist had penetrated their closeness, they had never married, each other or anyone else, and if they were having an affair, no one could be certain of it. However, he was her impresario in the grand tradition, the man who guided every move she made, and taking the part in *Chronicles*, with its single magnificent key leading role for one female star, had been the first decision she'd made for herself as soon as her contract with Cope had expired.

Spider Elliott, Zach thought. He might just know something about Melanie Adams, and at this delicate point any piece of information could be useful, whatever he'd told Roger about not talking to anyone. As if he'd call Wells Cope! Spider was different. He checked his watch and told his secretary to try to reach Spider at Scruples Two, trying not to remember how many times he had called Gigi there.

"Spider, hi, this is Zach Nevsky."

"Zach! How are you? How's Montana? Tell me about it."

"I'm fine, Montana's gorgeous, but I wish *Chronicles* had been set in the summer. I didn't know the ultimate meaning of wind-chill factor until I got here. I'm such a New Yorker I thought Montana was the Wild West; now I've discovered it's lower Canada. The snowdrifts here are twice as tall as I am. Enough about me, how are Billy and the twins?"

"They're all wonderful, blooming, thanks. How's your picture going?"

"Getting there, so far mostly on time, and just about on budget, the dailies look great, but there's one item I wanted to talk to you about."

"Shoot."

"You know Melanie Adams is on the picture?"

"Come on, Zach, the whole world knows."

"She's difficult. More than most. Used to having things her own way, naturally, and spoiled by Wells Cope. I'm about to go to the mat with her, and I figured you might have some wise words, considering that you've known her longer than anyone else."

"Wise words? Zach, I'd be the last person on earth to have any intelligent notions on the problem of dealing with Melanie Adams. Better you than me, guy. I'd help if I could, but I never knew her to please anyone but herself. I haven't seen or spoken to her in, oh, maybe six years, sometime after her first film was released."

"Yeah, but, Spider, according to what I hear, you're the man who knows all about women."

"That's a highly overrated reputation—no man on earth knows more than a little about women. My reputation depends on my understanding just that. In any case, I never had a clue to what made Melanie tick—she's an original."

"You always get the credit for taking the pictures that brought her to the attention of Hollywood," Zach protested.

"I understood how to light her, Zach, that's all. It wasn't hard. I turned on the lights and pushed a button on the camera, her face did all the rest. No way to get a bad picture of her. No fucking way. Listen, maybe this will help. Before Valentine ever met Melanie, she told me, judging on the basis of the way she was behaving, that she thought Melanie must be empty. Then, after she met her, Valentine decided that Melanie was essentially sad. She pitied her, God knows why, because she didn't like her. 'Sad' and 'empty,' Zach, words from a woman who had instincts that were right on the ball. Maybe that'll help."

"It will, Spider. And I thank you, really thank you."

"You're entirely welcome. Wish I could have told you more."

"Will you give my best regards to Billy? And kiss the kids?"

"Sure. Take it easy, guy, and try to stay warm. 'Bye."

As he hung up the phone, Zach Nevsky knew two new things besides what Spider had told him. Spider Elliott had been unforgettably in love with Melanie Adams, he could tell that from his voice when he'd talked about her. Spider also knew that things were over between him and Gigi. He'd never so much as mentioned her name . . . the dog that didn't bark. Well, what the hell had he expected, Zach asked himself furiously. That Gigi wouldn't have announced that she'd kicked him out to one and all; that she'd have carried on, for months, as if things were all right, just because . . . because of what, for Christ's sake? Over was over. But, Jesus, it had been hard, not asking for news of her. He'd wanted to desperately, just to say 'How's Gigi?' but he didn't trust his own voice. If he could read Spider over the phone, chances were that Spider could read him.

Spider Elliott put down the phone and put his feet up on the desk. He was deeply disturbed by Zach's call. In the seven years of her explosive stardom, he'd avoided every Melanie Adams film. She'd damaged him right to the core of his being when she'd disappeared abruptly from his life, with only a foul, lying letter as explanation. She had been his first love, his first true love. No matter what had happened since then, like anyone else whose first love had been thrown back in his face with contempt, he had never completely recovered from the memory of her gratuitous cruelty. Only Valentine could have nursed him through the emotional crisis Melanie had caused.

He'd put Melanie out of his life, even when she'd tried to lure him back, using all her blandishments, and afterwards he'd discovered his love for Valentine, a totally different kind of love, a mature love, a reciprocated love. Then, little more than a year later, Melanie had come back again into his life. Valentine had died while she was working late, driven by the heavy responsibility of completing Melanie's costumes for *Legend*.

Melanie hadn't literally killed Valentine, he realized that, he'd come to terms with it, but it was a fact that if Melanie Adams hadn't existed, Valentine would still be alive.

And if Valentine were still alive, he and Billy wouldn't be married. Spider sighed in wonderment at the twists and turns of his life, a life in which Melanie Adams had been the thread of fate. All that he'd accomplished in life, all that he mourned today, all that he cherished today, existed either because of her, or in spite of her, but was, in some way, determined by her. If Melanie had been a girl with normal emotions, Spider was certain that they would have been married long ago and still married now. He'd probably be a successful fashion photographer, for that was where his greatest talent lay, and she'd still be a model, or more likely, given the supremacy of teenaged models, she'd have retired to have children.

He wished Zach Nevsky didn't have to deal with her, Spider

thought as he got up and looked out of the high windows of his big office in Scruples Two at the last red glow of the winter sun drowning itself in the gray rim of the Pacific. He wished Zach Nevsky hadn't called and brought up old memories. He liked Zach, always had, no matter why or how he had split up with Gigi, for reasons that weren't clear even to Billy. Gigi Orsini could be trusted to take care of herself, Spider decided. Zach Nevsky, with all his power, was no match for Gigi . . . that much he *did* know about women.

Melanie Adams realized that Zach hadn't asked for this meeting with her alone in order to discuss her performance as Lydia Lacy. She had become the best judge of her work, and the role of a very young and virginal music teacher who causes a blood feud between the two most powerful men in a small town in Montana was one well within the range of several other actresses, but she'd accepted it for two reasons: she was playing opposite Clint Eastwood and Paul Newman, and it was the very first major part that had been offered to her at the moment she had finally fulfilled her contract with Wells Cope.

While she was still unknown and unwary, with no confidence in her potential, Wells had seen the power of her beauty, he had brought her from New York to Hollywood, he had had her coached, he had had her tested, and immediately after he'd seen the dailies of her first movie, he had signed her to a four-picture contract.

She had been eager then to sign a deal that would protect her from all the lurking threats and unknown private agendas that can entrap any new girl in town, particularly when the town is Hollywood. Wells had promised her that he would "invent" her, and with his acute intelligence, his undisputed power with the studio, and his ability to curb her ravening impatience and pick exactly the right roles for her, he was responsible for a career in which she had not made a single misstep.

Melanie Adams had desperately needed a mentor, and in Wells Cope she had found not just that mentor, but the only man she was ever to know who was content to make graceful and exquisite love to her without demanding any response, the only man who could immerse himself in her beauty, possess her at his leisure, and never ask any questions about whether she loved him.

All Wells wanted in return was to own her. When had she realized that she was his creature, she wondered. How long had it taken before she saw that although her leash was flexible, silken, invisible, and allowed her to roam, it was made of steel and soldered around her neck? When had she begun to rebel, and when had she realized that short of being self-destructive, which tempted her not at all, she could win only the smallest of victories?

She could spend as much money as she chose, but she wasn't trusted to pick out her own dress for the Academy Awards. She could live anywhere in the world, she could buy a houseboat in the Vale of Kashmir, but she had to report for work on the day Wells appointed, for as long as he decided he needed her, in the role he had chosen for her from hundreds of scripts she was never given to read. She could, and had, rejected Wells sexually when he'd begun to bore her, but when she reached out and took the other men she wanted, he was neither surprised nor, it seemed to her, even interested.

On the other hand, Wells condemned her to long periods of leisure—the curse of certain of the greatest stars—leisure she loathed, although she kept it filled with acting classes—until he finally settled on a project he deemed worthy of her. She could marry, but what would marriage be but another layer of ownership? What husband wouldn't expect something of his wife, even if she was Melanie Adams?

She could always fall in love, Melanie thought with a shrug, Wells couldn't prevent that, but she had never been "in love," whatever that meant, and she knew by now that it was not her destiny. All her life she had been adored, from earliest childhood she had been told how she was loved, love washed over her in endless, demanding, suffocating waves from every direction. She resented it, she struggled uselessly to reject it, it affected her as if she were being force-fed an ever-full bowl of melted chocolate. No. No to love.

Acting was all she was good for, she had to have acting or her life wouldn't be worth living. This knowledge made her resign herself to being an object of love. It was the price she had to pay.

Children? Melanie Adams shuddered. If there could be anything worse than to be owned by Wells Cope, it would be to be owned by children, whose birth was the one irrevocable act in any woman's life. At least a legal contract eventually had to come to an end, but the unthinkable ties of motherhood were lifelong, a child was the one person in your life you could not exchange for a more satisfactory substitute. She had never understood, never even considered it possible to understand, how any woman could be so unimaginative, so un-self-protective, as to want a child. Of course, there was no accounting for the slave mentality of other women, she realized. They needed to be needed. Even beautiful women wanted children. It was simply incomprehensible.

All she asked, she told herself, was to be free, for no one to have any rights over her, never to answer questions, and, more important than anything else, to have some final proof that she existed, *really and truly existed,* outside of other people's inadmissible, inescapable need of her.

She was able to find this proof that she craved with such anguish only in acting before a camera, surrounded by a crowd of people whose only interest was in what she did, not in who she was—people who paid her to be there on the spot, not, thank God, for love but for their own eventual gain.

Only when she felt herself being used to become someone else, someone who was essentially *not* Melanie Adams, only when she was asked to throw herself, body and soul, into another being, did she feel that she had exercised the capacities of her heart. Only her craft quieted, during the time that she was practicing it, her anguished life-long search for a true sense of her own existence. Only when she was acting did she approach, but never arrive at— did she come close, but never close enough—to happiness.

For Melanie Adams, as well as for Eastwood, Newman, and the Rowans, four of the most comfortable houses had been rented in Kalispell. Other cast members, the union crew, and members of the production staff of *Chronicles* were put up in a variety of welcoming motels, but all of the extras were drawn from the local population.

At six o'clock in the evening, Zach drove the short distance from his suite at the Outlaw Inn through the well-plowed streets of the residential section, whose lawns were watched over by elaborate snowmen, and parked in front of the rambling Victorian house that Melanie occupied with her personal hairdresser, a woman named Rose Greenway, who had styled Melanie's hair from the beginning of her career. Rose had become her indispensable assistant in many matters, her confidante, and, as far as Melanie was capable of friendship, her friend. When Melanie left Wells Cope, she took Rose with her.

It was through Miss Greenway that Roger Rowan had made all the arrangements for Melanie's comfort during the shoot, which included employing a special vegetarian gourmet cook, a full-time masseuse, a personal publicist based in L.A., who regulated the access of the international press to the star, and a personal dresser who cared for her costumes. Wells Cope had surrounded her with all the luxuries of stardom, and Melanie had learned to take immensely good care of herself.

"Come on in, Mr. Nevsky," Rose Greenway said as she took his parka and his fur hat. "Miss Adams said to go right on up, she's expecting you. The door's open. Just close it behind you so the steam from the humidifiers doesn't escape. This mountain air," she added disapprovingly, "is really too dry for Miss Adams's skin."

"I know, Miss Greenway," Zach said to the familiar complaint, and mounted the stairs and entered the large front bedroom with its bay windows, part of the half of the second floor that Melanie Adams had turned into her living quarters. It was the first time he'd been on the second floor of the house, and he expected it to be decorated with the same abundance of Sears' Best overstuffed but nondescript furniture that filled the downstairs. However, Melanie Adams had transformed the room with dozens of thin paisley shawls in a multitude of sizes and a wide range of exotic colors and mysteriously compatible designs. She had draped every surface with them, the sofas, the chairs, the tables, even the headboard of the double bed. Every lamp wore a paisley scarf over its shade, the curtains at the windows were covered in paisley, there were white fur rugs scattered over much of the wall-to-wall carpet, and the open bed revealed embroidered Italian linen. The duvet, Zach decided as he prowled around the empty room, probably had been stuffed with the choicest feathers of ten thousand ducks. There was a large fire in the fireplace, and a profusion of green plants everywhere. Votive candles in small hurricane lamps provided points of light here and there; the evocative deliciousness of Chypre filled the air from four green Rigaud candles.

"Come on in," Melanie Adams called from behind the open door that led to the bathroom. "The water's fine."

Cute, Zach thought.

"Thanks. I'll wait till you've finished your bath," he answered, and sat down on the largest of the sofas. He closed his eyes, and breathed in the luxuriously perfumed air, in which the warmth of the heat and the man-made humidity mingled with the subtly scented candles. All he could hear from the bathroom was the regular sound of a sponge being squeezed in and out and a muted splashing, as well as the drip of more water being added to the tub.

A visit to the gardens of the Alhambra, he asked himself? A romp in a sultan's harem? The most elegant little whorehouse in Persia? Whatever this was meant to be, he'd get pneumonia when he went back outside if he didn't take off his sweater and his flannel shirt in this heat, Zach thought, as he stripped them off and relaxed in his jeans and his T-shirt. Interesting little operation Melanie had going here, he thought. Confound and confuse, a good way to spare herself confrontation. On the other hand, she had never had to deal with anyone but Cope himself before, who lived in famous style, so this must all be for her own pleasure . . . pleasure . . .

By the time Melanie felt she had let Zach wait long enough and emerged from her bathroom, her hair wrapped in a turban of toweling, her thin white silk robe clinging to her moist body, wrapped tightly at her fragile waist, no trace of makeup on her astonishing face, he was deeply asleep.

She looked at him in disappointment; her entrance was wasted. But, on the other hand, this was a good time to catch him at a disadvantage, to inspect him more carefully than she could while they were discussing the part or working on the set and she was aware of his eyes evaluating her with their bright compelling intelligence. Even unconscious, with his flow of self-assurance cut off by sleep, Zach somehow remained at the center, Melanie thought. It would be impossible to ignore his presence in the room, difficult even to turn her back on him, for no matter how quietly he slept, Zach radiated a kind of pure physical energy. It came, she speculated, largely from the sheer size of him, the grace of him as he lay there, the rude life of his black hair, the thickness of his neck, the arrogant molding of his head, the rough edges of his face with its prominent cheekbones and a nose that looked as if it had been broken a half-dozen times. Sleep had not tamed Zach Nevsky.

Yes, she wanted him. She had wanted him from the beginning, but after she and Wells had stopped being lovers, he had insisted that she never have an affair with her director. Chief among his reasons was that she would lose her advantage, the advantage she owned because her director must, inevitably, ache to have her. And that aching, like a strong current of water imprisoned by a sheet of ice, would work for her, would give the director the motivation to attain heights that he had never reached for another actress, to become more brilliantly inventive, to stretch himself, to think ceaselessly about her scenes, to improve them, to make her surpass herself.

It was not by accident that Melanie Adams was known as a director's wet dream.

However, Wells Cope and his instructions and control were behind her now, Melanie told herself with deep pleasure. She was on her own, and Zachary Nevsky would give her a chance to test Wells's theory. Why should Wells be right? What if an affair with her director gave her even greater advantages than withholding herself?

Zach started and opened his eyes to find her inspecting him with an intent look in her eyes that he recognized and understood.

"Nice bath?" he asked, instantly awake.

"Lovely, thanks," she said, stretching her arms behind her back. "You don't know what you missed."

"I'd rather shower."

"That's so silly, yet I've never known a man who took a bath. One of life's greatest pleasures is wasted on an entire gender."

Melanie's voice had never been trained by a coach, never lost that touch of Louisville, the haunting hint of sweetness that created its own climate, a semitropical climate of tantalizing, far-off music and delicately tangible invitation.

Melanie sat down on a low chair near the couch and crossed her legs, letting her robe fall open high on her thighs. She unwound her towel turban and shook out the long curly hair she had just finished brushing, a heart-stopping tumble of light maple-sugar-brown hair with red lights in it, hair that changed in every light, with every move she made, hair whose exact color had never been properly named, although thousands of attempts had been made.

"It's quiet here," Zach said, suddenly aware that they were sitting in a deep hush broken only by the small sounds of the fire.

"Rose took everybody out for pizza and the movies after you came," Melanie answered. "She does that every Friday night, even when we're on location. Would you like a drink?"

"No, thanks."

"I'm going to pour myself some sherry . . . you're sure?"

Her voice was innocent, disarming, with a hint of humor in it. Melanie rose and went to a table where there was a tray bearing several glasses and bottles. Zach watched her move. She was aware of every step she took, of the exquisite shape of her wrists and hands and fingers as she picked up the small wine glass, of the miraculous tilt of her throat and her chin as she sipped, of the enticing pout of her lips as she pressed them to the edge of the glass, of the faint circles of her nipples riding high on her firm pointed breasts, of the shadows of her thighs leading up to a thrilling tangle, impossible to miss under her white robe, since the fire behind her provided the brightest source of light in the room.

She knows as much about lighting as any actress in the world, he thought. Does she think I'm that easy?

"You get the part," Zach said abruptly.

"What part?"

"Violet-tressed Aphrodite."

"Now that is a compliment . . . or is it? After all, I'm not auditioning."

"You'll never need to. Aphrodite has 'blandishing persuasion which steals the mind even of the wise'—or so Homer said."

Melanie crossed the room and sat down on the arm of the couch, close to Zach, dry-mouthed but holding her rising excitement in check, judging exactly the slight forward inclination of her spine that would enhance and reveal the swell of her breasts, knowing to the millimeter how the flesh of her thighs would spread softly as she pressed them into the arm of the sofa.

"Melanie, I've wanted to have a private minute with you for some time now," Zach said earnestly, turning toward her and allowing himself to scrutinize her face openly. Never, he thought, never had anyone had skin of such ravishing transparency, such passionate luminosity, a skin far more perfect without makeup than he had ever seen it on a screen.

"Have you indeed?" She didn't allow herself the gratified smile she felt rising to her lips.

"I don't know if you realize that the only reason I took this picture was because you were going to star in it. I believe—I *know* —that you're the greatest actress of your generation," Zach said honestly.

"Why, thank you." Melanie permitted herself a modest acknowledgment of something she had been convinced of for years. Somehow she hadn't expected this to start with the usual dance of compliments.

"Lydia Lacy," Zach said, finally lowering his eyes from her face, "is an eighteen-year-old virgin music teacher, utterly innocent, and so virginal that it hurts."

"That's not news to me, Zach," Melanie said, her voice becoming wary.

"What you don't know is that Ackerman, that criminal old fart, had the unbelievable stupidity to raise the question of whether you could play a convincing eighteen. Ackerman! He's got to be a hundred and ten . . . but he's still the studio boss. I had to take a meeting with that doddering, meddling, ancient oaf, he kept saying that you were almost twenty-eight and why couldn't we get a young girl to play the part—as if any young girl existed who could do the brilliant job you're doing—he nattered on about how the story is based on the premise that Eastwood and Newman, these two old guys, will do anything, literally anything to each other, because they're driven insane by Lydia's absolute youth. They'd kill to possess youth in such pure flower."

"And you came here tonight, now, two months into production, to tell me this? Your sense of timing is bizarre. No, incredible," Melanie said ominously, rising and folding her arms in front of her breasts.

"Frankly, I never dreamed you'd ever have to know. Why should you be burdened with hearing what passes for thought process with Ackerman? I was wild with rage . . . but you don't scream at Ackerman, not if you value your life. Those first two weeks, when I was sending the raw stock to the lab in L.A. to be developed, and getting the dailies back here a couple of days later, proved that he was fucking insane. I know you make it a rule never to go to dailies, but you'd be thrilled with them. You looked more like seventeen than eighteen." Zach paused and looked embarrassed.

"Just what are you trying to say?"

"Then I had a phone call from Ackerman. You know that the studio brass always sees the dailies before they send them back to us? Anyway, Ackerman phoned and said that he'd noticed a few signs of . . . I can't believe he had the nerve . . . but that senile old bastard called it . . . 'wear and tear.' He actually accused me of working you too hard, of not giving you time to get a good night's sleep, considering that you have to be on the set at six in the morning. He's been around for so many centuries that I suggested that, with all due respect, maybe there was something wrong with his eyesight. He told me that the other guys in the screening room agreed with him. I told him you hadn't had to shoot at night since we'd been on location, and he started to ramble on about collagen . . ." Zach broke off and looked fixedly at the fur rug nearest the couch.

"Collagen! What did he say *exactly*?"

"His son-in-law is a dermatologist, specializes in injecting collagen, you know, the stuff under the skin that makes a baby's ass look so good, that luscious, round, innocent stuff that seeps away, just simply disappears year by year, God knows where, no matter how perfect anyone's features are . . ."

"I know what collagen *is*, for Christ's sake! What did he *say*?"

"His exact words? Ackerman said, and I quote, 'It's a question of collagen. Just because there isn't a single line or flaw on your skin doesn't mean that your collagen level is unchanged. Even a three-year-old kid has already lost collagen.' Unquote. He told me that his son-in-law insists that *everything* depends on your getting a good night's rest . . . especially considering your dry skin. He said that he'd send you the latest safe-to-take sleeping pills from his own doctor if you needed them. Also the facial specialist of your choice. He told me we weren't lighting you well enough, and when those particular dailies got back here, the cameraman and I jumped on them together . . . we saw what Ackerman was talking about. We've been lighting you to hide the circles under your eyes . . ."

"There are no circles under my eyes."

"Not to the naked eye, no. But the camera sees them. Very, very faint, Melanie, but still circles and a sort of generalized, hard-to-define . . . right there on the edge, kind of maybe-yes, maybe-no, but as Ackerman put it, the faintest, almost invisible, but definite amount of . . . wear and tear. Lydia Lacy, eighteen-year-old virgin music teacher, wouldn't look like that, not even if she'd been up all night long, doing whatever virgin music teachers in Montana did for kicks way back then."

Zach stopped on a note of finality, as if he'd said every word he had to say on the matter, and began to stuff his flannel shirt back into his jeans.

"You're telling me to cut it out with Sid and Allen," Melanie said without inflection.

"Oh, yeah. That too. Unless you can manage to fit them both in and still be on time to leave for the set at six in the morning after an honest eight hours of sleep every single night of a six-day week. If you want breakfast, that means bed by nine . . . alone."

"If Wells were here, he'd cut your heart out, you vicious, maggoty little prick."

"Look, Melanie, I blame myself," Zach said remorsefully, turning to face her. "If Wells were here, I bet you'd never dream of getting involved with—anyone in particular. He established a routine for you, he ran your life, organized you in a way I can't provide a substitute for . . ."

"I don't want a substitute for Wells," she said ferociously. "God damn it, Zach, this is the first time I've felt like a free woman since the day I met him. Can you begin to imagine what it's been like? I never have a minute to call my own. Either I'm working for Wells or I'm waiting to work for Wells. Five major films! Routine! It's stifling! Coming here, working for strangers, with nobody watching over me, nobody owning me, nobody I have to listen to and obey—this has been the most exciting experience of my life since I made my first movie."

"Sid and Allen are your way of making up for lost time?"

"Yes! Oh, you don't know what you're asking me to give up.

You have no idea! I've never . . . done anything like it before. They've been an . . . experiment, oh, definitely time-consuming, I admit, but . . . worthwhile." She smiled at him with that mysteriously meaningful mixture of wantonness and withdrawal that audiences waited for, holding their collective breath.

"So do me a really big favor and stop?"

Zach spoke gently, but even Wells Cope had never sounded so flatly positive of what was right for her, and every self-protective brain cell in Melanie Adams responded to him.

"Consider it done," she said quickly, dismissing the subject.

"Good. Listen, Melanie, I'll speak to Sid and Allen, there's no reason why you should have to handle them."

"Zach, don't you dare!" Melanie flashed out at him, flushing with the beginning of anger. "That's exactly the sort of thing Wells would have said. I'll do what you want, but that doesn't mean I don't know exactly the best way to manage this. *Get off my turf.*"

"Sorry. But when my star is involved, I can't help trying to make things easy for her. Forgive me?"

"Of course. Now, will you have that drink?"

"Thanks, but I have to get back to my place, I'm waiting for a phone call from L.A."

"Ackerman?" she asked suspiciously.

"No way. Ackerman will never know we've talked. Do you think I'd give the sonofabitch that satisfaction. It's my fiancée."

"Good," Melanie said, relieved. "And congratulations. I didn't know you were engaged. Have I met her?"

"I don't think so, she's not in the business." Zach leaned over one of her hands, raised it, and kissed it lightly. "Good night, Melanie. See you tomorrow, bright and early."

"Good night, Zach."

As he drove away, congratulating himself, Zach estimated that not only had he nipped a potential problem in the bud, but he'd added an additional twenty years to Melanie's future as a romantic star. She photographed a fast sixteen now . . . on the worst day she'd ever known. So in another twenty years she'd still look maybe thirty-five max, so long as she remembered to schedule her sex life properly. She could always give up dinner.

Melanie Adams owed him, not that she'd ever realize it. He knew her ego would never allow her to repeat what he'd said to anyone in the world, would not allow her to check with the cameraman, but just in case, he'd have a word with him before the evening was over.

In any case, as sad and empty as Valentine may once have seen Melanie Adams, those words no longer applied. She was on top of her life, as far as he could tell, and enjoying every minute of it, now that Wells Cope was out of the picture. She was going to squeeze every drop of juice out of her good-bye scenes with the two grips, that he recognized just from the light in her eyes. She was looking forward to the drama and the farewell fuck that would sweeten each kiss-off.

Fiancée. Where, Zach wondered, had he come up with that particular lie, of all the lies he might have picked out of all the multitude of lies he'd told tonight? It made a great excuse, an excuse that would keep him out of trouble with Melanie, because that kind of trouble was clearly there for the taking and that kind of trouble he couldn't afford. Even if he could afford it, he didn't need it. And even if he needed it, he didn't want it. How could he *not* want it? Not want Aphrodite? Was there something wrong with him?

Rose Greenway retired to her own quarters on Saturday night later than she would have liked. However, she'd had to wait up to admit Sid White and escort him upstairs to Melanie's suite of rooms. She was exhausted, as she always was after a week of getting up every day at 5:00 A.M. to dress and breakfast before Melanie's driver picked them up. They both reported to hair and makeup at 6:00 A.M., something she'd never grown used to throughout her years in the business, although she realized fully that they were working through the shortest days of the year. Tomorrow she'd sleep late, as late as possible, Rose Greenway thought as she pulled her quilt over her chin.

Two hours later she woke up abruptly, with the impression that she had heard some sort of noise. She listened intently, but the silence of the house was undisturbed. Nevertheless, something in her long, devoted years of watching over Melanie made her uneasy enough to get out of bed, put on her warm wool bathrobe, and go to check up on her, quite as irrationally as if she were the mother of a sleeping baby. She listened for a minute as she stood outside the door to Melanie's room. A strip of soft, flickering light lay on the floor of the hall outside of the door. The candles were evidently still lit, the vaporizers hissing normally. All seemed to be well, they were probably sleeping, Rose Greenway thought, yet somehow she couldn't make up her mind to go back to her own bed. On the other hand, how could she possibly enter the room? Melanie wouldn't thank her for even the quietest, most discreet of interruptions at this hour, even if she were alone.

She hesitated irresolutely and finally pressed her ear to the door for several minutes. There was such a total absence of sound, not even a faint snore or the noise of normal breathing, that she opened the door a crack, as silently as possible, her eyes directed at the pillows of the big double bed directly in her line of vision. The bedclothes had been tossed about, but no one was in the bed. She opened the door a little further and drew in her breath in horror too great for a scream. Sid White lay naked near the foot-board of the bed, sprawled facedown on the floor. Under him she could see some of Melanie's hair and the edge of her nightgown. Rose lunged forward and rolled Sid White off Melanie's body with all her strength, registering, in the small corner of her mind that wasn't intent on Melanie, the fact that the back of his head had been blown away. She staggered backwards at the sight of the fragile woman, over whom blood seemed to have been slopped from a bucket. Keeping herself from shrieking, Rose stripped off her robe, threw it over Melanie, and ran to the telephone by the bed and called the police. She dropped the receiver to rush back to Melanie, and then grabbed the phone again. The producer, she realized automatically, never forget to call the producer.

Roger Rowan and Zach were working at Rowan's house past midnight on a change in the production schedule for the following week when the phone rang. Rowan picked it up, annoyed at the unexpected ringing.

"Yes? Rose? *What!* Oh, Jesus, *no!* We're on our way!" He hung up. "Melanie's been shot, come on. Shit shit shit! I don't fucking believe this!"

"Is she alive?" Zach shouted as they ran for the car.

"*I don't know.* That hysterical bitch called me 'Mr. Cope' and hung up!"

9

Norma Rowan fluttered around in the waiting room, bringing her husband cups of coffee and candy bars from the vending machine in the hospital hall, while he sat in a plastic chair, obsessing over the *force majeure* clause in the production's insurance.

"There's not gonna be a problem about money," he fidgeted out loud for the tenth time. "It clearly states that if the production of the picture is interrupted by death, illness, disfigurement, or incapacity of any member of the cast, there's no problem with insurance guys. They'll pay whatever it costs, even if we have to shut down the picture for good."

Rose Greenway, huddled in the comfort of Zach's shoulder, continued to hiccup with irregular sobs, her shock and grief slowly abating with fatigue. Zach, finally offended beyond endurance, said in a low, coiled voice, "Just shut up, Rog. We don't know anything yet. Melanie's been in that operating room over two hours and all you can do is talk about insurance."

"It's the only bright spot!"

"You should be glad Roger has the best interests of the production in mind, Zachary," Norma Rowan screeched at him. "Where would you be if he weren't thinking ahead, I'd like to know?"

"He's up shit creek no matter what," Rowan spat accusingly. "*Who* wouldn't call Wells Cope? Who insisted on talking to Melanie? Who, for Christ's sake, let *her* talk to Sid White. Who couldn't leave well enough alone? Nevsky, our genius director, that's who, and you all know it. This fucking mess is his fault!"

"Which one of you people is in charge here?" The question came from a breathless newcomer, a very young, tousled man who looked as if he had been aroused from bed only a short while ago.

"Who the hell are you?" Zach asked.

"Oliver Brady, *Kalispell Daily Inter Lake*, heard there's been an accident."

"We have nothing to say to you," Rowan snarled.

"Melanie Adams in the hospital, and you people don't have a statement?" the reporter gabbled excitedly.

"Get the hell out of here!" Rowan screamed, lunging at him.

"I'll get rid of him," Zach said, taking Brady by the arm and walking him along a corridor. "I'm Zach Nevsky, the director of *Chronicles*. Who tipped you off? One of the medics? Had to be."

"You're kidding, right? Like I'm going to tell you my source. I know she was shot, multiple wounds, I know there's a naked dead guy who was found with her, probable suicide, police at the house investigating—it's gigantic news and I'm the first person to get it. I'm not going anywhere till I get more details. The press has a right to know. Who was that creep in the waiting room?"

"Roger Rowan, producer of the picture. He's understandably upset, sorry about that. I've never seen you at any of our press conferences," Zach probed carefully. "You new at the paper?"

"Yeah, here's my press card, if you don't believe me. I'm on the sports desk, but this is my story and nobody's getting it away from me."

"Nobody's trying to," Zach said soothingly. He'd never seen a reporter who was both so brash and so nervous. Oliver Brady was clearly overwhelmed by opportunity, but not so impressed that he wasn't standing his ground.

"We don't know Miss Adams's condition yet," Zach continued. "The doctors haven't told us anything, that's what we're waiting to learn."

"So who's the dead guy? Why was he naked in Melanie's bedroom in the middle of the night? Why did he shoot her? Rage? Lovers' quarrel? Kinky sex?"

"Who, where, when, what, why . . . you've got them all except the *why*." Zach spoke slowly, his mind working clearly and rapidly, trying to put the best twist possible on a story that was about to explode all over the world. So much depended on the nature of the very first report.

"Brady," Zach pursued, "by tomorrow there'll be publicity and security people from the studio swarming all over—they're on their way here by company jet now. Every major news source will have sent their own guys. You won't be able to get within a hundred yards of this hospital. Your paper will probably send their top man, not a young sportswriter. There'll only be pool coverage. But you're a smart, enterprising fellow and you deserve an exclusive."

"I've got it anyway," Brady asserted confidently.

"Sure you do. One tenth of it. Big fucking deal. The big boys will take your stuff, rewrite it, and run with the rest."

"Listen, Nevsky, I have more than enough, even if you don't answer a single question, don't try to bullshit me."

Zach paused and considered the question with a searching look at the excited young reporter. He sighed and said at last, "Brady, you make a convincing point. Got a tape recorder? Good, just keep it running. And remember, this is off the record. I shouldn't be giving you these details." Zach took a deep breath. This would be as delicate as making the plot of *Love's Labor's Lost* clear to a roomful of sixth-graders.

"Melanie Adams has been the victim of a crime of passion," Zach conceded with a sigh. "She's been having a very intense romance, a passionate love affair with a young man named Sid White. Sid White is dead, a suicide. Miss Adams and Sid White have kept their romance very private, but it's been going on for a long time. This was Sid White's first film job. He is—was—a lighting designer who was willing to work as a grip on the picture to be near Miss Adams. However, Miss Adams recently realized that she had to break off this romance. Sid White was becoming an emotional basket case, irrationally jealous and obsessively possessive of her. She worried about his mental stability, he was insisting on marriage and she wasn't willing to commit to that, love him though she did."

"She loved the guy? You jerking me off?"

"Absolutely not. Melanie Adams was genuinely in love . . . but she had become unhappily aware that Sid White was wrong for her. They had a real old-fashioned romance going, Brady. Miss Adams has always been a great romantic, hell, you can tell that from her choice of films."

"I've never seen one."

"Then ask your movie critic, Brady, for heaven's sake! Anyway, I went to see her on Friday afternoon to discuss the situation. I advised her to let me handle it, take care of it for her, but she wouldn't hear of my interfering, got angry when I suggested it. She was too softhearted, too much of an old-fashioned romantic, to listen to advice, she insisted on speaking to Sid herself . . . she said it was the right thing to do. Those were her exact words, Brady, 'the right thing to do' . . . shit, if only she hadn't been so romantic, so old-fashioned! So Sid went to her house tonight, obviously by appointment because Miss Rose Greenway, her assistant, hairdresser, and friend, with whom she shares the house, would never have admitted him otherwise. That was Miss Greenway in the waiting room, the other woman was Roger Rowan's wife."

"So what happened then? How come he had a gun?"

"God knows. How many people are carrying guns nobody knows about? And as I said, Melanie worried that he was unstable, possessive, irrationally jealous. All I can assume is that when Sid learned that Melanie Adams wouldn't marry him, in fact wanted to stop seeing him, he went completely insane. He shot her, he must have believed she was dead, and then he committed suicide. Like Mayerling . . . you remember Mayerling? No? It was a castle in Austria where the Crown Prince Rudolf killed the woman he loved madly, Maria Vetsera, and then killed himself. It was the crime of passion of the nineteenth century, Brady. A woman like Melanie Adams inspires that kind of passion, Brady, it's her unfortunate destiny . . . *Mayerling in Montana* . . . I feel as if history is being repeated here tonight."

"Mayerling in Kalispell . . . nah, 'Mayerling in Montana' sounds better."

"There's been a lot of historical interpretation of exactly what happened that night outside of Vienna," Zach continued, having hooked his fish, "whether Maria Vetsera consented to the suicide pact or not, but no one has ever forgotten that story. No one will ever forget your story, Brady. It'll make you! But don't get carried away. What happened tonight wasn't a suicide pact. Melanie Adams was fleeing Sid White when he tried to kill her. Rose Greenway called Roger Rowan, the producer, when she discovered the bodies, and we both went to the house immediately. When I saw Miss Adams lying there, I could tell that she'd been trying to protect herself. One of her hands was right next to her face, warding him off."

"I still want to know why she was wearing only a nightgown and why he was buck naked? Why not give him the kiss-off fully clothed?"

"Jesus, Brady, where's your sense of romance?" Zach hissed at him. "You'd better find one damn quick, or you'll be covering baseball for the rest of your life, scoop or no scoop. Why the hell do you think? I'll tell you why! Melanie Adams must have allowed that crazy guy to make love to her one last time because she was *sorry for him.* That's why! The worst thing she was guilty of was lack of judgment, being too softhearted, too romantic, too old-fashioned. Major mistake! He couldn't have her for himself, so he killed her to deprive the world of her. A typical crime of passion, selfish, insane passion. Christ! You're writing about Melanie Adams here, not batting averages. She's in that operating room, victim of a crime of passion, because of *romance,* Brady, and don't you forget it! I'm going back to the waiting room now."

"Will you phone me at the paper as soon as you know how she is?" Brady asked greedily.

"Oh no, I can't possibly do that. I've given you your story, you're asking too much. I don't have the authority to do that, Brady."

"Look, Nevsky, if you'll phone me and tell me her *exact* condition, everything the doctors tell you, I'll read you every word of my story over the phone before I file it. That's a promise. I want to keep my scoop."

"Fair enough. And, Brady, if your story is honest, if it doesn't embroider and speculate on what I've told you, *if it runs as exactly the story you read me,* and that's a big 'if,' I'll *keep* you on the inside. I'll be in touch whenever anything new happens. This is a story that won't go away, and it's to our mutual benefit to get it right. But you tell anyone where you're getting the information, and you're dead with me, Brady. Here's my direct line at the production office, you can call me any time, while the rest of the press waits for the pool announcements. If I'm on location, my secretary will get me to return your call. If I'm here at the hospital, I'll leave word to put you through. Give me your number at home and at work. The tabloid press is so full of lying shit that it's a relief to deal with someone who still has real journalistic values, even if you're no romantic."

"How do you spell Nevsky?"

"I told you this was off the record. Call me an 'informed source,' for God's sake," Zach said in exasperation.

"I still need to know how to spell it. You and the producer were the first at the scene of the crime of passion, Mayerling in Montana."

His very first performance in the role of Deep Throat, Zachary thought as he raced back to the waiting room. He wouldn't have been as surefooted, as clear on what he had to say to Brady—and what he had to leave out—if he hadn't heard a dozen location catastrophe stories from that wily fox, Vito Orsini. Gigi's father was the kind of producer who had all the true passion and reverence for film that Roger Rowan lacked, and he possessed a master hand with the media that he had developed in dealing with the suits who ran the studios. Ever since Vito had brought him out from Broadway to direct *Fair Play*, the film that he had saved for Vito, the film that had been Vito's first big success after a long dry period, the film that had made him the hottest new director in Hollywood, the two of them had kept up their firm friendship.

Still he'd only taken a first step, Zach realized, only shaped the way the story would be perceived from the beginning. Even if by some miracle Melanie was able to continue with the picture, the production had been complicated in a hundred important and unforeseen ways. Vito had faced such situations and worse over a long and bumpy career, and never compromised, never tried to put the blame on the director. Rowan showed every sign of doing both. He needed an ally here, someone who would anticipate every thought process of a Rowan or an Ackerman, Zach realized. He needed Vito Orsini.

Another half hour passed in silence in the waiting room until the two surgeons appeared wearily from the nearby operating room.

"She is going to be okay," the elder of them said. "We had to give her massive transfusions, it was touch-and-go, but she'll make it. She's in the intensive care unit now, on the critical list."

"Her face," Rowan screamed, "what about her face?"

"Untouched, thank God," the second surgeon said. "The bullet that tore open the artery in her wrist caused the major hemorrhage. A number of bones in her hand are broken, and there are multiple flesh wounds in her shoulder. We did what we could, but she's going to need specialized attention and eventual rehabilitation from a hand surgeon, you'd better fly one up here tomorrow. She's a lucky girl. If she'd arrived here ten minutes later, chances are that she would have been dead from losing that much blood. I've rarely seen anyone in such deep shock."

"When," Rowan demanded, "can she go back to work?"

"*Work!*" The younger surgeon was incredulous.

"These are movie people, Joe, don't be surprised," the elder surgeon said in disgust. "I don't know. It depends on possible complications I can't anticipate, on her physical and emotional strength, her response to the transfusions, a million factors, but until she's out of intensive care I can't begin to give you an answer."

"Make a guess, that's all I want," Rowan insisted.

"If it were me . . . I'd give myself at least six months to get back to normal," the doctor said, "and then I'd find another line of work."

As both men left the room, Zach and Rowan headed for phone booths in the hallway, Zach to call Brady, Rowan to call his agent. Zach was soon back with Rose Greenway, waiting for Rowan to complete his call. The producer emerged at last from the phone booth and joined his wife.

"Roger, I'd like to talk to you," Zach said quietly. "In private. Let's take a little walk in the hall."

"What is it this time?"

"Allen Henrick, the other grip Melanie was screwing. His story *cannot* get out, you understand that."

"Yeah."

"You should get Lou Cavona to meet us at the office as soon as possible. He's the one to handle Allen. Also, Sid was his brother-in-law and he doesn't know Sid's dead."

"I'm going to call Ackerman before I do anything. I have a responsibility to Ackerman."

"Roger, you'll have your chance to blame me for everything as soon as Ackerman wakes up. Why disturb him in the middle of the night? He won't thank you for it. Lou Cavona is important *now*, while we can still try to keep this in the family."

"Family! This'll be front-page news all over the world! Every radio station, every television station . . . it's only a question of time. God knows what that young punk is going to print."

"We'd better pray that he's a Melanie Adams fan."

Getting to remote Kalispell in February is not an uncomplicated matter, but, by the end of the day following Oliver Brady's story, a story that was picked up by the wire services and immediately circled the globe, the parking area of the local airport was filled with private aircraft ranging from large studio jets to many smaller charter planes, some of them old enough to have been retired decades ago. The manager at Glacier Park International Airport, aware that this was just the beginning of the influx, had arranged for a snowplow to clear two large nearby fields, and had hired a crew to lay out spaces on which to tie down dozens of planes.

In town, every single one of the more than a score of motels and hotels on Route 93 was busily hiring staff to clean rooms that had been shut up since the tourist season ended early last autumn with the official closing of the road into nearby Glacier National Park. Restaurant owners were on the phone trying to scrounge up supplies from wholesalers as far away as San Francisco, willing to pay inflated prices for an airlift of food, since they knew that they would be able to charge anything for a meal.

The earliest arrivals had come in on a number of large jets; Joe Irving, the head of production for the studio, with his chief assistants and secretaries, landed within minutes of a jet bearing a dozen insurance executives. They were quickly followed by the rest of the studio contingent: almost the entire public-relations department; the head of studio security and his assistants; the business affairs chief and his assistants; a large group of studio lawyers; Melanie Adams's agent and lawyer; Rowan's agent and lawyer. Only Ackerman, it seemed, was left holding the fort back in Hollywood, Zach thought, as his entire production department set itself to the task of snatching the best accommodations in town for the new arrivals before the newspaper reporters and network correspondents and their crews could pitch their tents. And that imminent invasion was merely the American media. Planes bearing press from Japan, from France, from Germany, from Britain, from every country in the world where American movies played, from every country where the names of Clint Eastwood, Paul Newman, and Melanie Adams were known, were on their way.

Vito Orsini, whom Zach had called in the middle of the night, had been one of the first to arrive in Kalispell, hitching a ride with the insurance people, and was now sharing Zach's suite at the Outlaw Inn.

"If I owned a house in Kalispell, know what I'd do?" Vito said, his eyes alive with fun. "I'd hold an auction between the Germans and the Japanese, three months' minimum rent, and take my family, kids and all, somewhere cheap in Florida until this story goes away. I'd pay for their college education in one easy move, and they'd get a great tan. Hell, even a heated garage will go for a fortune by the time the *Enquirer* and the *Sun* get here."

"Glad you're having such a good time, Vito," Zach grinned painfully.

"Glad it's not my picture," Vito retorted.

"Morally it is," Zach insisted. "It's mine, and since you're here to hold my hand, it's yours too."

"Thanks for your generosity, kid. Glad it's not my ass on

which no one yet has established moral rights. So what's the story?"

"Lou Cavona was a gem. He said that three generations of grips in his family prided themselves on surviving hurricanes, earthquakes, epidemics, sandstorms, snakes, rogue elephants, and typhoons, to say nothing of the madness of directors, producers, and actors. They've seen it all, done it all, and never blinked three times. But they were all Cavonas, his side of the family. Sid White was his wife's brother, he wasn't genetically a grip; Lou blamed himself for getting the guy the job. He feels terrible for his wife and family, but that's the last such favor he'll be doing her. He understands the trouble we're in just as well as Ackerman does."

"What about the other grip?"

"Lou took care of Allen Henrick, I didn't ask him how and I sure don't need to know, but Henrick is on his way back to L.A. to work on another picture. Since Henrick is a married man and wants to stay that way, he'll keep his mouth shut, probably tell his wife he had frostbite of a delicate extremity. Lou said the other grips won't talk to press under pain of torture and getting kicked out of IA. He can deliver that."

"But what about the rest of the crew and staff? Shit, once the media starts digging, it'll only take one observant waitress from Craft Services to start the rumors."

"I know, Vito. But they'll only be rumors, they won't be *the* story, the one everyone's heard and absorbed by now as the truth. That's the most we could ever have hoped for."

"You did good work there, kid. Mayerling in Montana! For shame!"

"A combination of directing high-school plays and inspiration from some of the horror stories you've told me."

"I ever tell you about my Mexican dog, *Slow Boat*, back in 1975, almost nine years ago? No? That was one tight spot that Maggie MacGregor showed me how to get out of. The solution created her career. What's more, the murderer is still working full time and picking up the occasional Oscar. Don't ask! Is Maggie joining this circus?"

"Would she miss it?"

"Haven't laid eyes on her since the first sneak preview of *The*

WASP," Vito said, remembering how Maggie MacGregor, the most powerful television journalist in the country, had left his bed without so much as a good-bye word as soon as she'd learned of the enormity of his historic disaster, a picture that had given the word "flop" a new dimension a number of years ago. He'd had three successful pictures since, but Maggie had never returned to his life.

"Do you have any influence with her?" Zach asked hopefully.

"Maybe yes, maybe no," Vito answered. "It depends on whether she has a conscience or not. It's a neat question, kid. If a woman you've been fucking to her heart's content drops you dead just because you made a lousy movie, does she feel you injured her, or does she feel she injured you?"

"I'd say that depends on how she's justified it to herself," Zach answered, trying not to show surprise at Vito's revelation, since *The WASP* had been made while Vito was still married to Billy Ikehorn Orsini Elliott. "It could go either way."

"What about the local police?"

"So far, the doctors haven't allowed them to talk to Melanie. But she's responded so well to the transfusions that they've told me they can move her out of intensive care to a private room, at which point we can't stop the chief from questioning her."

"You have to coach her first. Tonight."

"Don't I know it?" Zach sighed. "I've been trying to decide how much to ask her to say."

"One line should do it. You read her the important parts of Brady's story, and then you tell her that all she needs to say is she doesn't remember a thing. *Nada.* She draws a blank for that whole day. Shock. One line, 'I don't remember.' Or maybe two, if she feels up to it. 'What am I doing here?'—a classic, I always love that line. That's *it.* Two foolproof lines. Now, will you just leave me alone with this script? I've got to read it again."

"Vito, even if by a miracle Melanie can be on her feet working in ten days, ten days, for Christ's sake, she'll be wearing a cast on her wrist and her hand'll be in a cast and a sling. There's no way anybody dreams she could possibly be up for it in ten days anyway. But Eastwood and Newman have stop dates that mean we'll lose them unless she can do the proposal scene with Newman and the big fight scene with Eastwood *before* those ten days are up.

Two major emotional scenes! We're going to end up shutting down the picture even though the insurance never pays a hundred pennies on the dollar. Joe Irving and the rest of the production group are viewing the rough cut now and they're going to love what they see, I guarantee it. That makes it all the worse."

Vito shook his head at Zach with diffused tenderness and superiority. "Look, get out of here so I can think. Okay, okay, ask me the thing you really want to know."

"Ah, shit, Vito." Zach looked at him in mute appeal.

"Gigi's fine, kid. Career going wild, another new account, only two traffic tickets in the last month."

"Vito . . ."

"Yeah, there's a guy. What did you expect, you pathetic asshole?"

"What kind of guy?"

"Somebody she works with, that's all I heard. Gigi hasn't managed to have time for personal conversations since you and she broke up. I suspect she plain doesn't want to tell me, because she knows we're friends." Vito shrugged. "I did gather that you don't even know as much about handling women as I do. Welcome to the club."

Had Melanie Adams even understood what he'd told her yesterday, Zach wondered, as he followed the Kalispell chief of police and the doctor into her room. She hadn't uttered a word as he'd read her sections of the newspaper article and told her what to say, but had only lain there with her eyelids closed, no expression on her pitiful, drained face. She'd been aware of his presence—she'd whispered his name when he was finally permitted his three minutes alone at her side, and she'd nodded slightly when he left her—but otherwise she'd been utterly silent and almost as white as if she were dead. How much sedation was she under? Would she remember how important it was not to talk to the chief?

Zach leaned against the wall in the hospital room, while the head surgeon and the policeman sat in chairs on either side of her bed.

"No more than a few minutes, Chief," the doctor said, "and if I think it's too much for her, I'll have to ask you to stop."

"Right, Doc. Miss Adams, I'm sorry, but I have a few questions I have to ask you," the policeman said in a hushed voice, turning on his tape recorder. Melanie turned her marvelous eyes to him in startled wonder. His mouth opened and nothing came forth. He shook himself mentally and started over.

"Miss Adams, on the night you were shot, did Sid White say anything before he went for his gun?"

"Sid . . . how is he? Where is he?" Melanie asked imploringly. Zach straightened up, the hairs on the back of his neck rising in horror. She didn't remember yesterday.

"He's, well, he's . . ." The policeman stopped. He didn't want to announce Sid White's suicide to this poor woman.

"He took his own life, Miss Adams," the doctor said carefully.

"No! No! Oh, my God . . . poor sweet Sid . . . poor lost Sid, I was so afraid for him," Melanie murmured in heartbroken tones, "he was so impulsive, so tormented, he wasn't strong enough for this world . . . not like . . . the other."

" 'The other'?"

Zach closed his eyes and all but fainted standing upright.

"Others, others . . . people in movies, officer. He was a gentle, beautiful soul and I loved him."

"Miss Adams, he shot you," the policeman persisted.

"He couldn't have known . . . what he was doing," Melanie whispered. "He could never have wanted to hurt me. He must have been insane. And now . . . Sid's . . . gone. That proves his love . . . all those months . . . I kept telling him there was no reason to be jealous . . . but he never believed me . . . oh, Sid, if only you'd believed me . . ."

"Did you tell him it was over between you? Was that the motive?" the policeman asked.

"It had to be. What else could it have been? I should have listened to Zach . . . he wanted to get rid of Sid . . . I was a fool . . . I loved him so much that I listened to my heart." Tears appeared in her eyes.

"Chief, for Christ's sake, leave her alone now," the doctor said angrily.

The chief rose hastily and left the room with a longing backward glance at the sight of greater beauty than he'd ever see again. The doctor took Melanie's pulse, and then bent his head to listen to her heart with his stethoscope, just time enough for Melanie to look Zach full in the face and give him an all but imperceptible wink.

"*She milked it!* Vito, she would have carried on for hours if the doctor hadn't stopped her!"

"See why I love actresses, Zach?"

"I had a near-death experience. And she knew it. She *caused* it!"

"You gotta love 'em."

"But this one? She's on a whole different level of the beast. Actresses are my specialty, but I know when I've been slapped on the wrist and sent back to the minors."

"That's why you're going to be able to finish this picture, kid. If she was doing Duse today, she can do the Eastwood and Newman scenes before the ten days are up, no problem."

"Paul proposes to her during a sleigh ride, and the fight scene takes place outdoors, on the steps leading to Clint's mansion."

"Not anymore. See here, on page eighty-eight, where I've marked it, that's where she's going to be thrown from a horse—a stunt double, naturally—and be injured. The proposal and the fight scenes will both take place in the hospital, with her in bed. Hair, makeup, period nightie, period cast and sling. When she's back on her feet, which I predict will be sooner than anyone thinks, you can get her and the horse, not actually getting on, just about to. And from then on you're home free, she plays the rest of the picture with a cast or sling or whatever. New costumes are your only problem."

"But, Vito!"

"But what?"

"Melanie's a piano teacher! It's important in the book."

"The shots of her giving lessons, you've got them, right? Great, so from now on she'll start to teach singing—she can sing, can't she?—if she can't, you'll dub her. Don't be so literal-minded. The year I won the Oscar for *Mirrors,* the thing people remembered most about the film was Dolly Moon's water breaking when her Best Supporting Actress Oscar was announced. People don't read the book and then compare it frame by frame with the movie—

ninety-five percent of *Gone With the Wind isn't* in the film. Cheer up, Zach, no book is sacred. Who won the Pulitzer last year? See, you haven't a clue. Why isn't your scriptwriter here anyway? Get him here tomorrow, he can sleep on the floor."

"Vito, for the love of God, how can we film in a hospital room? Melanie has the biggest one in the hospital, but the cameras, the crew, the lights, the cables—it's an impossible fit."

"How much would it cost to rent the operating room for a couple of days? In fact, why doesn't the studio plan to build the hospital a new wing? Do well by doing good? You can build your set in the operating room, working nights. They can set up with a stand-in, wheel Melanie's bed in just for the takes, and forget about master shots. Close-ups only. I did it once in Sicily at the beginning when I was still making spaghetti Westerns."

"Have I ever told you I loved you?"

"More or less. Come on, Zach, I'll buy you a drink."

The bar of the Outlaw Inn was so crowded that Zach and Vito had to search for a table. Since the production was shut down until decisions were made, everyone but the busy studio arrivals seemed to have time on their hands and nothing better to do than gather and gossip and think about their paychecks mounting up.

"Grab that booth," Zach said, as a group of cheery wardrobe people got up to leave. They slid in as the others slid out, with the unmatchable expertise of men who had spent their early years in New York and ridden the subways daily.

"What are you having?" Vito asked Zach.

"A Negroni, sweetheart, what else?" said a woman's famous voice as Maggie MacGregor joined the party. "You bought me my first one, remember, pussycat? Rome, 1974, at the Hostaria dell' Orso. I'll never forget it." She leaned over and kissed Vito on the lips. "If they don't have Campari in Montana, I'm going to be very disappointed. What the hell are you doing here anyway?"

"I figured you'd show up, so I've been camping out waiting for you," Vito said, laughing. He was astonishingly glad to see her, and if she wanted to start out by remembering the first time she'd interviewed him for *Cosmo*, when she'd been an unknown magazine writer, an interview followed by two weeks of lovemaking and deeply friendly mutual appreciation, it meant that any interim unpleasantness could be considered buried.

"As usual, you look like the best kind of cross between the young John Huston and the young Vittorio De Sica," Maggie said, approvingly checking Vito out and noticing that his flash, his toughness, and his quality of bronzed warmth hadn't suffered by either the passage of a few years or the drop in temperature. His short, curly hair was just as thick as she remembered, and of course his aristocratically large Italian nose and full mouth were as boldly Latin as ever. "Trust you, Vito, to wear heavy deerstalking tweeds and a cashmere vest in a place where everybody else is dressed like lumberjacks. Did you bring your astrakhan coat? Who's this gent?" she asked, pointing at Zach.

"Maggie, may I present Zachary Nevsky, the director of *Chronicles*."

"I loved *Fair Play*, Zach." Maggie trained all the force of her round, dark, Betty Boop eyes on him, weighing and judging eyes that had cajoled and terrified half of show business into admitting things they had never planned to reveal on the most public of forums, her interview program. At thirty-two she was in the prime of her prime, divinely voluptuous in all the vital places, utterly poised and an addictive presence to more than three-quarters of all Americans who watched television news shows in prime time.

"Thank you, Maggie," Zach said respectfully.

"What exactly *is* Vito doing here?" she asked him.

"Ah . . . Vito . . . well—"

"I came up to persuade Zach to direct my new picture, Maggie, and when the fireworks happened I decided to stick around and watch."

"What new picture?" she demanded imperiously.

"It's top secret, too soon to announce it, even to you, love, but Zach has given me his word, haven't you, Zach?"

"Sure have," Zach said, knowing he was now committed to a picture he'd never heard of, as tightly as if he'd signed a deal memo. This was a neat answer to the question of how easy it had been to get Vito to jump on a plane. Well, such an exchange was less than he already owed Vito for *Chronicles*.

"So you'll be working together again. That's wonderful—keep me posted. Say, Vito, do you remember the time we had dinner together at the Boutique of La Scala in Beverly Hills? Am I crazy, or was Billy pissed off that night about our reminiscing about the Mexican dog? I've always wondered about that . . . she's never liked me, still doesn't, but, my God, when I called to tell you that you'd won the Best Picture Oscar the day before the ceremonies, didn't that make up for it?"

"Oh, you know how Billy used to—"

"Didn't she realize that nothing really happened *that* time?"

"Listen, folks, I've got to run," Zach said, getting up abruptly.

"Something I should know about?" Maggie queried automatically, never taking her eyes off Vito.

"My CPR class, wouldn't do to be late for that," Zach said, and left the bar in a hurry, before a hysterical bellow of laughter could fight its way out of his chest.

"He's cute," Maggie said, "very cute indeed."

"Taken, Maggie."

"How taken?"

"My daughter. He's family."

"Well . . . in that case . . ." Maggie's momentary spark of interest disappeared.

"It's so noisy in here I can hardly hear you," Vito complained. "Why don't we have our drinks someplace quiet, like your room? We have a lot to catch up on. I'm sharing Zach's suite or I'd ask you there."

"Come to my place. We can kick off our boots, order dinner from room service, and just relax. Nothing exciting is going to happen here tonight."

"You're staying here too?"

"Well, obviously, Vito," Maggie said in amazement. "I have the Presidential Suite—my network knows how to treat a girl."

By the time dinner was served, Vito had made Maggie believe that it was her idea to make an hour-long special on the saving of *The Kalispell Chronicles.*

"Funny, it's not the movie itself as much as the human interest that I'm fascinated by," he said as they lay entwined, having postponed food for an intensely thorough reunion.

202

"The attempted murder-suicide? But, Vito, that's the story that everyone's covering. There's going to be so much written about it that people will be sick of it in ten days. I almost didn't bother to come, but the program department insisted."

"I agree, you've seen one attempted murder-suicide, you've seen them all, even with Melanie Adams as the victim. What interests me is what's going to happen next. Here's this actress who's enjoyed the easiest and quickest rise to stardom in film history. She's never had anything bad happen to her. Sure, she's a huge talent, sure, she's exquisite, but we both know those are things she was born with. And there's something so basically *unfair* about that. She'd led a charmed life. You weren't born to one and neither was I, and neither were most people."

"I'm listening."

"So I want to know *how* this trauma is going to affect her. She can't just carry on as if nothing happened, it's not humanly possible. One night in her bedroom she faced an ultimate nightmare, a murderous man with a gun, running her down, shooting at her *face*, narrowly missing killing her. That's something she'll never get over, *never*. She can't help but realize how close she came to dying, or at the very least losing her career. How has this experience changed her? I don't think anybody is ever going to get that story."

"Oh, tosh. Melanie'll hire round-the-clock bodyguards like a lot of people, and get some big German shepherds, and if she has some sense, which I doubt, she'll be a lot more careful about the guys she lets into her room at night. Maybe she'll go into therapy, like all the other stars, but that's not a story."

"Maggie, you amaze me." Vito tied a bedspread around his waist and picked up the phone to order dinner. He knew her so well he didn't have to ask what she wanted to eat.

"They said a half-hour wait," Vito announced. "Want a walnut or a piece of this delicious complimentary fruit?"

"Uh-huh. Why do I amaze you?"

"Because you can get a story no one else can get and increase your 'legendary power,' to quote those cover stories on you in *Time* and *Newsweek,* and all you're doing is lying there looking sexier than ever and saying the obvious things."

"The hell I am!" Her pride was stung.

"You just did. You took the point of view of the average housewife reading about this. So Melanie Adams almost got shot by a jealous lover. Yawn. I should be so lucky, look at her anyway, just as rich and gorgeous as ever. Yawn."

"Hmmm."

"What does that mean?"

"When I say 'hmmm' instead of 'bullshit,' that means you might be right. Tell me how you might be right. I'm too exhausted to figure it out for myself. You certainly haven't slowed down with age. What are you now, Vito, nineteen?"

"Forty-eight. I have slowed down a little, but you inspired me, Maggie."

"There's still hope for the human race. So tell."

"It's the eternal question of the before-and-after syndrome. We all know, or think we know, what Melanie was like before. We'll never know what she's like after. We'll never have a heart-to-heart talk with her, only what the PR people let us know . . . unless *you* get to her. We'll never know what it felt like for her to suddenly discover that the person she thought she was—one of the most celebrated and protected women in the world—was, in reality, nothing but a helpless cipher begging for her life. Will she ever feel strong again? Will all the bodyguards in the world take away her feeling of vulnerability? Those are your kind of questions, Maggie. I can hear you asking them. I can hear you asking her what she wants to be remembered for, what she wants as her epitaph."

"I'm still listening, but I haven't had that click yet."

"*Does she still have courage?* Not an actress kind of courage, but a human kind of courage. That's what I want to find out. And you can't ask that, you can only *show* that."

"How?"

"Zach has figured out how Melanie can do two of her biggest, longest, most emotional scenes, one with Paul Newman, the other with Clint Eastwood, lying on her hospital bed nine days from now. Only if she's willing, only if the doctors let him, of course, and he won't know until the last minute. These scenes would be draining under the best of circumstances, performed by an actress in the best of health. Now, Melanie absolutely does *not* have to

204

make this effort. Nobody expects it of her. Nobody would blame her if she used all her energy to recover from the shooting. Nobody would hold her accountable for the picture being shut down. And she knows all that. But will she make a try? Will she want to give it her best shot?"

"I don't know," Maggie said thoughtfully. "Personally I might, I might not, but I'm no Melanie Adams. You're right, Vito, it is interesting."

"It's going to be tough to make it happen," Vito went on, as if he hadn't heard her. "It'll take a miracle of timing from the crew. Zach's going to use the operating room as if it were a film set and work in there. Provided that Melanie has the guts and will-power to go through with it, she can save this picture single-handedly. Now *if* she can do that—she's got something special. If she even tries to do it and breaks down under the pressure—which I'm inclined to think she may, considering that she only got out of intensive care a day ago—*it's just as interesting as if she doesn't.* Not as heroic, but more human. In any case, don't tell me you wouldn't like to get all that behind-the-scenes action on television."

"What makes you think that they'd let my crew come in and get all this, if it's going to be so hard to do as it sounds?" Maggie was torn between suspicion and covetousness.

"Because Zach's the director, and the director calls the shots."

"Why does he need all that extra trouble, a television crew breathing down everyone's neck, shining their lights at everything that moves, asking annoying questions, getting in the way? He'll have a job and a half making the whole thing come together as it is."

"Because his future father-in-law will ask him nicely."

"Bullshit! Just what's in it for you, lover?"

"He'll be a lock for an Academy nomination for best director, who knows, maybe an Oscar. And that's good for my next picture. Very good. Plus, as I told you, Zach's family." If he said that once more, Vito reflected, he was going to start believing it himself.

"See, Vito, you can never fool me for long," Maggie crowed, delighted. "I knew you had to be getting something for yourself. But it's a hell of an idea and if you can fix it, lover, I'll do it and we'll run an hour in prime time."

"I'll get on the case after dinner," Vito promised her. "If it ever comes."

Just what, he wondered, *was* his next picture? He'd just guaranteed Zach and *Chronicles* a new treasure of publicity, he'd captured a possible Oscar-winning director . . . and he didn't have a single book or screenplay up his sleeve. Something would be magnetized to him, he thought, as he went back over to the bed. Why waste his energy on thinking about properties while Maggie was lying there purring so prettily at having figured him out? He and Susan Arvey had called it quits after Curt Arvey died suddenly and she became head of the Arvey Studio. They'd agreed that their business relationship was too important to spoil with sex, and there had been no one since then.

Room service, Vito reflected, had said a half an hour or more, which meant at least an hour before dinner. Maggie had learned some fascinating moves since *The WASP* ended their relationship. Was it all the fresh air, was it the Presidential Suite, or was it just Maggie that made him so horny?

The mass of the media, as Maggie had predicted, had gone home by the end of little more than a week's frenzied digging for details, endless informal interviews with everyone on the crew they could capture, many formal interviews with a patient Rose Greenway, a nastily impatient Roger Rowan, a fluffed-up Norma Rowan, and every doctor and nurse in the Kalispell Hospital. The rumors about Allen Henrick had surfaced and floated for a few days and eventually drifted to the bottom for lack of any hard proof. No one had been allowed inside the Kalispell Hospital, no one had been permitted closer to Melanie Adams than a photo taken of the window of her room, Newman and Eastwood declined to be interviewed, and Zach Nevsky had been too busy to talk to anyone from the press.

Maggie MacGregor had been as busy as Zach, but her loyal crew had the talent of invisibility and the forthcomingness of a religious order vowed to silence. In a fur hat pulled down to the collar of her fur coat, fur-lined waterproof boots, and sunglasses, Maggie hustled about on her errands almost unrecognized by the rest of the media, who took her continued presence as a compliment to the importance of the story on which they themselves were working.

All of the television equipment was moved, piece by piece, into the hospital at night and stowed away.

Zach planned to film one of the big scenes on a Friday and the other on a Saturday, waiting until the last possible dates before the schedule would cause him to lose Newman and Eastwood. Either Melanie could do it or she couldn't, but it would be too much of a risk, he decided, to ask her to work until she absolutely had to.

As he worked on the infinite number of details that went into bringing off his plan, he became aware that Wells Cope was in Kalispell, staying at a private house he had managed to rent. He was being allowed, at Melanie's request, to visit her for a few minutes each day. Cope kept out of Zach's way, never intruding on Zach's turf, never even having a drink in the Outlaw Inn bar, but he had been spotted here and there by dozens of the production staff.

"What's he up to, best guess?" Zach asked Vito.

"He can't be protecting his investment, Melanie doesn't owe him a thing anymore. Since that's the only motive I'd ever count on with Cope, I'd have to say he's more sentimental than I thought. Maybe he just came to visit a sick friend, for old times' sake. Hey, maybe he's in love with her. Ever think of that?"

"Give me a break, Vito."

"I'm as mystified as you are. So long as he stays out of the way, there's nothing we can object to. You said Melanie didn't seem upset by him, didn't you?"

"Yep. It's almost as if he isn't here, according to her. He brings flowers, asks her how she is, talks about the weather, and leaves."

"That's fucking sinister," Vito said after a considering pause.

"Be serious."

"I am serious, kid. He knows about our plan, I assume."

"Oh, sure, she didn't make any secret of it. He thinks it's a great idea, gives me a lot of credit, says it's what he'd do himself."

"That's even more sinister than I thought."

The day after Melanie had triumphantly completed the second of her big scenes, brilliantly directed by Zach Nevsky, she gave Maggie the long private interview for which Maggie had been preparing.

"Well?" Vito asked, as Maggie emerged from the hospital room, after her crew had hauled away all traces of their presence.

"There won't be a dry eye in the house. She made *me* cry." Maggie blew her nose indignantly. "What courage! You were right, Vito. Am I glad I listened to you. And don't worry, I have some terrific stuff with her and Nevsky, she gave him all the credit."

"Stick with me, kid."

"I sometimes . . . almost . . . wish I had. But it's too late now, isn't it, Vito?"

"Afraid so, my darling. But think how many times we'll meet again. And in what strange places."

"Nevsky, do you have a minute?" Wells Cope asked, approaching Zach outside of Melanie's room.

"Now I do," Zach said in irritation. "Been enjoying your stay in Kalispell, Cope?"

"More than you know. But I have a bone to pick with you."

"Do you now?"

"Indeed. When you first found out about the grips, you should have gotten rid of both of them immediately. *At once!* The minute you knew who they were. That was criminally stupid of you, Nevsky."

"Christ! That's easy enough to say in hindsight, Cope. You've got a bloody nerve."

"Hindsight? I had to do it on four pictures, Nevsky, and I expected you to have as much sense."

"You . . . you mean she makes a habit . . . ?"

"Oh, good Lord, you didn't believe her when she said it was the first time, did you?" he asked, looking at Zach's face. "By the Almighty, you did, you fell for it. Oh, really, what innocents they allow to make movies these days. She gets off, as they put it so delicately, on jealousy, Nevsky."

"She said . . ."

"She said she wanted to be free, didn't she? To be her own

208

woman? She's always said that. She thinks she doesn't want to be loved or needed, but that's just her way of saying she's the most selfish woman in the world. Melanie needs love . . . and then she wants to kill it, to grind it in the dust, to watch its death throes, to listen to its final cries of anguish. And then, when that's no longer amusing for her, she *needs* to repeat the process. Over and over. It's a very dangerous way to find pleasure. I've told her often enough, but she won't stop and I can't make her. So I get rid of the grips—it's always grips, thank goodness, never actors—and I keep getting rid of them until the picture's over. I must have bought summer places for half the shop stewards in the IA by now."

"Wells?" Melanie's voice called from inside the room. "Come in here, and bring Zach with you."

Melanie was sitting up in bed, still made up for Maggie's interview. "Did you tell Zach our news, Wells?" she asked.

"Not yet. I was getting around to it."

"When we finish here, I'm going to make another picture with Wells," she said in her imitable valuable cadence, her fabled climate of seduction. "He's the only person in the world who understands what an utter monster I am, and I'm the only one who understands what a twisted beast he is—and we forgive each other —so we might as well work together. I've thought about it a lot while I've been getting better—oh, don't look at me as if I've been hypnotized, Zach."

"He thinks I'm some sort of Svengali, darling."

"I need Wells and he needs me. But of course the rules are going to be different now. One film at a time, no more multiple-picture deals. Wells is going to let me choose the scripts I want to do, he's going to let me decide when I want to work and when I want to play, and he's never going to tell me what to wear to the Oscars."

"It sounds like the best of all possible worlds," Zach breathed incredulously.

"And I owe it all to you. That's what I told Maggie, on camera. I knew it would drive Wells mad with jealousy. He pretends not to care, but I know him too well to believe that."

Zach looked at Wells Cope and saw a quickly suppressed flicker of pain in the man's eyes, as if the bright point of a poignard had jabbed his skin. He could almost pity him, Zach thought. But only almost.

"You both deserve congratulations. I hope you have a long and happy life together."

"Thank you, Zach, darling. You *are* divine. Too bad I was put out of commission . . . I had such lovely plans for you."

" 'Only grips,' Wells?' " Zach asked. "Are you so very sure?"

10

By the last week in April, as soon as photography had been completed and the cast and crew had packed up and left Kalispell, Maggie MacGregor's much-publicized news special appeared on the network, drawing such enormous ratings that even Maggie was astonished.

To Gigi's surprise, instead of insisting on taking her out, Vito invited himself for dinner that Friday night. After dinner he announced that she and Davy were to join him in front of the television set, resolutely overturning Gigi's variety of flustered objections. Vito wore a convincing poker face that Gigi, more sensitized than anyone in the world, recognized as personal involvement. Her father was an incorrigible case, Gigi realized, with his way of appropriating the spotlight wherever it was. You might imagine this TV special was one of his own productions, she thought with the special emotion that Vito always aroused in her now, a combination of undemanding, amused love and acute clear-sightedness.

As she had matured from the girl of sixteen who barely knew her father, to the woman who had observed him more and more closely over the years in his many incarnations, usually over a meal they shared alone together, Gigi had become something of an expert on Vito Orsini, not, she realized, a subject that anyone was likely to grade her on, but nevertheless useful if you were his only child.

"Dad, why are you more interested in this show than you should be?" she attacked blandly, as they waited for the show to begin.

"Zach's going to direct *Long Weekend* for me this summer."

"I've never heard you mention anything called *Long Weekend*," Gigi said, ignoring Zach's name. "Where is it set—in the Congo, in Australia, in Patagonia?"

"In Malibu. A fast forty-five-minute drive from here, or three hours, depending on traffic. Never try to drive to Malibu after Thursday night or come back before Monday afternoon, hence the title of the screenplay and the rationale I gave Zach when he asked."

"Zach Nevsky?" Davy asked, curious. "What's he like to work with?"

Vito glanced swiftly at Gigi's face and got no message at all from her serene expression. She's even worse than I am, he thought, appalled, she's a disgrace. She shouldn't be allowed out on the loose without a warning sign around her neck. And she used to be such a good kid. Living with Billy all those years ruined her, he thought in a heartfelt moment of paternal feeling. This poor boy hasn't got a clue. Doesn't he realize he's absolutely wrong for Gigi, too normal, too nice? One day—and soon—he'll bore her, just as he's bored me, in spite of his sense of humor, in spite of his pleasantness. Undiluted worship, even of my own daughter, gets tedious. It's *unhealthy*, for God's sake.

"Considering his line of work," Vito informed Davy, "Zach's a hell of a good fellow. I can understand why Gigi and he were planning to get married, even if they did break up over some silly misunderstanding six months ago."

"DAD!"

"What?" Vito asked, all injured innocence. "You mean Davy didn't know all about him, so what's the big deal? You kids, you're so stiffly compartmentalized—hey, life is a snowball gathering snow, you roll where you roll, and everything you pick up is what makes you what you are."

"You sound like a bad imitation of a fake New Age guru," Gigi sputtered furiously. "Or Dershowitz defending a serial killer."

"Quiet, baby, Maggie's starting her introduction. I don't want to miss a word."

"Oh, fuck Maggie!" Gigi raged.

"Now, now, baby, Maggie's been fucked good and plenty, you don't have to feel sorry for her," Vito said calmingly, infuriating Gigi further.

"When did you start calling me 'baby,' you fraud?" she demanded, turning on her father.

"Shhh," he said, with a finger to his lips. "Let's have some quiet here."

For the next hour they watched, mesmerized, talking only during the commercials, as the behind-the-scenes footage unfolded and the interviews took place.

"Wow," Davy said when it was over, "if the rest of the picture is as good as that, it'll be the hit of the year."

"Oh, please," Gigi retorted, "Melanie was chewing the scenery."

"Gigi, you're nuts," Vito said, "she was fantastic, even I bow down to her. She had every bit as much strength and passion as those scenes demanded. I second Davy's 'wow.' She'll get an Oscar nomination for certain, with a good chance of winning."

"I didn't mean the scenes from the film," Gigi snorted. "They were . . . convincing—but spare me all the kissy-kissy stuff, the eyes filled with grateful tears while she was so sweetly whimpering to Maggie that she owed it all to Zach, I mean did she really have to cling to his hand and look at him so adoringly? He's just a director, for God's sake, he didn't create her talent."

"I don't think she was putting it on," Davy protested. "She meant every word of it."

"Oh, bull, she was sickening. And Zach looking down at her

as if Melanie had just given birth to the Christ Child and he was the Three Kings and all the animals rolled into one . . . it was a *stunt*, that's all. Now we know she can act lying down as well as standing up, what else is new? Doesn't every woman have to, sooner or later? I thought that part of the interview was grade-A bathos. I'm surprised Maggie didn't ask tougher questions. And for *Maggie* to tear up? She should be deeply embarrassed."

"Well," Vito said, getting up to turn off the television, "I'm just glad I signed Zach to direct while the getting was good. 'Bye, kids, I'm off. Thanks for dinner, Gigi. Come and kiss me good night."

"What the fuck are you up to, you rotten, meddling blabbermouth?" Gigi hissed angrily in his ear after she kissed his cheek.

"Me? I just wanted a home-cooked meal, baby."

"It's the last one you'll get in my house, you revolting old maid!"

"How come you never told me about Zach Nevsky?" Davy wanted to know as soon as the door had closed behind Vito. His eyes had narrowed into two thin question marks, and his beautiful mouth had thinned and aged.

"It's nobody's business," Gigi said. "Especially not my damn busybody father's."

"I've told you I've been in love twice before, but not seriously —I could never have hidden an involvement that almost led to marriage." He gave a sort of barking laugh that was the opposite of amusement.

"I have a different attitude about that than you do, Davy," Gigi said with a long look that took him in frowningly, intently, realistically. "What's past is past. We started out fresh. I wasn't interested in your other romances, but you insisted."

"Insisted?" He faltered at the word, and then shook his head stubbornly. "It's not insisting to tell someone you love the important things about yourself."

"I never asked you for details, never ever. But you were the one who was curious, right from that first day, remember? You were the one who asked me all those personal questions—"

"That was Archie and Byron's idea of a joke, and you know it perfectly well."

"You were certainly ready to take advantage of it," Gigi fumed.

"Let's get back to Nevsky," Davy said stubbornly, with a meanly calculating look. "How long were you together before you broke up with him?"

"That has absolutely nothing to do with anything!"

"Did the two of you live here? Is that why you have such a big place?"

"Davy! Shut up! I refuse to be tormented with questions!"

He was caught up in an ugly but utterly involuntary mood. "Don't kid yourself that I believed that story about your 'need for privacy'—I knew something was going on that you wouldn't share with me."

" 'Share'! Now there's a word I loathe and detest! Shall we invite in the neighbors and all get down on the floor and form a circle and 'share' our childhood traumas with each other, Davy? Is that what you want?"

"Stop trying to avoid my question." His voice was distorted by the sticky panic and hatefulness of a jealous lover. "All I want to know is why you never told me about Nevsky. Why did I have to hear about it from your father? I feel as if a part of . . . of *everything* . . . has been stolen, distorted, alienated . . . because you never wanted to tell me of your own free will."

"I still don't want to! Is that enough to satisfy you?"

"Gigi! Don't do this! You're going away tomorrow to work on The Enchanted Attic, and you know how I feel about that—the very least you can do is tell me about Nevsky." He grew more and more petty and demanding in his rending distress, unable to stop himself.

"Davy," Gigi said, "this is getting ridiculous and absurd—demeaning to both of us. You were miffed at Archie and By at the office Christmas party because they kissed me under the mistletoe . . . they kissed everybody, even you! Each time I've gone up to San Francisco for Indigo Seas, you've been suspicious of the Collins brothers, the most devoted family men I've ever met. You were jealous of Ben from the first time he came to the agency to look

215

over the setup, and you've been getting more and more jealous and possessive ever since, even though you know there's every reason for me to work on The Enchanted Attic since it was my idea."

"Don't you belong to me? At least a little, considering?"

"Considering that you want to marry me? I've told you and told you I have no intention of getting married. I'm not ready! I may never be! I don't belong to anyone! It's intolerable. Don't ask me questions like that!" Gigi vibrated with her need for freedom, her craving to extricate herself from an ownership she had never wanted.

"I can't help it," he pleaded, "it's not something I can decide to *not* feel, don't you realize that?"

"I don't want to mean so much to you! I should never have started this!"

"No," he flung at her, "*you* shouldn't have!"

"Oh!" she cried, stung. "You mean it was all my idea? You had nothing to do with it, you went along to be nice to me?"

"I fell for you from the instant I saw you. I didn't know I could love anyone as much—but you flirted like mad, you know goddamn well you did, you encouraged me right from the start. You let me make love to you *on the rebound*, didn't you, Gigi? On the rebound from Nevsky. That was why it all happened so suddenly. And you don't have to answer me, I know I'm right."

Davy's face was contorted with such grotesque suffering, such absorption in his darkened vision, such concentration on his pangs and perceptions of his injuries, that Gigi couldn't stay in the same room with him for another minute. He was intolerable. If he'd been a snake she'd have stomped on him without hesitation. A proposal of marriage was a handcuff.

"I've got to pack," she said, turning to go into her bedroom, "I'm exhausted and I don't want to continue this conversation. I'll try to call you from New York." She closed the door firmly behind her.

David Melville stood irresolutely in the center of the living room for a minute, and then, afraid of Gigi's reaction if she should come back and find him still there, went down the stairs to drive home.

Now he knew why she had never let him move in with her or been willing to move in with him; now he knew why she had never let him spend an entire night in her bed and wake up with her in the morning; now he knew why she insisted that he go home to sleep; now he knew why she only wanted to make love on the sofa in the living room; now he knew a million things he had never wanted to know, but had feared without daring to ask himself why.

Gigi was too angry to go to sleep at all that night. She filled a suitcase with jerky movements and then dumped its contents on the carpet in irritation, knowing that she was taking all the wrong clothes for New York. She rummaged through her closets in disgust, finding heaps of other clothes that were just as unsuitable. She tried, without interest, to invent new combinations of old things, turning California dressing into Manhattan dressing, and then jammed a selection of clothes into her suitcase at random, since it didn't matter what she looked like anyway on a strictly working trip that would be as short as she could make it.

She was so furious, as she got ready to go to bed, that her hands shook as she brushed her teeth. She should have known her father was up to something when he proposed coming to dinner at her place instead of picking a restaurant, something he'd never done, although she'd invited him often enough. He knew perfectly well she wouldn't want to watch that infernal show of Maggie's, but he'd been so persistent that she'd been trapped.

But to tell Davy about Zach! It wasn't a secret, why the hell should it be, but who'd asked her father to get into the act? What was he up to? What right did he have to be up to anything? But Vito never said anything without a reason. Granted, he didn't know about Davy's sick jealousy, but he'd talked about her and Zach as if they'd been children. "Some silly misunderstanding" indeed! Patricide had never been so understandable or desirable.

As far as Davy was concerned, it was over. Tonight had been the end. She wouldn't go through another one of these scenes. It was becoming impossible to remember the Davy with whom she'd had so much fun during those first months at FRB. Now, whenever she stopped at Bagel Central, the big food table in the main corridor of the agency, to trade office gossip with the group that invariably gathered there, he'd trail along as if by accident, and if he found her in conversation with any man, from the latest office boy to Archie himself, he'd join the talk, using all sorts of subtle but unmistakable body language to indicate that there was something more than creative teamwork between them.

She was as furious with herself as she was with Davy, Gigi admitted, several hours after she turned off the lights and fruitlessly settled down. She should never have had a personal relationship with anybody at the agency. Now they'd simply have to find new working partners. They could never work together in the same old easy, compatible way, after tonight. That would mean going to management and explaining enough to persuade Arch and By to break up the most productive team in the agency. But better to be embarrassed than tormented, she thought, better to be damned as unbusinesslike than to have to deal with a jealous man. He'd get over her; he'd already been in love twice before, by his own admission.

Anyway, what made her so foolish as to believe that such a faithful man existed? Maybe Abelard, but who knows what would have happened to his love for Heloïse if he hadn't been castrated? No way he wouldn't have dumped her for another pretty face sooner or later. Some local version of Melanie Adams would have come along, and Heloïse would have been toast. Not even history . . . just a footnote.

Gigi ground her teeth in disgust at the memory of Melanie, lying in bed, toying delicately with a single rose, the courageous, fragile, exquisite queen of convalescent Sarah Bernhardts, while Zach bent his rough, dark head before her in Magi-like worship. *Pul-eeze!* She knew Maggie was capable of stage-managing anything, but this was too fucking much, over the top, although the public would fall for it, not knowing the players as she did.

Or did she? She'd heard Zach's mordantly witty opinions on actresses often enough to know them by heart. But he'd always left room for a few rare exceptions. What if Melanie was one of them? Wells Cope had surrounded her with so much mystery that her personality was an enigma. *What if Melanie Adams was what she seemed to be?*

At that thought, Gigi turned on the light, got out of bed, and searched her bookcase. She needed something solid to read, something that would tide her over till morning. Jane Austen? Yes, Jane would be perfect, transporting her to a world in which sex was never mentioned, in fact didn't exist at all, and advertising and filmmaking were as undreamed of as disco dancing, miniskirts, or the entire state of California. The well-worn volume fell open to the first lines of one of her favorite novels. "It is truth universally acknowledged, that a single man in possession of a good fortune, must be in want of a wife."

You too, Jane! Gigi threw the book down as if it were on fire, went to the kitchen, and ate an entire box of corn flakes and milk, crunching down as fiercely as if they were made of coconut shells.

Ben Winthrop had sent a limo to take her to the Burbank Airport. He was on his way east anyway by private jet, he'd told her, to do some business in Philadelphia, so she might as well hitch a ride to New York, since they were both going to travel on Saturday. She'd have Sunday to catch up on jet lag before she started her round of meetings during the following week.

Gigi had become deeply involved in the development of the prototype Enchanted Attic, for Ben had virtually requisitioned her services from Victoria, who was in no position to refuse, since he had quickly approved an image-creating advertising campaign for the still-unopened chain, which was currently running in every prestige magazine published. According to Ben, the Mullers, the family who had started Kids' Paradise, had elected to retire to Sarasota, leaving their interest in the business in the hands of Jack Taylor, an experienced merchandise manager. Taylor, an ambitious middle-aged man, struck Gigi as someone who lacked imagination himself, but made up for it by providing her with an elaboration of details from which to choose. Ben had given her a free hand in creating the new stores, and although it frequently took Gigi away from her writing copy, she couldn't resist the opportunity to develop her concept to the fullest.

In New York, during the coming week, she had plans to meet with three interior decorators, each proposing a different scheme for the Enchanted Attics. Jack Taylor had contacted the creators of unusual toys and hand-made dolls from cities all over Europe and the United States, and they would be arriving to show her their merchandise. Silversmiths and other craftspeople of all types would be bringing her their designs for gift items made especially for the store, as would the designers of gift-wrapping paper and ribbons.

During Valentine's Day, Gigi had realized that the Enchanted Attic stores could carve out a second market, one that would be directed to men looking for romantic gifts at any time of the year. A woman of almost any age, she knew, was never indifferent to a really exquisite version of a little girl's present, and she was planning to be on the lookout for such items, from elaborate copies of Victorian dolls to exceptional stuffed animals. Gigi had taken a clue from Scruples and decided that The Enchanted Attics should be designed so that men would feel as welcome in them as women, and to counter the self-service policy of Toys "Я" Us, she had already decreed that each salesperson must be trained in an exact knowledge of appropriate gifts for every age and type of child. No one would ever be abandoned to wander the aisles wondering if something was too young or too old for a five-and-a-half-year-old tomboy.

But right now she didn't care if the first Enchanted Attic ever opened, Gigi thought. She'd finally managed to get fifteen minutes of numbed sleep just as the sun rose, and then her phone had started to ring, with Sasha and Billy full of last-minute advice about things she mustn't forget to do or buy or see while she was in New York. Billy had insisted that she be sure to wear no makeup on the trip and use moisturizer and lip gloss every hour to counteract the dry air aloft. As if she had the strength to worry about makeup, Gigi thought as she put on the gray sweatshirt and matching sweatpants that were the most comfortable things she owned.

Although it was her first trip in a private jet, Gigi got into the plane with the blankly languid look of someone who had never traveled in any other way. She drooped into her armchair and looked blindly out the window while Ben, looking absurdly collegiate in a Dick-Stover-at-Yale letterman sweater over an open-necked shirt, set himself up at the other end of the large main cabin, worked quickly on a computer, and ignored her. Gigi was conscious of extremely discreet understated luxury, of quiet, undemanding colors, of a steward who brought her tea and cookies and fruit, but as far as she was concerned, the interior of a private jet was merely a long, narrow room in the sky.

"You look droopy," Ben said, looking up from his work. "Do you want to lie down? The sofas aft make up into beds. Maybe you could nap."

"Oh yes," Gigi said gratefully. That made the difference. A nap. She had to have one. The world's most expensive nap. How much a minute, she tried to estimate, as she took off her clothes, put on an oversized silk pajama top that the steward had put out for her, and slipped under the covers. How much a minute? Who the hell gave a good goddamn, so long as the bed remained horizontal?

Gigi was still sleeping when the jet landed, refueled, and took off again. About three hours later she woke up, splashed her face with water, brushed her teeth, put on one of the bathrobes she found hanging in the closet, and staggered into the cabin, trailing Sulka crimson silk sashed at the waist.

"My God, I've slept almost all the way to New York! What time is it, Ben?"

"L.A. time?"

"You're right, it's a silly question. When do we land?"

"Sometime in the afternoon, depending on the winds." His smile seemed even more deliberately considered, more slowly introspective than usual, and Gigi's sense of his presence, as intent in repose as in action, took on an added weight because the two of them seemed suddenly very alone in a well-lit capsule outside of which lay an unthinkable vastness of space.

"Ben, I'm a little disoriented," Gigi said with a shade of impatience. "I'm not used to taking a nap in the middle of the day, so riddle me no riddles."

"I'm serious."

"Oh, stop!"

"You've been skyjacked."

Gigi looked at Ben Winthrop carefully. She had grown to know him well during the last few months of working with him, and raging whimsy had never been characteristic of him. Nor overstatement. He had a sense of humor, but he didn't make ridiculous jokes. In many ways his personality had the gift of perfect pitch.

"All right, I've been skyjacked," she said agreeably, sitting

221

down in the chair by his side. "Why not, after all? It's the week-end, people are supposed to indulge in mindless, healthy recreation. I'd still like to know where we're going, or are we flying around in circles?"

"Venice," he said. The furrows in his forehead deepened slightly and his basic blue, trustworthy eyes looked down his big, aristocratic, bumpy Boston nose at her with a gleam of some rare and precious amusement. He had never looked so much like a college girl's fantasy of the significantly sexy young English professor who would invite her into his office to discuss improving her grade on top of his desk, Gigi thought briefly, or would it be more comfortable under the desk?

"Venice Beach?" Gigi asked. "We can have dinner at Chinois on Main."

"Venice, the state of mind."

"Venice . . . Italy?" Her voice was so cautious it descended an octave lower than usual.

"It occurred to me that for your first skyjacking the destination should be worthy of the occasion."

"Venice!" Sparks of incredulous joy, tiny bursts of emerald fireworks, filled her eyes.

"So, no objections?" He sounded more anxious than she'd ever heard him.

"I don't have anything to wear!" Gigi wailed. "Oh damn, why didn't you warn me?"

"It wouldn't be a skyjacking if I'd warned you," Ben said reasonably.

"How come you *didn't?*" Gigi asked, realizing that her first reaction, although normal to her in any other travel surprise, was perhaps not the first matter of business. "Why'd you think you had to fool me?"

"Would you have come if I'd said 'Let's go to Venice'?"

"Maybe . . . I don't know. Why not, after all?"

"I didn't think so, somehow. You'd have had too much time to think about it. The agency would have had to be informed, Billy would have told you of the perils involved in traveling with a man—"

"What perils?" Gigi asked, her eyebrows disappearing into her bangs, the tilted tip of her nose almost bristling at the thought of

222

such an impossibility. "Billy would never say anything so boring and conventional, goodness, you don't really know her at all."

Gigi clearly remembered that one kiss Ben had given her on the night they'd met, one kiss that she had felt, so absurdly, was in some way seriously dangerous. He'd never tried to repeat it on any of the occasions they'd worked together on The Enchanted Attic, and by now he must have forgotten the whole strange moment. She felt totally safe with him.

"Perils indeed," she scoffed. "This is the twentieth century."

"Unless you're in a perilous mood."

"I don't even know what mood I'm in," Gigi said, the upturned corners of her mouth lifting into a considering smile that slowly deepened into a fine intensity, "except hungry, but that's not a mood."

"We can have dinner whenever you like. I was waiting till you woke up."

"Oh, Ben, I feel so divinely, beautifully, utterly free! Nothing but sky outside, Venice waiting out there somewhere . . . what more could a girl want?"

"Oh . . . quite possibly . . . a passport."

"My God!" Gigi's hand flew to her throat. She'd never owned a passport.

"There'll be one waiting at the airport in Italy . . . an old buddy in the State Department managed it."

"What a well-planned skyjacking," she mocked him. "Are you in the CIA?"

"No, but my old buddy probably is. He went to Yale instead of Harvard, which I always consider a suspicious sign."

"Why are you going to so much trouble for me, why are you being so adorable?" Her face was all vividness.

"Because I want to. Because it's fun. Because you need a vacation and so do I."

"Good answers. Consider them accepted." Gigi yawned, stretched herself out so that her back touched the armchair only at her shoulders and her rump, her bare legs stuck out on the carpet as far as they could go. Her head was thrown all the way back and her arms dangled limply.

"A little champagne wouldn't be unwelcome," she announced, gleefully and imperiously. "I'm on vacation now."

As soon as the jet landed at Marco Polo Airport, an official from the United States Embassy in Rome provided Gigi with her passport. The customs officials made haste to clear Ben and Gigi, and they walked down a wooden pier and stepped down onto the deck of a long, sleek speedboat, with a hull of gleaming honey-colored wood, that was waiting for him. Ben shook the captain's hand and greeted him as Giuseppe, as a deckhand heaped the luggage inside the cabin of the boat.

Gigi looked around eagerly. There was nothing to see but a great deal of ordinary sky, a very wide, very flat stretch of greenish water dotted by a few flat islands, and a blurred row of some sort of human habitation in the far distance. The air smelled vaguely salty, but not like sea air.

"Where's Venice?" she asked Ben.

"That way," he answered, pointing to the flat line of buildings in the distance. "We really should have arrived by boat, that's the grand classic way, but they put the airport out here, in the aptly named *Laguna Morta*."

"You should have kidnapped me and brought me here by yacht. I want my first impression to be grand and classic."

"Wait. Just wait."

The speedboat started suddenly, and Gigi almost lost her balance.

"Do you want to go into the cabin?" Ben asked. "It's windy."

"I'm standing right here, Ben Winthrop, until Venice shows up. I've seen enough paintings and photographs to know it when I see it," Gigi retorted as the wind whipped her hair away from her face. She put on the sunglasses she always kept in her purse, and held tightly to a railing, while Ben stood behind her. The journey over the wide lagoon was swift, but as they approached close enough to see the buildings clearly, the captain slowed the boat considerably.

"That's so we literally don't make waves," Ben explained. "We have to proceed at a crawl once we're near Venice. One of the reasons it's sinking is the way the water used to be allowed to pound the stones."

The dilapidated houses grew slowly larger, and flapping

clotheslines strung with newly washed shirts and dresses were the first visible detail of *La Serenissima*, "the most serene," the Bride of the Adriatic. Soon the speedboat entered a narrow canal and Gigi turned eagerly from one side to another, seeking out picturesque details, but finding only a vast number of cats, several unremarkable stone bridges, and hordes of screaming children. They turned a corner into a larger canal, and Gigi, dancing with impatience, was outraged to see that it was filled by a wide dirty barge piled high with crates of soft drinks and bottled water, clearing the sides of the dirty stones only by inches.

"Don't tell me," Ben said. "We should have taken a helicopter from the airport. How come I didn't think of that? Because there aren't any."

"Do we *have to* follow this thing?"

"We do."

"Isn't there a shortcut?"

Ben laughed at her face as their *motoscafo* slowed down even further. "When they built the canals they built them for the width of gondolas. You can't be in a hurry in Venice. You can run up a mountain in Nepal or dash across the Great Wall of China or even try to speed around the Place de la Concorde, but going through here, you can't move faster than the slowest boat in front of you, so sit down and wait."

Grinding her teeth, Gigi followed his advice. They were proceeding inch by inch. She shut her eyes in frustration. This could go on forever.

"Open up," Ben said, nudging her.

"Is that barge gone?"

"I promise," he said, amused.

Gigi opened her eyes and found herself floating on the Grand Canal. It was the most astonishing moment of her entire life. She was in the middle of a bewilderment, a dazzlement, a prism of every soft color, a composition of water and reflections unrivaled in the universe for gaiety and charm and iridescence, but above all for the fact that it simply *is*. She was stricken to the heart by the actual existence of the Grand Canal. She looked around her in speechless awe, feeling as if the speedboat had been transformed into a cloud-craft, confused and enchanted by the vistas of palaces and domed churches and darting water craft, all open to the harmony of pure radiance, the bath of light of the silvery, rosy shell of the treasuring sky.

"I know," Ben said, and put his hand on her shoulder. "You can never get used to it, no matter how often you come back."

She couldn't answer him. It was too much. Tears came into her eyes and traveled down her cheeks. He gave her his handkerchief silently. The *motoscafo* bobbed up and down, moving slowly as it crossed to the center of the widest part of the canal, turned right, and proceeded down the canal until it came to a landing stage of an exceptionally narrow palazzo with a many-windowed, faded, immensely frivolous pink and white stone face. A large, glossy black gondola with green velvet cushions was tied up to a green, white, and black striped pole.

Gigi gave her eyes a final wipe and looked up. "Is this the hotel?"

"Not exactly."

"Are we landing here?"

"We are."

"Are we visiting someone?"

"No."

"Are we spending the night here?"

"Yes."

"So this must be your own humble place?"

"That's right."

"You know, Ben, I'm beginning, after all, to wonder exactly what Billy would have said."

"Are you sorry you couldn't ask her?"

Gigi considered for a minute. Finally she said, without answering his question, "Somehow I feel as if I'm even more on vacation than before."

"How long have you owned your *palazzetto*?" Gigi asked as she and Ben watched the sunset from the deep balcony on the top floor. The interiors powerfully reflected the spirit of Venice without trying in vain to re-create it faithfully. It was, in a highly sophisticated sense, a deliberate folly. The rooms, tall and narrow and only two to each floor, had been intentionally underdecorated, the polished floors left largely bare, the fabrics simple, in order to highlight the

226

view of the Grand Canal, visible from every window. Yet, here and there, great gilded mirrors and a few extraordinary pieces of furniture, much of it inlaid in mother-of-pearl or inspired by the shape of shells, evoked far more decorative and eccentric centuries during which Venetians had filled their homes with loot from the entire known world.

Ben's room, balcony, and bath occupied the top floor of the palazzo, and the guest suite took up the floor beneath; the second floor, with the highest ceilings of them all, had been turned into a salon-library on the garden side and a dining room on the canal side. The pantry, kitchen, and servants' quarters were all on the first floor. All the windows at the back of the palazzo looked out on a tiny dream of a wisteria-wreathed garden filled with beds of miniature white oleander trees shaped into topiary balls, bordered by pink geraniums. The walls of the garden were latticed by climbing honeysuckle. The narrow house, which Ben told her Venetians insisted on calling a *palazzo*, although it was only a small palace, a *palazzetto*, made Gigi feel as if she were in a stage set that possessed all the amenities for living, a contemporary sketch based on a thousand years of history.

"About ten years," he told her. "I got a tip that it might possibly be for sale from a close friend, a fellow member of the Save Venice Committee, and I bought it sight unseen the same day . . . the same hour. It was in terrible shape, it took about three years to make the place habitable. I kept flying over for the weekend to check it out, and each time I found things in more confusion than before, with scaffolding and green canvas completely covering the façade, and the architect and contractor screaming at each other. I didn't know what I'd bought. Then one day I came and found that the scaffolding had disappeared, I could see the stonework for the first time, there wasn't a leak or a damp spot anywhere, an elevator had been installed, the floors and walls had been restored, and even the stove in the new kitchen was working."

"How long did you stay?"

"I had to leave for New York the next day," Ben said ruefully.

"You mean you only spent one night here?" Gigi was incredulous.

"Not even that. The place was empty, there wasn't so much

as a sleeping bag or a bottle of wine. I spent the night across the canal, over there to the right, at the Gritti. I was awake till dawn, hanging out of the window looking longingly at my empty *palazzetto* like a disappointed lover."

"What did you do next?" She was enthralled by a Ben Winthrop she hadn't known existed.

"Before I left the next morning I hired a decorator, hired a caretaker and his wife, arranged to install them in their own apartment on the first floor, and the next time I came I gave them a day's warning and stayed for an entire week. That's when I bought the motorboat and hired Giuseppe, the captain. It's not the only way to get around, but it's the most convenient."

"How much time a year do you spend here?"

"Almost a month, off and on, in short visits, whenever I have time."

"I just don't get it," Gigi said, shaking her head in puzzlement. "Why do you need to keep a whole establishment running when you're here so seldom?"

"I don't need it," Ben said, "I don't need it at all, but *I want it*. And it's worth it to me because it's a piece of Venice. I own part of the place that makes me happiest in all the world. *If I could, I'd own all of it.*"

"So just . . . being here . . . staying in a hotel wouldn't be enough?"

"Never," Ben said, looking across the canal to the lights illuminating the Byzantine domes, nine hundred years old, of St. Mark's Basilica. *"Never."*

He turned to Gigi and spoke intently. "It's the fashion to say that Venice isn't what it used to be, that it's merely one vast, decaying museum, only a sight for badgered tourists. For hundreds of years, writers have written tens of thousands of words lamenting the disappearance of the glory of Venice. They complain that there are no more Doges, they moan that Napoleon chopped down the trees in the Piazza San Marco, they're personally offended that Byron and Casanova aren't roaming the streets. It's as stupid as wishing you lived in the good old days of Elizabeth the First. Why didn't those writers just *use their eyes*, for God's sake, just walk across the Rialto and pinch the vegetables, have a coffee at Florian's or a drink at Quadri's, gossip, laugh at the pigeons, and enjoy themselves as the Venetians always have? Why couldn't they forget that this place is *Venice*, with all the impossibly romantic expectations that word arouses, and simply love it for itself, its unique, imperfect self? Today those carping writers are all dead and Venice is still the undisputed glory and wonder of Western civilization—still *alive*."

Gigi looked at him in amazement. Ben was exalted, transfigured. No trace remained of the businessman who could observe a stretch of green fields and acres of woods and see the perfect location for a mall.

"Signor Ben?" said a woman's voice. The caretaker's wife had appeared, preceded by a small knock. "The gondolier wants to know if you require him tonight."

"Ask him to wait, please, Maria."

"I suppose a full-time gondolier comes with the territory," Gigi observed.

"Don't get carried away," Ben laughed. "I have my choice—either my apartment in New York, my ski lodge in Klosters, and my little place in Venice, my jet, and my boat—*or* a full-time gondolier."

"You mean you had to draw the line somewhere?"

"We're not talking about drawing the line, we're talking about either one or the others . . . all the others. The gondolier works by the hour."

"Then I'd better get dressed," Gigi said, reluctant to stop looking at the marvels revealed by the darkness, which, as it fell and the moon rose, made Venice grow younger by the minute. "His meter's running."

She'd had no idea of how frightfully rich Ben was, jet, palazzo, shopping malls and all, Gigi thought, until he'd mentioned the gondolier. He wasn't joking about employing the man on an hourly basis. You had to be rich far, far beyond rich, like Billy, to cherish one meaningless little economy. Billy insisted that her chefs' assistants use every roll of kitchen paper down to the very last sheet that clung to the brown-paper holder. It made her feel real—earthy, sensible, reassuringly normal—she'd once admitted.

Trying to hurry, Gigi realized that when she'd packed she'd

clearly been in some sort of fugue state, as some shrinks would say, or, popularly speaking, out of her mind. There was nothing there, in all the crumpled bits and pieces she'd snatched out of her closet, that could be combined except a plain skinny black sweater, a black floor-length skirt, a wide black belt, and a pair of jet earrings. She put them on and surveyed the result with dismay. Her first night in Venice, and she looked ready for a black-tie funeral.

Rummaging through her suitcases in a final hopeless search, Gigi came across a small packet wrapped in tissue paper that Billy had given her. She pulled out a many-times-folded, tiny fabric bundle. She had to keep unfolding it seven separate times before she could spread it all out on the bed, a huge triangle of black net, flecked in a thousand places with gold threads embroidered into tiny squares and trimmed on all three sides with eight inches of scalloped gold lace. It was the scarf of a Geoffrey Beene evening dress that Billy had worn several times. There wasn't a wrinkle in the entire marvelous spill of it.

Excitedly, Gigi experimented with it. It worked as a mantilla, it worked as a sash, it worked as a cape or a sarong, a serape or a blouse. If you had the right underwear, it could work as a short strapless evening dress. But it worked best as Geoffrey Beene had planned, as a scarf simply *flung*—for that was the only right way to put it on—around her shoulders.

Gigi put on two more coats of mascara, applied fresh lip gloss, brushed her hair until it fairly spun off her head, flung the scarf over her sweater, and ventured forth, Venetian to the tips of her black velvet bedroom slippers, for she had even forgotten her evening shoes.

"What about all the people waiting for me in New York?" Gigi asked Ben the next morning, as they sat on yellow and green wicker chairs in the sun in front of Florian's and listened to the old musical comedy tunes played by the band in front of the café next door.

"I postponed them all. They won't expect you till you let them know you're on your way."

"What about the agency? What if they call me at the hotel I'm supposed to be staying in?"

"My secretary will field all calls and telex you here, there's a telex in my dressing room. You can dial direct back to California, nobody will know the difference."

"So if you push me in the canal, and I drown and disappear, it will be one of the unsolved mysteries of all time."

"I absolutely adore the joyous way your mind works." He grinned at her. She was wearing some of the new clothes she'd bought at the Versace, Valentino, and Krizia boutiques, with the rest filling shopping bags at her feet. Venice, the heart of it, was, among other things, Ben thought, the world's first and most beautiful shopping mall, and the men who'd paid for it had been the greatest merchants the world had ever known.

"There was this scary English movie . . ." Gigi's voice trailed off. That movie had been about another sinister, gloomy Venice, not this miracle of April sun and little children running around on the marble pavement, with pigeons eating out of their hands and colors like a rippling pool playing over the façade of St. Mark's, and the four bronze horses who pranced before it and winged lions everywhere she looked and the sound of bells always in the air.

"How long are we staying?" she asked.

"As long as you like. It's still only April now . . . the high season doesn't end till mid-October, and some people prefer Venice out of season. They say winter is the time to get to know Venice like the Venetians."

"Be serious. I know how busy you are."

"Don't ask me to be serious today," Ben said, "I'm much, much too happy."

"Because you're in Venice?"

"Because I'm in Venice, because the band at the café always plays the music I like, because we're going to the Accademia after lunch at the Danieli roof garden to see exactly one picture, my favorite Giorgione—you can look at it for as long as you like, for hours if that's your pleasure, but then we're getting the hell out of there because I'm following my Rule of One about how to live in Venice—every day you have to see one work of art, *only* one, spend at least an hour on the water, eat at least one fine meal, and buy one thing, it doesn't matter what. I'm happy to be here with a friend who's totally in my power because she can't go anywhere without me or she'd get lost; because there's polo at the Lido this afternoon if we're in the mood; because there weren't any telexes this morning; because they've started to play 'Tales of the Vienna Woods,' which always makes me feel like dancing—"

Ben took Gigi's hands, lifted her to her feet, and waltzed her off across the Piazza San Marco, around and around, scattering the pigeons and delighting the children and amusing the waiters and scandalizing the tourists and finally convincing the musicians that the new season had truly begun.

The next three days were spent according to Ben's Rule of One, and by the time they were over, Gigi felt she knew the city better than if she'd had a great guidebook and had spent every minute dutifully following its recommendations of the most important things to do and see. She had learned in her bones the essential rhythm of the city, and she knew the euphoria of Venice would always be there for her now, retrievable at will, no matter where she was or how old she grew.

As Gigi sat down to breakfast on the morning of her fourth full day in Venice, she found herself unexpectedly alone in the dining room on the second floor of the palazzo. She drank her orange juice slowly, fascinated as ever by the patterns of the busy water traffic immediately outside, patterns she was beginning to recognize, almost to anticipate. She finished her juice, put down the glass, and suddenly realized that her growing familiarity with Venice was matched by her growing confusion about Ben Winthrop. Dressed in colorful Italian sweaters and casual trousers by day, and elegant Italian suits at night, he wore them with such ease that his normal look, his still slightly Bostonian, professor-mixed-with-businessman look, had disappeared so entirely that she could barely believe he'd ever possessed it. His longish hair still had a mind of its own, refusing to grow in the direction his barber had planned, but his gray eyes held infinitely more blue than she'd ever realized before, perhaps because of the constant reflection of sea and sky, but the change in his appearance was merely a detail compared to his attitude.

It wasn't merely that Ben was in a devil-may-care mood, or that he was a busy man deliberately creating a rare free place in his life in which to relish every minute of a holiday, she reflected; it went deeper than that. Was it because he'd lost that "game face," that lack of self-revelation which was so much a part of his business persona? Since they'd been in Venice he hadn't, for a minute, struck her as the tough cookie she'd judged him to be when they'd first met, a gracefully and purposefully expressionless man who looked at everything with thoughtful consideration, his eyes weighing and judging.

Ben had become a boy, Gigi thought, a lean, powerful boy, his face getting tanner every day, a boy just under puberty, not quite thirteen, with learning and appreciation of art beyond his years, a boy in his enthusiasms, a boy in his unpredictability, a boy in his lack of self-consciousness, and, most of all, a boy in his relation to her. He hadn't shown the slightest inclination to kiss her again; when he grasped her to steady her arm as she climbed in and out of the *motoscafo* or a gondola, it was with a boy's helpful hand; when he stood protectively behind her on the slow-moving but aggressive ferry boat, the *vaporetto* that was as crowded as a subway, it was with a boy's sheltering body. When they returned to the palazzo at night after dinner, he escorted her to the door of her rooms and left her with a boy's kiss on the top of her head; when she appeared dressed in her new clothes, he greeted her with a boy's innocent admiration.

But how was it possible to reconcile this comrade, this pal, this gallant boy, with the very adult man whose kiss, so possessive and fierce, had frightened her only months ago?

As Gigi was reflecting on Ben in the dining room, he had stopped dressing to spend a minute on the subject of Gigi, to take stock of their situation, before the beginning of another day with her.

He congratulated himself that from the moment he and Gigi had started on their flight to Venice he had managed to maintain the flawless façade of a companion and buddy. Not once had he allowed himself to take advantage of Gigi's moments of high emotion or excitement, or even of the underlying condition of blissfully surprised joy in which she accepted all the details of the romance and beauty of their surroundings. He had *given* her Venice, Ben told himself, Venice at its most desirable, and, as he had planned, asked nothing in return, behaved like the best damned brother or uncle any girl could invent in her wildest dreams. He had not permitted himself to react a single time to the closeness and warmth of her marvelous animal presence, he had treated her a thousand times less personally than he would treat a glorious beast, if he owned one, although his hand burned whenever he touched her and he was overcome, a hundred times a day, by longings to grab her by her sweet, fragrant cap of hair and draw her close and cover her with kisses. Each day he had maintained his determina-tion to turn his lips resolutely away from her, and each day she had remained unperturbed, unquestioning, finding, as far as he could tell, his behavior perfectly natural.

What woman could have resisted the challenge he'd set her, he wondered, thoroughly dissatisfied with himself. He'd planned this trip to Venice with all the attention to detail he would have devoted to an important business deal, after letting months go by in which he and Gigi had worked together efficiently, lulling any ideas about his motives that Gigi might have entertained after that one mistaken kiss he'd been too quick to give, that kiss to which she'd reacted so badly, that kiss that had shaken his pride.

Gigi had accepted the fact that he'd trapped her into a trip to Venice with a certain swagger, a fearlessness. But, once established here with him, what woman on earth could not have been piqued by his seeming imperturbability in the face of what she *had* to know were her charms?

If Gigi were the kind of woman who played sophisticated games, he would have admired the perfection of her performance, but Gigi was what she seemed to be, he'd bet anything on it, and even if she had tried to, she would be unable to deceive anyone as experienced as he. Her reactions were pure, they welled up as soon as she felt them. How was it humanly possible that she hadn't made some effort, at the very least, to get some idea of how he felt about her? To ruffle him, to pierce his equanimity, to upset his self-composure. *To make him make his move?* All of the tests he'd set for her, all of the traps, had failed because she hadn't noticed them, but had gone blithely about her business of enjoying what-ever careful plans he made so that each day had its own rounded perfection. Yet, Ben thought, he had baited the hook so very well that it was simply inconceivable that this fish wouldn't bite.

And now the telex had suddenly sprung to life after days of blessed silence. "Just what I need!" Ben exclaimed bitterly, ripping the paper out of the machine so roughly that it tore.

Just what is it that you *do* want? Gigi asked herself as she munched her second piece of toast. You wanted freedom, and you have it in wild abundance; you hate possessiveness, and here there is no one who is trying to own you; you wanted to escape from the persecution of constant sexual tension, day and night, and you've acquired the company of the world's most correctly behaved and best-informed tour guide; you loathe being the object of jealousy, and now you have a boy who treats you like Huck Finn—shouldn't this be perfect, you ridiculous, perverse nut case? To be whisked off to Venice without obligation—to how many women in the world had that happened? Or could it be possible . . . that Venice without a little . . . flirting . . . was not Venice as it should be, not Venice whole? Did the nature of the city demand an undercurrent of flirtation, just as it demanded the ebb and flow of the tides, without which the canals would stagnate?

Gigi was aware that she was a flirt by nature, but she had not allowed herself to flirt with Ben Winthrop, not for a second. You do not flirt with a skyjacker who is also a major client, a man whose hospitality you are accepting under circumstances that are, as she didn't need Billy to tell her, highly compromising, and, above all, a man who has kissed you once, kissed you unforgettably, dangerously, passionately, so that if you flirted with him you'd be asking for trouble. Ben had his Rule of One, and she had hers: No flirting with Ben Winthrop.

And yet, and yet . . . when they had taken the long *vaporetto* trip up and down the entire winding length of the Grand Canal, each time the ferry stopped, bumping clumsily into one of the many floating landing stages, and Ben had been watchful to hold her upright, she'd yearned to lean back against him, turn her head, nestle into his chest, and stay there, instead of pulling away as soon as he'd cushioned the shock of the landing. Each time she'd watched him drink a cappuccino, she'd ached to hold his free hand; when a sudden brief shower had sent them into a church portico to take refuge, she'd just been able to resist the impulse to button her head inside Ben's oversized jacket; when he glanced down at a check she looked at his eyelids and thought only of touching them with her fingertips—but that wasn't flirting, Gigi assured herself, it was a natural need for tactile contact with a member of the opposite sex, something any woman would feel in this outrageously over-the-top city in which romance seemed a duty. A man and a woman in Venice together without a touch of romance was unthinkable. Even unpatriotic, considering her half-Italian heritage.

The only men she had flirted with in Venice—the only men who'd flirted back—were every waiter in every restaurant, Giuseppe, the *motoscafo* captain, Guido, the gondolier, and—by far the most satisfactory—Arrigo Cipriani.

Yesterday, before lunch, she and Ben had been suddenly beset by a craving for a real American hamburger. They'd strolled to Harry's Bar, the only place in Europe where it was properly made. There she'd met the owner, a friend of Ben's, and one of the great, subtle, almost subcutaneous flirts of the world, Gigi quickly realized, in spite of his dignified mien. By the time lunch was over he'd given her his red necktie, his signature, the only kind anyone had ever seen him wear, to sport with the navy blazer and white shirt she was wearing with her jeans, whipping a replacement out of his pocket. This morning she'd put the tie on again, liking its jaunty look, and it hung around the neck of a sky-blue cotton shirt that she was wearing under a Burberry argyle sweater she'd bought yesterday.

Thank goodness she had her charge cards with her, Gigi thought, as she ate her breakfast on the morning of the fourth full day in Venice. It was equal to Beverly Hills in temptations, the dollar was twice as strong as the lira, and most boutiques were open seven days a week. Two days ago she'd been unwary enough to linger outside the window of Nardi, the most famous of the Venetian jewelers, and Ben had dragged her inside to try on the huge emerald drop earrings set in diamonds that had caught her eye.

When she'd explained that she couldn't let him buy them for her, that a skyjacking, even the most luxurious one, simply did not include gifts of precious jewelry, he'd been obviously crestfallen,

236

but later in the day, when she'd allowed him to buy her a small, Swiss-made traveling manicure set, he'd been as pleased as he'd been disappointed at not being allowed to spend a fortune on the earrings. He could pay ten gondoliers for a century of full-time service for the price of those earrings. Didn't he have *any* sense of the value of money?

"Damn!" Ben came into the dining room and sat down next to her. "A telex came last night. I should rip that machine out of the wall."

"Do we have to go back?"

"Oh, nothing like that, that can't happen unless a mall explodes—I left instructions. This is something else. I'm involved in shipping, and suddenly there's a chance to pick up three freighters if I go out to Mestre this afternoon. The owner's badly overextended himself and he needs to sell them immediately for the value of the scrap metal. If I don't get them this morning, someone else will this afternoon."

No, Ben hadn't lost a sense of the value of money, Gigi thought, it just wasn't her kind of sense. Scrap metal—what a reason to interrupt a day in Venice!

"I'll leave you here with Guido as your chaperone, and I'll be back in a couple of hours," he continued.

"How far is Mestre?" she inquired.

"Half an hour tops, right on the mainland. I'll go to the railroad station by speedboat, have a car and driver meet me at the station, look over the ships and be back in time for a drink before lunch."

"Why can't I go with you?"

"To Mestre? It's totally hideous. Gray, grimy, industrial. You shouldn't waste a minute there."

"Really," Gigi insisted. "I need to see something hideous, just for a change of pace."

"Then I'd love it, but don't say I didn't warn you."

At the gate to the shipyard, Gigi and Ben were met by a guide who gave them each a numbered bicycle, a hard hat, and a pair of "safe shoes," like Dutch clogs with iron tops and rubber bottoms, that they put over their own shoes before they were allowed into the shipyard proper. The freighters were in a drydock about a mile away, and everyone used bicycles to get around the enormous yard, in which large metal ships of all kinds were being built nonstop in a terrible din.

At the drydock they stopped on the concrete and looked at the freighters on the vast floor of the drydock, far below them, just above water level, three identical, unpainted gray metal ships. They looked sad, Gigi thought, not only because they had been hauled up out of the water so that the vast amount of hull space below the waterline was visible, but because they were about to be torn apart and chopped up. Yet she could tell that their bows and sterns were elegantly, even poetically, designed, and there was something strikingly pleasant to the eye about the sweep of their lines, something as strong and graceful as their destiny was pathetic.

"Where *is* that owner, Severini?" Ben asked impatiently. "I want to finish this fire sale and get back by noon."

Within a few minutes two men sped up and jumped quickly off their bikes. They were obviously father and son, both exceptionally graceful, well-dressed, and equally grim.

"Mr. Winthrop, please do forgive me, I was on a long-distance call and then, to my horror, I found that all but the smallest bikes were gone. May I present my son, Fabio? He is a naval architect. We had to requisition these bikes, or we'd still be standing at the gate."

"I'm glad to meet you both," Ben said. "This is Miss Orsini, a hopelessly curious tourist."

"One would have to be, to come to Mestre," said the senior Mr. Severini.

As she shook hands with him, Gigi felt his pain, his panic, and his decency. He was a man in very grave financial trouble, no matter how well dressed. She and Fabio Severini walked away a short distance so that the business discussion could proceed in private.

"A naval architect?" Gigi asked. "In other words, you design ships?"

"Yes," Fabio Severini answered. "These three ships were my first commission. After my academic training, I was lucky enough to be granted an apprenticeship under the great Giuseppe de Jorio, in Genoa. Of course, I would never have attracted such a large commission if these ships had not been built by my father. Perhaps I would have first built a racing boat or a small yacht for some rich man. I will never know."

He leaned over a railing and continued to talk, as if she weren't there, never taking his eyes off the hulks of the doomed ships. "I've devoted most of my life to learning the only trade I've ever cared about. Some people consider that there is no finer thing to be than a ship owner, like my father. Our family has owned ships for hundreds of years, some of them the pride of Venice. But in my opinion it is equally fine to be the man who designs the ship."

"Of course," Gigi murmured, not knowing what else to say.

"I designed a new freighter, a freighter with proud and un-usual lines. Why should a freighter not be as beautiful to look at as any ship that sails on the ocean? That was my philosophy. I spent ten months here supervising the men who welded these hulls to-gether in the drydock, plate by plate, watching the ships grow upward, deck by deck—and now? Three boxes that float. Three boxes—marvelously shaped, totally seaworthy boxes—that soon will not even float, but will be reduced to raw metal. Their engines are still in Trieste, built under the license of a Swiss company. We pray that they can find a buyer. If not, our family business will be completely ruined. We paid one-third the price of each ship for each engine, the normal ratio. My father doesn't blame me, he blames himself for building three at once. The problem was not in the design but in misjudging the market."

"Boxes? I don't understand. Are they empty inside?" Gigi asked, without caring about the answer but unable to endure the silence that had fallen between her and this unbearably sad young Venetian.

"Yes, empty. The interior is always finished last. These ships are almost finished, but nevertheless they are useless. There are two celebrations in a shipyard when a ship is built, one when the first plate is put in place, another when the workmen that made it present the ship to its owner. There will be no second celebration."

"Couldn't they be converted to some other use?" Gigi asked, watching over her shoulder to see if Ben was anywhere close to concluding his deal.

"If we had the luxury of time, certainly," Fabio answered. "A ship is like what you call a stretch limousine in the United States. It can easily be changed, even made longer. It is built in many modules, one size module for a tanker, another size for a passenger ship, another size for a freighter, determined by the use you are going to put it to. But conversion takes money. A great deal of money. Not long ago the Mariottis—they've been in business forever—converted a huge container ship, which had sailed for years, into a passenger ship for eight hundred people. They scooped it out, leaving only the engine and hull intact, and then put in the decks, public rooms, and staterooms. Even a swimming pool. With all that work, they still cut in half the time that they would have needed to build the ship from scratch. Ah, look, my father is waving to us."

As Gigi and Fabio rejoined the men, she saw them shake hands on what must be a deal. The elder Severini looked at her and smiled in a combination of relief and despair.

"Good-bye, Mr. Severini and Mr. Severini," Ben said. "We've got to hurry back." As they carefully piloted their bikes over the many potholes and cables of the shipyard, Gigi risked a backward look and saw the father and son leaning over the railing and looking wordlessly at the three freighters. The father had put his arm over the son's shoulders. Ben was right, she thought, she wished she hadn't insisted on coming.

11

The sunset of the day on which Gigi and Ben had visited Mestre was of such outrageous beauty, even for Venice, that Ben directed Guido to take the gondola out to a vantage point in the middle of the lagoon and attempt to stay in one place as long as possible.

"He's on his mettle now," Ben explained with a grin. "While the boat's moving, it's relatively easy to avoid the worst of the waves from bigger craft, but you can't anchor a gondola, and there's a lot of water traffic around at this time of day. We should probably be wearing seatbelts. It would add a new scandal to Venice history."

"Is he thinking 'crazy Americans'?"

"Something ruder and more specific. Hold on!"

Gigi and Ben rocked as the wake of a *vaporetto* churning out to the Lido hit the gondola. Gigi glanced up at Guido, standing on his perch way above their heads, swiveling to look in every direction of the compass, his attention firmly fixed on identifying potential threats, particularly those coming from the police *motoscafos*; they were the only sailors in Venice who constantly broke the speed limit.

"Oh," Gigi sighed, "I know you don't believe in making comparisons to the past, but, Ben, wouldn't it be glorious if there weren't a single motor in Venice, if every boat on the water were a gondola? Just for a day?" The sound of her voice was so full of wistful need, so touched by her yearning for something impossible, that Ben Winthrop instantly seized on the moment he'd been waiting for, the moment when Gigi was ready, even if she wasn't aware of it, to respond to him.

"I'd rather turn back time to another day," he answered. "Not even a day, but one particular night and one particular minute."

"When?" she inquired idly, looking up at the lavender clouds mixed with pink and gold and trying to decide, before they changed, what color this sunset would be called if such an evanescent color had a name.

He took her chin in both of his hands and turned her face up toward his. "The first night I kissed you," he said, and leaned forward and gave Gigi the gentlest kiss she had ever received. "The night I kissed you too soon," Ben said, and kissed her again, even more gently. "The night I upset you," he added, and kissed her a third time, so gently that his lips barely brushed hers. "You taste like the color of the clouds," he told her, surprised to find himself so moved, surprised to find himself saying these words. "I've tried to remember what you tasted like ever since that night, and now I know . . . the most beautiful April sunset."

"In Venice?" Gigi faltered, unable to find any words that wouldn't sound flirtatious.

"Anywhere in the whole wide world."

"*Oh.*"

"Do you think you might give me a kiss?" he asked humbly.

Gigi leaned forward to kiss him very softly, as he had kissed her, when a wave slapped the gondola suddenly, jolting her forward, Ben caught her in his arms and she found herself with her nose mashed on his earlobe. Guido's voice, apologizing and swearing, was heard above them.

Gigi burst out laughing. "My intention was friendly," she whispered to Ben, extricating herself from his neck but remaining in his arms, "but a gondola's too . . . tippy." Would this count as flirting, she wondered?

"Guido, take us back to the palazzo as quickly as possible," Ben shouted.

Never had a gondola ride been so bumpy or seemed so long. Guido plied his oar at his highest speed. Ben held Gigi wrapped tightly in his arms, his face buried in the top of her head, kissing her hair over and over as he had prevented himself from doing for so long. She could barely think in words; rocked like a baby, she was all darkly vivid sensation, as if she were made of humming wires and intoxicating impulses that were shot through with honey and heather and pink wine. Under Guido's glance they walked decorously from the landing steps into the palazzo. Gigi stopped inside the front door and turned to Ben with sudden shyness. She'd definitely gone too far to retreat to her former position, she thought with what was left of her rational powers, but what about all her good resolutions? Ben's eyes were tender and imperative, Gigi thought as she looked up at him, eyes she didn't know, certainly not a boy's eyes.

"Now what?" Ben asked her, with a certainty that belied his question.

"I'm not . . . sure," Gigi answered, wishing desperately that women could still faint and answer such impertinent questions the easy way.

"I . . . I don't . . . . . . oh, Gigi, if you don't like me a little, I don't want to make love to you . . . not without knowing the consequences . . ."

"That's a chance you'll just have to take," Gigi murmured, as inscrutably as possible, since she couldn't look away from his eyes. "I guarantee nothing . . ."

"You've already broken your own rule," Gigi said softly as they entered Ben's bedroom, where his bed stood on a raised platform that faced three long Gothic windows framed in lacy stone. "The Rule of One—one kiss—"

"But today we didn't visit a work of art—we have to make up

for that—and my rule never said anything about one kiss," he said in a husky voice he hardly recognized, "never, ever just one kiss." He led her to the center window and turned her so that her back was toward the Grand Canal, while he stood slightly away from her. "I've thought of kissing you right here, with my eyes open, so that I could experience two great pleasures at the same time."

"But diluted," Gigi objected with a low, mocking laugh. "You can fulfill either the sense of touch or the sense of sight, but not both at once—unless you're kissing a statue . . ." She moved toward him, reached up, and pressed her mouth to his in a snowstorm of tiny, chaste, determined kisses that made him close his eyes in rapture. "Choose," she commanded, and he kept his eyes shut and claimed her mouth so thoroughly that soon her lips felt as if they were made of some new, never-before-known material, roses on fire.

"Oh, Ben . . ." she sighed. "I shouldn't flirt with you like this."

"You're right," he agreed, his voice shaking with impatience as he took her to his bed. "It's too much and not enough . . . let's skip flirting. We can flirt later."

"Later?" Gigi wondered. "Later . . . ?"

"You're flirting again," he muttered as he undressed her. "Good God, you're beautiful . . . oh, hopelessly . . . incorrigibly . . . unforgivably . . . so beautiful . . . so much more than I'd imagined . . ."

"You imagined?" Gigi breathed accusingly, with her last resources. "Is that what you've been doing, daring to imagine me like this?"

"Nothing else. I might as well have been in downtown Mestre since we came, for all I've really noticed of Venice, oh, Gigi . . ." His lips claimed her breasts as completely as they had claimed her mouth, and soon, so soon that they were equally astonished yet equally unhesitating, he claimed her entirely and, in claiming her, caused her, unmistakably, to claim him. They were both so dense with desire that they could have ignored a cyclone, so light with desire that they could have floated out of the Gothic windows on a puff of air, so fierce with desire that they could have bitten each other to draw closer together, yet still so tentative that they trembled with each rapid step in the most ancient of dances.

An hour later, when the sunset had long passed, Gigi spoke again. Her voice sounded strange in her ears, as if it had been taken apart and put back together in some better, more interesting way. "Now that you know the consequences of making love to me . . . are you glad you took the chance?"

"I'm still not a hundred percent sure that it was enough of a chance," Ben Winthrop said consideringly, his hands parting her unresisting thighs with a masterful grace that had nothing to do with his tone of voice. "I'm going to have to risk it once more . . . to make absolutely certain."

"Shouldn't we . . . start in the gondola . . . like the first time?"

"Not unless you want to." He kissed her as gently as he had in the gondola. "We could just pretend." The fish had bitten, Ben thought. And caught the angler.

"Why pretend?" Gigi gasped as he entered her again. "Oh, Ben, this is real life, isn't it?"

Hours later, blazing with erotic secrecy, they sat in a semicircular booth, ordering dinner at that most elegant of all Italian hotels, the Cipriani. Its indoor restaurant enjoys a charm possessed by no other hotel restaurant in the world; a surrounding view of water and sky with the noble Palladian vista of the dome and tower of the cathedral of San Giorgio Maggiore across the lagoon in the background.

"Being here is exactly like being on a ship," Gigi said, breaking the silence in which they were held, happy prisoners, a silence made up of having too much to say and not knowing where to start, or even if they should.

"Uh-huh," Ben agreed, his eyes on her, not glancing in the direction of the floor-to-ceiling windows from which they were separated by several tables.

"No, it is. Just look, do look and you'll see what I mean."

"I do know this is one of my favorite places," he declared while he intently observed Gigi's bright head as if it were a rare and ingeniously made flower on which a petal was missing. Was this it? Was he in love? He'd never felt like this before, God help him, Ben thought in a confusion of intense happiness and equally intense wariness. He was so habitually thrifty with his emotions that he was deeply mistrustful of them.

Ben hunted in the pocket of his jacket and pulled out a black velvet box. "I forgot," Ben said, opening it and taking out the emerald and diamond earrings, "I completely forgot until just now. I couldn't resist buying them anyway. Since you wouldn't let me give them to you, will you wear them for me, here, tonight?"

"That depends," Gigi said thoughtfully, not taking the huge, desirable jewels from the palm of his hand, not even looking at them, looking around the room as if it held an answer. On what *did* it depend, she wondered distantly as she played for time. From the instant that Ben had kissed her in the gondola, she'd been unable to rely on her brain. Where now was the girl who'd so wisely meditated, this very morning, on the reasons for not flirting with Ben Winthrop? How had she been swept away so quickly into precisely the situation she'd been scrupulously careful to avoid from the minute she'd found herself on a plane to Venice? She'd had a choice, even after he'd kissed her, she'd had a choice right up till the minute she'd gone to his room. Was this love? With Zach she had never had to ask herself that question, with Zach it had always been love from the first moment. With Davy she had known that it was not. With Ben she only knew that she didn't know.

"Depends on what?" Ben repeated, as she paused.

Gigi shook herself mentally and remembered something she'd forgotten. "On whether you'll look out of the window now or not. I mean *really* look, not just outside but also at the tables near us and *at* the windows too, not just through them, look as if you're seeing the entire thing for the very first time, taking it in as a whole."

"For how long?"

"Three minutes."

"Here." He handed her his wristwatch. "You can time me to the second as well as tell the phases of the moon, the time in twelve different zones, the signs of the zodiac, almost anything except the chances of the Celtics."

"I have zodiac karma," Gigi said while she watched Ben looking intently across the room. "I always have the most promising horoscopes. Even in different magazines."

246

"I have parking-space karma," he answered, moving the focus of his eyes beyond the busy waiters and well-dressed patrons to the dark sky and water outside. "I can always get one, in any city at any time of day. May I give you my parking-space karma? Or isn't that allowed either?"

"I don't think you can give away your personal karma."

"Who says so? As a matter of fact, my karma automatically comes with the earrings—when you put them on."

"Oh no, I don't think so. Not unless I give them back to you at the end of the evening, without the slightest objection from you."

"You're such a stickler for form," he complained, knowing she had read his intention.

"Form follows substance."

"I believe that what you're actually trying to say is 'form follows function,' which doesn't apply. Aren't the three minutes up?"

"Almost. What I'm actually trying to say is that if I wear the earrings tonight, I'll only be borrowing them for a few hours. Understood?"

"Absolutely. Can I stop now, and look at you?"

Gigi looked at his watch, waited two seconds, and said, "Time's up."

Ben turned his eyes away from the windows and stretched out his open palm. With a series of deliberate and leisurely movements, Gigi took off the small jet earrings she was wearing, put them in her purse, took each of the heavy, dangling emeralds from his hand, and fastened them one by one to her earlobes.

"If stars could dance . . ." Ben said, unable to take his eyes off her, or to finish his phrase. "Don't you want a mirror?" he said instead.

"I remember exactly how they looked when I tried them on," she answered, moving closer to him on the banquette. "I'm feeling self-conscious enough just now without looking at myself. Don't you want to know why I wanted you to look at this particular space as if you'd never seen it before?"

"Is it some kind of ritual?"

"On the way back from Mestre I suddenly had an idea, maybe

the most interesting idea I've ever had—I was going to tell you about it when I'd thought it over, and then . . . oddly enough . . . it went entirely out of my mind. Then, when you brought out these earrings, for some reason my idea came back, fully formed."

"Fully formed," Ben repeated mechanically, saturated with a feeling of privilege as his eyes caressed and possessed Gigi.

"You're not paying attention," she cried, and slid away from him.

"If I do, will you come back here?"

"First, listen," she said solemnly. "This is serious. Those three freighters you bought today do *not* have to be junked and sold as scrap metal. They're exceptionally graceful ships with particularly elegant hulls. True beauties. They could be turned into an entirely new kind of cruise ship—"

"What! Who the hell's interested in cruise ships?" he interrupted, astonished and almost offended at the way her mind worked at the damnedest times.

"You are, Ben Winthrop."

"Darling, for Christ's sake, I told you I had interests in shipping, but I never said anything about cruise ships, that's a totally different industry. Why are we even talking about it?"

"Oh, I know you're not interested," she said dismissively, waving away his objections, "but you should be. Imagine a cruise ship that's the equivalent of the Cipriani: elegant but not too large, exclusive, wildly expensive, and perfect in the smallest detail. A ship that would constantly give you the experience of being in this restaurant. Those freighters we saw could become ships like that, with only one class and only one kind of accommodation—*suites* —super-luxurious suites carrying a strictly limited number of people in the greatest possible style at the highest possible prices."

"How," asked Ben, suddenly shifting into another gear and giving her an entirely different kind of attention, "just exactly *how* would you know that there's any need for that kind of ship?"

"From the Collinses, the owners of Indigo Seas—they adore taking cruises, all of them, as a family, and they do it twice a year, leaving the kids at home. Yet they never stop complaining about the small size of the first-class staterooms and the fact that the big cruise lines all carry three classes of passengers. People pay tremendously different prices for their tickets, but essentially, once on board, they all get the same trip and use the same public rooms and restaurants."

"But they need three classes in order to operate at a profit, like planes."

"No, as I see it, the real problem is that they start out with such enormous ships that their huge operating expenses force them to fill up too many staterooms," Gigi said. "Ben, I know it sounds undemocratic, and I'm not saying it isn't, but now, as ever—maybe more than ever—people with enough money to take really expensive trips want to mingle with people who have the same amount of money. It's just like the people in this room, busy looking each other over and delighted to see that everyone is as rich as they are."

"How do you know that?"

"Since I've put these earrings on, I've had about a dozen appraising and deeply approving glances from people who looked at me before and let their eyes just slide by me without any more interest than they'd give any other girl. Well," Gigi amended, striving for punctilious honesty, "maybe a little more, but not much. But now, wearing these emeralds, I'm more than merely acceptable, I'm one of them, and they're thrilled to acknowledge it."

"Assuming that what you say is right," Ben went on, "the fact is that freighters simply aren't cruise ships."

"Those freighters aren't necessarily freighters, either. What they really are, Fabio Severini told me, are 'empty boxes that float,' " Gigi insisted. "*They could easily become cruise ships.* He also told me that it takes only half the time and half the money to completely refit a ship, once you've built the hull and the engine. There are three engines in Trieste that were made especially for those ships—"

"You're sure?" Ben's voice became casual as his mind started to race at her information.

"Positive. His father's trying to sell them—"

"That's hopeless, those engines are custom-designed for particular ships, and take years to get."

"Oh no! Then the Severinis are finished." Gigi was surprised at her sense of loss at this knowledge. Yet she'd been afraid of it all along. The ruin of the Severinis' family-owned ship building business was one of her strongest reasons for wanting to save the freighters. But if they could recoup the money they'd paid for the engines, they would still have capital to work with. The freighters wouldn't be a total loss.

"Ben, if *you* bought the engines—you've already got the hulls —then you could convert them into the most perfect little gems! Hire the best ship designers in the business! In one step, you could own your own cruise line! Why not? Give me one reason why it's not a great idea." Gigi was aflame with her particular kind of enthusiasm that felt utterly at home in seven-league boots.

"Hey, calm down, darling. There's more to running a cruise line than just owning the ships."

"There's more to building a mall than just owning the land!"

"But I know all about how to do that already." His voice was strangely blank, Gigi thought, considering her wonderful new idea.

"Don't you want a new challenge, Ben?" she probed, trying to engage his imagination.

He didn't answer her. He didn't even hear her question. Ben had an uncanny gift for knowing the exact moment at which any new idea and the climate of the times were in magic sympathy. Gigi had stumbled upon such an idea. He had already appropriated it.

As he sat there, looking absentminded, Ben Winthrop's brain was sorting through the names of the experts who would tell him which key people to hire away from established cruise lines; he calculated the fire-sale deal he could make on the engines; he took a dozen mental notes on a dozen subjects related to cruises on which he needed to educate himself rapidly, for he knew, *precisely*, that in 1984, rich people were making and spending money as they had never spent it before in modern times. The cruise industry had not yet responded to this new wave of shamelessly lavish spending. There was a great deal of money waiting to be made, and no time to be lost.

"*Ben!* You're not even listening to what I'm saying," Gigi cried, aggrieved. "Just think—you could call it the Winthrop Line."

"And I suppose you'd want to call the first ship the *Winthrop Emerald?*" He responded all but automatically.

"Well—it might be sort of corny . . . still, it might be something to consider. How do you feel about it?" If she could get him thinking about giving a ship a name, Gigi told herself gleefully, maybe he'd begin to consider the cruise-line idea seriously.

"I like it," he said, suddenly turning to her and snapping into a completely different mode of attention. "It's easy to remember, and it will commemorate the way you look tonight. When you christen the ship the *Winthrop Emerald,* maybe you'll let me lend you the earrings again for the occasion."

"You mean—you're going to do it! *You are!* I can tell from your eyes! You're not teasing."

"Of course I'm not," Ben said with surprise. "I'd never joke about a business matter. Gigi, it's a superb idea, an idea waiting to happen, but let's not even discuss the advertising budget until I know more about a business that's still a mystery to me."

Gigi's mouth fell open. She hadn't been trolling for another account, it hadn't crossed her mind. On the other hand, fair was fair, it had been her idea. Did she want to see it go to Chiat/Day? She was far from possessing the kind of total professionalism for which he gave her credit.

"There's only one problem," Ben said with a sigh of regret. "This is the equivalent of having a mall explode. If only you hadn't mentioned it tonight . . . if only you'd had your stroke of genius a few days later. We'll have to start back first thing tomorrow so that I can get into it immediately."

"I'd have to be leaving anyway," Gigi agreed mournfully. "I haven't wanted to admit it, even to myself, but there's a definite limit to the amount of time I can be expected to be spending usefully in New York. Archie's probably foaming at the mouth in impatience as we sit here."

"If we leave tomorrow, we pick up six hours between here and New York. You and Jack Taylor can work all weekend on The Enchanted Attic, and I'll send you back to L.A. on Sunday in plenty of time to have a decent night's sleep before you have to be in the office. I'll telex my secretary the minute we get back from dinner, and she'll line everything up for you. Vendors don't mind hustle."

"Oh, Ben, I don't know whether to laugh or cry. I feel so

torn. I'm thrilled about the *Winthrop Emerald* and I'm miserable about leaving Venice."

"Darling, darling—don't you understand that we'll be back, many many times? You never have to say good-bye to Venice."

"Have you heard from Gigi?" Sasha asked Billy as they sat in the twins' nursery, observing their children having their first play date. It was such a warm day that the three babies were wearing only their diapers and little cotton shirts. All of them were at the stage of the lightning-crawl, and they had been enclosed on a soft rug inside a huge octagonal playpen with clear Lucite panels. Hal and Max, Billy's nine-month-old twins, were fascinated by little Nellie, who was two weeks older than they were. Although there were two of them, each outweighing her by at least five pounds, the tiny girl was clearly dominating them by the divine right of females.

"Sort of," Billy answered. "I called New York, and the hotel operator told me she was out, and then I got a message from Ben Winthrop's secretary, telling me she'd be phoning at eight the next morning."

"Why is that 'sort of'? Didn't she call?"

"No, she called, but she had almost no time to talk," Billy replied, irked. "I thought she'd want to tell me all about what she'd accomplished, but she said it was too complicated to go into till she got back. When I think of some of the really complicated things we've discussed on the phone! Ha! The Enchanted Attic is the least of it, believe me. I had the feeling she couldn't wait to get off the phone."

"I had the same kind of conversation with her. Unsatisfactory and rushed. I think she's either becoming a workaholic or goofing off and having fun in New York and doesn't want to admit it."

"Oh, Sasha, come on, you know as well as I do that Gigi's not the type to goof off," Billy objected. "She's consumed by that project, she's consumed by all her damn projects. First she invented the antique lingerie and then Scruples Two, then she left to be a copywriter and practically invented a new kind of bathing suit, and then she had to go and invent a new kind of toy store. Look at our kids . . . do they look to you as if they need more toys?"

Billy had provided three boxes of new Keds in bright colors

for the children to play with, knowing that any baby was more interested in the box than in anything it might contain. After they had munched wetly on the boxes and explored all their possibilities, there were the irresistibly chewy shoes and laces, objects that always kept her teething twins quietly busy for minutes at a time. When they tired of shoes, she had three pairs of unbreakable plastic sunglasses to give them, for her own sunglasses attracted them passionately, and, as a final treat, a bowl filled with ice in which three well-washed silver dollars were being kept cool for the ultimate in gnawing pleasure.

"They're not playing with the boxes," Sasha said, "they're playing with Nellie, or hadn't you noticed? They're *investigating* her. Do they think she's a toy? Some sort of doll?"

"They've never been this close to another baby before. Anyway, Nellie's smart enough to take care of herself."

"Of course she is," Sasha said, "she was born smarter. It's the nature of the beast."

"She's a girl," Billy observed, without hurt feelings. "What do you expect?"

"Oh, Billy, girls may start out smart, but not all girls stay so damned smart!" Sasha said, and burst into violent tears.

"Good God, Sasha, you poor thing! What's wrong, for God's sake, what is it? Tell me what's wrong," Billy begged, holding her shoulders in a strong grip, but it was a long while before Sasha recovered enough to be able to utter a single word. Finally she wiped her eyes, blew her nose, and rallied enough to speak.

"We're getting divorced."

"Oh, Jesus. Oh, Sasha, I am *so sorry.*"

"But—you're not surprised, are you?"

"Not . . . no, not entirely. I felt there was something . . . I didn't know what, but I know both of you so well . . . I'd hoped . . ."

"I've hoped and hoped until I've gone almost mad from hoping. It's really and truly hopeless. Billy, it's been going on for months and it got steadily worse instead of better—I held out until I was sure, but I filed for divorce almost three months ago. Josh moved out then. Did Gigi tell you what was going on?"

"Not a word, not even a hint. But the last time Spider and I saw you and Josh, we both noticed that he wasn't . . . oh, you put up a good show, but Josh didn't, he looked so haunted, so . . . grim . . . and then you've always been busy when we called, and we wondered why."

"He's sick, Billy, poisonously sick with jealousy of men I slept with before I met him. And he has good reason."

"How the hell can you say that?" Billy asked incredulously. "Is Josh out of his mind?"

"On that subject, yes."

"What are you talking about? Sasha, you've got to explain!"

As rapidly as she could, but not sparing herself in any of the details, Sasha told Billy of Josh's visit to New York and his discovery of her past. Her voice was matter-of-fact, but her eyes didn't meet Billy's, and she kept shaking her head slightly from side to side in self-disapproval, not realizing what she was doing.

Billy listened silently, watching Sasha carefully. When she had finished, Billy grabbed her hands and squeezed them tightly.

"Now you listen to me, kid. Josh has done a lousy stinking number on you. He's got you thinking that you've been one really bad girl. I hear all your well-reasoned justifications, but what I *see* is that somewhere along the line since this whole thing started, you've bought into his line of utter shit! Josh is a giant asshole, and if he were in this room I'd strangle him with my bare hands—in front of the kids if I had to—and no jury in the world would convict me!"

"Billy!"

"You should know what I was like before I met Vito. Josh would think it was a thousand times worse than anything you ever did. I picked out men—Ellis's male nurses—and *hired* them with only one idea in mind, fucking them. I never wanted to get to know them well, it didn't even matter if I liked them, as long as they attracted me physically. The point was the fucking. Pure fucking. You *dated* your lovers, you had relationships with them, dinner, dancing, jokes, romance—I wouldn't have been caught dead in public with mine, and they weren't lovers, we never talked, they were nothing but bodies with cocks attached. And that went on for years and years."

"*Billy!*"

"Well, at least I've managed to make you smile. Or is that

254

shock? In any case, it's an improvement. You know something, Sasha, you were never a Great Slut, you were a *Great Rake*. Spider fucked just about every model in New York in his day, and his day lasted for a decade, until he met Valentine. He was a Great Rake, and so were you. I wasn't a slut . . . I needed sex the way I needed water, and I found the only way to get it while Ellis was dying. And before I met Ellis, when I was living with Jessica in New York, I had my own Great Rake period, believe me. So let's have no nonsense about jealousy being acceptable for whatever people did *before* they met each other. It's *unacceptable*, and if Josh can't get that, there's nothing to do but get divorced, and the sooner the better. If you ask me, he's just too old to change, too old and too bound up in a very strict background of traditional virtues."

"It's more than that, Billy, it's even more than jealousy. He might have been able to cope with the jealousy one day, but it was the *shame* that finally made me make up my mind. Josh wouldn't go anywhere with me because he was afraid of meeting someone who knew about my past. He *felt shame* that he was married to me."

"Damn! If only you'd told him before you got married!"

"There would never have been a marriage."

"That's exactly what I mean. You could have been spared all this. Who *needs* his crap? Oh, Sasha, what can I do to help you?"

"Are you kidding? *You've done it.*" Sasha started laughing and crying at the same time until Billy found herself heartily joining in, deeply moved by Sasha's plight. As they both recovered, they turned to their forgotten children, who had been quiet throughout their companionable fit of emotion.

"Do you see what I see?" Billy asked.

"How did they all manage to take their diapers off?"

"The twins untape themselves whenever they can . . . they hate diapers and they figured it out all by themselves, no matter how sticky the tapes are. Spider says they're mechanically minded."

"But Nellie doesn't know how!"

"Either she's just learned—or they took it off her. She's much more interesting than the Keds. Either way, who cares? They're too young to play doctor."

"Is anyone ever that young?" Sasha asked suspiciously.

"Yes, Sasha, absolutely, positively guaranteed. I'll show you the book where it says so."

Gigi felt as if she'd been away for a period of time that had no relation to hours or days as they are counted in Southern California. She parked in her specially assigned space behind Frost/Rourke/Bernheim and tried to get back on course as she walked toward the agency entrance on the first Monday morning in May. She'd arrived home last night, not quite eight days after she'd left, with barely enough time for a few hour's sleep.

She must be late, she realized, as she rapidly greeted Polly and received a complicitously meaningful look in exchange. Gigi felt dizzy with two sets of jet lag, a brain full of memories, and a heart spinning with unanswered questions, but she was certain that the word "Venice" wasn't tattooed on her forehead. The only explanation for Polly's I-know-what-you've-been-up-to look was that she was congenitally suspicious. Gigi walked with purposeful rapidity past Bagel Central and headed directly to her office through the usual gossiping crowd, making a tightly polite greeting grimace that indicated that anyone who stopped her to say hello would regret it. She intended to get the Davy Melville business over with while she was still operating under a full head of steam.

The office was empty. Every sign that Davy had worked there had vanished, from the photo blow-ups on the walls to the espresso machine, from his drafting table to his bowl of organic fruit. Gigi stood in the middle of the room, relieved that Davy had had the sense to get a new partner before her return. Her desk intercom rang.

"Gigi? Archie. Could you come into my office for a moment?"

"I'll be right there," she said, and marched back down the length of the corridor. What's with him, she wondered. No "Welcome back, Gigi," no "Glad you're home"?

"Great work, Gigi," Archie said, looking up from his desk.

"Thank you." How did he know already that she'd done great work, Gigi asked herself. There was an office grapevine like a python that grew fast enough to choke a grown man in five minutes, but it was only Monday morning and she hadn't spoken to anyone yet.

"Yup. Terrific work. Davy was only Byron's right arm and left nut, that's all, until he met you. Now he's performing the same functions for Jay Chiat, who will probably criticize and scare him into doing even better work than he was doing here."

"Oh, shit, he quit." Gigi flopped down into a chair, stunned.

"Yep, a week ago today. He came in here and told Byron and Victoria and me that your personal relationship had reached such a painful point that he couldn't work with you, and he couldn't stay in a place where he'd see you again every day. We gathered that you'd been . . . oh, let's say . . . trifling with his affections."

"Give me a break, Arch, Davy was into emotional receivership. What am I supposed to do, marry someone I'm not in love with so you don't lose a key creative?"

"I expect loyalty from you, Gigi, but not to that degree. What I would suggest is that as a member of a creative team you refrain from engaging in physical contact beyond what would be considered appropriate to office behavior."

"Gee, Arch, did you ever think of becoming a copywriter? The U.S. Marines' training manuals, for instance, could use you. You have such a thoroughly light way with words. I was wrong, okay, I should never have let things go so far with Davy, I know that very well. Much too well. I'm sorry as hell that he felt he had to quit, and I'd like to request a female teammate in the future so that I don't get carried away by my uncontrollable lusts, my unleashed emotions, and my ferocious sexual demands, which, obviously, Davy was absolutely powerless to resist, hard as he tried to."

"But he said—"

"He never knew the real truth, poor boy. Davy was my sex slave, Arch. I forced him to fall in love with me by bewitching him with a combination of magic spells and potions known as the Orsini Curse. It started way back in Florence, Italy, and Savonarola was its first victim. Does that cover this unfortunate episode? Or would you like to put me in the stocks next to Bagel Central, where everybody can see that I'm punished for my sins, not that they don't know all about them already, with elaborations too horrible to contemplate. I'll never live it down. Now I understand why Polly gave me that very odd look."

"There has been a fair amount of talk," Archie admitted, breaking out his gorgeous flimflam-artist grin, delighted that he didn't have to scold Gigi anymore. He and Byron had flipped a coin to decide who would get the task neither of them wanted, although it obviously had to be done.

"Why can nothing go on in this office," Gigi asked querulously, "without everyone instantaneously getting a cockeyed version of it?"

"It's one of life's little mysteries. I think it's something in the bagels. How'd it go in New York?"

"We're all set. The first twenty-five Enchanted Attics will open within two months, seventy to eighty more over the summer, the last ones in the fall. Ben's people will discuss the new set of media buys with Victoria. Oh, and by the way, I don't know how big it's going to be, but I seem to have developed another new account for us."

"*What?* Gigi, that's fantastic!"

"I do hope it will help make up for the loss of Davy," Gigi said demurely.

"What's the account?" Archie asked eagerly.

"The Winthrop Cruise Line."

"What's that?"

"At the moment, it's three empty ships sitting in drydock outside of Venice, and three engines sitting in Trieste."

"Oh," Archie said, deflation clear in his voice. "When you said the Winthrop Cruise Line, I was expecting something big and exciting. I thought maybe Ben had taken over a bunch of huge ships."

"In a year, Archie, my friend, a jewellike new ship will be sailing the seas, soon to be followed by two more, ships that will set the standard for glamour, luxury, spaciousness, and expensiveness, each catering to no more than a couple of hundred rich people who could afford to spend lots of money on second homes but don't want the bother or responsibility. Is that exciting enough for you?"

"Hey, listen to this!" Archie said, busy scribbling. '*When your second home is the seven seas*'—how about that for the copy line?"

"I liked it when I wrote it down on the plane yesterday. Here's a list of twelve copy ideas, it's at the top."

"Gigi—"

"Yes, Archie?"

"I have a problem. I don't know whether to beg you on bended knee not to be such a cocky smartass, adorable as you are, or . . . whether to ask you to have dinner tonight, now that you're no longer, so to speak, involved."

"I vote for dinner, Archie, since, after our discussion, I realize that you couldn't remotely intend to pursue or initiate any colleague-to-colleague contact, either emotional or physical, that might be misinterpreted by either party engaged in said contact."

"On second thought . . . why don't we make it a big lunch, to celebrate the new account? I'll call Byron and find out if he's free to come with us," Archie said, laughing helplessly. "I'm not sure I trust myself to live up to your moral standards. Oh, and when Byron asks you out, as I happen to know the bastard is planning to, can I count on you to tell him the same thing?"

"Gee, I hope I'll remember," Gigi said earnestly. "But if there's a full moon—well, all bets are off. That Orsini Curse I told you about? You see, Archie," Gigi said, scurrying to the door of his office, "it's stronger than any individual, and," she added, as she escaped into the corridor, "the women in my family are helpless victims of their own fatal power. It could happen to Byron—it could even happen to you, *sweetheart.*"

Victoria Frost stared at the pile of issues of *Adweek, Advertising Age, The New York Times* and *The Wall Street Journal* that lay on her desk. Each of them carried a story on the projected Winthrop Cruise Line that Ben Winthrop had announced at a press conference. Although none of them credited Gigi with the idea for inspiring the type of cruise ship he described, all of them, in the part of the story that concerned the award of the account to Frost/Rourke/Bernheim, mentioned Gigi as a "rainmaker" and included a few paragraphs on The Enchanted Attic, Indigo Seas, and the small but promising Beverly Hills Beauty Bar cosmetic accounts, a recent line Gigi and David had pitched and won, as well as the designer perfume account on which Gigi and David had been the creative team.

Until today, she had been considered the rainmaker for FRB,

Victoria thought, but from now on she'd be forced to share that position with Gigi in the minds of the advertising community. The Winthrop Line account was budgeted at fifteen million dollars; the first all-copy "teaser" ads would start to run as soon as possible on the premium-priced back covers or the inside front covers of every top prestige magazine in the United States and Europe. Ben Winthrop had told the press that he aimed to make the Winthrop Line, beginning with the *Winthrop Emerald*, into the equivalent of a string of five-star international resorts.

The agency had added over thirty-three million dollars to its billings since Gigi had arrived on the scene, Victoria estimated. Archie and Byron hadn't waited the customary year to review Gigi's salary, but had put their heads together and decided to give her an immediate bonus and triple her compensation. When they'd told Victoria what they thought FRB should do for Gigi, she had accepted it; the money Gigi earned wasn't a battle she could win. They couldn't afford to lose Gigi, but all the rationality in the world couldn't change a bitterness that her discipline in hiding her emotions had barely enabled her to mask.

The luck of that creature! The Enchanted Attic and Winthrop Line accounts were the result of Ben Winthrop's raging hard-on for her, did anyone doubt that? The smaller Indigo Seas, perfume, and Beauty Bar accounts showed only that people would always fall for flash and trash; Gigi's big accounts had come from her willingness to play the sex game, and that could turn against her as quickly as it had turned toward her. The chit was out of the office playing at spending Ben Winthrop's money far more often than she was in the office doing the job she'd been hired for, Victoria reflected savagely. Winthrop had given her the opportunity to excuse her absences on the grounds that he needed her to make a host of decisions, when it was obvious that what he really wanted was to have her easily available even when he wasn't working in Los Angeles. Victoria's animosity toward Gigi had grown with each of Gigi's triumphs, but she made herself treat the girl with an even correctness, a seamless lack of overt hostility.

Victoria had slowly come to understand that Angus Caldwell was the problem that drove her almost unbearably wild with impatience, not Gigi, who had used her twat so cunningly to conjure millions out of Ben Winthrop.

260

It was almost a year and a half since Angus had persuaded her to move to California, and he was still hesitating, still finding a multitude of reasons why it wasn't the right time to make the definitive break with New York. Yet, whenever they were together, no matter how brief it was, he made her realize that every other man she had anything to do with was third-rate, good only for minimal physical release.

Sometimes, Victoria brooded, she'd caught herself wishing Angus would die. She had loved him so utterly for so long, and with such absolute singlemindedness, that she knew that nothing less than death could force her to give him up. If he were dead she could probably go on with her life, such as it was, but while he was alive, and married to her mother, she would never know a moment's happiness. If Angus were dead, her love would never die, but it would become peaceful and painless, a source of timeless tenderness and memories, instead of a daily dagger-wound of jealousy and need and hunger. Perhaps, in time, she would find a place in which to feel gentle.

Oh, if only she had her life to live over again! By Christ, she would have picked the richest boy she met and married him. Love would have had nothing to do with it, so long as she was certain she could dominate him. Today she'd be the youngest social leader of the most desirable gilded communities, a triumphantly reigning young matron whose biggest problems would be deciding on the interior decoration of her fifth house, picking the name of her third child, and choosing her next lover. She would have led the life her mother had bred her for, and led it with such supreme style that she would have risen far above either envy or imitation. She would never even know how lucky she had been not to fall in love, hopelessly and permanently in love, with a man named Angus Caldwell.

But she didn't have her life to live over again, Victoria thought bleakly. She was thirty-two and she had nothing.

There was the usual pile of all the latest magazines on her desk, collected weekly by her secretary so that she could check out the ads of companies that might be vulnerable to a cold pitch. Victoria opened the latest edition of *Cosmopolitan*, finding herself on a page that was devoted to yet another quiz. *Cosmo* editors, she had noted, loved quizzes, or was it the *Cosmo* readers? Automatically, as she read the questions, she found herself answering them in her mind.

What is your idea of perfect happiness? Being with Angus openly and forever.

What is your greatest fear? That Angus will never leave my mother.

What living person do you most admire? No one.

What is the trait you most deplore in yourself? Stubbornness.

What is your greatest regret? Not belonging to Angus.

Who is the love of your life? Angus.

On what occasions do you lie? When I tell Angus I've never fucked another man.

When and where was your most perfect moment? The first time Angus and I made love.

What is the trait you most deplore in others? Giving up.

Which living person do you most despise? Myself.

If you could change one thing about yourself, what would it be? To stop belonging to Angus.

What do you consider your greatest achievement? Belonging to Angus.

What is your current state of mind? I am in Hell.

12

In early September of 1984, Zach Nevsky completed postproduction on *The Kalispell Chronicles* and immediately started work on Vito's new movie, *Long Weekend*. The film-business comedy was going to be filmed in and around Malibu. Most of the action during the twelve-week production schedule was going to take place in three separate houses in the Malibu Colony, a private, gated enclave of the rich beyond rich.

"We could have bought three beach houses for the rentals we're having to pay," Zach complained to Vito as they arrived on the site on the first morning of the shoot.

"Not in the Colony, unless you bought there years ago. You have to pay five or six million now to get a house on a sliver of land that's cheek-by-jowl with your neighbors. It's the most expensive beach property in the world."

"There's no privacy," Zach commented. "You'd think that's

what people would want, but here everybody can come and picnic or sail a kite on the beach in front of the houses, so long as they stay below the high-tide mark."

"The State of California owns the coastline, and the public has its rights. To me, the thing that's most ridiculous is that you can see into your neighbor's rooms through all the windows on both sides of most of the houses. And who are they? The very same hell-spawned pricks you've been doing business with all week. God, I hate this place," Vito said happily.

It had been a nightmare to arrange the furnished rentals, and only the fact that the official summer was over had made it possible. The houses they had been able to negotiate for were suitably spacious, and whatever was missing in their decor, the set dressers would supply. Vito felt as relaxed about the prospects of this picture as he could remember feeling at this particular nerve-racking stage of waiting, when everything was set and nothing had actually started to happen. Such deceptive peace—the peace of a film on which nothing has yet gone wrong, the peace of a certain war in which the first shot has not been fired—was doomed to be fleeting, even nerve-racking for anyone with imagination, yet on this golden September morning he couldn't help giving in to the sheer animal joy of finding himself on the edge of the North American continent, about to turn it into a mess of cables and lights and trucks and trailers.

Yeah, he loved this ridiculous, awful business, Vito reflected as he sat on the beach and watched from a distance as Zach dealt with the sixteen members of the cast who would be working on this first day, a party scene in which none of the principals were present yet. He was able—at least today—to keep himself from hanging around maddeningly close to the action in the style for which he was infamous among directors, who wanted a producer to be neither seen nor heard. Vito's blazing energy level was so high that he found it physically unbearable not to poke his nose into every nook and cranny of a film, staying on top of everything that happened, as tightly aware of whether the star's vegetarian lunch had been properly prepared, as concerned about the color of the star's wigs, as he was of how many pages of the script had been filmed by the end of each day.

264

Vito knew he drove directors up the wall, and he'd never worried about it. If they didn't like his style of producing, they didn't have to work for him. But in the case of *Long Weekend*, he had resolved to keep out of Zach's hair as much as possible. When Zach had first come to Hollywood from Off Broadway, he'd all but perched on Zach's shoulder during the entire production of *Fair Play*. Now Zach had become such an assured and brilliant film professional that Vito felt it was a sign of respect to lounge around on the sand with his sneakers off as if he didn't have a care in the world, as if he, the producer, weren't the man on whom all ultimate responsibility rested, for it was he who had found the property, arranged financing, and hired the cast and crew as well as Zach himself.

So, if he was so sure of Zach's ability, how come he hadn't taken his eyes off him in the last hour, Vito asked himself. Deliberately, and with a feeling of self-imposed physical duress, he turned his back on the scene in progress and forced himself to scan the horizon.

As usual, the Pacific at Malibu was flat and boring, without even a flock of kids playing to supply animation. They must all be back in school now, he thought, spying only one other person sharing the beach with him and watching the actors. Wouldn't you know it, he thought, filmmakers can't even work a couple of hours without attracting a rubbernecker. By tomorrow there'll be a whole group of them and by Wednesday there'll be a crowd that will have to be kept back by some sort of barrier. He looked at his watch. Still a while till the lunch break, when he planned to grab a bite with Zach and find out how the first morning had gone.

Vito got up and strolled in the direction of the solitary watcher. If he didn't talk to someone, he knew he'd be unable to keep himself from stealthily approaching closer to the temptation of the set, and he wanted to have at least one morning of noninterference under his belt on which to congratulate himself.

"Mind if I sit down?" he asked the woman, who was sitting, as he had been, on the sand, clad, as he was, in jeans and a faded denim jacket.

"It's a public beach," she said, agreeably enough, without looking at him, her eyes intent on the filming.

Vito sat down and glanced at her, looked away quickly, and then, cautiously, looked back. Could you fall in love with a profile, he asked himself in total wonder and total terror.

"It's a nice day," he heard himself saying. Maybe she would turn around and he'd see her full face and it would all be over, an illusion, a trick of the light and the angle, or else she was the one girl he'd been looking for all of his life without knowing he'd been looking.

"That it is." She didn't turn, not by so much as a quarter of an inch. She had dark hair, pulled back carelessly and knotted with a bit of bright yellow wool; the one eyebrow and eye he could see were equally dark; her lips, bare of makeup, were a soft pink. Her skin was very white, with the luscious matte quality of a gardenia, and there was a flush of pink where the sun had touched her cheekbones and her nose. He'd never been so moved by a profile in his life. It possessed a nobility, a purity, and a sadness that transcended all of its individual details, Vito thought. What vile beast had made her sad, he asked himself, overcome by an irrational feeling of protectiveness.

"You're going to get sunburned," he said, "if you don't watch out."

"I put sunblock on a little while ago," she answered, unmoving, "but thanks for thinking of it." She smiled faintly in acknowledgment, still watching the actors, and Vito's heart turned over. It felt as if it had literally flip-flopped in his chest, he said to himself in horrified fascination, and he hoped that was physically impossible.

"You seem very interested in filmmaking," he managed to say.

"In this one, yes. For some reason I've never seen Zach in action before."

"Zach," Vito said flatly. He was fucked, totally fucked.

"He's the director, see that tall, great-looking guy with broad shoulders in the white T-shirt, that's Zach, the one who's telling the cameraman something. Just look how dynamic he is, on top of everything, totally in his element. He's just so beautiful, I love to watch him," she said fervently.

"Yeah."

"Do you have the time?" she asked.

"It's about eleven-thirty," Vito said. Eleven-thirty on the day the world started and ended in two minutes of conversation.

"I came early to watch, but time seems to stand still when you watch a movie being made. Zach warned me about that. I'll starve before he's ready for lunch."

"You're having lunch with . . . the director of the picture?"

"Right. He told me that it would probably be okay the first day. He said he'd be too busy later on, discussing the morning's work, so it wouldn't be convenient for me to come out."

As she spoke, the woman turned her head toward Vito and he realized that the desolation he had felt before had been happiness compared to this. Her profile had only warned of the fascination of her full face; the delicate indentation that led from the base of her nostrils to the top of her vitally alive upper lip was the most perfectly shaped fraction of human flesh that he had ever seen or imagined. And her eyes. Jesus, he should never have looked into both of her eyes. He should have gotten up and walked away and never come back. No disguise has ever been invented that can hide the expressions of a person's eyes, and these were so lively, so humorous, so sportive, in spite of a certain desolation, that they told him he would die for this woman who belonged to Zach. Not die to have her, because that was impossible, but die to defend her, to keep her from harm.

Unable to move, although he wanted to run for his life, Vito watched Zach stop the action, give the cameraman some final instructions, and walk toward them, putting on a sweater as he advanced.

"Hi!" he yelled from a distance, and the woman got up and ran eagerly to Zach. He put his arms around her and lifted her up off the sand in a great bear hug and kissed her on both cheeks in a way that spoke of many exchanged kisses, many exchanged confidences, many hours of happiness together. Zach and the woman approached Vito smiling, and Zach put his arm around Vito affectionately.

"We finished early," Zach said, "and I knew my little one here would be dying of hunger. Come on, let's go eat. There's a little place down the beach that's supposed to have great hamburgers."

"No, thanks," Vito mumbled. "I have to get back to the office."

"Oh, for Christ's sake, do you think I don't know what torture you've been going through all morning?" Zach said, laughing. "Just give me a break and don't do it this afternoon, my mind is half on my work and half on wondering if you're going to explode from not messing in my picture. You might just as well drive me crazy one way as the other."

"I'll come back tomorrow. You and . . . your friend . . . well, I don't want to butt in."

"Huh?" Zach looked puzzled.

"You have a lunch date, Zach."

"Well, so what? Why can't you join us?"

"This lady has a lunch date with you," Vito said, at the end of his rope. "Two's company, Zach, didn't we make a picture with that name?"

"Vito, what's wrong with you. Sunstroke?" Zach asked.

"Vito? *Vito Orsini?*" Sasha cried in amazement.

"Sasha, are you going crazy too?"

"Sasha—*your sister?*" Vito asked, wondering if he'd forgotten how to pray.

"No, Sasha my grandmother. What the fuck did you think? It's not possible that you two . . . haven't . . . met . . . before . . . is . . . it? I mean, how *could* it be possible? It's impossible. Totally impossible. Gigi would have introduced you years ago."

"But she didn't, did she, Vito?" Sasha said, blushing for almost the first time in her life, and looking down at the sand, unable to meet his eyes.

"No, she missed the chance, somewhere along the way."

"Bad, bad Gigi. And to think I used to consider her my best friend."

"Cruel Gigi. I'm writing her out of my will this afternoon."

"Look, guys, you two go and get lunch, or whatever you have in mind," Zach said, throwing up his hands. "And don't bother to come back!"

In the car on the way to lunch, Sasha kept sneaking quick peeks at Vito while she chatted nervously, since he seemed incapable of saying more than a word or two.

"You're sort of like a figure out of mythology," she said. "I've been hearing about you for so long from other people that after a while I decided you were sort of an Italian-American Zeus and never appeared except to a choice swan or two, not to mere mortals."

Why, Sasha wondered, looking at Vito's powerful profile, his inborn attitude of total authority, his commanding look that made her think of a leader of a band of fearless outlaws, a man beside whom even her own superbly vigorous Zach seemed almost tentative, why had Gigi never introduced her to this one particular magnificent human being? Jealousy was the only possibility. Gigi, that horrifying bitch, understood her taste in men too precisely not to have known that Vito was meant for her.

"I mean, think of all the times we might have bumped into each other," Sasha continued, rattling on after a brief pause, "all those years I lived with Gigi in New York . . . but of course you were working in Europe then . . . and later, when the two of us shared an apartment out here before I got married . . ."

"But Gigi said—"

"I'm divorced now."

"Good."

"Good? Most people say, 'Oh, I'm so sorry.' "

"Bullshit. Josh was wrong for you. Nice guy, but all wrong."

"How do you know him?"

"When I was married to Billy, he handled our pre-nup and our divorce."

"Oh. *Oh!* I forgot all about that. It was so long ago, ages before I met Gigi. Well, that's really amazing, that makes another connection. There's Gigi, Josh, Spider, Zach, Billy . . ."

Had Billy been utterly out of her mind, Sasha thought. She'd let this glorious bronzed pirate, this conquistador, *this dazzling man,* of all the men in the world, get away? How could she possibly be content with Spider, darling Spider, but just another big, blond All-American sweetie-pie, after she'd been married to Vito? It was unthinkable, beyond her imagination. But of course that marriage had lasted only a year, so obviously they hadn't been right for each other to begin with. Billy could be so blindly, stupidly stubborn . . . Vito must have been too strong for her, too right about too many things, unwilling to let her follow all her extravagant rich woman's impulses that so often led to some kind of mixup. They must have been hideously miserable together, she thought with a leap of pure joy.

"Did Zach say a little place *down* the beach?" Vito asked.

"I don't remember, we're driving *up* the beach. We just passed Trancas."

"What about here? I know you're starving."

"It looks fine." Starving, Sasha wondered, why would she be starving?

They pulled into a simple, rather shabby beach hotel with a restaurant facing the water. Vito secured a round table in the corner on a screened porch where an awning flapped idly in the sea breeze. They both studied the menu earnestly.

"Anything look interesting?" Vito asked.

"Everything, anything . . . maybe a chicken salad." She could just play with it, Sasha realized, she wouldn't actually have to try to swallow.

"What about a drink first?"

"Oh, yes. Please. What's good before lunch?"

"Champagne, dry sherry, either Tio Pepe or La Ina, Lillet, Negroni, Bloody Mary, Cinzano . . ." Had he been a bartender in a former life, Vito wondered as he rambled on, but she wanted to know, so he was telling her. Anything she wanted to know he would tell her. Anything.

"Cinzano, please, on the rocks," Sasha said, seizing on something she didn't know if she liked, just to make a decision.

"Waiter, two Cinzanos on the rocks and a chicken salad for the lady—"

"Why don't we wait to order? Unless you're hungry."

"I'm not. I was before, but I'm not now," Vito said.

"Me neither. Phantom hunger," Sasha said, wondering what she meant.

"Yes. That's what happens when . . ." Vito stopped, looking for the courage to proceed. It was now or never, and if it was never he might as well know before he got in any deeper, not that it was possible to get in any deeper than he was already.

"When what?" Sasha asked, holding her breath.

"When . . . two people meet and discover that they have an

270

involuntary relationship," he said, lifting his head and looking into her eyes, which were as dark as his own.

"As opposed to . . . voluntary?"

"As opposed to existing because of other relationships, meaningless relationships because they're not chosen freely; as opposed to normal social life or any kind of responsibilities or civilized conventions. *Involuntary* because they are real and absolute and they exist in and of themselves and can't be escaped. Because they are destined."

"Oh," Sasha barely breathed, unable to sustain his gaze.

"I wasn't supposed to meet you . . . until today," Vito said firmly. "You weren't supposed to meet me . . . until today. And I do *not* believe in that sort of thing. I am not any kind of Buddhist or a follower of a Tibetan sage or a believer in reincarnation or any other sort of organized believer, come to that. But this is different. Isn't it?"

"Oh, yes. Yes. *Yes.* Hold my hands."

Vito grasped both of her hands in his and they sat silently, trembling, alternately looking at each other and back to the table-cloth, until they felt resolute and steady enough to continue.

"There's something I have to tell you right now," Sasha said, with an expression of painful determination, remembering her vow to herself.

"You're not, you can't be, oh, even if you are, it won't change the way I feel—"

"What on earth are you talking about?" Sasha asked, astonished at the sudden look of dreadful anxiety on his face.

"You're sick, there's something wrong—that's what you have to tell me, isn't it?"

"Oh, Vito. I've never been better in my life!"

"Thank God! Nothing else matters. *Nothing!*"

"It matters to me. I have a past that involves lots of men."

"I once had a conversation with Billy," Vito said, "before we got married, and I told her that I didn't want to know a word about her past, because I could be a jealous man. I've gotten wiser since then, and a lot less jealous, but I continue to think that whatever you used to do is none of my business."

Sasha listened to him and paid no attention. "I had three

lovers, never more, I gave them each a different night, twice a week, but never on Sunday," she insisted stubbornly.

"I hope they realized how lucky they were. The only thing I'd like to know is . . ."

"I knew you'd have a question, I just knew it," Sasha wailed.

"Were any of them as old as I am? I'm forty-eight."

"Most of them were in their forties, a few in their thirties, late thirties. I've never been attracted to young men."

"Well, that takes care of that." Vito sighed deeply in relief. "Do you want to know about my past?"

"No. Not one word. It wouldn't make any difference."

"Good." He'd hate like hell to have to tell her about Susan Arvey and Maggie MacGregor, Vito thought, but he would, every word, if she asked. He would never devalue the truth with her. And all the others, even the ones whose names he couldn't remember, way back to the very first girl when he was in high school. He'd have himself hypnotized if necessary, and regress.

"Oh, Jesus," he said, remembering something important.

"What?"

"I'm a terrible father."

"But Gigi adores you," Sasha protested.

"That's because she's an angel. I neglected her disgracefully when she was a kid. Her mother and I were divorced when she was a baby, and I never even bothered to realize that she needed a father. I was too busy with my career to spend time with her, I thought if I paid child support I was doing my share, I was a shit and a half as her father and there's no excuse for it, nothing you can invent or imagine, no matter how hard you try."

"But you're sorry now?"

"Of course I'm sorry! It's the great regret of my life. Now I take her out to dinner when I'm in town and she has time for me, and we have long talks—grown-up stuff—but think how different it would have been if I'd been around when she was growing up. Think what she missed. Think what I missed."

"She'd have a father complex that would ruin her life."

"You think so?"

"I'm positive. Ask her, if you don't believe me."

"I believe you. I believe you about everything." He truly did,

Vito realized, mesmerized. He understood suddenly that he'd never really trusted a woman before.

"Well, then . . ." she said lightly.

Why did Sasha have that teasing fountain of dark enchantress light in her eyes, he asked himself frantically, that smile which curled her lips so provocatively? Didn't she have any idea of the danger such a combination was to him?

"You haven't eaten lunch," Vito said hastily, looking away.

"Neither have you."

"Could you have dinner with me tonight?" Vito asked.

"No."

"Why not?"

"Because it's too long to wait."

Vito thought intensely about what she'd said. She hadn't eaten lunch, but it was too long to wait to eat dinner. It seemed, to his love-crazed mind, that there was only one meaning possible in her words, but he simply could not find it credible, in this world or in any alternative existence, that it was possible for him to meet Sasha Nevsky, the same Sasha who was Zach's sister and his daughter's best friend, this very morning, and then make love to her this very afternoon, with only one Cinzano to punctuate the occasion. It wasn't a possibility. With some women, yes. With most. Back before he'd met her, back when he was another man, he would have seized the opportunity. But not with Sasha. She was too desperately important. However . . . there seemed to be no other next step for them to take, not reasonably. They'd settled all the other questions. Yet no man could ask her to do such a thing. No woman would consent. Could he? Would she?

"Yes we can," Sasha said. "Nobody can stop us. We're going to make our own rules. Right now. That, if I'm not mistaken, is what these beach hotels are for."

"You . . . read my mind."

"It's the first time that's ever happened! In my whole life! I'm never psychic. Oh, Vito, you *are* in trouble."

"Do you think you're not?"

∽

Sasha felt as if the universe had been reduced to one bed, as if the bed were a great white downy bird on whose safe and friendly back she and Vito were lying in a trance of love, swooping around to the music of a slow tango, watching the continents change color below them in the light of the setting sun. The setting sun . . .

"Zach!" Shocked, Sasha sat up in bed suddenly. "We forgot him! It must be almost night—he said not to bother to come back. Did he really mean it?"

"No," Vito admitted indolently, drowning in memories of a palette of sensations which he'd never equaled. How could he have imagined that he was as much in love with her earlier as he was now? He roused himself with difficulty as Sasha shook him.

"No conceivable way Zach wouldn't expect me back to find out if he'd completed the day's work, to ask how the crew was coming along, what kind of performances he was getting—you have the most adorable breasts in the galaxy."

"Fitters' breasts," Sasha said, distracted from her worry about Zach. "When I was a lingerie model, they always used to fit the new bra patterns on me because my breasts are . . . so they said . . . perfect."

"Fitters, swarming all over your breasts? They must have been men of iron will."

"Female fitters."

"It's a good thing you were wearing baggy denim at lunch. I would have been too awestruck to tell you all the things I absolutely had to tell you."

"That means you fell in love with me for pure reasons."

"Reason had nothing to do with it, pure or impure. People don't love because it's reasonable, or the world would be a different place, more peaceful and a hell of a lot less interesting. Your breasts are a bonus, your bottom is beyond description, everything else is too perfect to talk about, but if you had an ordinary, average body, a totally indifferent body that nobody would look at twice, I'd love you just as much because I couldn't love you more."

"But you're going to love me more every day," Sasha said with certainty.

"Of course, I know that. I'm just talking about right now, this minute."

"Right now is what I'm worried about," Sasha sighed, kissing him on his warm right shoulder. She felt as if it were the first man's shoulder she had ever noticed, as if this particular transcendently powerful configuration of muscle and skin and sinew were being created by her lips. During the six months of waiting for her divorce following the miserable months after Josh had gone to New York, during which he hadn't touched her, she'd been celibate. Now, after the thunderbolts and lightning of Vito, she knew she had never been made love to properly in her life. He was a Zeus indeed, she'd been right in her first impression. She felt like a newly devirginized virgin. She struggled to be practical.

"Darling, what about Zach? And I have to call home to check on Nellie with the nanny, and that's just the beginning . . . oh, the thought of it!"

"The thought of what?"

"All those people we know together. If only we were true strangers with no hellish mutual friends or family or connections. You have no idea how bizarre this is going to seem."

"I have a pretty clear idea," Vito laughed tenderly. "Drama is my business, and 'bizarre' is an understatement. Here's what we're going to do. We'll get married tonight, in Vegas, and then we'll tell them. That'll remove nine-tenths of the hassle, because it'll be a *fait accompli* and they can't try to reason with us or ask us if we know what the hell we're doing or any of that ridiculous stuff people carry on about."

"Elope?"

"Sure. Millions of people do it, and they couldn't possibly need to more than we do."

"Not tell *anybody*! Oh, yes!"

"Nobody but Zach."

"Oh, why do we have to tell *him*, of all people?"

"It's a question of honor. He's your only male relative. I can't carry you off without informing him."

"But he's my big brother, I'm his baby sister, he's the only one of the whole family who encouraged me, who always made me feel I wasn't hopeless all the time I was growing up and nobody in our intolerably talented family thought I was anything but a pathetic little mouse—I worship him—*he'll kill me!*"

"Let's find out." Vito looked at his watch, reached for the phone by the bed, and called the number that had been set up in Malibu for the production. In a minute he had Zach on the line.

"Hi, kid, it's me. No, I don't care if you wrapped or not. I don't care if there was a tidal wave and all the houses we rented are gone. I don't care if the script girl gave birth to triplets on the beach—Sasha and I are getting married tonight, I thought you should know. Uh-huh. Uh-huh. Uh-huh. So why didn't you say something at the time? Anyway, we're off to Vegas on the seven-o'clock flight and we want you to come with us and be our witness, make sure the rabbi is a real rabbi or whatever. Why a rabbi? Your mother, you idiot, she'll feel better if it's kosher. Great! See you at the plane. You'll be back in plenty of time to start tomorrow at the usual time. Yeah, I'll tell her. 'Bye."

"What didn't he say 'at the time'?" Sasha asked, gasping with curiosity and admiration at how Vito had disposed of Zach.

"He said he knew we'd get married as soon as he introduced us, it was just a question of how soon. He said he'd been directing love stories most of his adult life, so it was impossible to hide anything from him. He mentioned *Romeo and Juliet*, among others. If you ask me, he's giving himself a lot of credit, hindsight's easy, but what the hell, that's why Zach's great. He never takes his eye off character, never overlooks the human condition. Oh, he said to tell you he loved you and you were doing the right thing. He said that if you look in Ecclesiastes you'll see that there's nothing new under the sun. And not to worry yourself sick about Ma. That I could have told you myself."

"Ma! Why did he have to remind me, I'd forgotten Ma." Sasha shuddered. "I may have no sense of reality left, but if you think that Tatiana Orloff Nevsky, who runs my family with more power than any pope ever ran the Church, four feet ten inches of pure moral authority, the eldest of five younger sisters who are just as petrified of her as I am, if you think—"

"Ma's taken care of," Vito grinned. "I'd heard so much about her reign of terror from Zach that I figured she could give me some production tips, and I went to visit her one day when I was in New York. We hit it off right from the beginning, she said if she weren't too old she'd set her cap for me and I told her I was up for it, but she just laughed. Said she couldn't be tempted, even by me, I should have come along a decade ago. But she let me pick her up

—talk about tiny—and kiss her good-bye. Zach said that was like getting the Croix de Guerre."

Sasha's mouth fell open in astonishment. *"She let you pick her up?* Nobody, but nobody, not even Zach, is allowed to pick her up. She's very sensitive about being the smallest one in the family. In her head she thinks she's taller than I am, so picking up is forbidden."

"Well, I wasn't in the family then. And the next time I see her I'll snatch her up right away and establish a new Orloff-Nevsky tradition. Tatiana and I will flirt heavily, unless you object. I'm her type."

"Better you than me," Sasha said in surprise and joy. "Now I've got to call and check that Nellie's fine and tell Nanny I won't be back till tomorrow. What should I say if she asks questions?"

"Tell her you met an old friend. Tell her it's a surprise party. Then just hang up." Vito lay back on the pillows and looked at Sasha, her long meshes of silky black hair falling over her white arms as she dialed the phone, and wondered what his past life had been about. All the chasing after scripts and book rights, all the casting sessions and fights with directors and the nagging, predictable war without a truce that every independent producer conducts with the studios, his Oscars and his Oscar nominations and all the money he'd made and lost, although, thank God, he'd had a few extraordinary years in a row and had saved damn near every post-tax dime he'd made after the disaster of *The WASP—Fair Play* alone had made him rich for life—but what had it all been *about,* before Sasha? It had seemed important at the time, that's all he was sure of. Now there were only two things on his mind. Getting something to eat and getting married. If necessary in reverse order.

The next morning, Sasha phoned Gigi at the agency as soon as she and Vito were newly presentable.

"Gigi, it's Sasha. I've got to see you, it's really important. Can we have dinner tonight?"

"Oh, honey, I can't possibly, not tonight. The Collins brothers are in town and they're taking all of us to the Orangerie for a big celebration because of the success of their newest Abbondanza line."

"How about lunch? Gigi, it's something that really can't wait."

"Well, I was going to work through lunch, I have a ton of stuff to do, but okay, sure. What'd you do, get a bad haircut? Or, oh my God, don't tell me Nanny quit?"

"No, nothing like that, nothing to worry about. Just something we have to talk over."

"Why can't we talk on the phone?"

"Because we can't! Meet me at the Dôme at one?"

"Right. But it'll have to be quick."

Sasha hung up the phone and turned to Vito. "Good news, she won't have much time. She has to get right back to the agency after lunch."

"If you could see how frightened you look, darling baby, you'd laugh. Gigi won't eat you alive. I'm the one who's terrified."

"You don't look it." Vito had put on his producer gear, one of his superbly made suits in a fabric so clearly expensive and tasteful that it made bankers and studio executives feel that they weren't dealing with anyone too riskily creative. He was expert at dressing for the enemy, never so dapper or overly fastidious that he seemed to care excessively about his clothes; never falling into the trap of dandy-hood, so that in spite of the fact that his custom-made shirts were the finest that Charvet made, and his ties and shoes were minor works of art, they never ventured beyond well dressed into the dangerous area of eccentricity. No studio executive could accuse Vito of looking as if he worked at his clothes, although with his distinctively Italian features and a body on which everything hung with Italian style, he could easily have created that impression with one false note of flamboyance. He had settled for looking unplanned, as if the undeniable quality and fit of his clothes were an accident, something that had just happened, fallen onto him out of his closet while he was getting dressed.

"Too bad Zach isn't here to protect us, but he can't leave the set," Vito said, knotting a tie with purposeful nonchalance.

"He wouldn't come anyway," Sasha said. "He hasn't seen Gigi since she kicked him out."

"So my brother-in-law won't be caught dead in the same room with my daughter?"

"We have a major family feud and we haven't been married

278

twenty-four hours. Eloping doesn't solve everything." Sasha pulled down the corners of her beautiful mouth. "Not only that, I had to get all dressed up or Gigi would know that there's something odd going on even before she sits down at the table."

"I don't care if anybody in my family never talks to anybody in your family till the end of time, so long as they stay out of our hair."

"Who, exactly, is in your family?" Sasha asked, looking at her restored self in a full-length mirror. The sophisticated surfaces of her hair and her makeup glittered and flashed as they had never glittered before, she was wearing her most elegant fall suit, and she looked confidently ready to enter a ballroom full of inevitably lesser beauties.

Vito stood next to her, tall, tough, yet every inch a grandee, seeming as sure of himself as any conductor of a great orchestra, possessed of the same magic authority that holds together every element in the performance of a symphony or the making of a film. They couldn't stop looking at each other in bashful wonder at what a handsome pair they made.

"You and Nellie and Gigi and Zach and your mother and all your relatives," Vito said.

"They're my family too, so how can they never talk?"

"I've just realized that you may have one fault."

"Already?" Sasha demanded, affronted.

"You make sense."

Gigi raced into the Dôme ten minutes late, and was led, by one of the young women who worked at the headwaiter's desk, through a long, mirrored corridor where tables lined both walls and every word that was said could be overheard. Beyond lay two smaller rooms, the last one for people who wanted ostentatious semiprivacy and the middle one for people who wanted to talk comfortably without being overheard, but still feel as if they were in a restaurant and not in a chic Siberia.

Vito had chosen a table in the middle room so that Gigi's reactions would be reduced by her high visibility and the fact that she'd be surrounded by four other tables of people.

"Sasha, I'm sorry I'm late. Dad? How wonderful! You look

fantastic. In fact you both do. But, Dad . . . what are you doing here?" She kissed both of them and sat down next to Sasha.

"Did you tell him?" Gigi hissed at Sasha out of the side of her mouth.

"Tell him what?" Sasha quavered.

"That you have to talk to me, of course," Gigi snapped. "Really, Sasha! Dad, listen, Sasha and I have something we have to talk about. I hate to ask you to join your own table, but I don't have much time."

"Actually . . ." Sasha said. She stopped dead and looked at Vito in worshipful despair.

"Gigi," Vito said, "Sasha wanted to tell you something herself, but she's been struck dumb, so I'll tell you for her."

"Can I order first? Whatever it is, I have to get back to the office in three-quarters of an hour, and I don't want another bagel lunch like yesterday." Gigi studied the menu, one of the longest in town. "This is so complicated. What are you having, Sasha?"

"We're having the veal and chicken sausages with the warm potato salad," Vito answered.

" 'We'? Who invited you? Dad, you're horning in on a girl-friend lunch, you're not supposed to do that. Where are your manners?"

"Actually . . ." Sasha said and stopped again.

"Actually, I was invited," Vito said.

"Sasha, why did you invite him? You're insanely polite. How can we talk while he's listening? Sorry, Dad, but you'll have to consider yourself uninvited. I love you, but go away, just for now. We'll invite you another time, I promise."

"Gigi, Sasha and I got married yesterday."

"Very funny. What do you think about the Chinese chicken salad? Good choice?"

"Gigi," Sasha said, "we really did."

Gigi put down her menu and looked at both of them. She looked closely and then she leaned back and looked at them from as much of a distance as she could manage. She cocked her head and studied them as if they were a rare form of animal. She put her elbow on the table, rested her chin on it, and contemplated them slowly and at length.

"Oh, wow," she said quietly. "Oh, wow."

"I know it'll take you a while to get used to the idea—" Vito jumped into her silence.

"You and Sasha, you two don't even know each other! I've never introduced you, you've never mentioned each other to me. Zach and I used to kid about it. Do you both realize what that means? I must have unconsciously known this would happen, I must have seen it coming a mile away! I mean—*why* did I never introduce you? There's got to be a reason, doesn't there? You're perfect for each other! *Just perfect.* It's the best thing that's ever happened to either of you—but why didn't I just introduce you sooner, that's what I can't understand. God, I must have wanted to keep you all to myself, *both of you,* what an evil, jealous, withholding rat-fink I am! I hate and despise people like me. *Oh!*"

Gigi started crying and kissing them simultaneously, all over their faces like an agitated puppy, so that their table was the focus of a dozen pairs of fascinated eyes and ears.

When she could finally speak, she asked, still sobbing, "How long have you known each other? How'd you manage to keep it a secret from me? Not that I blame you, considering how I'd kept you apart. I guess it must have felt sort of . . . delicate, dating each other, especially waiting for Sasha's divorce to become final." She blew her nose and dried her eyes, her tears overcome by curiosity.

"We met yesterday," Vito said proudly.

"*Now* you're kidding me."

"On the beach, out at Malibu. Vito picked me up."

"I didn't even know who she was," Vito added.

"Then how could you be married?"

"We eloped to Vegas last night," Sasha answered.

"Oh, how sad! All alone, just the two of you. But how romantic! Just the two of you on the spur of the moment—crazy love . . ." She shook her head in a multitude of emotions.

"Actually, we had somebody as a witness," Vito said with a sinking feeling. She'd have to know eventually.

"Who?"

"My . . . brother," Sasha said.

"ZACH! You invited Zach to your elopement and you didn't invite me! How could you do a thing like that?" Gigi shouted. "I was home all last night, all you had to do was call and I'd have been there like a shot—I'm so insulted—my feelings are so hurt—"

"But Zach introduced us!" Sasha protested. "He literally chased us off the set—that's where we picked each other up—and told us to get out of his hair and have lunch without him. If it hadn't been for Zach, it wouldn't have happened—not as quickly, that is. Zach was directly responsible for, well,—Gigi, *you know* what I mean, and then Vito got all heavy-duty Italian about things and decided he had to ask the permission of a man in my family, for my hand in marriage, and there was nobody to call but Zach, who promptly decided to get all Old Testament about it and barged in and simply insisted that he come with us to Vegas to make sure we got a rabbi and didn't sneak off to some judge or Elvis impersonator. Really, Zach is just as unreasonable as you said, Gigi. Worse, if anything."

"Well . . . in that case . . . I suppose I understand, a little. I certainly wouldn't have cared about a rabbi. But I get to give the reception, not Zach, is that understood?"

"Absolutely."

"Totally."

"I just realized," Gigi said, turning pale with excitement, "I have two stepmothers now, you and Billy! You've got a tough act to live up to, Sasha, my girl. I expect some heavy-duty competition for my favors. And . . . my God . . . sweet little Nellie is my sister and Zach is my—oh, shit!—what is he? I don't want him, whatever he is."

"Your father's brother-in-law, or your stepmother's brother, definitely not your uncle, if that's what you're worried about. At least I don't think so." Sasha thought of her mother and how she would know some absolutely specific Old Testament word for Gigi's relationship to Zach now that Gigi, all unknowing innocence, had been irrevocably drawn into the Orloff-Nevsky circle.

"Well, praise Yahweh. Say, are we going to eat, or are you both so much in love you live on air?"

"We'll order now," Vito said. "And, Gigi, don't tell a soul until we tell you it's okay. You're the only person who knows. I'm going to deal with Billy and Josh."

"You have many talents," Vito said in admiration, after Gigi had rushed through her meal and left them alone with each other. "You certainly know how to handle Gigi. What a spin you put on the Zach story, it might have been fatal otherwise."

"That's what best friends are for," Sasha said smugly. "I didn't want her to feel bad."

"I thought I was your best friend," Vito complained.

"You're my everything."

"So will I or won't I get the spin?"

"You'll get the unvarnished truth, dearest love. You're old enough to take it."

"I guess that's the first installment."

"You wanted to see me, Vito?" Josh Hillman looked at Vito coldly. "If it's a legal problem, there are firms that specialize in industry law, we handle very little of that."

"It has nothing to do with the film business, Josh," Vito said, staring with much harder coldness at this man who had been, until a month ago, his wife's legal husband, although, from what little Sasha had told him, he had never deserved to be married to her for a minute.

"Then how can I help you?" Josh asked unwillingly. He had no reason to ask Vito to leave his office immediately except a powerful desire to do so, and that, for a man as formal and punctilious as he, wasn't enough.

"I came to tell you that Sasha and I were married yesterday."

Josh was struck by a feeling of blatant savagery such as he had never before felt in his well-ordered, conservative life. He jumped up and came around his desk at Vito, his fists clenched.

"How dare you!"

"We love each other. You have no further rights over what she chooses to do."

"You filthy son of a bitch! *I know all about you,* I know who you are and where you've been, you unsavory bastard, I know how you treated Billy and why she divorced you and how you forgot you had a daughter until Gigi was sixteen. I know how Billy financed *Fair Play,* I know how hard she worked on *Mirrors* and the way you rewarded her for your Oscar, I know why she had no problem in becoming Gigi's legal guardian, I know you for the lowlife, bloodsucking, stinking piece of dirt you are—and you think for one minute that you can get away with marrying my wife?"

"Sasha is not your wife. I understand your feelings, but she is no longer your wife. You caused her to divorce you." Vito spoke evenly and took no step backward.

"For fucking good reasons, Orsini, as you'll find out."

"I know all about her love life in New York, it's the first thing she told me, right off the bat, so there'd be no problems about it later. Look, Josh, Sasha and I are one of a kind about what we did before we met each other. We understand that jealousy is born when you love someone, that it's natural, pardonable in its own way. But we're different from you—for us, when an old love is dead, it causes no more jealousy. It's over, finished, forgotten. It doesn't live on as a cancer, eating us up day by day, and killing the new love. Sasha is mine now, and I don't care how many other men she slept with before me. I'll make her happy, I promise you."

"Do you think I give a fuck about your promises? Do you think you can patronize me with dusty philosophical observations? Do you think I don't know that you must have been sneaking around behind my back with my wife long, long before I found out what kind of woman she really was? And do you think for one single second that I'm going to let my daughter be brought up with you around? I'll sue for sole custody, and I'll win. Sasha is an unfit mother, God knows you've proved yourself an unfit father—Nellie will be taken away—"

"Josh, shut up. You're screaming like a madman. Call your secretary, I have someone waiting in your anteroom you should talk to before you continue to embarrass yourself."

"The hell I will. You don't give the orders around here."

Vito walked around Josh, reached over the desk to the intercom, buzzed and said, "Please send her in."

The door opened and Billy walked into Josh's office.

"You were right," Vito said to Billy. "I do need you."

"Do you know what this prick has done to me?" Josh attacked Billy immediately, accepting her appearance without surprise, so lost was he in his frenzy of anger.

"I've known for several hours," Billy said, sitting down calmly. "And I think it's perfectly splendid."

"Billy, you're out of your mind," Josh shouted. "You've been brainwashed. This is *Vito*, the man you told me to get out of your life at all costs."

"I remember who he is, I loved him enough to propose to him. And I remember you, Josh, and I know who you are. You're a good and dear friend to me, someone whose counsel I value, someone I'd be lost without, but right now you're not acting like the Josh Hillman I recognize."

"I won't let him near my daughter!" Josh raved on as if she hadn't spoken. "He's stolen my wife and now he wants to steal my daughter! He has no idea of what I can do to him, I'll bury him with legal bills, Nellie'll be eighteen before I give up custody—"

"Josh. Sit down and calm down." It had been a long time since Billy Ikehorn had spoken to him in that tone of voice, and from years of dealing with her at her most dictatorial and impossible, from years of automatic obedience, Josh responded enough to sit on the chair behind his desk.

"You and Sasha are divorced, Josh," Billy said emphatically. "You know, as a lawyer, exactly what divorce means. If you call her your wife, it's because you happen to be temporarily hysterical. You're not thinking like the Josh Hillman I trust, the Josh Hillman who's a pillar of the Los Angeles establishment, the Josh Hillman everyone comes to for help and wisdom."

"Billy, if you think I give a flying fuck for my image, you're crazy! I want justice, I want to make them suffer for what they've done to me."

"My God, Josh, you are a pathetic case," Billy said without changing her exacting tone of voice, more fit to lay down an injunction than for any other purpose. "You want justice? For what? What injustice have you suffered when a wife you wouldn't forgive, wouldn't touch, wouldn't try to understand, finally left you, without you trying to stop her? What injustice have you suffered when she's found someone who loves her unconditionally?"

"You don't understand! " Josh broke in passionately.

"I'm afraid I do," Billy answered. "It's an old story. You still love Sasha, but you couldn't manage to forgive her, no matter how you may have tried—if you tried. You don't want her to be happy. *Ever.* You're eaten up from head to toe with jealousy because she loves someone else. You want to ruin that happiness out of distorted, dark, venomous jealousy. You'd kill them both if you could."

"How can you, of all people, try to reduce this to mere jealousy? Don't you remember what Vito was like after he won the Oscar?"

"There is no such thing as 'mere jealousy,' Josh—I've been there and I know. I've also come to one single conclusion after half a lifetime in Hollywood: there should be a year's period of grace for everyone who wins an Oscar, it's a dangerous time for them. Vito didn't handle it well, but not as badly as some others."

"But what about Gigi?" Josh raged on, his mania unabated. "You told me yourself what a rotten father he'd been. Why should I allow my daughter anywhere near him? You can't expect me to forget that, that above all. No, Billy, I'm sorry, but no, never, he'll never live in the same house with Nellie. Never! I'll fight them to the end!"

"Vito, would you leave me alone with Josh for a minute?" Billy asked.

As soon as the door was closed behind Vito, Billy moved her chair closer to Josh's and spoke in a low, intent tone.

"You weren't always such a perfectly upright innocent father yourself, were you, Josh? There was a time, my good old friend, not much more than seven years ago, when you divorced your wife of twenty years, breaking the heart of a wonderful woman who had done absolutely nothing to deserve it, and you gave her *complete* custody of your three teenaged children."

"What the hell has that got to do with it?" Josh was so astonished at this unexpected attack that his fury was checked in his surprise. "Joanne and I had reached a point of no return."

"As the French would say, Josh, permit me to laugh. You were a man of forty-two having a secret affair with a girl of twenty-six, you were willing to give up everything in life for her, including your three terrific children, you were madly, wildly in love, and you didn't give a damn about all your responsibilities or duties, parental or otherwise. You were going to start fresh, leave your old life behind . . . all for the love of a charming redheaded girl . . ."

"How? . . . You can't prove any of this . . . you're imagining . . ."

"Didn't you realize that Valentine and I were friends? Close, intimate friends? She told me, Josh, *Valentine told me everything*, including the fact that you fell in love with her the day you met her, doing business for me, if I'm not mistaken. Vito has only known Sasha *since* your divorce, I know that for a fact. I also know about that stolen week at the Savoy in London, Josh, that week you spent with Valentine, I know about Valentine's apartment where you were with her during those many evenings Joanne was told that you had to work late, I know about the weekend when you, still very much married, took Valentine to New York and went to Lace's party—even John Prince couldn't resist telling me that little tidbit—don't look at me as if I'm a ghost. Valentine told me because she needed to tell someone and she knew I'd never repeat a word. She told me because she loved you very much. I know that she'd have married you . . . if she hadn't found out that she loved Spider more. Valentine and *Spider*. My Spider. I could indulge in a wallow of disgusting jealousy myself, if I'd let myself, but I won't."

"Jesus, Billy—you knew, you knew so much and you never said a word . . ."

Billy got up and stood behind Josh and put her arms around his shoulders. "You've been unlucky in love, my dear, but you're still the most attractive bachelor in town . . . there's hope for you yet. Third time lucky . . . I know you never loved Joanne, not like Valentine and Sasha, so we won't count her."

"Billy . . . I don't . . . I just don't know what to do."

"Accept it, Josh. Vito knows what he should have been to Gigi, he knows it so deeply and so clearly that he'll be the best stepfather Nellie could have. He'll make up for everything Gigi missed, and more. And you'll have joint custody, that's always been in the agreement. Just accept it. Let it go. You've caused enough pain . . . you've had enough pain."

Josh sighed deeply and put his head on his arms. Billy stroked his hair quietly, as if he were a child. Finally he looked up. "I guess you're right. Hell, I know you are. But you tell him. I don't want to see him again."

13

ould she ever get used to flying commercial airlines again, Gigi wondered, as Ben's Gulfstream III carried her to New York. It was mid-September, and during the past summer, when he wasn't in Los Angeles, he'd frequently had her picked up and flown to meet him for the weekend wherever he happened to be. She felt as if she had slipped unnoticed into the back door of a doubt-free establishment, like that of the time of Queen Victoria, when all the rulers of Europe were related to each other and knew themselves to form a group that transcended nationality and made a class unto itself, with its own immutable laws and customs. What separated the rich at the piercing tip of the ultimate point of the needle of the pyramid of American money, from the rich seemingly just below them—yet in reality miles below—was the effortless ability to maintain a private aircraft with two pilots in a constant state of readiness, not merely a company plane.

Winthrop Development, Ben's company, had three executive jets of its own, so that the widespread web of malls could be visited by his employees at a moment's notice, but the Gulfstream was Ben's personal property, and he used it as casually as a kid jumped on a bike. She was getting used to being spoiled very quickly, Gigi reflected. She no longer felt the same quality of thrill when the limo drove up to the end of the landing strip at Burbank Airport and the chauffeur jumped out to carry her luggage into the waiting plane, where the steward stood at the top of the short flight of steps to welcome her aboard. A thrill, yes, decidedly she still felt a luxurious, cosseted thrill, but it diminished each time, and she suspected it could vanish slowly into an expected convenience, as it had for Billy twenty years ago.

This present trip would keep her in New York for almost a week. There had been so much progress made on the planning of the *Winthrop Emerald* that Ben now wanted her to see what was going on in the big downtown warehouse he'd bought and converted into the center for all American operations on the cruise ship. He'd taken time, whenever he could get away from his malls, to make himself an expert on the business during the summer, but he'd been reluctant to share any of the details with her until he felt he had a total grasp of them himself. This visit was, Gigi realized, a sort of unveiling, a show-and-tell of what he had created. She had expected to be more involved, as she had been with The Enchanted Attic, but she'd been busy enough with her own work at the agency that she hadn't bothered to pay much attention to the sort of quietly gleeful secrecy he'd thrown over the project.

Actually, Ben's attitude about the *Winthrop Emerald* paralleled in certain ways his attitude toward her, Gigi told herself as she pensively consumed the smoked Scottish salmon with thin slices of buttered brown bread that the steward had just offered her. There was a kind of possessiveness involved in both, a possessiveness that involved obtaining exclusive control. She didn't mind that he kept the ship all to himself, like a child with a new toy, but every time they were together she had to be on the alert to keep him from maneuvering her into the position of his choice.

When a man wanted to do everything for you, including marry you, but you weren't sure you loved him, you had to keep a clearly marked distance between you, Gigi reflected. The pain of her experience with Zach—a pain she somehow couldn't yet manage to put behind her, hard as she tried—had taught her that, if nothing else. Of course, the problem was that the more successfully she sustained this crucial distance, the more Ben wanted to break it down. If she'd been trying to snare Ben Winthrop, this catch of catches, she couldn't have planned her moves more shrewdly, but she still was no more sure that she truly loved him than she'd been that night at dinner at the Cipriani. Whenever she thought about marriage to Ben, she found herself struck by a blankness of imagination as thick as a dense fog. Was this what men felt when they told women that they weren't ready for commitment, or was it just her practical streak that had so often prevented her from building castles in the air?

Or was it because Sasha had nicknamed Ben "Mr. Wonderful"? The expression annoyed Gigi, yet something in her was in sneaky agreement with Sasha's worldly opinion—now illogically but definitively suspended in the single case of her father—that every man, no matter how good he seemed, was too good to be true.

Damn it, Ben *was* wonderful! Intelligent, surprisingly thoughtful about pleasure and beauty, always so good to look at—he'd have been wonderful even if he'd been poor, except that Ben Winthrop was somehow impossible to imagine separated from the aura of his money. What the hell was wrong with her, feeling the need to defend him from an invisible Sasha, even taking a perverse pleasure in trying to find faults in him?

She must be committable, but as the plane flew high above the Mississippi, Gigi thought about what had happened two weeks ago, over the Labor Day weekend, when she and Ben had joined a house party of his old Harvard friends and classmates on Martha's Vineyard. There had been six couples in all, so close to Ben that he was godfather to each couple's oldest child. There had been plenty of room for all of them, parents and children, in a huge, rambling, shabby clapboard cottage on a bluff above the sea. The time had been jammed with simple pleasures—sailing, walking, talking, and eating, pervaded by an atmosphere of camaraderie and shared experience, yet hadn't she been aware at all times that Ben was the unacknowledged yet unquestioned top dog of the group, the first among equals? And hadn't he not only reveled in it, but expected it as a tribute to his success?

There hadn't been any particular event she could actually point to, but as a stranger to the group, Gigi had noticed clearly how Ben's opinion on any subject became the general opinion in spite of any amount of laughing disagreement; how all the very pretty, thirtyish women listened to his compliments with more enjoyment than they did to those of their husbands; how, when Ben tired of sailing, somehow they all agreed to head into shore; how, when Ben felt it was the moment for a drink, everyone discovered they were parched for their chosen brew, tall glasses of iced vodka and Doxee's clam juice; how, when Ben had a notion, at the last minute, that it would be fun to abandon the dinner that had been cooked for that evening and go out for lobster, everyone concurred after a minimum of playful debate.

Simply innate leadership? Or just a good sense of timing? Perhaps. Yet what about his habit of arranging—designing—moments for himself? It seemed to her that it had started that first time they'd made love, when he'd wanted to kiss her and look out at the Grand Canal at the same time. A perfectly harmless and poetic fancy, surely, much less planned than the Nardi earrings he'd "bought anyway" and produced from his pocket at the Cipriani. Obviously he had never accepted as serious her earlier refusal of the emeralds. If Ben Winthrop wanted to give someone earrings, by God, she'd get earrings, although Gigi had made him keep them in his possession ever since, consenting to wear them on only a few occasions.

Was she . . . in any way . . . part of an . . . artistic arrangement . . . he'd made for himself, Gigi wondered. Someone he'd *appropriated* because she fit into a picture that he'd constructed? Or was she being absurdly unfair, mistaking his genuine manifestations of love for those of control? Maybe he simply didn't know how to show love any other way. *Damn Sasha*, it was all her fault that she was even asking herself these questions! He was all she could ask for in a lover . . . and yet . . . and yet . . . didn't he always choose the time and place?

On the Vineyard, over that weekend in the big tumbledown

family house, their hosts had considerately given them separate bedrooms, yet he had come to her that night, an hour after everyone else had gone to bed, come unexpectedly to her room right next to the master bedroom, awakened her, and fallen upon her with such a surging wave of passion that there was no possibility that the people on the other side of the thin wooden wall hadn't heard his moans as he thrust, and the way he'd cried out violently in his moment of orgasm. When he'd grown hard again, too quiveringly hard, too needful to resist, she'd made him swear to remain silent before she'd allowed him to take her once more, but in the oblivion of his powerful spasms he'd been unable to master himself, and he'd screamed again.

Breakfast, with that group of near strangers, had been deeply embarrassing for her because of the impeccable behavior of everyone in the big kitchen, who all seemed to have heard nothing at all. Nudges and winks would have been easier to take than their pretense. One laugh, and she would have felt released from her constraint. She had been as angry as he was remorseful; she hadn't let him near her the rest of the weekend, and he'd accepted her punishment without a word of objection. Still, she could imagine what they must have said among themselves, that band of close-knit, impenetrably silent, friendly young wives, when they got back to Boston.

Ben, of course, never worried about what anyone said or thought. In his apologies he told her he'd never felt such physical passion for anyone, and that the worst the other women would think, if they thought about it at all, was envy because their own husbands hadn't made love to them twice that night. If being in New England made her more Bostonian than the Bostonians, he would respect her feelings, he'd promised solemnly.

Gigi got up to stretch her legs with five laps of a dog-trot around the cabin of the jet. She had to admit, she told herself as she stopped and leaned on the padding of an oval window and looked down at the clouds, those unforgettable sounds Ben made had, at least, drowned out her own gasps of delight, for he had learned her sexual secrets with astonishing quickness, and even while she was worrying about her hosts in the next room, she hadn't been able to keep from making one hell of a lot of noise herself. She only hoped he'd suffered mightily from the punishment she'd imposed on him that weekend, because, damn him, it had been all but unendurable for her.

The next afternoon, on the day Gigi was to visit the Winthrop Line headquarters, she dressed carefully in her most impressive big-city drag, since this would be her first official visit as the representative from Frost/Rourke/Bernheim. She'd bought a new suit from Karl Lagerfeld's fall boutique collection for Chanel, the couture house he had recently joined with a free hand to revitalize the grand old business, which had become dowdy since the death of Mademoiselle Chanel herself. It was made of a cream tweed, with a wraparound skirt and a cardigan jacket, both pieces trimmed in cream and black plaid, worn with a black silk blouse with a giant floppy collar and a heavy gold chain belt low on her hips. As she checked herself in the mirror, Gigi felt that the jaunty, relaxed 1920s lines of the suit were exactly suited to her many-layered bangs, her chin-length bell of swingy hair, and her black lashes, almost thick and long enough to need untangling so they wouldn't trap flies. Mademoiselle Chanel wouldn't be ashamed of her, she decided as she set out, trying to remember to slouch in appropriate flapper fashion, although her quick, dancing walk didn't accommodate itself to slouching.

The first person to whom Ben introduced her in the converted warehouse in lower Manhattan was Erik Hansen, a man of sixty-three, the key man in the entire operation, head of the management team Ben had assembled.

Hansen, who had been hired away from the Royal Viking Line, was one of the three top executives in the cruise world. He had accepted this new job only because he faced retirement and had far too much energy left to consider leaving the business in which he was a king. The Winthrop Line had given him lifetime financial security as well as a ten-year contract. He was a man of medium size, a walking furnace of brisk purpose. He had a wiry build, wiry white hair, and a wiry grip. It came as a surprise when he gave her a quick, warm smile, suddenly a wiry grandfather.

"This is the man," Ben told her, as they all had a cup of

coffee in Hansen's office, "who knew exactly which key men were worth stealing, and he's already filled his wish list. When Hansen came calling, they listened."

"Is that the way it's done?" Gigi asked curiously. "Theft?"

"It's the only way," Hansen said. "Cruise ship owners, like Mr. Winthrop, raid the competition all the time when they build a new ship. There are just so many top men, and everyone wants them. Mr. Winthrop made it easier by giving me a free hand with salaries. We're also planning the finest officer and crew accommodations and recreation space on any ship afloat, which will lure the best people from other lines, since their lives are spent on board."

"Each executive we've hired brings his own following with him," Ben added, "so we've almost completed our top and middle echelons. They're all in this building now. Our hotel manager, Eustace Jones, who comes from a famous British tea clipper family, is working upstairs, and so is Per Dahl, the Norwegian captain."

"But why do you need them now?" Gigi asked. "The maiden voyage of the *Emerald* isn't scheduled for a year."

"They have to be consulted every step of the way," Hansen answered. "The complications are endless. For example, the chief engineer, Arnsin Olsen, is all-important while the navigation, communications, electrical, and waste treatment systems are being designed. Since he reports to Captain Dahl, the captain is here too, to add his expertise. As we speak, André St. Hubert, the *chef de cuisine*, is breathing down the neck of the restaurant designer, Antonio Zamboni, to make sure that he doesn't plan to install the dishwashers where the stoves should be. Although St. Hubert reports to Jones, the hotel manager, on the other hand, he must make his decisions with his chief chef, Paul Vuillard, and the head maitre d'hotel, Gianni Fendi, as well."

"Fendi? Vuillard, St. Hubert? No Americans?" Gigi asked.

"Americans are singularly unsuited to an elegant restaurant atmosphere." Hansen favored her with a wiry grin. "Cruise ships from all over the world go to Italy for their top service personnel —headwaiters, waiters, wine stewards, even busboys. They are simply the best. The Portuguese are good, the French are often too snobbish to do anything but cook, and the Spanish have no tradition. The stewards and chambermaids will be Scandinavian, the officers and captains Norwegian, Danish, or English, the hospital personnel Swiss. The casino is run, as everywhere afloat, by an Austrian company, just as the beauty salon is owned by an Englishman, who has concessions on all ships."

"But won't the *Emerald* fly the American flag?"

"The international flag," Ben told her. "That gives us the right to hire who we please."

"Aren't you going to hire *any* Americans?" she demanded.

"Of course," Ben answered, "for the orchestra, the entertainment staff, and the gym trainers. But I'm considering Greeks for the *corps de gigolo*. They have charm, enthusiasm, and endurance." He winked at her look of outrage.

Hansen coughed, ignoring the interruption, and continued his point about the kitchens. "You see, Miss Orsini, the chief engineer, Arnsin Olsen, must work closely with the chief chef. There are vital matters such as the sizes of the meat lockers, the tanks to hold fresh lobsters, the caviar storage compartments, even the space allotted to breakfast cereals—pampered travelers cling to their favorite cereal, and there's no shopping center in the middle of the South Pacific. The use of every inch of the ship is a subject of intense discussion. Every one of these men is a specialist, each one demands more space for his own supplies than is possible, and they all have to work together because each detail ends up connected to every other—the size of the wineglasses, for example, must correspond exactly to the size of the racks in the dishwashers."

"Of course," Gigi said, nodding as patiently as possible. Dishwashers? What was the ship going to *look like*, for heaven's sake? A floating Kmart?

"It sounds like the United Nations," she said. "Who's the boss?"

"The owner, Mr. Winthrop, is the boss, and I report to him. He has to make all the final decisions, since he pays the bills. Naturally it would be easier if he could take a year off from his other activities and live in Venice, but since he can't, we've brought Porta Margera to him. Once all the plans are completed and we have everything we need, down to those wineglasses I mentioned, the ship will be fitted out in the drydock."

"I think Miss Orsini is going to faint unless she sees some

designs," Ben said, standing up. "I recognize a certain look in her eyes."

"Not faint, scream," Gigi whispered to him, as he took her arm to lead her out of Hansen's office. They bypassed the first floor, which was devoted to offices and accountants, taking a newly installed elevator up to the second floor, which was one vast space crowded by a hundred draftsmen working at computers.

They walked up and down with Arnsin Olsen, who showed them the way in which the lower part of the 540-foot length of the freighter was being used: fuel tanks filling the bottom of the ship, separated by a double bottom from the tanks of drinking water, bath water, and cooking water that filled the next deck. There was a complicated desalination system for treatment of sea water used in the air-conditioning system and for scrubbing the decks and doing the laundry.

Gigi looked at incomprehensible computer designs for the between-decks spaces that would contain all the pipes, electrical wiring, and telephone lines of the ship.

"I didn't realize it was going to be so complicated," she said to Ben, while Olsen's back was turned.

"Neither did I," he responded, "and we haven't seen so much as a stewardess's cabin yet. This stuff's all below the waterline."

"Can't we—?"

"Not without being rude. Olsen is very proud of this," Ben answered her unspoken question. "You started this, now be patient." He put his arm casually around her waist, managing to give her a firm pinch on the ass in passing.

"Stop that!" she said in a low voice, conscious of the interested eyes of the squadron of draftsmen who were discreetly enjoying the novelty of this visit.

He gave her another healthy pinch. "Malls don't have to cross oceans, carrying picky passengers. It takes at least fifty thousand computer drawings to plan one ship, and that's only to help the engineers and designers find the best solutions to the space, not to replace the human design process, so you deserve far worse than a little pinch or two."

"Miss Orsini, would you like to see the *Sizione Maestra?*" Olsen asked.

"That depends," Gigi said cautiously. It sounded like the sewage system.

"The master section drawing, through the midship, deck by deck."

"Please! Lead me to it!"

She and Ben took another elevator, accompanied by Hansen and Olsen, to the third floor, where even more draftsmen worked at even more computers. They went to a large office at the back of the room, where Gigi was introduced to Captain Dahl, Eustace Jones, and a third man, Renzo Montegardini, the naval architect in charge of all the design work necessary to turn the empty hull of a freighter into the finest cruise ship that had ever sailed the seven seas.

Montegardini, Gigi saw at once, was more central to this entire enterprise than anyone except Ben, who merely signed checks. Even Hansen deferred to this tall, gaunt man in his fifties, who wore clothes as well as Vito Orsini did, and had an immediate charm. As he bent over her hand to kiss it, she felt as if she'd been knighted.

"So, at last I meet the young lady whose genial inspiration caused me to leave my dear Genoa, my beloved studio, my apprentices, and my other clients."

"You make me feel guilty," Gigi said, using her eyelashes with unrestrained abandon.

"Do not waste your sympathy on me, most kind and lovely Miss Orsini. I am a convert to the New World. I love New York, my wife loves New York, even my wife's cats love New York. And this is truly a magnificent challenge. Always before, I have worked on a ship from the first rough sketch. Here the problems are fascinating, but since the lines of the ship are splendid, there is no problem that cannot be solved."

"Then you approve of the ship's lines?"

"I salute them. I doubt that I could have done much better myself, and nobody in Italy has ever called me a modest man, except, of course, my wife, who knows my inner self. However, all other things remained to be done. I started with the funnel—but you know that—"

"I know nothing!" Gigi exclaimed, and then remembered her

manners. "Except about the fuel storage and the water storage and the kitchens . . ."

"Ah, these engineers, they always start with practical matters. A malady professional, even a mania, but we forgive them their obsessions, since a ship must sail. You see, Miss Orsini, the funnel is paramount. It sets the silhouette of the ship, the signature of the ship, the style and romance of the ship, much like the cut of your enchanting jacket from my wife's friend Lagerfeld." He turned to the back wall of his office, where a covered painting hung.

"Be still, my heart," Gigi breathed into Ben's ear.

"The funnel?"

"Renzo, you fool. He didn't say he was married, did he?"

Ben planted his hand firmly on her ass and left it there while Montegardini drew back a cloth from a painting of the *Winthrop Emerald*. Gigi's heart battered her chest in excitement and joy as she studied it and tried to see what it could possibly have in common with the gray freighters she had seen in Mestre.

Yes, the configurations of the bow and the stern were identical, but everything else belonged to another universe. Four new decks rose from the former main deck, sweeping back from the prow of the ship in one clean, positive line toward the great twin funnels that stood athwart the stern, their shapes a statement of adventure and grace she had never expected, and one that she recognized was entirely individual. The entire ship was white except for the single slash of emerald green that traversed every foot of the longest point of its hull, from prow to stern. There was a wide emerald green band on each of the white funnels, just below the round metallic smokestacks. Each of the four new decks was striped by a continuous line of blue window glass. In the middle of the topmost sun deck rose a tall structure like an angular open staircase, on which signal flags were flying. Although the painting was made of the ship at rest on a still sea, it seemed to be plunging forward, as if it were a spacecraft rather than an object that had to obey the laws of gravity, yet at the same time it proclaimed man's profound and simple relationship to the sea.

Suddenly, Gigi realized that she had been standing in a roomful of silent men, gaping without any verbal reaction at the picture of the *Winthrop Emerald*. She turned to Montegardini with a gesture of despair. "I don't know what to say."

"You've already said it," he told her, smiling. "Four minutes of silence, that tells me I've succeeded."

"Beyond any dream," she told him.

"Gigi," Ben said, almost impatiently, "I knew you'd love it, but you've got to look at the *Sizione Maestra.*" He held up a sheaf of large sheets of rustling paper, held tightly together by metal clamps at one end. "Until you've seen these, you really haven't got a clue—"

"*Ecco,* Bennito, I have a feeling that Miss Orsini has seen enough of these drawings for now," Renzo Montegardini said. "She looks as if she may be suffering from the famous fatigue of the blueprint. Why don't you show her the model suites, the fully appointed section of the restaurant, and the owner's suite, and then come back downstairs, if Miss Orsini still cares to look at these master plans today?"

"It's not blueprint fatigue, it's bliss," Gigi said. "But you're right, I don't want to spoil the impression of the painting by looking at the innards of that glorious ship right away."

"Whatever you say," Ben said, putting down the master plans reluctantly. "You coming with us, Renzo?"

"How not? I must see if *la bella signorina* approves."

"You've made another conquest," Ben muttered at Gigi as the parade of men followed them back to the elevator.

"How come he calls you by your first name and nobody else does?"

"He calls everybody whatever he chooses. He's the naval architect, the artist, and we're just the drones."

"Poor darling drone. How I pity you. But after all, it's your name on the side of the ship."

"He allowed me that much," Ben agreed, as they stood in the back of the small elevator, packed now by Montegardini, Olsen, Hansen, Dahl, Jones, St. Hubert, and Zamboni, none of whom intended to miss a moment of Gigi's reaction to the model rooms. Ben's hand was now pressed between the cheeks of her ass, although nobody could notice it, and his middle finger was moving firmly in an insistent rhythm, held back from its objective only by Gigi's firmly clenched muscles and Monsieur Lagerfeld's tweed.

"I won't get out of the elevator unless you stop that," she said, her low voice pitched to be unheard by the others, who were busily arguing all around them. "They're so polite that they'll stand back to let me go first, so we'll be stuck right here into the middle of next week."

Ben withdrew his hand as they stopped at the next floor. When they emerged, followed by the six men, Gigi looked around and, with a rapid glance, took in a group of model rooms that would take at least an hour to inspect in detail.

"Tell me about the owner's suite," she queried, turning away to question Ben. "I didn't know there was going to be one."

"There'll be one on each ship, twice as big as each of the other suites."

"All for you, poor drone?"

"Only if I'm aboard, otherwise for the most VIP of VIPs."

"Could I see that first, please? Just the two of us?"

"But—"

"Aren't you the man who signs the checks?"

"Gentlemen," Ben said, "I'm going to show Miss Orsini the owner's suite myself. We'll join you in a minute."

The model rooms had been designed to the precise scale of the ship, so that their walls, like partitions, stopped well short of the high ceilings of the warehouse. As Gigi stepped into the owner's suite, she heard the solid thunk of the door as it closed behind them, yet at the same time she could hear the conversation of the men who had been left to mill around outside and look for imperfections.

"Alone at last," she said to Ben, twirling around and around and kicking off her shoes.

"Come on, sweetheart, stop kidding. Isn't this incredible! Look at it, for God's sake, have you ever seen anything like it? And this is just the bedroom. Wait till you see the sitting room, the kitchen, the dining room, the sun deck, the baths, and the walk-in closets. There's almost a thousand feet of space here. Every detail's complete, except for the things that the design teams are still looking for in Europe."

Gigi crawled to the middle of the quilted beige silk bedspread of the enormous bed and flopped down so that she lay at full length. "Great mattress. Just come over here first and give me a tiny little kiss. I absolutely have to lie down for a second, I'm dizzy."

Ben, shrugging in impatience, sat down next to her, bent over, and kissed her briefly on the lips.

"Oh, better than that," Gigi whispered. "You can do much better. Try to revive me, I'm wiped out."

Laughing, Ben too lay back on the bedspread and put his arms around her.

"Was it the desalination system that knocked you out, or Renzo?"

She raised herself off the bed and stripped off her jacket. "I think it might have been the elevator ride," she murmured. With one quick gesture she unhooked her wraparound skirt and flung it on top of her jacket. "Or maybe I'm pinched black and blue. I'd better find out the extent of the damage." As she was speaking, she rapidly unpeeled her panty hose and her panties.

"What the hell's come over you?" Ben hissed at her. "There are a bunch of guys right outside this wall. They can *hear* you."

"Not if I keep my voice down," Gigi said in her softest tone, as she bent over him in a quick motion and unzipped his fly. "Not if you don't make a silly big old fuss."

"Stop that!"

She straddled him before he knew what she was doing, and looked into his eyes. "Do you remember that old song, *'Only Make Believe'*? I think it goes, 'Only make believe I love you, only make believe you love me.' Something like that," she murmured, humming softly. "Only make believe we're alone, dear, only make believe you want me so . . ."

"You're nuts!"

"Yes . . . oh, yes, Ben, the spirit of the high seas has penetrated me. I'm making believe that the wall goes right up to the ceiling and nobody can hear us," Gigi whispered with a wicked, merciless smile as she put her warm fingers into the fly of his shorts and imprisoned his penis in both her hands.

"Don't!"

"Quiet, they'll hear you," she admonished him, exploring the dangling length of his limp penis adroitly, each stroke of her hands reaching the soft bulb of its head, lingering there an instant, and circling it before returning to follow its almost instantly expanding length and width all the way down the base. She wasted no time on unnecessary refinements or teasing moments or alternating pressures or interesting caresses. She wanted his penis as big and hard as it could ever get, and she wanted it fast. Fast and quick and now.

As soon as she felt him filled and pulsating, as soon as she knew he was well beyond the point of any self-control and couldn't possibly push her off and zip himself up, she bent her lovely head and took just the fat, velvety tip of his penis in her mouth and sucked on it as strongly as she could, using her tongue and the succulent pulling membranes of her lips and cheeks with every ounce of savage energy she possessed, while she held his shaft in a firm grip so that he was imprisoned by her fingers, all sensation concentrated in his most sensitive spot. At the same time, she listened intently to the rhythm of his panting ragged breath. The instant she could tell from the tightening of his muscles and the change in his breathing that he was beginning to approach an orgasm, she pulled her mouth away and slid upward on her bare knees so that she was able, in one quick motion, to take his whole burning penis between her legs, sinking it in deeply and fully, for she had been ready to open easily to him since she'd closed the door of the owner's suite.

She looked down at Ben as she rode him, her breasts thrust forward under her blouse. His eyelids were clenched together in an ecstasy of excitement. "It's up to you," Gigi muttered, as she plunged up and down with relentless animality. "It's up to you how much noise you make." She never took her eyes away from his face, watching the stern concentration of pleasure spread over his features in a grimace that grew and intensified every second. His teeth were grinding and he had grabbed her bottom in both of his hands so that he could push upward into her, but she struggled successfully to retain her dominant position so that she could observe him closely. She watched as his mouth grew grimly tighter and tighter in his effort not to cry out, and she redoubled her frenzied motions until he was galloping, all will lost, toward an irresistible climax. He bit his lower lip so mercilessly that she was afraid he'd draw blood. Only then did she cover his mouth with hers so that she muffled the low, barbaric sounds that escaped as he was finally overcome by a huge, wild burst of release. As she felt him coming inside her, she permitted herself the exquisite climax she'd been holding back since she'd taken him in her mouth, but a silent climax that he was too lost in restraining the sounds of his own mad delight to notice. As soon as she could move, Gigi rolled off Ben and looked innocently up at the warehouse ceiling.

He opened his eyes, barely able to focus.

"Why?" he croaked.

"Why? I thought that was what you wanted . . . the elevator . . . the hand on my ass . . . your finger . . ."

"You're . . . simply . . . crazy."

"I must have got my signals scrambled. But just think, now you've learned how to come without screaming the house down. That could come in handy someday."

"Bitch!"

"Right on! And don't you forget it!"

"Oh, God, I love you!"

"Why, thank you, Ben. Oh, dear, I can't find my panties."

"Never mind them. Get dressed for heaven's sake. Oh, shit, the bedspread!"

"I can't leave this room looking less neat than when I entered it. What would people think?" Gigi found her clothes, piece by piece, exactly where she had thrown them, and dressed quickly. She went to the dressing table that faced the bed and inspected herself, nodding from side to side in disapproval.

"What's wrong now?" Ben asked imploringly, as he mopped and smoothed the bedspread.

"Being on top has its advantages—my hair's fine—but I have an unmistakable just-fucked look."

"Oh, stop, stop! You've had your revenge. They won't even know the difference."

"Renzo will, and all the others too, even if each one of them is a virgin."

"Then stay in here and cool down. Take a shower or something. I'll tell them you don't feel well, you have a headache."

"But I feel simply terrific," Gigi announced as she put on fresh lip gloss. "I'm ready for the rest of the tour. You'll have to replace that spread, I don't think sperm comes out with a damp cloth, and I seem to have . . . ah . . . leaked." She slipped into her shoes and walked to the door of the suite. "Coming?" she asked him over her shoulder as she stepped out.

"Gentlemen," she announced, "the view of the owner's suite has refreshed me. I feel like a new woman—shall we continue?"

As soon as Gigi had left for New York, Victoria Frost put into motion a plan she had been mulling over for many months. When Archie and Byron had first tried to hire Gigi, they had promised her never to go after the Scruples Two account. Gigi had been determined not to solicit that juicy piece of business, billing thirteen million dollars a year and certain to grow larger, because she knew that, because of her, Spider and Billy would feel obligated to give it to FRB whether they wanted to or not.

This prospect compromised her bid for independence and her family connections in a way that made her squirm merely in contemplation, she'd explained to Arch and By. She hadn't even considered their offer of a job until they'd agreed to the condition. Both of them had made sure that Victoria knew that Scruples Two was off limits.

And all of them were dead wrong, Victoria decided.

In the first place, there was no possible conflict of interest; Gigi wouldn't be doing business with herself if the agency worked for Scruples Two, since she didn't share in the agency's profits. In the second place, the copy that Gigi had written for Scruples Two was one of the major reasons that the catalog had been such an instant success. And in the third place, Gigi's unprofessionally squeamish shades of feeling, such a quaint excess of standoffishness, had no place in the advertising business. Arch and By should never have agreed to her conditions, but at the time they'd needed Gigi too much to make the necessary arguments that would have convinced her how coy and oversensitive she was being.

More than enough time had passed since then—almost a year. Gigi had had far more than her unfair share of success on her own, to make that early agreement as meaningless as it was stupid, Victoria decided. It was time for her to step in. She had done her homework on Russo and Russo, the agency that currently had the Scruples Two account. There was no need to say anything to

Byron or Archie until she'd been successful, she thought, as she telephoned Spider Elliott and made an appointment to meet him in his office.

"Welcome to Scruples Two," Spider said as Victoria was shown in. "It's not every day that I meet Gigi's boss . . . not that Gigi can be said to have ever had even one, in the usual sense of the word. It's an exclusive club, you know. A caterer named Emily Gatherum and you and me. And my wife, of course, but she hasn't been to the office since our boys were born."

"I've heard so much about the twins," Victoria said glowingly. "When Gigi and I have our girl-talk lunches together, she often tells me what new stunts they're up to, she even shows me photos, for all the world like a doting aunt. You must be so proud of them."

"I'm totally gaga, but I understand that's normal. What would you like to drink—coffee, tea, something cold?"

"Nothing, thanks. Mr. Elliott—"

"Spider, please. Nobody calls me anything else."

"And I'm Victoria."

Spider never looked at a woman without automatically re-dressing her. When he'd been running Scruples, even the most self-assured clients had rarely dared to decide on an important dress without his approval. Victoria Frost, he saw immediately, would never have needed to ask his advice. In her double-breasted coat-dress of crisp beige wool, she projected an ultimate combination of efficiency and authority. She could be nothing but an extremely successful businesswoman in that dress, yet it was so excessively chaste that paradoxically she created an impression of drama. Strange how Gigi hadn't mentioned that she was a beauty, in the classically severe ballerina mode that other men so often found intriguing.

As Victoria received her first impressions of Spider, she couldn't help regretting that this was one man with whom clearly she could never enjoy a secret afternoon. Every bit of knowledge she had about male manners, signals and codes computed into an instant understanding that Spider Elliott would never respond to her on a sexual basis. He was taken. As taken as a man could be.

"Spider, I'm here to talk about the Scruples Two advertising," Victoria declared, with the kind of confidence that immediately puts another person into a receptive frame of mind, just as the first notes of a great musical performer reassure the audience and settle them down to listen. "I've been studying your campaign intensively for the last four months, and I'm convinced that Russo and Russo simply aren't doing as good a job for you as we could, at Frost Rourke Bernheim."

"Is that so?" She doesn't waste time getting to the point, Spider thought.

"It *is* so. They're not the most compatible mix for you. They fall short of being your ideal marketing partner. I'll bet anything that the creative team is male."

"You're right about that, but bright, bright guys. They do great graphics. I like 'em."

"With all due respect, bright isn't enough. Advertising is a business in which it's axiomatic that only the bright survive. And I don't have to tell you that great graphics can only go so far. They have to be the *right* graphics or it doesn't matter how good they are."

"Uh-huh."

"You're selling a single product," Victoria continued, feeling herself quickening the smooth rhythm of the pitch, "a catalog that only interests women. The one and only point of your advertising is to get more women to send away for the catalog. No man in the world would look through a Scruples Two catalog unless he were a drag queen, and yet you, a man, are using the creative ability of two fellows with male minds in male bodies. There's too much testosterone floating around in that creative mix, Spider."

"You really believe that men can't write great ads for women? What about the reverse? Can women write ads for men?"

"Sometimes an extraordinary woman can. My mother, for instance. She had as many accounts that appealed to men as to women. But her heyday was decades ago, and women have changed. People don't walk a mile for a Camel anymore—or at least they know they shouldn't—and women today have changed, particularly the women who buy from your catalog, working women, young mothers with jobs, busy women executives who have no time to shop. They're a whole new breed, Spider, and there's a whole new set of needs and wants, a new set of priorities. Most important, there's a new set of fantasies . . . women's fantasies."

She paused for a split second to make sure she had his full attention, before she went on.

"There isn't *a man alive* who can really be aware of what's going on in these women's minds, and how they want to perceive themselves in terms of image."

"We know all that, Victoria, or the catalog wouldn't be so successful."

"Oh, it's dead right in the catalog, I agree, but you're using copy based directly on what Gigi created. I have a complete set of Scruples Two catalogs, and the copy has barely changed since she left; you've just jiggled her words around and applied them to the new items."

"That's true enough." Not just true, Spider thought, but too true. He'd been concerned about it for several months. He hated to rely on repetition, but nobody could write Scruples copy like Gigi.

"But the ads in the magazines have changed," Victoria continued easily. "They just . . . miss, in my opinion. They're as good as Russo and Russo can produce, but they're not going to get better —they need a new direction. You also need serious new media planning. You're not in many of the best hot magazines for your particular customer, you should be advertising on selected television shows, for your sales figures you're not spending enough on advertising."

"What is it that you're proposing?"

"I'd like to make a pitch for your account."

"I'm a little confused here. Would it be Gigi who'd be doing the creative work?"

"Of course, or I wouldn't have dared to come here. Gigi's quickly become our top creative on the copy side—aside from Archie Rourke, of course—Gigi's a woman and she's intimately familiar with the product. Obviously she'd be our first choice, although we have other female creatives with enormous talent. What we'd do is put all the creative resources of the agency to work before we made our pitch—we'd want to see ideas from everybody, male and female and every sex in between—it's what's charmingly called a 'gang bang'—but I know that Gigi would come up with the best stuff."

Spider got up from behind his desk and sat on it, his arms folded, looking down at Victoria.

"Does Gigi know about this?" he demanded sternly.

"No. She took the job with FRB on the condition that we not solicit you. But that was a long time ago. Now she's more than proven herself; no one can doubt that she can stand on her own two feet without any help from anyone here. That's why I took it upon myself to make this solicitation."

"If we listen to the pitch and still decide to stick with Russo and Russo, will she be embarrassed?"

"Hah! Gigi? I have yet to see her embarrassed, Spider. She won't take it personally. She's become a different person since she used to work here. She's highly professional."

"You're sure of that? The Gigi I know, as workmanlike as she was . . . could be emotional."

"I'm sure she still is. But the agency business quickly teaches you to leave your emotions at home."

"Well . . . look, you make a lot of sense, Victoria. I like the way you think. And most of all, I miss having Gigi's brain to call on. But we need fresh catalog copy too, not just the ads or the media buys. Would we be able to ask her to spend time on that?"

"It goes with our becoming your marketing partner, Spider. Not at Russo and Russo, but at FRB."

"Victoria, I'll be frank. I'd do anything to get Gigi back working on Scruples Two. I haven't been really happy with Russo and Russo. I don't need a 'gang bang' or anybody else's input, and I know your graphic guys are tremendous, especially Bernheim. Promise me a team of Gigi and Bernheim, and I'll give you the account."

"You make quick decisions," Victoria said, smiling calmly, hiding her shock and triumph well.

"Only when the offer's irresistible," Spider said, and put out his hand to shake on it.

As Victoria Frost left the Scruples Two offices and stood in the elevator going down to the valet parking level, she felt her spirits rising higher with each descending floor. Gigi would spit blood when she found out . . . but there was nothing she could do about it . . . management was management, and the opportunity to capture a thirteen-million-dollar account—soon to be much bigger—on a cold pitch couldn't be rejected for one individual's personal reasons. God, but it made her feel at the top of her form to kill two birds with one stone! Gigi and Scruples Two. If only Spider Elliott weren't so wedded to that wife of his, she could have killed three birds this morning, Victoria told herself in soaring good humor. But you can't have everything.

She wished she had somebody to talk to, Billy thought, as she swam laps in her pool all alone except for any one of the six gardeners working on the eleven acres of gardens. She'd promised Spider not to swim by herself, but if she got a cramp, at least one of them would hear her call for help, she rationalized as she started her fourth set of fifty laps, feeling deeply sorry for herself.

Gigi was in New York; Sasha was off in Santa Barbara with Vito for a few days, although they couldn't take a real honeymoon until *Long Weekend* had finished production; Dolly Moon, her best friend in Los Angeles, was on location in Maine, playing in a divorce comedy opposite Alan Alda, and Jessica Thorpe Strauss, her oldest friend of all, from the days before she'd even met Ellis Ikehorn, had taken off on a European vacation with her husband, now that their five kids were back in school. She simply was not in the mood to talk to any of Spider's six sisters. Everyone she truly cared about had deserted her.

The twins were just beginning their long afternoon nap, and Spider was busy running Scruples Two. Talk about the dead center of the afternoon, Billy told herself as she churned up and down, this was unquestionably it. She hated swimming, but she had to exercise or she wouldn't be able to fit into the giant roomful of clothes she owned, not that she had anywhere to wear them. The obscenely silly, petty, unimportant problems of a poor little rich girl . . .

Disgusted with her thoughts and herself, she climbed abruptly out of the pool, thirty defiant laps short of her goal, roughly toweled herself dry, wrapped herself in a terrycloth robe, put on sneakers, and set off rapidly for her walled garden, her private sanctuary at any time of the year. If she was going to be alone, she might just as well be alone in the place she had planned for solitude, Billy thought, looking apathetically at the glorious blooms of early fall that filled the garden Russell Page had designed for her in a palette of whites.

Fall was a rotten time of year, Billy decided, even here, where all was beauty and peace. Beauty and peace had their place, but not in the autumn, when her East Coast blood ran more quickly than ever in some sort of involuntarily programmed anticipation of the excitement of this season that always felt like the true beginning of the year. Autumn, when all the galleries had new shows; autumn, when the round of parties started; autumn, when people came back from vacation instead of going away; autumn, when the plays opened; autumn, when you bought a new wardrobe . . . to bloody hell with California, where autumn was the forest-fire season and where there was nothing new under the hot sun except more of the same beauty and peace.

She needed something to do with herself, Billy realized as she sat on the old bench beneath the arbor of wisteria, its leaves now turning yellow and its blooms long gone. She'd been totally plunged into motherhood for more than ten months. Hal and Max were the center of her life, after Spider. While she was pregnant she had decided not to try to choose among her options of full-time motherhood, part-time motherhood, and returning to work. She'd opted to give herself a chance to find out what she wanted, since she possessed, as so few women did, enough money to pick any path or combination of paths.

Now she knew that full-time motherhood wasn't the answer. Not if she could judge by the vile and self-pitying mood she was in, the mood she'd been in for weeks longer than she'd admitted to anyone, including herself.

Even if she wanted to stay home and be with the twins, she'd be frustrated because they were so deeply involved with each other and their newfound world that consisted of searching out and destroying everything in their path, like miniature soldiers set forth to carry out a scorched-earth policy. They needed her far less than before, and gave her far less of their attention.

Without question, Billy assured herself, it was a sign of superior intelligence that they took everything apart to find out what it was—the toilet flush had been their latest project—but that didn't make wreckage as fascinating to her as it was to them. Now that they had started to walk, becoming upright from one day to another, with a future in Olympic sprinting clearly evident from the beginning, even Nanny Elizabeth had demanded reinforcements, and a fast-moving assistant nanny had been added to the nursery.

She could, of course, return to Scruples Two and the job she had shared with Spider, Billy thought, except that Spider had, in the last year, expanded his activities to include hers. Face it, she told herself, he had taken over. Taken the fuck over. Completely. She didn't blame him . . . not really . . . his abilities had always been greater than his responsibilities, but she couldn't walk in and get her old job back, because her old job had been absorbed into his job and he didn't even realize it. He'd be shocked if she told him how little time he spent now discussing the operations of the catalog with her, preferring to forget them when he wasn't at the office, exactly like the typical businessman returning home to the little woman.

"And what kind of a day did you have, Spider, darling?" "Oh, the usual, sweetheart, you know, details, details, tell me what the kids did today, tell me what's new." The only thing he didn't ask was "What's for dinner?" but that was probably only a question of time.

She had been naive not to have anticipated it, Billy realized. From the day she'd met Spider, from the very first day ten years ago when he'd toured Scruples with her and detailed every last thing she'd done wrong in running and decorating her cherished boutique, he'd been the man with the answers. He'd conned her into giving him and Valentine a free hand, and made it into a raving success that no other store had ever equaled.

When that era was over, Spider had come back from his sailing trip around the world and talked her into lending the name of Scruples to the catalog, although she'd been violently opposed to the idea when Gigi and Sasha thought of it. He'd been brilliantly right. Again. Had she ever done anything that Spider hadn't forced her into, Billy wondered. Had she really let him dominate her to that extent for a decade? Yes, by God, she had, she realized as she leapt off the bench and paced back and forth in the walled garden. She'd been led around by the nose by this man, love him though she did, as if she were without a brain in her head, as though she were merely a rich woman, a woman he knew was going to listen to his advice, be convinced by his charm and his tra-la-la, and follow his lead. A rich doll. She, Wilhelmina Hunnenwell Winthrop Ikehorn Orsini Elliott, a rich, dumb, dependent dolly babe.

Well, fuck that! She had an idea, a good one too. Billy rushed out of the garden, not even bothering to lock the door behind her, and strode for hours through the woodland glades and gardens of her eleven acres, thinking as hard and fast as she'd ever thought in her life.

14

A re we going out tonight?" Spider stopped inside the door to their sitting room and looked at Billy in confusion.

"No, darling, why?" When he walked through the door, she had turned toward him with such an eager swirl of anticipation that his first thought was that he'd come home late on a night they were supposed to be meeting friends for an early dinner.

"You're all dressed up and you look as if you can't wait to get going somewhere."

"Do I?" she asked. Billy knew exactly why he was so surprised. She had grown so excited in the course of developing her new idea while she was prowling around the gardens this afternoon that she'd worked herself into a state of flying exhilaration. She felt too jubilant to put on any of the casual comfortable clothes she'd grown used to wearing all day long, even right on through the pre-dinner hour when she and Spider played with the children while they had a drink. Usually she'd change into another pair of jeans and a fresh shirt only when Hal or Max had made her messy enough to go to the trouble.

Two hours before Spider came home tonight, Billy had stormed all four of the twenty-five-foot-long racks in her closet, a thirty-foot-square room carpeted in ivory, each rack-bearing wall padded in lavender silk, pushing aside one hanger after another in search of something to wear that went with her elated mood and yet wouldn't require that she get into panty hose and real shoes, which would look ridiculous for an evening at home. It couldn't be daytime, it couldn't be fall or winter, not in this weather, it couldn't be formal, and she was feeling too charged up to wear any of her long, elaborate, at-home robes. Was it possible, Billy asked herself, that a woman who had first appeared on the Best-Dressed List at the age of twenty-three should now find herself with nothing to wear for an evening at home with her husband? Was that what having kids did to you?

Finally she'd found the perfect ensemble tucked away in the rack where she kept her sportswear: slim pants and a long, flaring tunic with a deep oval neckline, made of a heavy oriental silk in an astonishing blaze of color that lay somewhere on the thin line dividing shocking pink and hot pink. It was almost a costume, especially with the matching velvet slippers she'd once had made to wear with it, back in the days when it had seemed important, even vital, to own a special pair of shoes for every separate piece of clothing she owned.

After she'd showered and brushed her blunt, heavy, wild curls back off her forehead, Billy realized that the color she was wearing demanded more eye liner, more blusher, and more lipstick than she normally used. Once she'd applied her makeup it was clearer than ever that something, some final note, was missing, and she'd gone to her vault to find a piece of jewelry to complete her outfit.

It had been so long since she'd worn anything that children couldn't possibly pull off and put in their mouths that she'd almost forgotten the numbers of the two separate combinations of the vault's intricate locks. The heavy door swung open and Billy looked in a state of semi-shock at the trays and trays of black velvet that were piled on the shelves in stately order. Well, yes, she realized that she had jewels, she'd had them since Ellis Ikehorn had started buying them for her as an emperor would bestow gifts on a newlywed empress, but there were so many . . . she had forgotten how much she owned.

When had she had time or occasion to wear all of these, she asked herself as she pulled out one tray after another, each tray bearing its load of treasure, the jewels all in their allotted places for quick inspection. Not plain gold, it looked awful on pink, and of course her diamonds were out of the question, Billy knew, putting back everything that was wrong. Not her emeralds, either, and somehow not her rubies, which she liked with pink or red, but not with this particularly powerful pink, which overwhelmed them. Her always-right pearls looked too conservative tonight, even the black ones, and her semiprecious collections, the turquoises and corals, the aquamarines, the amethysts and tourmalines, the citrines and the jade—none of them worked when she held them close to the silk and glanced at herself in the mirror. That left sapphires, the obvious choice, but hardly what one would call your obvious pink and blue combination, not when she'd put on the enormous sapphire earrings with a large baroque pearl hanging from each extraordinary gem, and the double ropes of sapphires and baroque pearls that fell so perfectly into the neckline of the tunic.

Everyone knew that you had to wear your jewelry next to living skin or it lost its glow, Billy thought righteously, or was that story just about pearls? Weren't you even supposed to swim in salt water with pearls at least twice a year? Never mind, at least she looked like herself again, didn't she?

She inspected herself from all angles in her three-way mirror. After she'd lost the lumbering weight of her early years, Billy had been able to wear and carry any clothes ever designed, thanks to her height and the slim, long lines of her limbs, but tonight, after so many months of dressing for staying at home and being with children, she caught her breath in delight at the sight of her reflected image. Oh, she looked—if she said so herself and there was no one else around to say it—she looked—and there was no other word to use, so she'd have to use it—*magnificent.* Magnificent in the way Lorenzo de' Medici or Sultan Soliman had the word "magnificent" attached to their names, "magnificent" as in great and lofty and royally lavish, as in grand and splendid and sumptuous.

There was nothing wrong with magnificent, Billy thought, as she waited for Spider. He hadn't been treated to his wife in her magnificent manifestation in too long a time . . . this should be a lesson to her in not taking her husband for granted. He'd never known her in her consistently magnificent days, when she was Ellis's wife and Ellis had wanted that for her, but he'd certainly seen her in many magnificent moments. He must have been wondering what had happened to her, perhaps even asking himself why childbirth had catapulted her into appearing as a perpetually practical housewife and mother instead of the woman he'd married.

Billy was standing in front of a balcony door, looking out at the seemingly endless pathway bordered by noble sycamores that led the eye into the gardens below her, when she heard Spider's step at the sitting room door. Deliberately, she didn't turn until she felt him right behind her.

"My God! I know what it must be," Spider said, holding her at arm's length as he inspected her. "There's only one reason I can think of for you to look so beautiful and excited."

"Aren't you going to kiss me?" Billy pushed forward against his strong arms, but he easily held her off.

"And ruin your lipstick? Not until you tell me if I'm right— you're pregnant again!"

"Oh, come on, Spider! Is that the only reason you can think of for me to look beautiful?" she exclaimed, deeply disappointed.

"It's the best reason I can think of, but it's not the only one," he said, amused at her reaction.

"What's another?"

"The twins did something new they've never done before, like discovering why people use napkins, or maybe you found a new hairdresser who'll come to the house, or you just had a great massage, or, hell, I don't know, maybe you've bought the kids that dog we've been talking about . . ."

"Your imaginative powers astound me," Billy said, hiding her exasperation. "Do you want a drink?"

"Love one. Where are the kids?"

"They're playing in their playroom with their two nannies, and having a marvelous time prying up the floor tiles one by one.

Actually I was hoping we might have a few relaxing minutes alone together when you got home, instead of the constant struggle to keep Max and Hal from drinking out of our glasses."

"Hell, darling, I don't mind that. If the little buggers do manage to get a taste, it'll probably put them off liquor for life. Aversion therapy. Why don't you call Nanny Elizabeth on the house phone and ask her to bring them in? If I don't see them now, they'll be asleep by the time we finish dinner."

Pregnant again, Billy thought wrathfully as she used the house phone, pregnant again . . . as if the twins weren't enough, as if the only reason a woman would make herself magnificent for her husband could possibly be to announce that her womb was still in working order. Was that what she was to Spider, a uterus on two feet, like some new kind of toaster oven that popped out warm infants? Or, even worse, someone who only looked her best when she had a piddling household accomplishment to bring to his attention? Or a new hairdresser? Apparently so, damn that condescending son of a bitch! He had no idea to what depths of taking-her-for-granted he'd slipped into.

Still, she was as much to blame as he was, she had to be fair and admit it, Billy thought as she sipped her drink and the twins climbed over Spider as if he were a jungle gym, ignoring her familiar presence. She'd been blindly immersed in what some Victorian writers called "baby worship" for more than ten months, and heavily pregnant for months before giving birth, totally concentrated on her fascinating reproductive powers, so naturally he'd lost his sense of who she really was. *So had she.* She felt as if she had just awakened from a long coma.

Still . . . wasn't that forgetfulness convenient for him, this man with a firmly established history of telling her what she'd done wrong and then fixing it with his superior powers? Hadn't he accepted her staying home with astonishing rapidity and not a single protest? Yet, in justice to Spider, wouldn't any man behave in the same way? Wasn't that the way the bastards were genetically constructed from the day they were born? From *before* they were born? Even Spider Elliott?

Well, so be it. She didn't intend to allow him to remain in his throwback-to-the-1950s mode for longer than it would take to explode that particularly odious little time capsule of typically male thinking. She'd have to keep her new idea to herself until after dinner—she was too enthralled with it to be able to eat and talk about it at the same time.

Why was it, Billy wondered, as she and Spider went back upstairs to the sitting room after dinner, that no matter how many rooms a house had, no matter how many corners had been arranged just so that people could sit and talk, you always found yourself migrating to the same intimate quarters, which invariably turned out to be the smallest room in any house?

She felt his arms close around her waist as soon as the sitting room door was shut behind them.

"Okay, so you're not pregnant," Spider said. "But is there any reason why I shouldn't get you pregnant tonight? Just think, we could have three kids under the age of two. Or even four, if you got lucky and had another set of twins."

"Now there's a truly appealing idea," Billy replied in what she assumed he'd understand was a resoundingly negative response, but as he pulled her back toward him, his busy, peremptory hands told her that he'd missed her irony. The trusty trouser snake, she realized, was deaf to nuance.

"You're resplendent," he said, kissing the back of her neck.

Resplendent, Billy thought, flinching, a word that had always brought to her mind the picture of a dowager wearing a diamond tiara, a word that had only two meanings for her: old and rich.

She pulled away and stood looking down at the group of antique Japanese cachepots in which African daisies were massed, dozens and dozens of the multicolored Gerberas, tonight confined to a selection of brilliant yellows that clashed gorgeously with the hot pink of her tunic. She selected one and played with its petals. Finally she spoke.

"Spider, I have an idea and I'm dying to tell you about it."

"I have a better idea and I'm dying to demonstrate it to you," he answered, taking the Gerbera out of her hands and kissing her purposefully on the lips.

"Spider, I'm serious!"

"So am I," he pursued, ignoring her words and kicking his charm up a few notches. "Seriously horny."

Billy moved quickly and took refuge behind a heavy table. "Sit down and listen to me. You're always horny."

"Only when I see you."

"Then it'll keep, won't it? Please, please pay attention."

"For how long?" he bargained.

"Until I've finished, and I wish you'd really listen and not make me feel as if you're just marking time until you can jump me."

Spider gave her that damned smile which always made her want to curl up in his lap.

"I'm at your command, mentally alert, so long as you keep your distance. I'll take a chair, you can have the sofa. You might consider putting a paper bag over your head . . . on second thought, don't bother, I'll just look at my knees. Now, what's your idea?"

"It hit me this afternoon. I was thinking that I had to find something to do with myself, that just staying home wasn't the answer, and I found myself considering redecorating—"

"Why not? A completely new look—it'd be fun for you."

"I started to consider redecorating," Billy continued, shaking off his words, "and I realized that what I wanted was real work, not spending more time ditzing around on something that I'm perfectly happy with the way it is."

"If you want work, what's wrong with your old job?"

"My old job simply doesn't exist anymore, Spider. I've been phased out. I can't complain—after all, it's been almost a year and a half since I was involved in Scruples Two full-time. How many people have you hired since then who do some of the things I was doing?"

"Let's see—we hired Dodie away from Bill Blass to work full-time with Prince, and we hired Fabienne and Serena and Tracy to do the accessory buying and keep finding new pieces to copy for Gigi's antique lingerie; there's Mary Anne in charge of maternity clothes, plus Sasha expanded her department, she has six assistants instead of four, and she'll be back part-time by the beginning of next week—"

"So there isn't any place for me."

"Hell, darling, we own the business, we can create any kind of place you want—the only reason we took on so many new

319

people is that the amount of business we're doing is increasing almost faster than we can control it. Joe Jones walks around looking worried and saying "Inventory, inventory," out loud to himself all day long, as if he'd never had to deal with it when he was marketing chief at L.L. Bean—yet their inventory must have been more complicated than ours—"

"Spider, Scruples Two is something I can look at now and say to myself, 'We did it,' " Billy interrupted. "I can look at each new catalog with satisfaction and think, 'Spider and I, working together, accomplished this.' It's a solid, ongoing achievement in which I invested a huge amount of myself, it exists in the form I helped shape, it's mine and yours and Gigi's and Sasha's, a joint effort that will continue as it started, but that's not enough."

"What *would* be enough?" Spider scrutinized her face with loving curiosity.

"I want to do a *new* catalog. My own catalog, built from scratch, something that doesn't exist . . . that's never existed."

"What kind of catalog?"

"A decorating catalog. I want to call it 'The Scruples Home,' and I want to commission a small group of the top furniture designers in the world to design compact, exclusive collections of furniture in the moderate but not cheap price range that Scruples Two sells clothes at, and I want—"

"But where's the market?" Spider broke in. "People don't shop for furniture by catalog, not our kind of customers. They want to go and pick it out, sit on it—"

"Have you ever actually been to the furniture department of a department store?" Billy demanded.

"Actually . . . I don't think so . . . in New York I just sort of accumulated some junk for my loft—a couple of palm trees and a mattress—in L.A. I took whatever furniture came with the two houses I rented, then I moved in here, furniture heaven . . . no, I haven't."

"You're lucky—even Bloomie's in New York, with its model rooms, drives you wild with frustration. Trying to get a salesperson and make some sense out of the stuff you see is a lesson in total confusion. If you can stay the course, hours later you end up exhausted and depressed, convinced that you've made expensive mistakes. The Scruples Two customer doesn't have time to waste in department stores, that's why she's buying from our catalog."

"Right. But what about using interior decorators?"

"Spider, they're not for the busy working mother, any more than she can afford to hire a personal shopper."

"If you say so, God knows, interior decorators are one of your areas of expertise."

He looked, Billy thought, as if he were repressing a desire to indulge his sense of the ludicrous at her expense. Didn't he realize how earnestly she'd thought this through?

"The whole point of buying from a catalog," Billy said, watching Spider carefully, "is to get a rock-bottom price, because essentially a catalog is nothing more than a convenient and well-presented warehouse."

"I know all that, Billy, it's my business," Spider said impatiently. "You still haven't answered my question."

"The Scruples Home would present the basics, the essentials for five different kinds of homes: urban traditional, classic modern, American country, French farmhouse, western ranch house. Five perfect sofas, five perfect armchairs, five dining tables for multiple uses, five loveseats, five coffee tables, five headboards, and so on—you get the picture—and they'd all be able to be used together or separately, our principle of mix-and-match that makes the Prince collection so successful." Billy looked at Spider to see if she could get any feedback from him, but he looked as puzzled as before.

"Spider! Pay attention! Our Scruples customer could decorate by herself, without leaving her home. She could finally find that French country headboard she's always wanted but never could find, she could order the elegant loveseat from one of the collections and a modern expandable dining table from another, and get her place finished at last—we're assuming that she isn't living in crates—or if she's just getting married or starting fresh with a one-room studio apartment, she could do all the indispensable basics from The Scruples Home, and when she has the time to spend, she can stamp it with her own individuality with things she picks up here and there at flea markets and junk shops. *But she'd have her basics at wholesale.*"

"That loveseat," Spider asked, "what would it be covered in?"

"I figured plain muslin upholstery on everything upholstered, plus a choice of slipcovers."

"*Slipcovers!* Jesus, Billy, that's asking for inventory disaster. How many different fabrics would you have to carry to give your customer enough of a choice?"

"I think six would do it to start. Some sort of neutral, washable, textured fabric, like a duck or a seersucker, a black and white stripe in cotton, three basic mixable color choices in solid cotton, and one great floral. The customers could add sets of slipcovers as they went along. When needed, I'd keep adding new fabrics." Billy spoke proudly. The slipcovers, she knew, were her most amusing and innovative part of the entire idea. They were dirt-cheap to manufacture, practical to use, and fun to switch around.

"Look, let's not talk about the slipcovers yet," Spider said, trying to control his vision of Billy ending up with tens of thousands of yards of unwanted fabric. The next thing he knew, she'd be starting a remnant store. "What sort of pricing are you talking about?"

"Based on what I saw when I did this place with my decorator, the low-end wholesale on a decent three-pillow sofa would be about six hundred; a good, solid farmhouse table that would seat eight people would run about four-fifty—"

"But didn't you redecorate about three years ago?"

"More or less."

"Oh, Billy, Billy—prices have zoomed since then, and you're talking about major money here, even at what used to be the low end. Anyway, how did you happen to find out about low-end prices?"

"I went everywhere with my decorator—I didn't trust him to make a decision without me—and we were doing the staff rooms."

"Staff! Billy, aren't you playing lady of the manor? You're planning a furniture catalog for the Scruples Two customer, a tasteful woman with a healthy middle-class income. She's not going to furnish in stuff intended for your live-in help."

"Damn it, Spider, do you think I bought anything that wasn't really comfortable and good-looking for those rooms? Do you think I expected the people who work here to live in squalor? Is that what you think of me?"

"Calm down, darling, of course I don't. I just think you're being impractical, basing this on your taste, not that of real people."

"You're wrong," Billy flashed. "I'm turning my back on what I buy for myself. I'm using my taste but not my extravagance. The chair you're sitting on was five thousand dollars in plain muslin, before the fabric was ordered from France, which added another nine hundred dollars, plus labor costs for quilting and upholstery and shipping and sales tax. And that was minus the decorator's one-third markup. Believe me, I okayed every single bill."

"Lord have mercy, lady. You do have expensive taste."

"I can afford it," Billy snapped. "That chair is comfortable beyond belief, built to last until doomsday, the fabric is hand-screened pure linen, the upholsterer was the most expensive in California—the Scruples Home armchairs won't *look* all that different—an armchair is an armchair—but I have no illusions that they'll be the same. They won't be stuffed in hundred-percent down, or built by hand, or detailed in the same way. Spider, you can buy an excellent reproduction of an antique chest of drawers for five hundred dollars, or you can buy the Philadelphia original at auction for a million bucks—"

"Don't tell me they give the same pleasure."

"They *both* give pleasure! Spider, here's where you're just not getting this idea, where you're just not listening. If I hire the right designers, the best designers possible at any price, and give them a firm mandate to make handsome but uncomplicated furniture, and if I strictly limit the choices and sell a lot of pieces, this thing will fly!"

Spider got up and walked over to the desk and started scribbling on a pad. As he worked, Billy watched him silently, feeling her fury building at each unasked-for scratch of his pencil.

"The way I figure it," he said finally, "your basic fully furnished living dining room would run into at least four thousand dollars and change, and that's without even a lamp to see what you've bought."

"Carpets, lamps, accessories—of course I thought of them for another department in the catalog, surely that's obvious," Billy said defensively. "There are all sorts of terrific items available at low prices that you haven't a clue about—"

"And how would you know, oh, princess of the eight-thousand-dollar armchair?"

"Because I subscribe to shelter magazines, from the most expensive to the cheapest, I always thought I should have studied to be a decorator—"

"Aha! Now I know where all this is coming from! So you wanted to be a decorator—you never told me that—I wonder why. The Scruples Home is just as impractical as Scruples was the first day I walked in there and found an exact reproduction of the Paris Dior showroom, smack in the center of Beverly Hills."

"Spider, will you *never* let me forget that? This is totally different, this is based on everything I've learned from Scruples and Scruples Two. I've had a liberal education in marketing, and there's a real need for this—"

"Hold on a minute," Spider said, putting his hand up in a peremptory gesture, as if to stop traffic. "Scruples Two has a money-back guarantee, no questions asked, or we wouldn't do any business. Right? So your customer orders everything for her living room–dining room, and when the pieces come, she finds out that she just doesn't like the way they look—maybe they're the wrong color or size because she measured wrong, or her husband doesn't like them or whatever—what does she do now—send them back?"

"Yes." Billy glared at him. "I'll find a way."

"Oh, Billy, have you even thought about the added cost of shipping all this stuff to her in the first place? And have you realized how big a warehouse you'd need? Something the size of Kentucky, if you want my opinion. And how does your customer unpack the crates when they're delivered and get the stuff in the house—if she works, how can she even make sure she's at home when they're delivered, come to think of it, and, worst of all, if she decides to return something, how the hell does she pack it up? These are all bulky items—a three-pillow sofa isn't something you can return to sender at the post office. Trouble, Billy, you're buying nothing but trouble. And what happens when you make a mistake —we've made plenty at Scruples Two, so you'd be bound to make mistakes—and no one wants a French country headboard and you're stuck with two thousand of them, or everyone wants them and you need twenty thousand of them in a hurry?"

"How many more pails of cold water do you have ready to

dump on my idea?" Billy was physically assaulted by his words. She looked at him and hated him.

"I hate to be negative, but somebody has to tell you that it simply isn't a practical plan. It's a lovely fantasy, a well-meaning fantasy, but it isn't businesslike. Scruples Two was businesslike from the very beginning. You didn't think it was, until I convinced you, but this . . . no, it won't work."

"It will!" Billy said passionately. "I'll do it with my own money and you'll see!"

"Yeah, well, of course there's always that choice, isn't there?" Spider drawled, in a voice that had suddenly gone absolutely flat.

"Why are you using that particular tone with me?"

"You don't understand the first thing about finance, you've never had to worry about meeting a payroll or borrowing, but I don't know a bank that would lend you a dime on this proposal. If you want to spend your own hard-earned money on it, be my guest, but when you get into deep shit and come complaining to me, just don't say I didn't warn you."

"I promise you that." Billy turned away with loathing from the sight of Spider's blond head, and walked out on the balcony.

Why the fuck had she ever told him? Why hadn't she just gone ahead and commissioned the designs herself? Had the catalog designed, set the whole thing in motion? When she'd bought the best corner in Beverly Hills and built Scruples, she had done it without asking, telling, or consulting anyone, and a great store and a great mail-order business had both been based on that impulse she'd had years before she'd laid eyes on Spider Elliott, Billy thought, shaking with rage.

Every bit of the marketing help he'd given her, help that he'd been highly paid for and could never stop reminding her of, could easily have come from someone else, hired for that purpose just as she had hired him.

Billy felt her nails digging into her palms in the excess of her fury. This whole thing was *unforgivable*. Because she had married Spider, he had the illusion that he'd become her boss. He thought he'd created Scruples Two all on his own, this ignoramus who'd never bought more than a potted plant since he'd left home, who'd been perfectly content living in rented, furnished places until he'd moved into her beautiful house with only a few clean shirts and now had the bloody nerve to set himself up as an expert on what would and wouldn't work in home furnishing.

Billy hardly moved as she gave herself over to the thoughts that drummed in her head. She could buy a hundred of the best people in the decorating world to give her advice on the Scruples Home catalog, she could hire the editor-in-chief away from any decorating magazine to set up a phone service to help the customer pick colors, measure walls, do all the things Spider thought were so impossible to achieve . . . Why didn't he want to be helpful instead of immediately pissing all over her idea?

As Billy stood rigidly on the balcony, looking at nothing, Spider came out behind her and put his arms around her tightly.

"I know you're angry," he said. "I shouldn't have been so positive about everything. Maybe it could work, who knows? Why don't you get your feet wet first, start on something smaller, like a Scruples bed-linen catalog or a Scruples bath-accessories catalog, and if those work out, then get bigger by stages?"

"Those catalogs exist, I get them by the dozen. And I don't start small," Billy said, so angry she could hardly utter the words. How magnanimous of him to offer her the sop of scalloped sheets and soap dishes. How thoughtless. How disrespectful. *He had no respect for her.* He never had, not now, not since she'd known him, superficially perhaps, but not deep respect.

"I'm tired," Billy said, jerking out of his arms. "I'm going to get ready for bed."

As she took off her clothes and sat down at her dressing table to remove her makeup, her anger and frustration continued to grow. Billy put on a bathrobe, picked up a book and went to read on a chaise longue in the bedroom, unwilling to get into the same bed with Spider until he was fast asleep. Double beds were an invention of the devil.

She was rereading the same line over and over, her malignant, assaulting, wrathful thoughts mounting and expanding, when Spider appeared from his bathroom in his pajamas.

"Good book?" he asked, trying to create a normal atmosphere before he went to sleep.

"Not particularly."

"Then why don't you come on over here and lie down next to me and let me apologize more effectively?"

"You have a remarkable sense of humor. I'd rather read. Even a bad book."

"Have it your own way." Spider turned to write something down on the small notepad that normally lay on his bedside table. "Have you seen my pad?" he asked Billy.

"No. Why? Are you thinking of more itty-bitty catalog ideas for me?" she asked. He reduced her, damn him, he *reduced* her!

"I've given up on that, thanks. I just want to remind myself to call Russo and Russo tomorrow. I can't delegate that particular job to anyone else."

"What job?"

"Didn't I tell you? I've decided to hire Frost Rourke Bernheim to handle the Scruples Two account, so I have to give the Russo boys the bad news."

"*You what?*" Billy let the book drop and jumped up.

"I just told you what. I'm changing agencies. Victoria Frost came by today and convinced me that we're with the wrong agency. A most impressive dame."

"*I* hired Bill and Ed Russo. I discovered them," Billy yelled at him. "They're my friends and you know it. Advertising was my department. How *dare* you fire them without talking to me about it?"

"Shit, Billy, you haven't been participating in daily decisions since before the kids were born. The Russos aren't doing a good enough job, and that's that. I don't ask you how to zip up my pants in the morning."

"What a crappy, infantile cliché. You sound eight years old. Did you remember that Gigi made it clear that under no circumstances was she going to solicit our account when she changed jobs?"

"I did. Victoria said Gigi was comfortable with it now."

"Oh, Victoria told you that, did she, and you believed her?"

"How could she lie about it?"

"I don't know, but I'm certain that Victoria Frost is no expert on Gigi, they can barely be civil to each other."

"That's not the impression I got," Spider said grimly, watching Billy in disgust. Did she have any idea how she looked, laying down the law as if her first husband's money had earned her the right to decide anything she chose?

"You fell for Victoria Frost's pitch, and now you're ready to trample on Gigi's feelings the way you trample on mine. Listen to me, Spider. I own as much of Scruples Two as you do. You can't ignore me. You can't put me in your pocket and go your merry way. You *will* call Victoria Frost in the morning. You *will* tell her that you've changed your mind. Period. You *will* consult me about choosing a new agency. Period. You *will not* fire the Russos until I've looked into the problem and decided if they should have another chance. *Do you hear me?* Just because you don't respect Gigi doesn't mean that you can get away with not respecting me."

Spider walked over to her and took her by one arm, holding her in a painfully rough grip, making it impossible for her to move away.

"No one can respect a woman whose way of making her point is withholding sex, screeching like a fishwife, and displaying her amazing aptitude for pussy-whipping."

"Take that back!"

"I will not!" he shouted. "It's the truth. And you know it."

"Get out of my bedroom. Go sleep somewhere else. You make me sick. And don't forget a single one of my instructions." Her voice was pulverizingly arrogant.

"Billy, you don't want to do this, believe me."

"Don't tell me what I want. You don't know what I want. You don't know me. Unfortunately I know you only too well. You're contemptible."

"I'm out of here," Spider said, in a tone so calm and condescending that it made Billy want to kill him with every muscle she had. "I'm leaving so that I don't put you over my knee and give you the good spanking you deserve."

In the morning, when he went to his bathroom, Spider found a sheet of paper next to his shaving mirror.

I'm going away, and I don't know when I'll be back.
You're getting along perfectly well without me, and there is
no reason to stay and keep house for you. I don't know why
you have no respect for me, but it's clear that you don't from
what you say and the way you act. I will not tolerate that.
I'll send for the children soon.

There was nothing else, not even a signature. Spider rushed into Billy's bathroom and saw evidence that she'd packed some of her makeup. In her closet, the mess of clothes on the floor showed that she'd been in there picking out enough to fill a suitcase.

He called down to Burgo O'Sullivan on the house phone.

"When did Mrs. Elliott leave?"

"A limo came for her about an hour ago, Mr. Elliott."

"Thanks, Burgo. Please tell the chef I won't be having breakfast at home."

She'd be on the first plane to New York by now, Spider figured. Going to ground at Jessica's, no doubt, her usual refuge in times of trouble. It was just as well, all things considered, although her note was ridiculously dramatic. God knows, he didn't want to see her today.

As Spider shaved, he told himself that Jessica had a way of making Billy listen to things she wouldn't take from anybody else. It was Jessica who'd made her understand Vito, of all people, at least long enough to stay married to him for more than a few weeks. It was wise, much-put-upon, much-loved and loving Jessica who understood the art of compromise that Billy was too bloody rich and too incredibly stubborn to accept without a fight to the finish.

She'd send for the children, would she? Over his dead body, she'd send for the children.

Filled with righteous indignation, Spider rushed off to his office where his first act was to call the Russo brothers and tell them that they no longer had the Scruples Two account.

"There's just one problem," Sasha said to Vito as they walked on the sand in Santa Barbara, hand in hand. "Gigi's going to have to invite Zach to our wedding reception—at the place they lived in together."

"He's only one guest out of a whole crowd. Gigi doesn't have to do anything but say hello to him—not even good-bye, if he leaves without making a point of it, as I'm sure he will," Vito said reassuringly. "But she can't expect him not to be there, he's practically a relative now or something. Even if Billy were giving the reception, they'd both have to come—it's for us, after all."

"Honestly, wouldn't you think people could just get along with each other after they've broken up? It'd be so much easier for everybody, and so much more civilized."

"No, actually, I wouldn't. How do you feel about Josh coming?"

"Oh, my God! Gigi's not going to invite him too?"

"She's known him forever, and politeness demands that she invite him," Vito said, and gave a judicious sigh. "But—I warned her that he was off our list."

"You *are* rotten, Vito, you said that just to torment me."

"I adore tormenting you. You torment so enchantingly."

"Don't push your luck, big boy."

"You have a certain low streak of Jean Harlow in you, Sasha, or is it Mae West?"

"You remind me of—of—George Raft."

"Now you've gone too far. You've provoked me."

"And just what are you going to do about it?"

"Wait and see."

"Wait till when, Georgie?"

"Now is as good a time as any."

"Vito, no, not on the beach! Stop it!"

The FRB offices were empty at six the next evening, except for Victoria, Archie, and Byron, who had sent everyone home early and were sitting around a table in Victoria's office, reaching the end of their second bottle of celebratory champagne. The men were in their shirtsleeves, and had long since discarded their ties. Even Victoria had unbuttoned her all-but-ecclesiastical white blouse, rolled up her sleeves, and put her stocking feet up on the table, in the joyous spirit of the moment.

"What's so funny about you is that you're both so inconsistent," Victoria Frost said, breaking the kind of dreamy, relaxed silence that sets in toward the end of a state of high euphoria. "You're concerned about Gigi's reaction to my getting the Scruples Two account, but you don't worry that she got The Enchanted Attic and the Winthrop Line by sleeping with Ben Winthrop— although how much sleep they got is debatable."

"Her business," Archie said, and broke into song. "There's

330

no business like her business, there's no business I know, everybody's da that certain da da . . ."

"Accounts that depend on sexual . . . heat," Victoria said,
trying to choose her words carefully, since Archie and Byron had
had much more to drink than she, "sexual . . . tension . . . between the client and a creative, are risky at best—what happens
when Winthrop gets tired of her? That's going to be a problem, it's
just a question of time. He's big game. At least we know that
Spider Elliott is only interested in her work."

"Big game?" Byron asked. "You mean Arch and I aren't big
game? I have news for you, there are a lot of women who'd disagree, right, Arch?"

"Big game in the sense of big rich. No offense, Byron Bernheim the Third, you have comfortable expectations, but you're
light-years away from big, big, *big* rich. One day Gigi's little affair
will end." Victoria was certain of her assessment.

"Not necessarily," Archie insisted. "I've seen them together,
and the guy is crazy hooked on her . . . has a serious jones for our
little Gigi. It could end in marriage."

"So then Gigi will become the client's wife, she'll stop working, and move into a totally different life," Victoria continued.
"The first thing she'll begin to think about, when the honeymoon
is over, is moving the accounts to another agency where they
didn't know her when she was a working girl. There's nothing
clients' wives enjoy more than that kind of meddling, no matter
how little they know about advertising. And Gigi'd be a thousand
times as bad . . . she knows too much."

The three of them sat in silence, thinking of all the horror
stories told about clients' wives, tales that were a part of advertising
lore. Clients' wives were universally dreaded, and a Gigi established inside the client's tent would be much more of a problem
than a Gigi merely having an affair with the client.

"Oh, balls, let's not spend another single second worrying
about it," Archie said expansively. "Forget the whole thing. We've
got too much to celebrate. Victoria, don't be such a downer, tell
me about Harris Reeves again. Tell me exactly how it happened,
what he said and what you said."

"Are you serious, Arch? Like a bedtime story?" Victoria
smiled so voluptuously that her face took on an erotic expression

331

that made both Arch and By remember exactly how she'd looked the night she'd recruited them in her apartment in New York.

"It hasn't sunk in yet," Archie replied. "I feel like a kid who just got the whole circus for a birthday present. A real three-ring circus with elephants, lions, and bareback riders. Or maybe a casino of my own, with a racetrack thrown in. Come on, Ms. Frost, baby, don't make me beg."

"Yeah, come on," Byron insisted, "I gotta hear it again too."

"This morning, when I got in, there was a message to call Harris Reeves at Beach Casuals in New York." Victoria stopped deliberately to enjoy the look of impatience on their faces.

"I'm begging, Victoria," Archie pleaded. "Begging!"

"Me too. Please, Victoria, more gruel!" Byron cried. Just his luck, he thought, to be in business with a world-class cock teaser, even in the office.

"I returned his call, but he was out to lunch. Since he's the CEO of the biggest swimwear company in the country, I sat around all morning biting my nails and waiting to call him again, wondering how long he took for lunch. At eleven, California time—am I drawing this out enough for you two kiddies?—I called him back and got the man himself. Seems he takes a short lunch. I told him I was returning his call and asked what I could do for him. And he said . . . and he said . . . let's see, what is it exactly that comes next?"

"Victoria! I'm going to wring your exquisite fucking neck!" Archie menaced her.

"Why, Archie, if you do that, you'll end up in the gas chamber," she giggled.

"*Victoria!*"

"Oh, all right. I'll indulge you. What babies you are! And he said he was exceptionally impressed with the work we'd done on Indigo Seas and he'd been keeping track of the increase in their sales and I said thank you very much, and he said that he'd had his VP in charge of advertising check us out completely and heard nothing but good things about us from Joe Devane and others, and I said thank you very much, and he said his current agency had gone stale, they'd had the account without competition for ten years and he'd warned them but they were stone cold dead in the water, couldn't come up with anything exciting and new, and I said nothing except 'ummm,' and then he said that he wanted us to take on Beach Casuals. Like that. Just over the phone, just like that. While I was still trying to say something sensible, like 'Thank you very much!' Harris Reeves said that he wanted us all to fly to New York next week to meet with his people and I said we'd be thrilled and delighted and what was a good day for him and he said Wednesday and to count on being there till the weekend so we could meet everybody involved, have discussions, all that jazz, and I said thank you very much again, and he said he felt Indigo Seas was a conflict and I said of course it was and naturally we'd resign it and he said fine and eventually we got around to the usual looking-forward-to-meeting-you formalities and the phone call was over. Are you boys happy now, or do you want me to go through it again?"

"You left out the best part," Archie complained.

"She did it on purpose. She wants us to lick her feet," Byron chimed in. "Take off those panty hose, Victoria, I'm all yours."

"By. I'm touched, but no thanks. Maybe, just maybe, I'll give you a rain check."

"Screw the rain check, Victoria, give us the best part!"

"The account bills ninety million dollars a year."

"Ninety million," Archie breathed reverently.

"Ninety million," Byron repeated, "ninety fucking million. What a fucking *win!*"

"No," Archie protested, "You can't call it a win because there was no competition, what a fucking *steal!*"

"No," Victoria said. "No, children, we didn't steal it from anyone. It's a fucking *windfall!* That's the beauty part. Nobody gets ninety million on a windfall, not even my mother!"

"Jesus, Victoria, I'm glad you were the one Harris Reeves talked to," Archie said. "I'd have had a heart attack—if you can get one from good news."

"I got the impression of a man who wasn't happy with his VP in charge of advertising," Victoria said, almost to herself, "a man who has simply taken over the situation, a man who runs a very tight ship and doesn't let anyone have any real power but him. You can imagine how that VP felt when Reeves made the call. He started Beach Casuals from nothing more than thirty years ago, and he's right, his advertising has become institutional."

"Are you going to call the Collins boys and resign the account," Archie asked, "or do you think Gigi should? She's the one with the relationships up in S.F., maybe that'd be the best way to do it."

"Archie, resigning an account for a conflict that's at least ten times bigger than they are is strictly a management responsibility," Victoria told him sharply.

Did Arch or By think that she would give anyone else in the world the pleasure of telling Indigo Seas that they weren't big enough for Victoria Frost, she wondered. And, oh, when Gigi came back, all full of herself and that overpriced cruise ship her boyfriend was building, wouldn't she have a nice first day back at the office?

Victoria poured them all another glass of champagne and made a toast.

"Here's to Frost Rourke Bernheim, the agency that understands business reality."

"Business reality!" They lifted their glasses, clinked them together, and drained them.

"I'm opening another bottle," Victoria announced. "You greedy kiddies hogged the first two."

15

As soon as Billy stepped through the high gates and set foot on the cobblestones of the spacious courtyard of her private house, her *hôtel particulier* on the Rue Vaneau in Paris, she knew she had fled to the only place where there was hope of finding some ease for the plucking physical pain in her heart and for her ceaseless contemplation of the wounds to her spirit. The purchase of this house, almost four years ago, this house she had never lived in, had been a capricious action, even in her own judgment, but at the time she had been ripe to surrender to the first object of temptation that came her way after her divorce from Vito Orsini. She had bought it within days of seeing it, at the inflated asking price of eight million dollars, a willful act of pure folly, because she had known at first sight that it was destined to be hers, this welcoming gray stone nobleman's residence that had been built hundreds of years ago for a Parisian family and had never changed hands until she fell in love with it.

"Madame will be pleased with the condition of the house," Marie-Jeanne, the wife of the *gardien*, Pierre Dujardin, both of whom lived in the gatehouse, assured her, after they had greeted each other. "Every morning I said to Pierre, 'What if Madame Ikehorn drops in today, without warning, just as she did while she lived in Paris?' And believe me, Madame, every night before we went to sleep we were satisfied that everything, from the last pipe in the cellar to the last slate on the roof, all was in order."

"Thank you, Madame Marie-Jeanne. I'm very grateful, I knew I was leaving my house in good hands."

"It has been too long, Madame, since we have seen you."

"Yes, I agree," Billy replied, "but my life is complicated."

"Of course, Madame," the *gardien*'s wife responded.

Did Mrs. Ikehorn not realize that to abandon such a house, to leave it standing absolutely empty in the middle of the most desirable and aristocratic residential neighborhood of Paris, to leave the stables with their stalls crammed with a veritable treasure of antiques, still packed in their crates, was the sign of a life that was not just complicated but unquestionably crazy? However, she and Pierre were paid well and promptly every month, and their own gatehouse, in which Madame Ikehorn had installed the same modern heating and new kitchen as she had in the great house, was the envy of every *gardien* in Paris. Nevertheless she was delighted to see Madame Ikehorn again, it was reassuring that she had returned and not sold the house to strangers.

"Does Madame intend to stay in Paris long?" she asked.

"I'm not sure," Billy answered. "Certainly for a while. Madame Marie-Jeanne, I'll visit the house alone, if you don't mind."

"But naturally, Madame."

As soon as the double doors had closed behind her and she found herself in the circular entrance hall, Billy was caught again by the special atmosphere of her house, a rare fragrance of civilized lives at their most charming and leisurely. The house was as graciously lavish with its perfect proportions as it was touchingly human in its calm acceptance of the work of time. The cobwebs and peeling paint that had disguised the house when she first saw it had been swept away, the sagging parquet floors and the moldings,

336

crumbling with damp, had all been carefully restored to their original classic elegance, yet there was no hint of newness. The thick old glass of the French doors lent its lavender tint to the flood of gentle morning sun that spilled onto bare, gleaming floors and well-swept, if empty, fireplaces. The original mirrors, set into their paneled frames on the walls, still offered reflections that traveled backwards to a slower, more glorious time; the floors still creaked slightly with every step she took, with a sound of welcome and a promise of peace.

Billy toured all twenty rooms in a trance of rediscovery that gave her stripped soul some release from pain. Eventually she reached the new winter garden that she had built at the back of the house, through which she could see over the walls of her own evergreen garden into the vast park of the Hôtel Matignon, the residence of the Prime Minister of France. She sat down on the wide, built-in window seat and lost herself in reflection.

The last time she had set foot in this room was before Christmas of 1981, and all her thoughts had been concentrated on moving in and celebrating the holidays here with Sam Jamison, the sculptor from San Francisco, who had known her only as Honey Winthrop, a schoolteacher from Seattle.

She had lived that deception successfully for almost a year, so that Sam wouldn't know who she was and treat her with the special attitude all men used toward her when they realized she was that envied and scorned oddity, that gossip-attracting freak, that both more and less than human creature that the world makes out of any independent woman of vast personal wealth.

All men, she had believed at the time, with the exception of Spider Elliott, the very same man who had sneered at her a day ago as the "princess of the eight-thousand-dollar armchair" and mocked her so scornfully, so belittlingly with his characterization of her financial stupidity based on her "hard-earned money" when he knew that the last time she'd worked for a paycheck was twenty-two years ago, and a junior secretary's paycheck at that.

Christ, what was there to choose between them, Billy asked herself. Sam and Spider both, when you got right down to it, fatally factored her money into their love for her. Spider had been able to hide it for years, behind an attitude that she was, as he'd put it in a letter to her, a "basic creampuff" whom it hadn't taken long to "whip into shape." Sam had seen her one night at the Paris Opera and discovered her true identity. He had instantly withdrawn from her, rejected her absolutely, even after reading the agonized letter of explanation she had sent him the next day. He was convinced that she had arranged for the amazing success of his new exhibition by getting her friends to buy his sculptures. He hadn't given her a chance, not the benefit of a single doubt. But, she thought, at least Sam had the excellent excuse that she had consistently lied to him for nine months.

Which was better, a man like Sam who rejected you because you hadn't treated him as an equal, or a man like Spider, who treated you as if you couldn't possibly be his equal, as if all your struggles to achieve anything would have been doomed without his help? No, not which was better, but rather, which was worse?

Let them both rot in hell, Billy thought, as she marched through the house and looked for the *gardien*.

"Monsieur Pierre, I have decided to sleep here tonight. Please be kind enough to search in the stables and find an armoire, a table or two, a mirror, some vases, candlesticks, and two chairs, and arrange them in one of the smaller bedrooms, one next to a bath."

"But, Madame," he protested, realizing that his formal greetings must be postponed for the moment, "there are only antiques to be found in the stables, certainly no bed for Madame to sleep on."

"It will arrive within a few hours," Billy said.

"In Paris? Hah! That would be a miracle." He laughed out loud at the mere idea of such promptness.

"You'll see. And thank you, Monsieur Pierre, the house looks marvelous."

"Thank you, Madame, you too look marvelous. It gives me joy to see you return."

"Until later, Monsieur Pierre," Billy said, hurrying through the gates to the car and driver that waited for her outside.

"Until later," he echoed. Madame did not look marvelous. Madame looked . . . if it was possible for such a beautiful woman . . . Madame looked ravaged.

In the furniture department of the Galeries Lafayette, Billy secured the services of a harried saleswoman by the simple method of pressing a thousand franc note into her hand and saying that she would like immediate service.

"What can I do for you?" the saleswoman asked, with her first smile of the day.

"I have need of a bed with a good mattress, two pillows, good lamps, bulbs, candles, bed linen, towels, lightproof curtains for two windows, a rug—oh, a hamper for a bathroom—if I think of anything else, I'll tell you."

"But these things are all to be found in different departments, all over the store," the woman said, scandalized by this list. "I work in furniture only."

"I also want someone to hang the curtains, install the bed, and do anything else that's necessary. I live on the Rue Vaneau. All this must all be delivered at once, so that the work is completed by the end of the day. There will be another two thousand francs for you when it is done, and something generous for the deliverymen and installers."

"Of course, Madame, it will be my pleasure to serve you. I shall accompany you to the other departments."

"You understand," Billy said in her perfect French, "I am a crazy American, that explains all, does it not?"

"Oh, but no, Madame is not crazy, only perhaps, a little impulsive."

"That sounds exactly like what they'll put on my tombstone," Billy said. "Let's start, I have no time to waste."

As she raided the great department store, Billy reflected that it would have been a great deal easier to stay at the Ritz, where she had lived in the four-room Windsor Suite for so long, but that was the first place where anyone looking for her would telephone. She had spent the first night in Paris in the airport hotel and arranged to be picked up today by the same discreet car-and-driver agency she had used during her months with Sam Jamison, when she had lived a double life of such maddening complexity that it was made bearable only by a wild sexual and emotional passion.

What I did for love. There's a song like that, Billy thought, as she tested a mattress, and it must have been written for other women as foolishly deceived as I am, but surely not one of them was as hopelessly mistaken in her emotions. And, quite probably, none of them was French.

No more than four years ago, Billy had discovered how to manage to preserve two separate identities. In one of them she was the American millionairess Billy Ikehorn, who occupied the best suite at the Ritz, a flighty socialite who spent her time being fitted for clothes, shopping for antiques, attending parties, and spending most of her nights, scandalously, who knew where? In another she was simple Honey Winthrop, a Seattle schoolteacher on sabbatical, who spent her days doing research on Voltaire and slept, five nights a week, with Sam Jamison in his rough studio near the Place des Vosges, a vibrant, offbeat part of Paris.

Now, in the capsule she had created around herself, she had a single life and a single bed, now she was expected nowhere, she had no shopping, no lunch parties, no fittings at Dior or Givenchy, no lover, no lies to tell, no car and driver—nothing but an almost empty house and caretakers who were discreet enough never to question her comings and goings. Within two days Billy felt certain that she was slipping through the cracks of Paris like smoke, observing but never observed.

The area around the Rue Vaneau was like the dark stone in the luscious peach of Paris, so utterly without tourist attractions that it was almost as quiet as the countryside at night, although if she listened closely she could hear the unceasing rumble of the surrounding city, its softly brilliant invitation to gaiety, the allure of its lights, the impatient sound of taxi horns—almost, she imagined, the conspiratorial laughter of men and women.

But on the Rue de Varenne, the nearest cross street to the Rue Vaneau, stern policemen guarded the Prime Minister's residence, allowing no car to park. Nothing interestingly commercial flourished, with the exception of a famous shoe-repair shop, the Cordonnerie Vaneau, to which all the old aristocracy brought their riding boots and handmade shoes; a tiny cheese store; a few small florists; several hairdressers; and, here and there, simple bistros that depended entirely on the local inhabitants for their clientele.

She was safe from meeting anyone she knew, Billy concluded,

so long as she confined her peregrinations to the area between her house and the Luxembourg Gardens. Above all, she didn't want to run into anyone who would recognize her and ask her what she was doing in Paris. But there was every reason to believe that even now, at the height of the fall tourist season, no one would have any reason to seek out the quiet, gray, narrow, rather melancholy streets that lay in this part of Paris. All the best hotels and the great shopping as well as most museums and famous restaurants were located on the Right Bank; the amusing little antique dealers, chic bistros, and galleries were elsewhere on the Left Bank, closer to the Seine. Her immediate *quartier* was grand indeed, if you knew its secrets, but uninviting, somber, and even unfriendly unless you had *entrée* into one of the great stone mansions and embassies that hid their interior gardens from the passer-by.

Billy felt driven by a need to walk until she dropped. Only constant motion kept her from the kind of thinking that she wasn't ready to confront. She could escape the workings of her brain by walking for hours on end, but pavement alone could not satisfy her. Standing on the Rue Guynemer, the outer limit of the district to which she had confined herself, she looked across the street and covetously eyed the tempting vista of the vast Luxembourg Gardens, which lay behind sharply pointed, gilt-tipped bars. There was a little-frequented side entrance directly opposite her. All she had to do was cross this street to find herself in one of the biggest parks in Paris, an utterly bourgeois park where only the most leisurely and curious tourist would stray.

The leaves had already turned to that special shade of faded golden rust that is the uniform autumn color of Paris trees. Billy felt an acute need, a positive thirst to feel the cleanly swept surfaces of the pleasant pathways of the Luxembourg under her feet, to lose herself in the seclusion of the gardens that the Chartreux monks had established in 1257, to sit on a little slatted chair and look up at the open sky. Only schoolchildren, young mothers, students, and retired people frequented the gardens during the week, she remembered, although large families came from all over on the weekends, drawn by the marionette theater and the large, hexagonal, shallow basin in which generations of children had sailed their toy boats.

She looked in both directions, darted across the street, and within seconds she was within the formally laid out but almost empty confines of the Luxembourg. She drew a deep breath of freedom and began to stride quickly under the old trees, letting her fancy decide which crossing to take as she reached the end of each *allée*, only stopping to sit down when she was finally worn out.

She was hibernating outdoors, instead of in a cave, Billy realized, driftingly, grateful for the uncomfortable chair, for it would have been unthinkable to sit on the grass in a Paris park. No one in the world knew where she was, and unless she dropped dead on this chair, no one would ever know, since, in accordance with French regulations, she always carried some sort of identification papers with her whenever she went out of the house. When she'd lived here before, she'd kept a photocopy of her passport in her wallet. Today she had only her driver's license and a few hundred francs in the pocket of her slacks.

She needed this time of mindless solitude before she would be ready to take the next step in her life, Billy knew. If she had tried to simulate isolation in her walled garden at home, she could never have achieved the feeling of complete escape that was possible here, six thousand miles away, in the middle of a park that was shared by strangers who all had their own lives to lead. She would have been attached by a hundred strings to the house that lay outside the walled garden, and the people in that house and the problems that had driven her here. She had been frighteningly impulsive all her life, she knew that only too well, and this flight to Paris, abrupt as it might seem, had been a way of postponing any action. It was counterimpulsive, Billy thought soberly.

Should she be troubled in any way by finding herself so utterly alone? How ridiculous she was. A woman with a house within a brisk twenty-five-minute walk, a woman with a banker just across the Seine at the branch of the Chase on the Rue Cambon, a woman who had only to hail a taxi and appear at the Ritz reception desk to be given any service she asked for, a woman who could be on the Concorde to New York tomorrow and on the plane back to Los Angeles an hour later, was hardly cut off from the world. The Luxembourg was not Tibet.

No, on the other hand, realistically she *was* alone, for she was all by herself, and nobody but the *gardien* and his wife knew she was in Paris. The fact that she had resources to change that condition quickly was no reason to deny that she had gone to ground here, in the center of the most civilized dot on the globe, as effectively as if she had burrowed deep into a cave in the wilderness. She had fled by instinct after the fight with Spider. This was her own chosen place, a place she had never shared with him, a place that she knew in a thousand deep ways in which she could never know Los Angeles, even if she had been born in California and never left it during her lifetime. Los Angeles might change its skin ten times over without affecting her, but a modern building erected in central Paris diminished and distressed her.

How long would she stay? Perhaps the same instinct that had brought her here would tell her if she should stay forever, Billy reflected, and made her way back to the Rue Vaneau where she showered and changed to an equally inconspicuous sweater and pair of pants, before she went out for her early dinner. At the moment the most pressing problem she was willing to consider was whether to start her meal with a plate of plump Brittany sardines in oil, the vegetable soup of the day, or a slice of Paris ham, a succulent pale pink, cooked on the bone. She had walked enough to eat anything she wanted, Billy realized, although, in some strange way, she had lost her appetite. Probably jet lag.

For the next five days Billy walked for six hours a day, slept ten hours a night without remembering a single dream, and ate brief, simple meals without appetite. She lived in the moment, rejecting all introspection with the help of a pile of mystery paperbacks, one of which was always in her shoulder bag. The only interruption to her routine was a visit to the small hairdresser two streets away, confirming her belief that it was impossible to be badly coiffed in Paris. She became so bold in her anonymity that she occasionally permitted herself to sit by the sailboat basin and observe the misadventures of the miniature regatta. She listened to the placid gossip of the mothers and the grandmothers with their knitting, and managed, by fierce concentration on this small local drama, to think successfully about nothing at all. Eventually, one afternoon, she was so lulled into weary relaxation that she found her eyes closing as she sat in the October sunshine. She pushed off her sneakers and dozed deliciously.

"They say that if you sit here long enough you'll see everybody you know," Sam Jamison's voice remarked as he pulled up a chair and sat down next to her.

She had dreamed it, Billy told herself in a scurrying leap of disbelief, and didn't bother to open her eyes.

"Are you still calling yourself Honey Winthrop?" It was his voice, just as speculative, just as humorous.

She kept her lids firmly closed, without a flicker of recognition, but she knew she was awake.

"It's the most direct shortcut from my studio to the Boulevard de Montparnasse, since you inquire," Sam continued. "And what, you're probably asking yourself, would I be doing going toward Montparnasse in the afternoon? Would you believe that I'm on my way to see a framer who's making a base for a new piece I recently finished? I was planning to go on Saturday, but it was too nice out today to spend time indoors. I can see you agree with me, or why would you be here? I didn't have any idea that you'd returned to Paris. I never left, you know. No, you wouldn't know, would you? Unless you read the art magazines. I had a show in L.A. last year, but I didn't invite you, it didn't seem like a great idea at the time—"

"How dare you sit here and babble like a fool?" Billy demanded furiously, opening her eyes and turning on him. "Where do you find the nerve to talk to me? You're annoying me in a public place, and either you move or I will!"

"At least you're still mad," Sam replied. "If you'd just laughed at me, I'd have been crushed."

"Don't flatter yourself," Billy said, gathering her wits as she tied her sneakers with trembling fingers. "Do you really believe that I'd give enough of a damn about you to stay mad for three years? You have an incredibly exaggerated idea of your importance."

"It depends," Sam said slowly. "It depends on just how rotten and stupid I was. I think you could have stayed mad at me forever without getting close to how mad you deserved to be."

"If that's supposed to be an apology, keep it! It doesn't interest me."

Billy jumped up and started walking rapidly in the direction of the Medici Fountain. He followed her easily, physically unchanged from the sinewy redhead she'd allowed to pick her up and call her "babe" and throw her naked on his bed an hour after she'd met him.

Sam put one of his strong sculptor's hands on her shoulder and stopped her in the middle of the path. "Please! Honey, don't run away! If you're really not mad anymore, couldn't you just give me a minute to explain?"

She was trapped, Billy realized. If she didn't give him his lousy minute, he'd spend the rest of his life thinking he still meant a great deal to her, and catering to his ego was the last thing she wanted to do.

She looked at her watch. "I can spare a minute," she said. "But don't call me 'Honey'—it was a nickname, and I always hated it."

"What, then?"

"Billy."

"Billy Ikehorn . . . I remember that last night when you told me who you were. Is that still who you are?"

"Close enough," she said brusquely.

"Billy, I read your letter but I didn't believe you."

"That's not new news." Billy shrugged in indifferent disdain. "Henri told me, after you practically spat in my face at Lipp's."

"But don't you see," he pleaded, awkward but determined to have his say. "I'd just sold five big pieces of sculpture in one afternoon. *Five!* More than half the show, the first I'd ever had in Paris, and I'd been working on them for years. I'd gone from being an unknown to being an unheard-of success. *Of course* I was convinced that you were behind it, anybody in the art world would have been, much less me. Since then I've sold just about everything I make . . . but, for God's sake, Billy, that was the very start of it—and it was right after I found out how rich you were. Are. Be fair, you had never told me the truth about yourself . . ."

"I told you why I'd lied in my letter." Billy was implacable.

"I only had minutes to read it before the first piece sold. Those first clients—I fucking couldn't believe in them! Years of trying, and suddenly, out of the blue, a triumph? On that scale? Billy, with each sale I believed in myself less and less. I felt . . . Jesus . . . like a kept man! Like your gigolo, your toy, your spoiled darling who couldn't cut it on his own. It was the worst afternoon of my life. I tracked down every last buyer, I grilled them about their relationship to you—they thought I was nuts—but finally I proved to myself that you'd had nothing to do with it. But by that time you'd disappeared. *And I've never, never forgiven myself.*"

"Big fucking deal," Billy said, relentlessly.

"It was," he answered, helplessly. "It was a bigger deal than I ever knew."

"If you felt so guilty about the way you treated me, why didn't you write? You knew a letter to the Ritz would have reached me."

"I . . . it's hard to explain . . ." He blushed deeply, as he always had when he was moved.

"Good-bye, Sam," Billy said, turning quickly. She didn't need to know. She didn't want to know.

"No, wait, it *was* your money, damn it!" He was abrupt, almost breathless. "I thought that if I wrote, after being so . . . such a total shit . . . so utterly heartless . . . those cold, terrible things I said . . . you'd think I was doing it . . . oh hell!—*because* of the money, like all those other guys. I knew that wasn't my reason, but in your letter you said that every man you'd ever known was changed—by the money—I was afraid that you'd think I was . . . another one of them."

"You were always too damn proud, Sam. It's a vice in you, not a virtue."

"Do you think I don't know that?" He gripped her arms with both his hands. "Look what it cost me—I've never been able to fall in love again. And believe me, I've tried!"

"Sam, don't exaggerate. It isn't like you, and it doesn't make anything different or better. There are a thousand mixtures in the world called love, you can make any claim you want, it cuts no ice with me."

"Billy—you were the only woman for me. *You are.*"

"Nicely said, Sam, but it comes a little late, doesn't it? Your apology—if that's what it is—is accepted, but words are cheap. Let's say good-bye here, this isn't my direction anyway."

"I'm not saying good-bye! Not after finding you sitting sleeping in the sun between two old ladies. I almost ran away before I got up the courage to speak to you. I stood there for ten minutes, just shaking in my boots and gawking. Look, can't we just talk, just sit somewhere and have a drink? I know who you really are—

346

I even know who I really am, a miserable moron who didn't believe in himself enough to trust you. Can't we at least have a drink together, for old times' sake? Please, Billy, just let me look at you for a little longer, that's all I ask."

"First it was a minute, now it's a drink."

She'd been rash, Billy thought. She'd stayed too long on this shady, sun-dappled path, she'd looked too long at Sam's fine-grained skin and his beautiful, nearsighted gray eyes under his heavy reddish eyebrows, she'd let her eyes linger on the hollows below his cheekbones where she had loved to lay her lips, and the long mouth she'd kissed so often, she'd let him stand too close to her and touch her, and had discovered that she remembered how good he smelled.

Still, what had she to lose? Why shouldn't they have a drink? She had time, he had time, and it was the hour for having a drink. Not only that, but it was getting chilly, and soon the gates to the park would be locked. Old friends, even old lovers, aren't to be dismissed forever because of a misunderstanding, no matter how serious, not when they have apologized so handsomely, were they?

And she was tired of reading her paperback.

Her answer was in her silence, Sam thought with a flash of realization.

"Which way is your way?" he asked quickly.

"Back there, on the other side of the boat basin."

"We're not far from St.-Germain-des-Prés," Sam said. "Do you want to head to the Flore or the Deux Magots? Or would they be full of tourists this time of year?"

"By now you must know Paris as well as I do. You said you'd never left—this is my first trip back."

"I really don't know it well at all," Sam confessed. "Before we met, I'd seen enough of the major tourist attractions to satisfy me. After you disappeared, I finally learned French, and when I started to believe I had real money, I moved to a bigger apartment, right around the corner. I still work in the old studio—I stick pretty close to home unless I have to travel to another country whenever my dealer's arranged a show. And even then I grumble."

"You sound like an old-fashioned Parisian," Billy laughed. "Many of them lived and died in their neighborhoods without ever having the curiosity to cross the Seine and see the other bank."

"I plead guilty . . . the Left Bank isn't my scene. Finding you here today was a wild fluke . . . if it hadn't been for that framer . . . well, it wasn't in the cards that you'd have paid me a visit in my studio."

"Not bloody likely, as they say in the movies. Still, never rule out coincidence. In Hollywood, screenwriters are allowed two coincidences per screenplay—after that they're in trouble."

"We'd better hurry," Sam warned her, "or we'll be in real trouble. I can hear that policeman telling people that they're about to lock the gates."

"There's nothing so annoying as the way they lock all the parks at the first sign of sunset," Billy replied. "It makes perfect sense, but I wish they wouldn't do it."

"Yeah, that's one of the things about the French, they have this reputation as romantics, but they stop well short."

"The truth is, they're the most sensible people in Europe."

"Except the Swiss."

"Except the Swiss," Billy agreed. "I'll bet you had an exhibition in Geneva."

"Zurich," he grinned.

"Sold them all?"

"All."

"That's wonderful."

"Thanks—where are we going? I'm lost."

"Oh, let's walk in this direction," Billy said carelessly. "There's bound to be a café."

She knew perfectly well where they were headed. She had to show Sam her house. Her experience with him wouldn't have come full circle until he'd seen the house she'd planned on their living in together, the stable block she had converted into a dream studio for him. Then he would know, in a way in which words alone couldn't explain, just how deeply he'd misjudged her.

"What's this?" Sam asked as Billy opened the high, grilled gates set into the ivy-covered wall on the Rue Vaneau.

"My folly. Good evening, Madame Marie-Jeanne."

"Good evening, Madame, good evening, Monsieur."

"Good evening, Madame," Sam said.

"Madame Marie-Jeanne, would you have the kindness to lend me a bottle of red wine and two glasses?"

"Of course, Madame. I will bring them directly."

"Thank you, Madame Marie-Jeanne."

"It is nothing, Madame."

"If you could just leave them in the winter garden, Madame Marie-Jeanne?"

"Of course, Madame. Immediately, Madame."

Billy and Sam walked across the courtyard, shaking with soundless laughter at the ritual of ordinary French politeness.

"You're just lucky I didn't introduce you," Billy sputtered. "That would have made another round of 'Madames' and 'Monsieurs' and probably some obligatory mention of the weather."

"Who *was* she?"

"The gatekeeper's wife. Wait, before we go into the house, I want to show you something else." Billy led the way to one of the long stone wings, higher by a few feet taller than the first floor of the house, selected another key, and opened the padlock on a set of wooden doors above which a splendid horse was prancing in an arched bas-relief. Lanterns, on graceful standards, stood on either side of the doors.

"Once these were the stables," she explained as she turned on the lights she had ordered installed overhead, great banks of halogen lights that brilliantly illuminated every foot of the interior, all the way from one end to another.

"It looks like a giant warehouse," Sam said, blinking.

"There are two dozen horse stalls, each one full of furniture waiting to be unpacked."

"When do you think it was built?"

"Sometime in the 1720s or 1730s."

"It's . . . amazing," Sam murmured, looking up at the distant ceiling.

"I think so," Billy said, deciding to not yet tell him why she had had such powerful lights put up at a cost, her architect had informed her, of illuminating the operating room of a hospital. "Let's go find that wine."

Billy and Sam sat on the built-in seat of the winter garden, and opened the second bottle of wine that Madame Marie-Jeanne had deposited on a tray on the floor, the Bordeaux she kept for special occasions, a 1971 Beychevelles.

"I could never have imagined the interior of a house like this," Sam said. "Unless you've been in one, even without any furniture, you don't expect such charm. I understand why you wanted to own it."

"Nobody else did, at the time, but then I didn't ask any advice."

No, he thought, you wouldn't have asked advice, would you, you glorious girl I thought was insanely generous when you wanted to give me a tiny bottle from the flea market? You, you wild and hidden beauty, so shy that I thought you lacked any ability to demand what you wanted, until you asked me to show you my work and it turned out that you wanted my cock inside you just as badly as I wanted to put it there; you who threatened to make me hard again in that pizzeria, when I desperately needed to eat so I could fuck you for the third time in as many hours . . . and you could have done it too, just with your voice, your words, if I hadn't stopped you . . . no, you wouldn't have asked for advice on anything so unimportant as buying a mansion.

"Do you see that pine tree outside in the garden, the tallest one?" Billy asked.

"Yeah, why?"

"That's where I thought we'd hang the Christmas tree lights. Christmas of 1981."

"Oh."

Jesus, why are you doing this to me, Honey? Don't tell me to call you Billy, he thought rebelliously. Isn't it enough to have brought me here, to this empty house, to be sitting here with me drinking wine, to be lying back against this window seat, far enough from me to keep a proper distance, but not so far that I can't see the shape of your nipples under your sweater and remember what your breasts looked like when you got on top and hung over me so that I could try to take them both in my mouth at the same time, those deep pink nipples that I could never manage to suck at once because your breasts were too big and too firm, too full to be pressed together? But remember how I used to try, Honey? How I loved to be under you, on my stomach, with you inventing new tortures, like the time you licked me from the soles of my feet to the backs of my calves, up and down, never going any higher, licking and sucking while I got so hard that I was afraid that I'd go crazy, come all over the mattress, but you never said a word, just kept sucking on that soft place behind my knee until, just in time, you whispered, "turn over," and stuck my cock in you with your hand and I came even before I was in you, Honey, before I shoved all the way . . . do you remember that?

"The trees in the garden are all evergreens," Billy informed him. "It was my one gesture toward California, to have a green garden all year long."

"Good thinking."

Oh, Honey, he cried to himself, what do I care about trees when all I can think about are those nights in my studio when we'd be sleeping in my bed and I'd wake up slowly, ever so slowly, discovering I had a hard-on and you'd have your hand on my cock, except that you'd be pretending to be asleep, and you'd be lying on your side, with your back toward me, with your legs gently scissored apart so that I could slide my cock into you from behind ever so slowly, as if I were afraid to wake you up, and I'd pretend that I didn't hear you breathing harder, and I'd move as gently as I possibly could, only pushing it in an inch at a time, until I was all the way up, with my balls pressed against your incredible flamboyant ass and then I knew that it was safe to reach around your hip and somehow happen to put my fingers between your thighs as if I didn't know what I was doing, and then . . . Honey . . . then I'd go straight for that fat swollen waiting bud, like a ripe berry, between your legs and, still pretending, I'd press my fingers up into your wet pussy, just to be sure you were filled with me, and then I'd keep them there, two or three at a time, and use my thumb on your bud and push into you from behind, faster and faster but never too fast, drawing it out as much as I could until I felt you come in my hand and around my fingers . . . oh, Christ, it was so good . . . and neither of us would ever say a word . . . not a word, not even the next day. We'd pretend it hadn't happened. That's what you're doing to me now, aren't you, Honey, pretending that you can't see that I'm sitting here as hard as I've ever been in my life, just waiting for you to make a move? That's what you're doing . . . I know you too well, Honey, not to know that.

"Billy, did you ever get married?" Sam asked roughly.

"Yes."

"Happily?"

"I thought so," she said briefly.

"You thought so? What does that mean?"

"I'm . . . not sure."

That's as lame an answer as I've ever given, she thought, that's almost an invitation. Not sure? If you're not sure, you shouldn't be here with this man you once loved, should you? You should be out in some decent little bistro, eating a good dinner and reading your tame little mystery story at the same time, one act canceling out the other, just as you've done all week, waiting for illumination to strike, waiting to see into the future, but you certainly shouldn't be here in this half-light with Sam Jamison. What would Spider think if he could see me now? What would Spider do if he knew I was here in this house whose existence I may . . . or may not . . . have mentioned to him years ago, this house that could be anywhere in the world, for all he knows about it? And what would he do if I had decided to take Sam up and show him the second floor? But I didn't, did I? If Sam ever realized that I'd brought him back to a house with only one bed . . . my bed . . . he'd . . . who's kidding who here? I could go on my knees to have him this minute, I could fling myself on him and open his fly and take out that stiff jutting prick of his, that big cock I know as well as my own hand, and plunge it into . . . oh, Christ, I want his mouth on mine, I want his cock in me, I must have been insane to let myself be here alone with him, I could rip off my clothes and spread my legs, right here on the window seat, right this minute, and let him touch me and suck me and open me up the way he used to, let him put it into me . . . he wants to so badly . . . does he think I can't see it? He's got to know there's enough light for me to see how swollen he is, how ready, how crazy eager, but he won't move unless I let him, unless I give him a sign, just the

352

smallest signal would be enough and then the future would be known, the die would be cast, I'd be out of my misery and I'd never look back. Never ever! Oh, this man still loves me, even without his telling me, over and over, I saw it in his blush, hours ago, and in his eyes, I know him too well to doubt it . . .

"Is that why you're here, in Paris, all alone?" Sam asked her. "Because you don't know?"

"Yes."

"Have you come to any conclusions?"

"Not yet. In fact I can't even think about it. Not sensibly."

"Why did you bring me here?"

"To prove to you that what I said in my letter was true, that I *had* been planning to tell you who I was as soon as the exhibition opened, that I'd been getting this house ready for us. I wanted to show you that the reason I refused to marry you was never that I didn't trust you."

"And the stables?"

"I thought they'd be your studio."

"But there aren't any skylights."

"The Beaux Arts doesn't allow any major structural changes in a building, even a private house, once they've classified it as a historical monument, like this one. That's why I had it so well lit."

"I see. And if I asked you to come home with me now and spend the night with me, what would you say?"

"I couldn't, Sam."

"Why not? *Why the hell not?* Christ, Billy, I love you, I've never stopped. Why can't you give me a chance? I want you . . . and don't try to tell me you don't want me, because I'd never believe you."

"I do want you . . . but I can't."

I really can't, Billy thought incredulously. I'm going mad just thinking about it but I can't move in your direction, damn it to hell, because I'm not the person I used to be . . . I've lost her . . . but I've found someone else . . . who needs her? . . . Someone who realizes that this is the first time we've ever been alone together in any honest way, someone who knows that some of the thrill is gone, now that Sam knows who I really am, and I know he knows. Would I . . . could I . . . do the things that Honey would have done? Or would I be worrying about Spider? Would Sam stop me from thinking about Spider Elliott? Could I ever possibly love him that much?

"You *can't*? Is that because you still love your husband?"

"It looks that way, doesn't it?"

"How far away is that lucky bastard?"

"Six thousand miles."

"I guess that gives me my answer. We're here, just you and me, here alone, across a continent and an ocean. He'd never know anything about it, would he? You'd never tell him . . . you're the world's best liar . . . but you can't. Because you can't—no other reason. Because, basically, you don't want to enough."

"That's the way it goes."

"Just my luck." Sam stood up to go.

"I'll let you out," Billy said. "The gate's tricky unless you know how."

"Just keep your distance, lady."

"Sam—I'm sorry."

"We're both sorry, but the timing's wrong. Our timing always was."

As they crossed the courtyard, Sam looked down at Billy walking several paces away from him. He'd never get over her, not completely, but now . . . at least he had a fighting chance. At least he knew she loved her husband.

"Billy, one thing, did it ever once occur to you that I could never have worked without natural light? That those magnificent stables would have been like a dark, gloomy prison cell to me, that I actually love walking up five flights to get to a loft where the daylight's pouring in?"

"I never thought . . . I was an idiot! But you could have kept your old studio—"

"Don't you remember how I used to get up in the morning and start working as soon as it was light, before breakfast, often for hours at a time? I still work that way, all I have to do is throw on overalls and walk around the corner."

"I certainly took too much for granted."

"Only that. No big deal."

"Actually it was a big deal . . . it was incredibly thoughtless of me."

"Don't waste any time on it—it never happened anyhow. Will you kiss me good-bye? Billy, Honey, love of my life?"

"I don't think that's a good idea. I've been called a lot of things in my day, but not utterly stupid, Sam darling. At least not recently, not . . . in the last week." Billy laughed softly and closed the gate behind her.

16

As soon as the Gulfstream had reached cruising altitude on its return trip to California, Gigi lay back in her seat and closed her eyes, her mind returning to the actual plans of the *Winthrop Emerald,* which she had learned to read and understand during the past week under the tutelage of Renzo Montegardini. It had been agreed that in order for her to know what copy points were the most important, she should be thoroughly conversant with the entire layout of the ship.

"The lowest deck a passenger will ever see is the Capricorn Deck, where they board," Montegardini informed her. "This formerly was the top deck of the ship when it was a freighter. Now it is mainly given to officers' accommodations, the galley, and the restaurant, so that diners will have the impression of eating as close to the ocean as possible. Also, since it is low and central, there is the added advantage of maximum stability."

"How do people decide where they want to sit at dinner?" Gigi asked.

"They make their own arrangements during the day, depending on their mood. The maitre d'hotel will comply with any request, from a table for two to a table for twelve, and dinner reservations may be made anytime from seven-thirty until nine-thirty, so that the restaurant can close at eleven-thirty."

"Is there a captain's table?" Gigi asked.

"But without fail. Unless there is a captain's table, where would the captain eat? Each night he will invite a different group of people to sit with him, unlike the old days of tradition, when the same people dined at the captain's table every night. Now look here, Graziella Giovanna, on the next deck up, the Gemini Deck, we have the first of the suites that make this ship different from all others. There are fourteen suites on each side of the central corridor of the ship, each one of them five hundred and sixty feet square. Suites are located on three of the five new decks, eighty-four of them in all, plus the owner's suite. The *Winthrop Emerald*, when full, can carry a maximum—a maximum, mind you well—of only one hundred and seventy passengers, plus an additional hundred and forty in crew. Normally a ship this size would carry more than twice that many passengers, with perhaps a few suites."

This girl disturbed him, Renzo Montegardini admitted to himself with the wryness of a man thirty years older than Gigi, a man of sophistication, a man to whom many opportunities had been offered by women, and many accepted with mutual pleasure. She took away his peace of mind, this girl who coiled herself over the blueprints with such a submissive desire to be instructed, her jeweled eyes alive with excitement through the black velvet fans of her lashes that were so deliciously artificial. As he outlined the floor plan of a suite with his architect's precision, he imagined that her shoulder would be as burning to the touch as her small nose would be cool.

"Each suite," he said with resignation, thinking of Ben Winthrop, "is made up of two rooms side by side. You walk in through a short hall, on each side of which is a pale pink marble bathroom and a walk-in closet with a safe for valuables. To cover the walls I used a combination of pale woods and tone-on-tone brocades in lighthearted pastels, which I specified should be quilted for extra soundproofing. I used inset strips of floor-to-ceiling mirrors extensively, to expand the space and reflect the sea."

"What about the portholes?" Gigi asked.

"*Cara* colleague," the naval architect said in shock, "in the crew's quarters, yes, many portholes, but in the suites I have designed floor-to-ceiling windows over which, at the touch of a button, a lightproof shutter falls at night, so the late sleeper is not disturbed. Portholes!"

"Who knew?" Gigi asked mildly. "What's the rest of the suite like?"

"Here, five feet beyond the entrance hall, you can see where a wall is built to separate the rooms. In the bedroom you find a king-sized bed that can be divided into twin beds, built-in night tables, and a long dressing table opposite the bed. The other room is multipurpose, with a television and VCR that rises from its cabinet at the touch of a button, a built-in bar, a writing desk, and a round table that can be used for breakfast or games. Every object, every piece of furniture, was chosen by the design teams to give a feeling of a festive holiday."

"Does that dividing wall stop here?" Gigi asked, putting her finger on the blueprint.

"Exactly, leaving the bedroom area private. When the two rooms are joined into one, all the space becomes a wide, comfortably furnished sitting room giving directly onto the sea, with room enough for thirty people to have cocktails—or for two people to be cozy together."

Her mouth, the naval architect thought, in that cozy suite, would be perilously soft and nervously thirsty as she bent her head back for kisses; her breasts were set high and round and far apart, like those in certain old engravings that had tormented him as a boy. She would have impertinent hips and a maddeningly childish frizz of hair between her legs. He sighed and thought of her age. And his age.

"What's on the rest of this deck, Renzo?" inquired Gigi impatiently.

"Boutiques and the port tour office, Graziella Giovanna. Above you will find all the necessary public rooms of any cruise ship, the ballroom, the big and little bars, the casino, the lending library, the spa, the beauty salon, the gym, a special bar called

Rick's Place, another intimate room for AA and OA meetings to be held during the day—essential amid the temptations of a cruise, and of course the pool, the deck chairs, and much space for the seriously athletic."

"What do I do if I'm walking around this sun deck twenty times and I get hungry?"

"The sun deck, which we will call the Zodiac Deck, I beg you, has an open-air Sky Bar with fresh juices for the health-mad. Here, at the prow of the Zodiac Deck, in the Equator Lounge, high above the captain's bridge, we serve snacks twenty-four hours a day, with an elaborate afternoon tea. If you find yourself still hungry, room service will be available all day and all night. You seem to have an excellent appetite, *piccola signorina.*"

"I used to be a chef," Gigi explained. "I adore thinking about food."

"A charming talent," he said, regret mounting each minute. Without appetite, what was beauty?

"Renzo, here," Gigi said, pointing, "these two huge, empty spaces at the stern of the Zodiac Deck, are they the bases of the funnels?"

"Indeed, yes. They serve no other function but that of style. And the open space behind them, totally at the stern, is another sun deck."

"What if the ship carried two large helicopters? Could you use the funnel bases as hangers? Could the helicopters land on that sun deck?"

"Certainly, but we have no plans for two helicopters. Why?"

"I've been thinking . . . let's say you're docked for the day in London—if a group of women wanted to visit a couture collection in Paris, rather than sightseeing in London, they could do so easily by helicopter and get back to the ship by dinner, couldn't they? Or if you were docked at Piraeus, instead of fighting the smog at the Acropolis, they could take a day trip to a Greek island or two— there would be a hundred ways to use them."

"Have you discussed helicopters with Ben?"

"No, but I will, now that you've told me you can accommodate them."

I could find space for even *four* helicopters if you could accommodate me, Montegardini thought, accommodate me with your green eyes open and imperious, accommodate me mockingly and flauntingly, with all your melting, absorbing, exasperating charms laid bare until I was as exhausted as the victor on a battlefield. He bit the inside of his lip and thought of Ben Winthrop again. A possessive man, utterly possessive.

"Renzo? Renzo! Don't you think you could carve out some space from the ballroom—it's really huge—and make a costume storage and fitting room?"

"For what purpose, my dear naval architect in training?"

"For masked balls. I think that there should be a masked ball on each voyage, a ball with a surprise theme, with different costumes each time. They'd have to be bought in advance, stored on hangers, and fitted to the passengers by clever alteration people. I don't see another inch of space available."

"And where would these alteration people sleep?"

"Perhaps . . . with the officers?" Gigi suggested in a purring, beseeching tone of voice that made him desperately try to think of his wife's cats.

"I will try, Graziella Giovanna, at this stage nothing is impossible."

"Oh, Renzo, you're an angel! If nothing is impossible, wouldn't you say that you could make the main dining room just a tiny little bit smaller, and add a private party room where people could plan special dinners, one night Chinese, one night Italian, one night—deli? They could reserve it before the cruise and hold birthday and anniversary parties there—wouldn't it be a good idea?"

"I'll see, most *cara* Gigietta, I'll try to see if it can be done," he sighed.

And you, my enchantingly nerve-racking girl, are a supple, artless devil, an instinctive passionate animal wielding your warm weapons without even realizing it . . . and I must absolutely throw you out of my office until I regain my senses.

Gigi found the study of the blueprints so fascinating that by the end of the week she had them all reduced in size and put into a portfolio with the *Sizione Maestra*, the painting of the *Winthrop*

Emerald, and a set of interior photographs of the suites. This package, with Ben's enthusiastic approval, was planned to be used as a special advertising supplement, bound separately and inserted into *Town and Country, Architectural Digest,* and *Vogue.* Through the use of selected Zip Codes it was possible to mail it to the areas where most of the future American passengers of the *Emerald* lived. The last page of this section bore only one line of type, an announcement that the maiden voyage of the *Winthrop Emerald* was sold out.

"You do not hesitate to count your chickens so soon in advance, *piccolla* Graziella Giovanna?" Renzo had asked, his eyebrows raised.

"The maiden voyage will be by invitation only," Gigi assured him, "direct from Venice to New York. Is that an offer you would refuse?"

"From you, dear and valued colleague, no offer would ever be refused."

Gigi, pad and pen in hand, sat in the jet bringing her back to California, writing a card to go with her gift for Eleonora Colonna, who was going to be sixty-five next week. In the course of the last year, Gigi had made many trips to San Francisco to work with the Indigo Seas designers, and to keep their ad campaign fresh and on course. Her friendship with the matriarch of the family had deepened steadily. Eleonora Colonna's guest room was where Gigi stayed now, whenever she visited San Francisco, and she knew the large, close-knit family intimately, from all three Collins brothers and their wives, down to the last grandchild.

During her five days in New York she'd had time to visit some of her favorite hunting grounds for antique lingerie, searching for the romantic, richly decorated, hand-sewn garments created in days when women knew the erotic provocation of suggestion and understood well that a minimum of titillating revelation created a maximum of desire. In a box at her feet lay a true find, a complete bathing costume dating from 1894, a hundred-year-old creation an emancipated woman wore into the water only after a bell had chased all the men from the beach.

It consisted of four pieces, the first a very wide floor-length cloak made of heavy white linen, deeply flounced and bowed at the hem, and tied at the neck under a double ruffled collar. This enveloping garment totally covered the bathing costume itself as its owner proceeded across the sand. Underneath the cloak, the brave bather wore a knee-length, full-skirted, tightly sashed dress made of thin linen, worn over separate drawers of even thinner linen, gathered below the knees, and falling almost to midcalf. Both dress and drawers were navy and white, with much contrasting embroidery in nautical stripes. The last piece of the ensemble was a striped navy and white band, with a bow on each side, that was intended to sit on top of the head.

It took Deauville twenty-five years to recover from the sensation caused by that mysterious Italian girl who appeared on the sands one morning and captivated the gentlemen of the town so instantly that within days there wasn't a pair of field glasses left to be bought in all of Normandy. No one knew her name, although that night everyone at the casino was buzzing about her, even the blasé croupiers. Soon a rumor started that she was named Eleonora. But was she a dancer or was she a duke's daughter? Was she a blue-blooded lady of virtue or was she an actress? All that could be discovered, by bribing the female attendants who rubbed her dry after her daring immersion in the sea, was that she had the body of a great courtesan, the skin of a young child, the face of an angel, and the modesty of a nun. Also, she was merely fifteen years of age. Crazed by desire, two young princes sent her presents by means of the bathing attendants. One sent her a diamond the size of a chestnut that had recently been the property of a baccarat-mad maharaja; the other sent her a diamond tiara that had been in his family for five hundred years. All they asked for was a rendezvous with Eleonora as she walked back to the closed carriage that waited for her at the edge of the sands. But she returned the presents without an answer. The two princes observed her through their glasses every day, their hearts so utterly captured that they thought of nothing else. One day, for a sum that would have bribed the President of France twice over, they managed to replace the bathing attendants, wearing their dresses and bonnets. Eleonora, who was not a chatterbox, noticed nothing strange until she returned from her dip in the ocean and went to the changing cabin to have her bathing costume removed. "Why am I waiting here soaking wet?" she exclaimed in astonishment. "Can't you see that this accursed dress is clinging to me? I shall catch la grippe if you do not make haste." But her attendants were so frozen with lust by the sight of the wet cloth outlining her gloriously voluptuous body that they were rendered incapable of movement. "Oh, well, then, I shall have to undress myself," she announced with an intoxicating shiver, and unbuttoned her bathing costume all by herself, for she was a clever and handy girl. At that moment both of the princes flung themselves on their knees in shame at what they had done, for they realized that Eleonora was the one woman each of them would die to marry—their mamas had feared that no such woman existed. Covering their eyes in remorse, they revealed their identities to Eleonora, who replied calmly, "In that case perhaps one of you would have the kindness to give me a towel." That night, at the casino of Deauville, Eleonora appeared with a prince on each arm. Even the sound of the roulette wheels stopped as she made a regal tour of the private rooms, clad only in her flowing white linen cloak with her long dark hair hanging loosely over her shoulders. Her ornaments were orange blossoms in her hair, for she was far far too young to wear diamonds. The next day Eleonora had disappeared from the beach, and so had the handsomest of the two princes, the one who had been the first to give her a towel. It is said, on reliable information, that they lived blissfully ever after, immigrating to the coast of California, where Eleonora became a princess long before she and her prince renounced their titles to become citizens of the United States. Eleonora's youngest daughter became the mother of Eleonora Colonna, another great beauty who understands the power of a wet bathing costume.

With all my love,
Gigi

At the bottom of the card, Gigi had carefully done one of her expressive, humorous little sketches of Eleonora at that brief, tantalizing moment for which the gentlemen with field glasses waited for so eagerly, when she was forced to emerge from the gentle sea at Deauville after her swim and rush toward the attendants holding out the billowing cloak in which they would rapidly envelop her.

Satisfied, Gigi tucked the card into the box and tied a bow around it. She rang for the steward to tell him that she was ready for lunch. She still had hours left to write cards to go with the amazing five-piece white lace Victorian "marriage set" she had found for Sasha and the velvet-collared Edwardian dandy's smoking jacket made by Charvet and obviously never worn, which she'd discovered for Vito. He'd have to grow a mustache to do it justice.

Gigi arrived at the agency so early on Monday morning that she expected to be among the first hungry souls at Bagel Central. She'd spent the kind of thrillingly sleepless night that comes from overexcitement, obsessed by the plans for the *Winthrop Emerald*. She'd realized that she was in overdrive at three-thirty in the middle of the night, when she found herself still planning how to con Renzo into making room for a regulation-sized Ping-Pong table on the part of the deck reserved for deck chairs. Ping-Pong was the only sport at which Gigi herself excelled, the only sport at which she believed everyone, no matter how unathletic, had a fighting chance. After another hour of feverish concentration on a cruise-long Ping-Pong tournament with fabulous prizes, it occurred to her that a Ping-Pong table could be put up and taken down in a few minutes, that it didn't need a space all of its own, and she finally calmed down enough to plunge into an hour of deep sleep, only to wake up at six as if a fire alarm had gone off next to her pillow.

"Hi there, Polly," Gigi said languidly to the receptionist, as she took a plate, hoping that bagels were complex carbohydrates, a question she'd never dared to ask because she feared the answer.

"Hi, stranger. How was New York?"

"Fantastic. How's life at FRB?"

"Wild. Listen, Victoria wants to see you pronto, the minute you get in."

"*She's* in already?"

"Everybody's in early today," Polly said with the air of someone who knows something she can't tell.

"Which explains why there aren't any bagels left," Gigi said with disappointment, putting two sticky cinnamon rolls on a plate and getting hot tea out of a spigot. She carried her breakfast to her office, empty for the moment of Lisa Levy, the talented art director who worked as her creative partner, and decided that nothing Victoria had to say to her was more important than nourishment. She hadn't made breakfast at home, and she felt light-headed. Her mouth was full when her phone rang.

"It's Polly, Victoria wants to know if you're on your way to her office."

Gigi chewed as quickly as she could and swallowed hastily. "How fast can I eat, for Pete's sake? I could choke to death here."

"Bring it with you, she's in a chop-chop mood."

"Screw that. Tell Miss Vicky I'll be in as soon as I've done my Transcendental Meditation and read 'Dear Abby.' Without my morning rituals, my day gets off on the wrong foot."

"Gigi, please, please, do it for me," Polly said.

"Oh, okay." If Victoria Frost thought she could spoil her morning, she was wrong, Gigi thought, as she walked down the corridor and into the big office in which Victoria reigned.

"Well?" Gigi said, stopping inside the door. Archie and Byron were standing around looking excited while Victoria tested a fresh pepper grinder that stood next to a large platter of bagels, cream cheese, and smoked salmon.

"Is this my birthday?" Gigi asked delightedly as Arch and By both moved forward to kiss her hello.

"It's a little welcome-home party," Archie explained. "We missed your cheery face, believe it or not, so we laid on your favorite feast to express our affection."

"Now I see what that rush was about," Gigi said to Victoria, feeling only slightly ashamed of her uncharitable thoughts. "Let me at it!"

"It was my idea," Byron said proudly. "Archie wanted to get a cake, but I knew what you liked best."

"You were right on the money, Byron the Third," Gigi said, helping herself lavishly. "Did you have a vote, Victoria?" she asked curiously.

"I was in favor of a kilo of Beluga caviar and lots of Dom Perignon," Victoria said, "but I was outvoted. I've never really understood bagels. Gigi, fresh pepper for that salmon?"

"Just a little," Gigi replied. When Victoria Frost thought of mounds of caviar, champagne, and Gigi Orsini in the same context, something wasn't kosher.

"Tell us about your week, Gigi," Archie said when they'd finished eating.

"Archie, why don't you tell Gigi about our week?" Victoria broke in smoothly. Wasn't it enough that she'd finally agreed to this absurd breakfast without anyone expecting her to listen to any of Gigi's effusions on cruise-ship data and decor? She'd been waiting for this moment since last Tuesday, six impatient days of imagining how Gigi was going to look when the realization finally came home to her that in her absence the agency had expanded by over a hundred million in billings, had changed from a newly created shop in which she had been indulged and petted and treated like a prodigy, to an agency in which she would merely be another employee, albeit a busy one.

Byron and Archie had made a case for the welcome-home celebration. In spite of her reassurances to the contrary, they'd felt some minor residual concern about taking the Scruples Two account while she was away. Archie had even suggested giving Gigi the title of "assistant to the creative directors," but Victoria had vetoed it.

"The time to give Gigi some sort of a title is when she comes up for her yearly compensation review," she'd insisted, and she'd made her judgment stick. How like the boys it was to want to rush the rewards to which Gigi would feel entitled. They'd already given her too much more money. A title was all they had left, but Arch and By had no talent for management, they had never understood the discipline of delayed gratification and the necessity of maintaining order among the creatives.

Little Miss Orsini would have to be rewarded, no doubt about that, but there was no point in overdoing it. Her head had been enormous even before her first day on the job; she'd waltzed in here full of attitude, but during those delicate days in which they were struggling to get over the hump of being a new boutique agency, there had been no way for business reality to be applied to Gigi— she'd turned into a one-man band. But now, with the gigantic acquisition of Beach Casuals, the picture had changed totally and Gigi was back in perspective. No more girl wonder, no longer the pint-sized procurer of medium-sized accounts courtesy of the easy generosity of Ben Winthrop, who undoubtedly congratulated himself every time he fucked Gigi that the IRS was paying for it, since advertising was a deductible business expense. Had Gigi ever realized she was the sexual equivalent of a business lunch?

"Why don't you tell her, Victoria?" Archie countered. "It's your baby, not mine."

"I don't care who tells me what," Gigi said, "if you'd manage to get to the point. I have so much to tell you about the *Emerald*."

"Gigi, it's almost a year that you've been here," Victoria said, launching, as she had planned to all along, into the role of leader that belonged to her by right.

"You must know that you've proven yourself as a copywriter with the ability to get new business as well," she went on. "We all realized that you were afraid of the smell of nepotism and favoritism when you insisted that we stay away from the Scruples Two account when you came to work here. However—"

" 'However'?" Gigi broke in. "I don't like the sound of that word." Now she knew the reason for the caviar and champagne.

"However," Victoria continued with a small smile, as if she and Gigi had a secret between them, "you've undoubtedly realized that you've had more than enough success on your own to render that particular scruple, for want of a better word, utterly unprofessional and deeply unfair to us, as your employers."

"Are you telling me I'm unprofessional, Victoria?"

"Just the reverse. When you were new and green, Gigi, indeed you were, but certainly not any longer. We all agree that you've become a true advertising pro." Victoria's smile deepened, as if the understanding between them were stronger than anyone realized. "Before you came here, before you understood the nature of the business, Archie and Byron made a hasty mistake. They allowed you to clip our wings and prevent us from going after an account we're uniquely qualified to service. Last week I went to see

Spider Elliott—he's been unhappy with Russo and Russo for a long time—and he positively jumped at the chance to have us handle the Scruples Two account . . . he didn't even want any other agencies to pitch it."

"Why didn't you check with me in New York before pitching Spider?" Gigi demanded hotly.

"Check with you? Come on, Gigi, as a pro you certainly realize that management doesn't find it necessary to ask your permission to go after an account. We took your agreement for granted."

"When did all this happen?" Gigi asked, her cheeks flaming.

"About a week ago—what difference does it make?"

"A week ago? Spider and Billy knew how I felt. They haven't called to tell me . . . you'd think that in a week . . ." Gigi felt utterly confused as she looked around and saw that Archie and Byron were beaming sunnily at her in spite of the solemn promise they'd broken.

"Undoubtedly the Elliotts agree with us that you're a big girl now and don't need to be babied."

"I can see why you can't write copy, Victoria, you have a knack of choosing offensive words," Gigi snapped.

Victoria ignored her. "You'll be working with Byron as art director," she said, "and you'll get a chance to do innovative copy for the catalog."

"I did innovative copy for the catalog for years, thank you very much," Gigi said, standing up, "One of the main reasons I came here was to get away from catalog work."

"Gigi, it's something you can do with one hand tied behind you," Victoria said impatiently. "Why is it so hard for you to admit that you've been standing in the way of our getting an account that wants us as much as we want them?"

"Thanks for the breakfast," Gigi said, "but you didn't need to fatten me up to cushion the news."

Quickly she turned toward the door so that she wouldn't have to look at Archie and Byron's smirking, betraying, self-satisfied faces. She'd believed that they were stand-up guys, but now she knew she'd been wrong, charming though they were. Wasn't charm an essential part of creative directors' equipment? She was

astonished and deeply disappointed that they'd gone sneaking behind her back or, at best, colluded with Victoria.

If Victoria honestly considered her such a pro, she would have
met with her about the best way to go after the Scruples Two
account, instead of waiting to pitch it when she was safely out of
town. And, Gigi thought, if such a meeting had taken place, she
now felt confident enough in her own abilities to agree with Victoria that Scruples Two was fair game.

"There's more news, Gigi. Sit down, don't rush off," Victoria
said quickly.

"What kind of news?" Gigi turned back and saw that the
three of them had identical expressions on their faces, expressions
of gleeful victory.

"Great news! Incredible news!" Archie said, "We've got
Beach Casuals!"

"I don't fucking believe it," Gigi said, stunned. She knew the
swimwear industry inside out by now, and she knew what this
meant.

"Believe it!" Archie exalted. "Believe ninety million bucks a
year!"

"Oh, my God—that's fabulous . . . glorious . . . . . . but
. . . but . . ."

"But what?" Byron said. "You know there are no 'buts' with a
ninety-million-dollar account."

"But . . . it's a conflict with Indigo Seas."

"Oh, for heaven's sake, Gigi, that's not a 'but,' " Byron
laughed.

"Nevertheless, there is a conflict," she insisted.

"Of course there is," Archie said, "That's why we resigned
Indigo Seas."

"The most incredible thing was that Beach Casuals happened
the same day as Scruples Two—we all sat around in here and got
drunk, we were so stunned," Byron told her. "You should have
been here."

"I guess you *had* to be here," Gigi said quietly, looking at their
excited, elated faces. "Did you have any problem breaking the
news to the Collins brothers?"

"Nothing I couldn't handle," Victoria said smugly.

"Did they ask if I knew about it?"

"I told them you were out of town. I'm sure they understood, they're in business like the rest of us."

"Not all of us," Gigi said slowly. "Count me out."

"What are you talking about?" Archie asked incredulously. "You've got to be kidding—count you out, what the hell does that mean?"

"A moment of truth, Arch. I've just realized that I'm not built to be in the advertising business. I haven't become the professional it's so convenient for you to tell me I am, I—"

"Victoria, didn't I warn you she'd be upset—" Archie sputtered.

"It's not about Scruples Two, Archie, it's about duplicity. It's about breaking a promise to me—a promise you and Byron made before I'd agree to take this job—breaking it because there was an opportunity to get the account and you didn't want to risk it by trusting me—"

"Wait, that was Victoria's idea, not—"

"It doesn't matter who planned it, you all went along, didn't tell me about it for a week, and then hoped that lox and flattery would make it okay."

"Shit, Gigi, don't you have any faith in yourself?" Byron asked.

"Tons of it, Byron, and I'd even have helped pitch for Scruples Two if I'd been asked."

"So that's the big problem—we didn't show enough faith in you," Archie rallied.

"This isn't about my ego, Arch, it's about my fitness for advertising. You guys are in a business that demands that when a big fish comes along, the little fish get dumped out of the aquarium. I get inconveniently attached to my little fish, I get attached to people who've been good to me, like Eleonora Colonna and her sons, and I'm proud of the way we've built the Indigo Seas business. I know they trusted me . . . you've destroyed that. You all knew how close I've grown to the whole family. I understand that you had to resign the account, but couldn't you—at the very least—have given me a chance to explain it to them?"

"That's ridiculous," Victoria said furiously. "You're not part of management."

370

"It's not ridiculous, and you know it. This separation of management and creative is totally artificial, a convenient way for you to get and keep power, Victoria. Do you think I can put everything I've got into being *merely* creative—understanding the products, really getting to care about the clients—and then leave them to your tender mercies when there's a business decision to be made?"

"That happens to be the way things are in this shop," Victoria raged. "This agency doesn't belong to you."

"That's why I'm out of here, Miss Vicky. I can't live with the way things work in this business—or maybe it's only in this particular agency. Don't bother to send me my personalized coffee mug."

Gigi walked out of the office, down the hall, and out of the building, and got into her car and drove home.

"So my poor baby's out of a job," Vito said, stroking Gigi's hand tenderly as she sat having dinner with him and Sasha that same night.

"Looks that way," Gigi said, giving him an unconstrained smile. "I may end up sharing Nellie's room."

"What's a family for?" Sasha asked. "Does that mean I can fire Nanny?"

"I wouldn't if I were you," Gigi advised her. "I quit catering, I quit advertising, but I don't have the guts to take up nannying. Anything except that, but thanks for thinking of me."

"Would you like to direct?" Vito asked.

Gigi snorted with amusement. Everyone in Hollywood— sometimes it seemed that everyone in the world, including the Archbishop of Canterbury and the Chief Rabbi of Israel—wanted to direct.

"I could use you," he said, only half-jesting.

"What's the matter with your current director?" she asked, finding that, as usual, she preferred not to use Zach's name if she didn't have to.

"There's something going on with him," Vito said, "that I don't understand. *Long Weekend* is written as a black comedy about Hollywood. Many of the characters are far from being lovable— they're in the industry, and you know what that means."

"People like you, Dad?" Gigi grinned impenitently, basking

in the happiness that surrounded him and Sasha with enough left over for anyone in their vicinity to be warmed by it. "Regular Boy Scouts?"

"Don't laugh, some of them are being directed to lean in that direction. The original blackness is turning bittersweet, and the original bittersweet is getting positively romantic. Once or twice, Zach's even verged on the sentimental . . . directing a valentine . . . and when I scream at him, he tells me he's directing it the way he feels it. God save me from directors! Who asked him to *feel?*"

"Can't we talk about something else?" Sasha asked peevishly. "After all, he's my brother and I feel vaguely responsible for him. Now I know why they say you should never do business with family. Let's talk about Ben Winthrop, boy billionaire."

"Gigi," Vito said, "wait a minute here, you're the person who thought up The Enchanted Attic and the Winthrop Line, aren't you? That has to mean, at the very least, that you have a great deal to say about the choice of an advertising agency. You don't intend to leave those accounts with FRB after the way they've treated you, do you?"

"I'm not going to try to take them away," Gigi said. "Nothing would be easier, but the more I thought about it, the more I realized that there's a big problem involved, something more important than letting FRB keep them."

"What could possibly be that important?" Vito stared at her, deeply offended in his well-developed sense of righteous revenge.

"Oddly enough, the very fact that I do have power over the accounts. I don't want to ask Ben to move them for my sake."

"Why not?" Sasha asked, openmouthed.

"I don't want to . . . *owe* him. If I ask him, he'd do it in a minute, but then I'd be . . . oh, damn, how can I say this and make you understand? . . . I'd be in his *control,* even more than I am now."

"Wait a minute," Vito said. "*You* control the accounts, but if you move them to another agency, you'd be in *Ben Winthrop's* control . . . because you used *your* control? Have I got it right, so far?"

"Exactly. But only so far."

"What your daughter is trying to explain, darling, is that Ben

372

Winthrop's money is being spent on Ben Winthrop's advertising, and she doesn't want to be in control of the way he spends his money."

"But Gigi wasn't shy about getting him to invest in the stores and the ships," Vito protested.

"But, Dad, that was *suggesting* how he spend his money, giving him an idea he was free to accept or reject. Once he'd made his decision, then the agency I worked for deserved the accounts, but I hadn't controlled his decision."

"Hmmm." Vito thought it over. "So, in other words, you're not planning to marry him, right? You're not going to become the client's wife. Otherwise you'd move those accounts so fast Victoria Frost wouldn't have time to shit a single ice cube."

"Sasha, how can you put up with this?" Gigi asked, laughing, but not denying Vito's insight.

"It gets easier with practice. Oh, Gigi, are you sure you aren't going to marry him? How can you let the man who has everything get away?"

"Oh, it's not over yet. I keep trying to imagine myself married to Ben five years from now, or ten years from now, but I can't manage to get a vision of it, clear or unclear. Something sort of blocks me, my imagination won't work . . ."

"Mine does," Sasha cried. "I see you and Ben leading the most glamorous life, all over the world—couldn't you borrow my imagination?"

"When you met Dad, did you imagine yourself married to him?"

"That's not fair! You know that's the first thing all unmarried women think about when they meet a new man. Is he or isn't he 'the one'? And if he isn't, would I sleep with him anyway?"

"Sasha?" Gigi repeated insistently. "Answer my question."

"I *intended* to marry him from the minute Zach introduced us."

"I rest my case."

"What Gigi's trying to say is that the jury's still out," Vito pronounced. "Don't give up on her, darling, maybe you'll get to fly in Winthrop's jet someday. I wish you'd break down and admit that's why you're so in favor of this guy—it only goes to prove what the industry has always known; the secret to any woman's heart is in *transportation*. If you have a jet and a limo, it doesn't matter what you look like or how horrible a person you are, you have to beat off the nooky with a stick."

"What about a yacht?" Gigi asked. "Or a cruise ship with a helicopter on board?"

"Couldn't hurt," Vito said, paying the check. "But sailboats, forget it. Sailboats are a turn-off. Transportation's gotta have a motor."

"Honestly, Sasha," Vito sighed, as they got into bed, "I don't know what's come over these kids—your brother and Gigi, they're both so full of lofty sentiments and tender, finicky feelings—this younger generation, they're just too pure to cope with the real world."

Sasha giggled.

"What's so funny?" Vito asked.

"Zach's my older brother."

"I can never remember that. There's something distinctly grown-up about you. I bet you'd never leave those accounts with Victoria Frost."

"I'd snatch her baldheaded with a song in my heart. Listen, darling, what's really going on with Zach? I stopped you from talking about it in front of Gigi, but I've got to know."

"Damned if I understand it. With any other director I'd say that he'd let himself lose his edge, that he wasn't hungry anymore, that he was coasting, or that his reputation had gone to his head. None of that could possibly be true about Zach, he's too fine a director, too committed to excellence, but this material demands constant, unrelenting bite, and his bite goes missing from time to time. I'm having to spend too damn much time on the set trying to second-guess him, with very little result. I lived to do that until I met you and found something that's more fun."

"Could he be having a midlife crisis?"

"Isn't he too young?"

"Not necessarily. Is he behaving like somebody going through a horrible divorce?" Sasha asked, more and more concerned.

"Yeah, a little, and a little like somebody falling in love with the absolutely wrong person, none of which applies, since he hasn't

374

dated in months and months . . . in fact since I can't remember when."

"Good Lord!" Sasha said, sitting up in horrified surprise at this unprecedented news. "Would you say he's depressed?"

"He certainly doesn't seem to be having any fun. Instead of spending his lunch break with me, he keeps listening to Elsa Worthy, who plays the matriarch, a bit part—she was a big star forty years ago and she's still got some of that old fire, that old charm—she's giving Zach daily installments of the story of her life in all its misery, like a soap—you don't suppose he's fallen for her?"

"That doesn't sound like him," Sasha pronounced, more and more troubled.

"And then he's forgetful. Forgetful! Would you believe that yesterday the first AD had to tell him that he was shooting a finished scene twice? And that's not the only time it's happened. If I leave the set for five minutes I start to worry."

"Why didn't you tell me about all this before?" she demanded.

"I didn't want to worry you, sweetheart. I hate to bring the business back home with me, the way I used to do. Officially we should still be on the honeymoon we never had. On Friday, when he called Ma—"

"WHEN WHAT?"

"When Zach phoned your mother to check in like a good son, the way he's been doing a couple of times a week—"

"Oh, Jesus, Vito! You mean to sit there and tell me he's calling Ma and he's not in a depression? He must be like the walking dead! Calling Ma is the last resort—we only call Ma if we're feeling absolutely suicidal! Oh, my God, look at what you've been saving me from—a brother who doesn't date—Zach without a girl!—who acts like he's getting divorced, who's suddenly lost his short-term memory, who listens to sob stories from the past, WHO CALLS MA—when were you planning to let me know, after he put a gun to his head and pulled the trigger?"

"Sasha, you're exaggerating," Vito said patiently. "You told me you've always been a little overboard about Zach."

"I know I am, but calling Ma! Vito, he's severely depressed!"

"Come to think of it, he hasn't been the same old Zach for a while now," Vito said, thinking back. "When I went up to Kalispell, and that was about ten months ago, this . . . change . . .

had already started. It hadn't affected his work, so I didn't pay that much attention, or maybe it's just that we had so much damage control to do that I didn't notice . . . but no, you're right, he *is* depressed."

"Ten months?" Sasha echoed. "I've been so preoccupied with Josh and the divorce and meeting you that I've barely been able to see Zach in all that time, but ten months of depression, getting worse all the time? Well, we know what miserable, vicious bitch we have to thank for that, don't we?"

"We do?" Vito asked in astonishment.

"Your daughter, your darling baby Gigi, that's who!"

"Hey, watch who you call a miserable, vicious bitch!"

"Sorry, darling, but she is. And what is she doing now, that ungrateful, spiteful, cruel tease, but toying with the affections of Mr. Wonderful, who's clearly nothing more to her than another scalp to hang from her belt, having already screwed that poor boy Davy Melville right into the ground and out of the office—"

"Wait! Hold it right there! Gigi's been having affairs with one guy after another, which isn't her style, and Zach's not fucking around, which isn't his style either, so—"

"How come when it's your daughter she's having affairs, when it's my brother, he's fucking around—"

"Have a little respect, Sasha, darling, and don't miss the point. Are you listening?"

"Breathlessly."

"Gigi and Zach are still in love."

After a silence, Sasha nodded her dark head up and down in respect and admiration.

"I'll never forgive myself for not putting my finger on it before you. And you'll always remind me, won't you, Vito? For the rest of our lives you'll hold this over me as proof of your superiority."

"Only when I have to," Vito said. "What are we going to do?"

"Fix it, obviously," Sasha said with her usual proud confidence in her powers.

"But how? This has been going on for almost a year."

"So much the better. If they haven't gotten over each other in that long, it's serious." Sasha closed her eyes and concentrated. "Let's not monkey around, we'll fix it the usual way."

"We abandon them on a desert island for a week?"

"Oh, darling, that's such a typical boy solution. We don't do anything. You hint to Zach that Gigi's still in love with him and I hint to Gigi that Zach's still in love with her. But be subtle! Remember, they're almost as smart as we are."

"The Much Ado ploy? I didn't realize that was still in use."

"It was working tens of thousands of years before Shakespeare, and it'll be working when they colonize Mars."

"But what if it doesn't work with Gigi and Zach?"

"We'll worry about that if it happens. Or I'll have to call Ma and let her fix it."

17

For two days following his fight with Billy, Spider Elliott lived in a monotonous, repetitious trance of self-justification, repeating her final words to himself over and over while his mouth seemed to shrink as it grew tightly bitter at the edges. His eyes were narrowed and their Viking blue was darkened in a frown of defiance; his normally open features were shadowed by the unmistakable hardness of someone nursing a killing rage and resolved not to show it. No one now, watching him bent ferociously over the work on his desk, would have imagined him as the prototype of the carefree California surfer he once had been. He was so elaborately polite to his assistant, Tommy Tether, that the self-assured fellow decided that Spider must be getting ready to fire him; on three occasions he inquired solicitously of Josie Speilberg about how her adored nephews were getting along in school, the first time he'd shown more than a passing interest in them, and he braked for traffic lights that had suddenly turned yellow a mere twenty feet away.

He spent every waking minute reviewing each terrible thing Billy had done since he'd known her, from calling him "a cock without a conscience" when she'd accused him of making a play for Gigi on the basis of a few innocent kisses, to trying to add a three-week cancellation clause to his employment contract when he'd first come to California in 1977 to work for her at Scruples. Oh, yes, even way back then, at first sight he'd been aware of Billy's potential as a pussy-whipper, way back then he'd told Valentine that there was no success he would accept if it meant working for a pussy-whipping woman, and by Christ, nothing had changed, not in Billy and certainly not in him. How could he have been fool enough to marry her, knowing what he knew?

In the middle of the third night, after forty-eight hours of self-perpetuating fury, Spider woke up from a dream about sailing that left him with a vivid sense memory of the feeling of the tiller in his hand and the sight of an endless expanse of ocean. As he lay in bed, trying to recapture the dream in all its details, memories of his days at sea flooded over him.

After Valentine's death in 1980, Spider had bought a small sailing boat and disappeared, with his two-man crew, sailing ever westward, dropping anchor at countless islands in the many bodies of water that lay between Los Angeles and Greece, fleeing introspection and blunting his pain by plunging himself into a daily contest with the power of nature.

During that almost two-year voyage of mourning and recovery, he had written only two letters, and they had both been to Billy. He had sent his mother postcards from various ports, but Billy had been the only person he'd felt the need to communicate with, the only person he'd continued to feel close to during that necessary trip into an oblivion of sky, sea, and sun, through which he had succeeded in accepting his loss and envisioning a future.

Now, wide awake, with his anger burned out, he realized in shock and terror that he felt a monstrously urgent need to talk to Billy, to put things right between them. There was no one in the world he could go to for comfort from the things Billy had said to him—and the things he'd said to her—but Billy herself.

In the last letter he'd sent to her during his voyage, Spider remembered, he'd written that when he returned there'd be no point in going back into business because he'd never find another partner like her, never find anyone who'd be as much fun to fight with as she was. Granted, he'd written from a remote Greek island in the Aegean Sea, Spider reflected with despairing anguish, but his brain cells must have been reduced to ashes for him to have written that.

Nothing had ever been more exactly, precisely, specifically *not* "fun" in his entire life than his fight with Billy. Whatever the dictionary opposite of fun was, that fight had been it.

As he paced the floor, he told himself that he would give anything to find himself back inside the thick bubble of thorough-going depression he'd felt when he and Valentine had fought, long before their marriage, over her mysterious lover. *That* had been fun, compared to the way he felt now. That had been merely a muting of all his senses, a free-floating grayness cast over all the good things in life, a self-pitying sense that he might as well be dead for all the reason there was to go on living.

That fight with Valentine, Spider suddenly remembered, was the first time in his life that he'd been deliberately cruel to a woman. And the last, until he'd been cruel to Billy.

Well, he'd more than broken his brief record now, hadn't he? He'd really gone for broke, he had about as much reason to be proud of it as the hunter who'd bagged the last lion on earth, or shot the last nightingale and cooked it for dinner. And sucked on its bones when he was finished.

Where the fuck *was* she? It was still too early to call her at Jessica's in New York, or in Maine where she might be with Dolly, Spider thought, getting dressed because there was no way he could possibly go back to sleep. People as conspicuous as Billy don't just disappear, he told himself as he made scrambled eggs for breakfast and discovered that he couldn't touch them. He swallowed cup after cup of instant coffee and watched the clock until 5:00 A.M., when he started phoning. Jessica, he soon found out from her housekeeper, was in Florence, and Dolly, in Maine, hadn't heard a word from Billy in a week. By nine-thirty Spider was in the office, waiting to grill Josie Speilberg as soon as she arrived for work. There was no point in standing on his pride and pretending to her that he'd somehow mislaid his wife, and was trying to find her out of idle curiosity.

"Spider, if I knew anything, I swear I'd tell you. I haven't talked to her in five, maybe six days."

"Could you try to track down Jessica Strauss in Florence for me, Josie? And anyone else you can think of?"

By the end of the day they had exhausted everyone who might know Billy's whereabouts, from John Prince in New York to the concierge at the Ritz and his fellows at every other major hotel in Paris, London, and New York. Billy, it was clear, had taken a limo to LAX and vanished.

"She'll be back Spider, remember the twins are here," Josie said comfortingly.

"Don't think I haven't been saying that to myself all day long."

"Nanny Elizabeth! I'll bet she knows something!" Josie said, and Spider went racing home.

"Mr. Elliott, you know I'd tell you if I could," Nanny Elizabeth assured him, "but there hasn't been a single sign from her. I'm beginning to worry myself. But in my experience, these . . . misunderstandings . . . they don't last long when there are little ones in the house. She probably had to take a few days away from everybody in the world—it's been almost a year since their birth, and that's a long haul for any woman, no matter how many people she has helping her."

"We should have taken a vacation," Spider said. "Damn, why didn't I think of that?"

"Mrs. Elliott wouldn't have left," Nanny Elizabeth replied flatly. "There was no chance you could have made her take a vacation unless you'd taken the twins with you. I've rarely seen a mother so . . . well, devoted to her children."

"Is that a bad thing?" Spider asked.

"Too much of anything isn't good. I always tell my parents to get away together, even if it's just a weekend now and then. The children won't know the difference so long as I'm here, and the parents need time alone. I said as much to Mrs. Elliott, several times, but she wouldn't hear of it."

"She has a mind of her own."

"Ah, yes, indeed, and a will of her own. She's an unusually stubborn woman, that's for sure, but I love her dearly."

"So do I," Spider said. "Oh, God, *so do I.*"

By the end of a week, Spider was so frantic that he was beginning to consider bringing in the police, although Josh Hillman's advice was to sit it out.

"What could the L.A. police tell you? We know she's not here. On the possibility that she might have doubled back from wherever she went, we've searched the records of every possible hotel and apartment hotel in the city."

"Maybe . . . if I went to the media?"

"Spider, for heaven's sake, you don't want to broadcast your private disagreements to the world! Don't go near the media. Billy would hate that more than anything."

"You're right, Josh, but I keep imagining . . ."

"You're being unnecessarily morbid. Billy is not the kind of woman who's self-destructive, I promise you. She's tough, Spider. Go home, play with the kids, and remember that in a few days this will all be a bad dream."

"Do you bill for that stupid advice, Josh? Shit, I'm sorry, I know you're doing your best. And I am going home—Nanny Elizabeth will just have to take care of me too."

Spider sat in the twins' nursery like a large, loving toy as they climbed over him, feeling that he wasn't going to move from the floor until they were taken away to be fed. No, he'd feed them himself, both of them, and bathe them too. Contact with their flesh gave him the only comfort he had, and he even got a glow from the feeling of their food in his hair.

"Bow-gow!" Max said to him with a look of heartrending appeal. "Bow-gow!"

"Boo-goo!" Hal cried hopefully. "Boo-goo!"

"You guys want a dog?" Spider asked. "A bow-wow?"

They stood, each holding onto one of his knees, their lower lips thrust forward in their determination to make themselves understood.

"Boo-goo!"

"Bow-gow!"

382

"Nanny Elizabeth, listen to this! They want a dog! They just said their first word! Bow-wow! Come on, kids, we'll go out and buy a dog. A bow-wow. Its amazing, yesterday all they could do was wave bye-bye and say 'mama' and 'dada,' and today they want a dog! Isn't that exceptionally intelligent of them, learning to express an abstract desire overnight?"

"Not considering the amount of time Burgo O'Sullivan has been spending with them recently, getting under my feet. I hate to have to admit this, Mr. Elliott, but their first word is an attempt to say 'Burgo.' He taught it to them just at the very instant they were primed and ready to learn how to speak. Boys are so late in their verbal skills. Very naughty of Burgo indeed, and I told him so, but the damage was done." Nanny Elizabeth sniffed in disapproval.

"Burgo? That sonofabitch, I'll fucking *kill* him when I find him!"

Spider sprinted off in search of Burgo, leaving Nanny Elizabeth thinking that poor Mrs. Elliott certainly had good reason to stay out of the way of a man capable of such jealousy. It was only another name, after all.

"Burgo! You come out of your room, you maggot, you coward, or I'll kick the door in!"

"There's no need to shout like that," Burgo said, emerging from his quarters with the calm confidence of an indispensable man.

"Where's my wife, you lousy bastard? Don't tell me you don't know, the kids blew your cover, you miserable turd! You've been hanging around them—since when are you so interested in children, you deceptive, malice-ridden—"

"I don't know where she is," Burgo said with dignity. "There's no need to insult me."

"*Yes, you do!*" Spider screamed, and seized him around his neck.

"She phones me, I don't phone her," Burgo sputtered. "Let go!"

"Why didn't you tell me? You know damn well I've been going crazy!"

"I probably would have been forced to in a day or so, considering my sympathy for any fellow man, no matter who he is or how he behaves, but my first loyalty always has been to Mrs. Elliott, and she made me promise on my mother's grave," Burgo said with dignity. "Fortunately, my mother is alive and well."

"What the hell did she say, Burgo? *What*, for God's sake?"

"Mrs. Elliott asks about the children, each time, and I report in detail, I ask how she is, and she answers that she's fine—she sounds perfectly all right—and then she hangs up."

"Thank God!" Spider sagged in relief. "Well, now that I know she's okay, I guess I'll have to wait it out until she comes home. She could be absolutely anywhere."

"One day," Burgo offered, "I did happen to hear her say something to a person she called 'Marry John' or some such foreign name."

"Marry John? How do you know it was foreign?"

"Mrs. Elliott didn't pronounce it like an American name. It was slurred, faster than she usually speaks."

Spider was on the phone to Josh Hillman before he'd finished his sentence.

"Josh, does the name 'Marry John' mean anything to you? The *wife of who*? Marie-Jeanne? Billy's been paying their salary for years? And you didn't think of them? Jesus, Josh, so what if the house is empty and uninhabitable? Since when would that stop Billy? Oh, you're sorry, are you—big fucking deal. Now give me that address, you absolute moronic *asshole!*"

"Lawyers!" Spider muttered to Burgo, planted a kiss on his forehead, and raced upstairs to tell Nanny Elizabeth the news and grab his passport.

Billy walked along the Rue de Barbet de Jouy, swinging an empty shopping basket. She'd gone to the best local wine merchant to replace the wine that Marie-Jeanne had lent her, and discovered what a rare vintage the 1971 was. He'd promised to find a case for her somewhere or, failing that, to order a wine equally as good.

"Do you have suitable storage space, Madame?" he'd asked. "If so, I can try to find you several cases."

"I have excellent cellars, Monsieur, but I must wait to decide about an order."

"At your service, Madame."

Should she, Billy asked herself, perhaps buy wine? Cases and cases of wine? The best vintages, the most rare, the great treasures? In Paris, even in an empty house, it didn't feel comfortable not to have wine right on hand in case anyone dropped by. There were always several bottles of champagne on ice in any proper French fridge; no one thought twice about asking for a little "coup" of champagne when they were offered a drink by a friend, because they knew that a bottle would be finished too quickly to go flat. She sighed, disappointed by the lightness of her empty basket.

Today felt like the first real day of fall, Billy thought as she turned the corner to cover the short section of the Rue de Varenne that led back to the Rue Vaneau. She'd put on a heavy crimson turtleneck and a pair of black trousers this morning, and the tails of a long crimson and black striped wool scarf bounced behind her. She wasn't in the mood for the Luxembourg Gardens, Billy realized, as if awakening from a fit of indolence that had held her captive.

She was in the mood to swoop down on the Rue Cambon and buy every single new suit in the Chanel collection. Every single coat, every last dress, every chain belt, shoes, oh, yes, dozens and dozens and dozens of shoes! . . . Uh-oh, she was in trouble! She couldn't show her nose in the Rue Cambon, right at the back entrance to the Ritz. At Chanel she'd run into at least five women she knew, especially now, in the middle of the afternoon, when everyone had fittings.

But what if she ordered her car and driver? There'd be only a quick step from the curb through the gray glass doors of the shop; she'd keep her sunglasses on, and wear a big silk square well forward to shade her face. She could phone the manager in advance and arrange to be led straight to a private dressing room . . . could she risk it? She felt as strong a desire to buy something—anything—as she'd felt when she'd bought her house, and she knew that such a mood was a certain sign of dangerous restlessness, of a feverish need to make things happen. She had cabin fever, she was like someone who'd lived through a dark Arctic winter or a long convalescence during which she'd been forced to stay in bed and do nothing but rest her eyes.

If only Sam hadn't sent that enormous bouquet of fall flowers.

And a card on which he'd written, "If you ever change your mind, if the timing is right someday, here's my new phone number. I'll always be here for you, my love. Sam."

He shouldn't have done that, Billy thought. It wasn't cricket. She'd made up her mind and it was staying made up, but it didn't help to have those flowers, arranged in a vase by Marie-Jeanne, standing on the floor of the sun room in a blaze of russet and gold, reminding her of Sam's hair each time she looked at them. She'd throw them out, along with the card, the minute she got home she resolved, turning the corner of the Rue Vaneau.

Slumped up against the closed doors to her house was a tall man in a belted trench coat, his long legs crossed at the ankle, as if he'd been there a long time. Billy stopped dead. His back was toward her. He hadn't seen her. She still had time to wheel around and retreat around the corner.

For an instant Billy apprehended Spider fully; transfixed and pierced by a visceral recognition, she saw him utterly present in the world, in dimensions of time and space, with all his history and all his strength and all his weakness, all his past and all their memories, the whole of Spider Elliott enveloped into a single unique person about whom she had an overwhelming totality of emotion. Suddenly, without the slightest attempt at thought, Billy discovered that she was released and running toward him as fast as she could. She watched him turn instantly at the sound of her footsteps and race toward her, and the world was changed forever.

"No, darling, no, not now, we'll talk about it later. Ah, Madame Marie-Jeanne, there you are. This is my husband, Monsieur El-liott." Billy blew her nose and wiped her streaming eyes, fumbling with her key and Spider's handkerchief and his hand, which she couldn't let go.

"Oh, Madame, forgive me! He rang, but I would not permit him to wait in the house. I did not know that Madame was expecting Monsieur . . ." Marie-Jeanne stopped while she was still ahead, looking at Billy for guidance, while she and Spider shook hands.

386

"Monsieur Elliott has surprised both of us." Billy turned to Spider. "Come in the house, my poor baby, you look ready to drop in your tracks, I've never seen you so exhausted."

"There wasn't a nonstop flight to Paris when I got to LAX, so I flew to New York by way of Atlanta, or maybe it was Chicago, I've lost track, and then I missed the Concorde and had to wait five hours in New York . . . I could have made it faster by rowboat. I need a drink—I'm about to fall down anyway, just from happiness. I want to kiss you for the next two days. Two weeks. Two months."

"Madame Marie-Jeanne, I wonder—would it be possible to borrow two bottles of wine from you, and two glasses?"

"Of course, Madame. Where would you like the tray, Madame?"

"Oh, in the sun room . . . no, on second thought, could you bring it upstairs and leave it on the floor outside of my room? And I think I noticed some debris and dead flowers in the sun room."

"I will dispose of them, Madame, and sweep. Carefully."

"Thank you, Madame Marie-Jeanne."

Marie-Jeanne hurried back to her house to find the wine and tell Pierre the latest. The tall, blond type in tennis shoes she introduced as her husband was even better looking, to her taste, than the handsome redhead of yesterday. Would tomorrow bring a tall, dark man with one black shoe? Working for Madame Ikehorn was better than going to the cinema. And the way things were going, she must remember to order more wine.

"Spider, please let's wait to talk till tomorrow, you're so tired you're falling apart," Billy said, concerned at his loss of weight and his sunken eyes, which were more evident now that he'd showered, shaved, and put on her white toweling bathrobe that didn't even reach his knees.

"I can fall apart later, first I have to get things straight with you," he said stubbornly. "It's all I've been able to think about, and I need it a hell of a lot more than sleep."

"I haven't let myself think about anything we said to each other that night," Billy countered. "I knew I was in pure denial, but at least I don't look as ghastly as you do. I ate and slept and walked my feet off . . . a week at a spa couldn't have been better for me."

"I didn't eat and I didn't sleep because I knew how guilty I was. I was vile in ten thousand and one ways I'll never forget or forgive myself for, but once I stopped being angry, I started trying to figure out why—*why* had I been such a bastard to you, why had I refused to give your plan for a decorating catalog the respect I'd give any idea of yours, *why* had I made those cheap, nasty digs about your money and acting like a Lady Bountiful and not knowing jack shit about finance?"

"Did you ever manage to figure it out?" Billy asked coldly, feeling herself flush at this reminder of words she'd been blocking out of her mind.

"Yeah, finally, after I realized that the only other time in my life I'd been cruel on purpose to a woman was when Valentine and Josh were having an affair."

"You knew about them?" Billy asked, taken off guard. "Valentine told me, but I thought no one else knew."

"She told me too—after we were married."

"We're both good about keeping secrets," Billy said thoughtfully, "if nothing else. But what does a brief love affair between two other people in 1977 have to do with you and me in 1984?"

"I was jealous of Josh—I didn't even know who he was then, just some mysterious lover who kept Valentine busy and preoccupied—and I didn't even know I was jealous because I didn't realize I was in love with her. I was eaten up with fury because she didn't have the time to work with me that she used to have, because her attention was turned away from me and toward someone else."

"So?" Billy asked, completely puzzled.

"When I came home that night—was it only a week ago?—I found you like your old self again, all glowing and splendid and carried away with the excitement of your new idea—I felt . . . *jealous* of its potential to take you away from me—"

"Oh, come on, that's crazy! You've never known me as anything but a working woman—"

"Since the kids were born, you've stayed at home with them and I've come back every night to a wife who's been right where I expected her to be all day long, doing what I expected my beloved everyday wife to be doing. I'd forgotten what it was like to live with an electric, high-flying woman who can make big things happen with a touch of her magic wand, a vastly powerful woman in her own right, who doesn't need me, who has the freedom to go after anything in the world that interests her—"

"Are you trying to tell me, Spider Elliott," Billy broke in incredulously, "that you, of all men, wanted me to stay home forever and take care of the children and wait for the high point of my day, the marvelous minute when you finally showed up for dinner?"

"Yeah. Ain't that a pisser? In my heart of hearts, that's *exactly* what I wanted. An old-fashioned wife like my mom. A return to the 1950s, basic, unvarnished, barbaric, against everything I thought I believed. Once the thought crossed my mind, a bell rang and it hasn't stopped ringing. I wanted you to be just like everybody else. I wanted to be the boss of you. *I wanted you to be the little woman.*"

"You're utterly pathetic," Billy said. "I've never heard such absurd crap in my life."

"But it's the truth," he said painfully.

"Oh, I know *that*," she said, scornfully, "I can hear it in your voice, the bell rang for me too . . . that's what's so god-awful. You, of all people!"

"Me, just an unreconstructed caveman at heart. Could I have some more wine, please? I'm still in shock."

"If I'd known that before we got married . . ."

"What?"

"I'd still have married you, you poor idiot. You, Spider Elliott, are like most other men on the planet, you've just hidden it better. And now that you know the hideous truth about yourself, you can work on crawling out of your cave, or at least you can remember you're a caveman, give yourself a sharp kick in the ass, and go back to acting and thinking like the enlightened human being I expect you to be."

"Yes, ma'am," he grinned, faint with gratitude, refilling his glass.

"And none of that! No fake humility. You'd better be straight with me or I'll remind you that you want a girl just like the girl who married dear old dad, you . . . you . . . *pervert!*"

"That song is kinda sick, when you stop to listen to the meaning of the words."

"Maybe it was written before anyone knew how sick that was," Billy said generously.

"Nah, the songwriter was Freud's nephew. He knew what he was saying. Listen, darling, I'm not finished."

"Don't tell me there's something worse?"

"I thought back to the beginning of Scruples," Spider said, drinking wine as he remembered, "and I realized that you'd been the one who'd seen the need and had the original idea for a different kind of boutique on Rodeo Drive and the drive and determination to get it built—all I'd done was change the decor and the point of view and hire new salespeople . . . details."

"But that's what made it a success, as you reminded me frequently."

"Still, it was definitely your baby. And Scruples Two was *my* baby—well, to be fair, Gigi had the original idea, but I saw the possibilities and talked you into it. Let's drink to that! Once you agreed, you threw yourself into the job, you persuaded Prince to design the capsule collections, you hired all the right people to run the technical side, and that's what made *it* a success . . . so we've been working hand in hand all along, sometimes one of us doing the more important part and sometimes the other. We've had a true and equal partnership in every way."

"Hmmm . . . true and equal? I could have told you that, but you wouldn't have listened. Why did you think the decorating catalog was such a terrible idea, if I'm not all that hopeless?"

"I don't! I think it could be huge, a major success—but I don't want it to become a mania with you, the way Scruples was when you started opening new ones all over the world. That's where you were making big money. You were at it twenty-four hours a day. You *did* earn it the hard way, don't lose sight of that. If you hadn't closed all the stores after Valentine died, you'd have doubled the fortune Ellis Ikehorn left you . . . and there's no chance we'd ever have enough time together if that happened. You have a way of throwing yourself into things that scares me."

"It scares me too. If you hadn't been here today, I'd own Chanel by now. Not just the clothes, *the whole company.* And I'm not kidding. In fact, I bet it'd be a great investment, now that they've hired Lagerfeld . . . you know, darling, we should really think about it seriously . . ."

"Look, all those problems I mentioned," Spider interrupted, finishing his glass, "there isn't one of them that can't be solved. Furniture must be delivered and returned thousands of times a day . . . why was UPS invented? Or we could buy a fleet of trucks . . . so what if you have to get rid of some fabric and a few headboards? That's what factory outlet stores are for . . . factory outlet . . . Billy, beautiful, gorgeous, wild and woolly Billy Winthrop, did you ever seriously think about the incredible possibilities of factory outlet . . ."

"How much of that wine have you had?"

"Almost a bottle? Bottle and a half?"

"Darling love, you're on a talking jag. You're drunk. I hope you remember everything you said tomorrow."

"But, Billy . . . factory outlet . . . hasn't even . . . been . . . explored . . ."

Spider staggered over to the bed, crawled into the blankets, and passed out.

After she'd watched Spider sleep for a while, Billy wrote out a list of provisions and sent Marie-Jeanne out to buy butter, bread, ham, cheese, and other delicacies that didn't have to be cooked, like a thick slice of paté and a cold chicken, so she could feed him the minute he woke up. Maybe then he'd be sober enough to re-think buying Chanel . . . it wasn't that bad an idea . . .

When he continued to sleep, Billy made herself a hasty picnic supper, and then, more weary than she'd realized, crept into the bed, and fell asleep so quickly that she only had a few seconds to feel the intense bliss of being in bed with Spider again. He was still sleeping when she woke up early in the morning. Enough was enough, Billy thought, and woke him up with difficulty.

"Where am I?" Spider asked.

"Paris, France. Who are you?"

"Spider something."

"What are you?"

"A caveman."

"Just testing," Billy laughed.

"Come into my cave," Spider ordered, grabbing her gently by the hair. "We cavemen can endure anything but separation from our mates."

"Is this house really empty?" Spider asked later, as he dressed to go down to the kitchen for a very late breakfast.

"Except for this room, yes. Most of the furnishings are packed up in the stables. I'd show you everything, but I can't wait to go home and see the boys. Let's call the Ritz and find out when we can get the first plane back."

"I'm starving!" Spider complained. "Let's not call until after breakfast, darling."

"But what if we miss the next plane just because I waited too long?"

"A day won't make any difference."

"That's easy for you to say . . . you saw them yesterday. Or the day before yesterday, I've lost track."

"Where's the coffeepot?" Spider asked as soon as he reached the new kitchen.

"There isn't one. Now that I think about it, there isn't a pot or a pan, just a couple of knives the workmen left, and a corkscrew, and my cup. There's a café down the next street—I'll send Marie-Jeanne."

"What did you do for breakfast?"

"I let the hot water run till the water was steaming, turned it low, and then held a tea bag under the faucet in the cup."

"My Girl Scout. Such a clever baby. How do you contact Marie-Jeanne, by smoke signals?"

"I think I hear her opening the front door. Madame Marie-Jeanne, is that you?" Billy called.

"Yes, Madame. There are more visitors asking for you at the gate. Shall I let them in?"

"A man, Madame Marie-Jeanne?"

"No, not precisely, Madame."

"A woman, then? Did she give her name?"

"She did not say, Madame."

"Let them come in, Madame Marie-Jeanne," Spider said in his never-forgotten photographer's French.

"Yes, Monsieur. I suspect they have followed me," Marie-Jeanne said as Hal and Max ran unsteadily around Nanny Elizabeth and rushed into the kitchen, almost knocking each other down in their hurry to get to Billy. They swarmed up her legs into her lap and grabbed her around her neck with fat strong arms.

"Mama! *Bow-gow*, Mama!"

"Mama! *Boo-goo*, Mama!"

"Spider, they're talking!" Billy said through her kisses and tears, "Oh, I missed hearing them say their first word!"

"They want a dog, Mrs. Elliott," Nanny Elizabeth said, beaming. "A bow-wow."

"How long have you been here?" Billy asked Nanny Elizabeth. "Did you just get in?"

"Oh, no, we took the first direct flight right after Mr. Elliott left. The boys enjoyed the trip immensely. We've been most comfortable in a suite at the Ritz, at Mr. Elliott's instructions."

"I told Nanny to bring them here today if she didn't hear from me," Spider explained. "I figured that if all else failed, they were my ace in the hole. I was going to play on your feelings for my paternal position."

Without regret, Marie-Jeanne gave up hopes of a tall, dark man with one black shoe. Monsieur was, undoubtedly, the husband of Madame, or, if not legally wed, at the very least the father of her children. Those two blond angels looked even more like him than they did like her. And they were just the right age to begin to learn to speak a civilized language.

Later in the day, leaving the children taking their naps at the Ritz, where they were now all staying, Spider and Billy returned to the Rue Vaneau to say good-bye to Madame Marie-Jeanne and look over the house one last time before she put it on the market. It didn't make sense to keep it, she'd decided sadly, not on the basis of a week's unexpected visit every three or four years, not when you couldn't even make a cup of coffee in the kitchen. It didn't fit into her life, this marvelous shell of a house in this much-loved city. The house deserved to be lived in and used. It was cruel to keep it empty.

"Will you show me around?" Spider asked as they paused

inside the empty courtyard, for the gatekeeper and his wife had gone to visit their daughter to relate the newest events of the day. He drew her cherished head to his shoulder, watching the vivid autumn light play tricks in her dark brown curls.

"I want to," she answered, her expression kindled in a flood of feeling he didn't recognize. "Come with me."

Billy led Spider through every one of the rooms of the house on the Rue Vaneau, pausing as she left each lovely space, as classic and permanent as a great piece of sculpture, turning to look back as if it had laid an invisible claim on her. She touched each of the mirrors softly and traced the carvings above the fireplaces and the moldings on the doors with gentle caresses of her fingertips. She stopped at the windows and looked out at each vista, bidding it adieu before she passed by for the last time.

"Poor Monsieur Delacroix," Billy sighed as they reached the empty master bedroom with its wide view of the glorious old trees in the park of the Matignon. At that moment the bell of the cathedral of St. Clotilde began to ring, signaling the start of the thrilling chorus of bells that sounded from every part of the neighborhood.

"Delacroix?"

"My decorator. The most frustrated man in Paris. Just when everything was ready for the installation, down to the last pair of curtains, just when we'd finished buying all the antiques—everything but things for the kitchen—I went back to New York. He never saw it furnished. I think it broke his heart."

"So you didn't move in?" Spider asked very quietly, disturbed by the depth of her love for this house that was evident in every gesture she made, even in the delicate, precise sound of her feet on the floorboards, a footfall as personal as a signature. He knew why she hadn't lived here. He remembered every word of that magazine article about Billy and Sam Jamison. This was where she'd planned to live with him, that poor stupid idiot who'd lost the most lovable woman in the world, thank God.

"No, somehow it didn't seem destined to happen," Billy said, trying valiantly to hide the regret in her voice.

"Maybe not then, but, speaking personally, *I* can't bear not to see it furnished. We're staying right here, in Paris, with Delacroix helping, until everything's been unpacked and placed properly and the rooms are filled with flowers and there's wood in the fireplaces and candles in the candlesticks, and a ton of food in the kitchen and someone to make a decent cup of tea—even coffee—and then, if you still love it even half as much as you do now, we'll live here until you feel like going back to California, and if you don't, we won't."

"Spider!" Billy exclaimed. "What about Scruples Two? You can't just leave it like that!"

"Of course I can. The damn thing practically runs itself. What's the point of hiring expensive executives if they can't function without you? And there's always the telex or the phone if they need to reach me quickly. We both have a tendency to get too involved in work at the expense of enjoyment. After you had the children, it was as if you were working two jobs plus a night shift."

"I couldn't stop myself." Billy shook her head in self-knowledge. "That's the way I do things."

"If I can learn not to be a caveman, you can learn to be a little less . . ."

"Compulsive? Isn't that the word you're looking for?"

"Compulsive and . . . obsessive . . . two halves of the same thing. Oh, Billy, we need to take some time for ourselves. There are so many things we might discover that aren't all work, but we'll never know if we don't spend a few months looking around . . . and, if you stop to think about it, this house owes you a roof over your head after you've kept it up in perfect condition for all these years. If you truly wanted to sell it, you'd have done it long ago. You've always hoped to come back here, even if you didn't realize it."

"You remind me of someone I used to know," Billy said, gravely considering him.

"Who?"

"Spider Elliott . . . the one who could always talk me into anything."

"Only because you wanted it too," he said as he kissed her until she was reeling. "Come on, let's go explore those crates in the stables. I wonder if Marie-Jeanne's husband has a hammer or a crowbar."

Holding hands, they emerged into the courtyard and saw Pierre and Marie-Jeanne returning from their visit.

"Monsieur Pierre, do you happen to have a hammer?" Spider asked.

"Of course, Monsieur. Can I help you?"

"As a matter of fact, yes, four hands would be better than two. Let's open some of the boxes in the stables and find out what's in them."

"*Eh bien*, Monsieur," Pierre answered, startled, "that's a job for twenty men."

"We'll get twenty men tomorrow, but I want to start right now."

"Madame is going to unpack, at last?" Marie-Jeanne asked timidly.

"Oh, yes!" Billy exclaimed, dazed with pure happiness. "We're going to move in, with the children and the nanny—and a dog."

"A dog! *Dieu merci!* I have wanted a dog forever! I am the only guardian's wife who lacks a dog. Ah, Madame, this calls for a little coup of champagne, does it not?"

"Oh, yes, if anything ever did! I hope you're keeping track of all the wine I owe you."

"*Restez-tranquille*, I am, Madame. But the champagne, it is our pleasure, Pierre's and mine. A large dog or small dog, may I inquire?"

"We shall see, but a true French dog, set your mind at ease, Madame Marie-Jeanne."

18

Ben Winthrop's going to be in town the night of the party I'm giving for you and Dad—would you mind if he invited himself? You still haven't met him," Gigi asked Sasha as they played with little Nellie in the garden of the furnished Brentwood house that Vito had rented until they could find a permanent place.

"Of course not. I want to finally lay my eyes on Mr. Wonderful, and who knows, maybe I'll be able to hit him up for a ride in his flying machine. How could he refuse a bride's request at her delayed wedding reception?"

"He won't," Gigi responded with confidence. "Where do you want to go?"

"Joyriding! Now that you're out of work, we could hop on to San Francisco for a gracious lunch, do a little shopping wearing white gloves and hats, like genuine San Francisco ladies, and pop back in time for dinner."

"I assume you'll lend me the hat and gloves? But San Francisco's a great idea—I can deliver my present for Eleonora Colonna in person. Sasha, I wish you wouldn't refer to me as 'out of work.' I quit Frost Rourke Bernheim."

"What's the difference?" Sasha asked, her sense of practicality offended. "You're not getting a paycheck at the end of the week."

"It's by choice, and you can't imagine how free I feel. And anyway I have so much to do, what with planning your party and then the Venice party, that I couldn't work at a real job anyway."

"The Venice party?" Sasha asked. "You mean the maiden voyage?"

"That's the *second* party, a year away. This one is in two weeks. It's basically a PR junket for the business and travel press. Ben sees it as an opportunity to show off Winthrop Development, using the cruise line as the excuse. He's invited all his key people from his company, including all of the guys I worked with recently in New York."

"What's the point, when the ship's still in drydock? You told me it's a sight only a ship owner could love."

"Whenever a ship is built," Gigi explained, "the first plate laid in the keel contains a good-luck coin from the owner. Ben's going to have that plate on the freighter replaced with another one, holding an American silver dollar, to commemorate the purchase of the three ships and the refitting of the *Emerald*. I'm organizing the whole thing with a big travel agency. We have to bring the press to Venice, then out to Porta Margera for the ceremony of the plate-changing, and back to Venice for the celebration at the Cipriani. Travel, food, and lodging for almost two hundred media people and several dozen of Ben's employees."

"Are you getting paid for this Venice caper?" Sasha asked suspiciously.

"Ben wanted to pay me, but I wouldn't let him."

"Gigi!" Sasha was scandalized. "As your former agent, I can't permit this."

"Sasha, I simply *cannot—will not*—be on his payroll."

"Oddly enough, I understand how you feel, what with things

398

so delicately poised, so . . . undecided between the two of you. Okay, work for free, I don't care. And I'm glad Ben is coming to the reception, because the sight of the two of you together, poised right on the brink of marriage, might be just what Zach needs, just the jolt of reality that's been missing in his life. He's been holding on to an emotional fantasy for too long, and he's driving poor Vito crazy with his mooning around. I'd do anything to get him over you. Oh, Nellie, that's an earthworm, baby, not a toy. Give it to Mama. Oh, Gigi, she's putting it in her mouth! Stop her, for heaven's sake!"

"Nellie, no," Gigi said gently, removing the worm from the child's grasp. "Here's a nice shovel, go dig."

"Yesterday she found an earthworm and gave it a bath in her cup of orange juice," Sasha said. "She didn't hurt it at all, she put it right back in the garden. Do you think Nellie's going to be a zoologist?"

"With a mother who's out of her mind, she'll be lucky if she survives her childhood."

"I don't think I'm crazy to wonder what Nellie's future holds. Nothing's impossible for a woman now, and by the time she's grown up—"

"Don't play games with me, Sasha Nevsky. I know you too well."

"Sasha Orsini, please. Do you have a block about sharing that name with me? And I stopped playing games years ago."

"Then what's this nonsense about Zach?"

"Would that it were nonsense. Vito's sick about him. He hasn't done his usual brilliant job on *Long Weekend,* and my poor husband has had to prop him up on an hourly basis to keep him on course. A black comedy is turning into a sentimental romance because the director is still emotionally involved with the producer's daughter—do you think that could make a film in itself? Maybe I should suggest it to Vito, it might not be too late to rewrite the script."

"Sasha, there is no reason I can think of, except malicious troublemaking, for you to say that Zach is still 'emotionally involved'—what a revolting expression—with me. I know you dearly love to make trouble, but I thought marriage to two men in rapid succession would have cured you of that."

"You have a really mean streak, Gigi, reminding me of Josh, just when I'm so happy. How could you?"

"I don't guilt-trip, Sasha, so stop trying. Why are you making trouble?"

"If Zach were dating, even *actresses,* it would never occur to me that he's still carrying a torch for you—do you like that expression better?—is it 1940s enough for you?—but he isn't. Zach Nevsky has retired from frequentation of the female sex since you and he broke up. I ask you, Gigi, is that healthy for a young male in the prime of life?"

"Where do you get all this garbage?"

"My husband spends the first hour after he comes home every night dumping it in my lap, that's where. Ask him. Do you think your father would make things up just to make trouble?"

"If it helped him make a film, sure. But this . . . it's pure mischief. The two of you are up to something."

"Good Lord, don't you think we have better things to do with our lives than flatter you about your fatal charms? How can you be so self-centered? Nellie! Stop that! Gigi, she cut that worm in half with the shovel! Oh, God, how could she do it?"

"She's going to grow up to be a serial killer, rare for females, but not unheard of. Or an exterminator. Put her in her playpen, for Pete's sake. She's like a giant fat hummingbird. Watching her is making me a nervous wreck. Now I have a faint idea of what Billy went through with the twins."

"Would you like to give Nellie her bottle? It's about that time of the afternoon."

"No. I would not," Gigi said through gritted teeth.

"Oh, come on, be brave, you'll have to do it someday. Almost every woman does, even Ma had to give us bottles, or maybe she nursed us until she could wean us directly to a cup. When Zach calls her next time, I'll ask him to find out."

"WHEN ZACH DOES WHAT?" Gigi's eyes popped in astonishment. She had a healthy fear of Tatiana Orloff Nevsky, the cantankerous, awe-inspiring, dominating dictator of the large Nevsky clan, whose evil temper was legendary.

Sasha sighed. "He calls Ma for a little maternal telephonic cuddle. Vito says he's been doing it twice a week lately."

"Are you lying to me, Sasha?"

"I'm telling you the absolute truth, on the head of little Nellie."

"But—no offense, but your mother's a terrorist. I respect and admire her, but I'm glad I'm not her kid."

"I know, but when you're really feeling desperate, almost as bad as Ma thinks you should be feeling, considering what a disappointment you are to her, she manages to dredge up a little sympathy. You have to be suicidal before you reach that layer, but it does exist. When I was going through my worst times with Josh, I called her too, and it made me feel better. At least I knew I *had* a Ma, terrible as she is."

Gigi digested Sasha's words in silence. This was a side to Ma she'd never known about.

"Zach's never," she asked hesitantly, "actually said anything . . . about me, that is . . . to Dad, has he?"

"Not a word. Not to me and not to Vito."

"You see, you're delusional."

"Just the opposite. It's as if he's erased you by an effort of will. Considering how much time he spends with Vito, that's remarkably suspicious. If Zach even once asked how you were getting along, just casually acknowledged your existence—but not to mention your name, over a period of a year, when he works with Vito on a daily basis—don't you think you're a little old to still be calling him 'Dad'?—when you're my best friend, in spite of all the awful things you say to me, to say nothing of being the love of Zach's life, I call that a sure sign that it's still too painful. After all, you can discuss Zach without any trouble, because you're in love with Ben, but my poor wreck of a lovelorn brother can't even pronounce your name out loud because he's never been able to deal with the fact that his life has to go on without you."

"The more fool he."

"That's exactly what I said to Vito."

"And what did my dear old daddyums answer?"

"Something adorable about how he would never be able to get over me, not in a lifetime, but then Vito's different from Zach, he's an adult, and Zach's a lovesick boy."

"Boy? Really, Sasha, being married to an older man has made you intolerably condescending. Zach's at least thirty-one."

"But still a boy at heart, a passionate, romantic boy, like

Heathcliff. Did Heathcliff have a last name, or was that his first name? Joe Heathcliff? Heathcliff Jones? Never mind. It's sad, but I try not to think about it. Here's Nellie, you can burp her, even if you won't feed her. There's nothing quite as satisfying as burping a baby, not just hearing the burp, but feeling it come up and *out*."

"If Nellie's old enough to run around and dissect worms, isn't she old enough to burp herself?"

"Sure, but why should I deprive you of such a choice moment when you're going to fly me to San Francisco?"

Victoria Frost curled up in bed and counted and recounted the treasure of her circumstances with a tightly cautious hand. The agency was now in a position to count on billing almost one hundred and ninety million dollars a year, and she'd rid herself of that brazen, smart-alecky little pest, that presumptuous, impertinent tart, that infuriating self-promoter, Gigi Orsini, without losing the accounts Gigi had brought in, except for Indigo Seas, which they couldn't have retained in any case.

In spite of Gigi's assertion that she was getting out of advertising, there had been a sense of tense waiting during all of last week while they expected to hear that Gigi had persuaded Spider Elliott to take away Scruples Two, and Ben Winthrop to strip them of The Enchanted Attic and the Winthrop Line. Eventually, through the grapevine and the trades, Victoria, Archie, and Byron realized that Gigi hadn't joined another agency and taken her accounts with her, as she so easily could have. Preliminary work on Beach Casuals and Scruples Two was proceeding quickly.

In addition, FRB had been invited to pitches by three important New York–based companies. Mounting any pitch cost money and time, and required total focus, but they were up for them as they'd never been before. Their reputation as a hot shop was now nationwide, not narrowly local, and all of this had been accomplished in less than two years.

There was no longer the slightest valid reason why Angus should hesitate to leave New York, Victoria decided. She had long ago realized that he was a man of habit, a man not boldly eager to take the next inevitable step in his life—didn't almost all men share that basic weakness?—but his passion had deepened with the infrequency of their meetings. She knew in every cell, in her bones, in each hair on her head, that no woman held such physical dominion over a man as she did over Angus.

Victoria turned on her back and thought of the men she'd dallied with in California. Each one of them had added another layer to her erotic authority and her sexual creativity. They had served her well. Whenever she and Angus were together, he drowned himself in her body in a way that was so unbridled in his lust that on occasion he frightened her. She *owned* this man. He belonged to her. The time had come to have him on her terms. His life with her mother was a painful farce, he'd told her that on a thousand occasions. She'd waited as long as she intended to. It was the moment to claim her own.

With her new success, it didn't matter, Victoria calculated, that many of Angus's accounts still wouldn't leave Caldwell and Caldwell with him, in spite of the endless time he'd spent laying the groundwork for the change. There was more than enough profitable billing for both of them here in Los Angeles. Equally important, there was a real need for Angus in top management at FRB.

Victoria's job was far too big for one person, although she'd worked hard and long to hide that fact from Archie and Byron. The two of them were busy hiring people for all the new creative work they'd won, but on her side of the business she still, as always, kept the number and influence of her own assistant account supervisors to a minimum, so that Angus would find his place in top management ready for him.

It was early on a Saturday morning. Victoria had been awake before dawn. Angus and her mother would be out in Southampton for the weekend, Victoria thought, looking at the clock on her bedside table, but it was still so early that her mother wouldn't have appeared downstairs for breakfast yet. *Now!* The hated bonds of years flew into bits in her flush of success and impatience. She sat up in bed, picked up her phone, and dialed the Southampton number.

"Mr. Caldwell, please, Joe Devane would like to speak with him," she said to the maid who answered the phone.

Within a minute, Angus was on the line.

"It's me. What room are you in?" she asked.

"The library, what the hell—"

"Don't interrupt. You've read about my getting Beach Casuals, haven't you?"

"Yes, but—"

"Angus, it's been almost two years. I won't wait any longer. I'm through with being kept on hold, this is not a life I can endure. There's no reason for you to stay where you are anymore, I need you here."

"The timing is wrong, you're in too much of a rush—"

"The timing will never be better. I'm coming to New York next week. We're having an informal meet-and-greet Tuesday morning with Harris Reeves, and then I have a short meeting with Joe Devane that afternoon. We'll be spending the next three days with Beach Casuals. That gives you plenty of time to tell her."

"I . . . listen, I—"

"If you don't tell her, I will."

"You don't mean that, Victoria—"

"Don't try me. Good-bye."

Angus Caldwell hung up the phone without another word. He shut the library door and closed himself in, still hearing Victoria's voice in his ears. This was the day he'd postponed and postponed, hoping—no, *believing*—that something would keep it at bay. She'd meet somebody out there, or she'd outgrow him, lose interest . . . God knows what thoughts he'd entertained, but he'd never convinced himself that this moment would really come.

Suddenly, unable to endure being shut up indoors with his fearful musing, Angus Caldwell walked quickly out of the great house, which had been built a few hundred yards back from the ocean. He walked down across the perfect greenness of the lawn and onto the sand, stopping only when he reached the lapping waves that were gentle this morning.

Angus Caldwell looked about him in every direction, and surveyed the gauzy, opaline morning mists lifting quickly over the ocean as the pearly blue light of another superb autumnal Southampton day grew brighter. As he looked up and down the wide beige beach, he named to himself the residents of each magnificently tended mansion, set well apart from one another behind clipped green privet hedges, on a stretch of coast that had no equal in the world. Each neighboring home belonged to a good friend, in each of them he was the most welcome of guests, just as he was at the Maidstone Club and the Meadow Club, membership in which created the special knowledge of an absolute privilege that could only be found in Southampton, a privilege that none of the other, lesser, new-rich Hamptons could ever match.

Angus took deep gulps of air, the clean tonic salt air of the Atlantic, and looked at his own weathered, shingled, white-trimmed mansion, a landmark house of deep bay windows and wide porches and intensely comfortable, deliberately casual rooms, to which he took a helicopter each Friday night with longing antici-pation—the same anticipation he felt on Sunday night when the time came to return to his vast, art-filled, elegant Fifth Avenue apartment, knowing that a good week's work awaited him. He felt, with each pulsing beat of his heart, how much it meant to him when the elevator door opened and he entered the magnificent reception room of the agency where he and Millicent had been in charge of hundreds of employees for so long. He relived the ritual of each morning's progression down the corridor to his own office, interrupted many times to speak to many people, never abusing his keen awareness that everyone in sight depended on them for their livelihood. Angus Caldwell scanned the vast horizon of the Atlan-tic Ocean and contemplated his half-ownership of an agency that would soon bill a billion dollars a year. He and Millicent were good bosses, he reflected as he bent to pick up a piece of driftwood; they'd honestly earned every one of the millions they'd made.

He enjoyed the best life of any man he knew, Angus Caldwell thought, but upstairs Millicent was still sleeping in her bedroom, Millicent, who allowed him all freedoms but the one he craved so persistently. If Victoria were here right now, he would have to find a place where he could have her, where he could find the release only she could give him, for the sound of her voice on the phone had aroused him unbearably, to the point of pain. No, he wouldn't be able to stop himself, even if he had to throw her down on the beach in full view of the house.

If you don't tell her, I will, she'd said. When the waves retreated, Angus made a sizable hole in the sand with the toe of his tennis shoe and watched as the returning waves gradually filled it up. He shrugged at this inevitable phenomenon and started jogging down the wide beach, moving smoothly and easily, a man who looked as if he didn't have a care in the world except getting enough exercise to prolong his enviable life.

Vito and Zach broke for coffee while the editor looked over the takes of a scene they were working on in the temporary editing room that had been set up in a motel not far from the Malibu Colony location.

"There were a couple of takes in there that looked better to me than what we just saw," Zach said hopefully. "We can make that last shot substantially better."

"I know we can," Vito said. "In fact, the more film you shoot the better this picture looks. There was a day last week when I thought the only thing we could do with this film was burn the negative and hope that the arson squad wouldn't catch us, but now it's turned into an interestingly mellow stew, an oddball semi-black comedy mixed with pure sentiment and a sexy dash of madcap romance. I hear Siskel and Ebert now. 'A Valentine to Hollywood —two thumbs up.' "

"If you're right, Vito, it will be because of some lucky breaks and the chemistry of the actors. I haven't been up to speed, don't think I don't realize it. I keep seeing Siskel and Ebert with their middle fingers up, and we wrap on Friday."

Vito laughed comfortably. "It's only a movie, as I keep telling you, Zach. Don't take it so to heart, kid. Each of us has had more than one project that didn't seem to work out right from the beginning. And sometimes everything can be going great and you've produced a stink bomb. Ever see *The WASP?* No, forget I asked! I don't want to embarrass you."

Vito laughed again and poured another cup of coffee. "*Long Weekend* started with a jinx on it. The people who live in the Colony were probably getting together every weekend, making little wax figures of us, and sticking pins in them and boiling them in oil. They never wanted this film located here, this place is their own incestuous secret. But they couldn't beat us, and by now they've given up. *Long Weekend* should have been called *Black*

Mass in Malibu. In fact, I think I'll register that title with the Guild tomorrow."

"Vito, why are you so relaxed? You make me nervous. Ever since I started working with you, every minute has seemed like a matter of life and death, and suddenly I've fucked up and you're taking it calmly—well, relatively calmly. This is not the Vito Orsini I know."

"One, you haven't fucked up, we've got a picture here. Two, I'm not the Vito Orsini you knew, and you have your sister to thank. When I go home to Sasha, it puts my life in perspective. And if I'm in time to burp Nellie, the pages we've shot during the day don't matter as much as they used to."

"You really adore that baby, don't you?" Zach asked curiously.

"What's not to adore? The only thing I feel terrible about is that I wasn't there when Gigi was that age. But now Gigi's such a pain in the ass, such a worry to me, that I'm frankly glad it never worked out for the two of you. Between her flakiness and your flakiness, it would have been a doomed combination."

"Thanks."

"Listen, kid, you don't blame me for wanting to see Gigi settle down with Ben Winthrop, do you? He's pushing it hard, but Gigi won't discuss the idea, hasn't even let me meet him. Sasha says I'm mercenary, but what father wouldn't enjoy the thought of his daughter marrying a guy who's young, rich, handsome, and, as far as I know, halfway decent? Sasha says there isn't a chance in hell of it happening because Gigi's such a sentimental mess, and even if she did marry Winthrop, he'd be taking advantage of her unstable condition, and what's more, it'd never last, because she'd only be marrying him on the rebound from you."

"Sasha's out of her mind!" Zach exclaimed in bitterness. "Christ, what's wrong with her? She's never dropped her sisterly attitude, her sick notion that I'm irresistible to women. That's because I remind her of herself, if you ask me. I thought maybe marriage would cure her . . . but apparently not."

"You know something, Zach? You and your sister are both menaces to society. Now that I've taken Sasha out of circulation, someone ought to keep you locked up. No man ever really got Sasha out of his blood—look at that miserable slime Josh Hillman.

And my daughter, one of the most down-to-earth people I know, is still so touchy about you that I don't dare mention your name in front of her or she gets this little vulnerable hurt look on her face and makes me feel like a thoughtless beast. She's never even asked me how this shoot is going, just because you're involved. Talk about a lack of consideration for your father! I invited her to come out to the set to visit, now that she's not working, and she wouldn't consider it. On other pictures, she used to bug me to let her see me work, even though I explained how dull it was. She's not emotionally able to cope with seeing you."

"Then I certainly won't come to the party." Zach's voice was abrupt.

"You *have* to come, Zach, you know you do. Sasha and I wouldn't forgive you if you didn't. Gigi's mentally ready for that. In fact she's physically prepared, she's even stopped living her life in the bedroom, like a recluse, and forced herself to use the rest of the house. I think that's a good sign. On the other hand, she spends the entire morning reading 'Dear Abby,' Ann Landers, Dr. Joyce Brothers, and her horoscope in every magazine she can buy. Does she think she'll find the answer to her problems with you in those columns? I expect her to start sleeping with a teddy bear any day now."

"Vito, damn it, I didn't break up with her, she broke up with me. It's not my fault that she's—whatever she is."

"I know, Zach. None of my former ladies behaved in Gigi's sloppy, lovelorn way. Hell, even Billy and I get along now. I'm producing my next picture for Susan Arvey, and Maggie Mac-Gregor and I have a genuinely friendly relationship."

"You and Susan Arvey! No shit!"

"Sure. What'd you think? I'm reformed now . . . but I had my day. And a majestic, glorious day it was. Thank God Sasha doesn't want to know about it or I'd have to tell her, and I suspect that she wouldn't appreciate the truth."

"What about Maggie?" Zach asked, fascinated.

"That's a really long-time thing, started way before Billy. How do you suppose I talked her into doing that special on you in Kalispell?"

"I didn't think. Or if I did, I figured it was because the situation was so hot. I should have been more suspicious."

"Not at all, things like that don't show up to the naked eye, only the informed one. Take it from a reformed and experienced fellow. I see Gigi, and I see a girl who hasn't got a clue to why she bought the video of *The Way We Were* and watches it almost every night she's alone at home."

"*The Way We Were?*"

"Okay, you're no Redford and she's no Streisand, but the theme, Zach, the theme of two people who can't live together, but who have a love that won't die—it'll get to you every time you watch, even if you know it by heart. Twenty hankies. Ever see the picture?"

"Yeah, once . . . it didn't make much of an impression," Zach lied uneasily. He rented *The Way We Were* whenever he felt he had to see it again, about once a week, maybe again on the weekends. He wouldn't let himself buy it. That way lay enslavement.

The night of Gigi's wedding reception for Vito and Sasha still held a touch of the sultry heat of the day, which had been unseasonably warm for late October. A full moon, truly orange, a moon that would be called a harvest moon in any other part of the country, hung low in the sky even before the sun had set.

Gigi had rehearsed her party for several nights, darkening the house and putting new bulbs in her small lamps that now all gave a soft pink glow. With the lamps on, she padded about, placing countless candlesticks and votive lights until she'd achieved an effect that was as festive as it was flattering. The areas of shadow were equally successful—mysterious, alluring, and promising. Everywhere the house issued a significant invitation. All the tree branches and all the vines that could be seen from the various courtyards of the three-story, up-and-downstairs house had been hung with lanterns that glowed in pinkish luminescence, and the balconies had been entwined with strings of tiny white twinkle lights.

Gigi had first considered decorating the house in an all-white bridal theme that would be doubly effective against the colorful confusion of her own multipatterned floral chintzes, but discarded the idea after some thought, in view of the fact that these were hardly first nuptials for either Sasha or Vito. Instead she'd gone to the wholesale flower market downtown and loaded a borrowed van with twenty dozen pots of the palest pink cyclamen and twenty dozen pots of the white and pink English primroses that had just come into full bloom. She'd made another trip to the Farmer's Market to buy pink fruit, but except for pink grapefruit, if it existed, it was hiding from her.

Apples, Gigi decided, crates and crates of them, in every variety of red. She could conceal the bottoms of the crates with flower pots, Gigi reflected, but some final grace note was still lacking. She wandered through the market, smelling and touching, until she found tiny bunches of green-leaved, pink and white radishes that looked pretty enough to be pinned on a lapel. She bought every last bunch available, hundreds of them, and tucked them, like frilly grace notes, into the crates of apples that her caterers piled up in carefully picturesque disorder wherever she found an appropriate spot.

Where to put the bar, Gigi wondered. Her catering experience at Voyage to Bountiful had taught her that every bar was a potential traffic jam. There were so many unnecessary rooms in her house that she was able to set up bars in four different doorways, in spots too small to encourage people to linger.

After much searching for something original to serve, Gigi had decided to be sensible and fall back on the time-tested safety of a classic hearty Italian buffet, Vito's favorite food. Was there anybody who wouldn't find something to his liking amid the variety of hot and cold antipasti, the five kinds of pasta, the osso bucco, the chickens with black olives, the sausages with peppers, and the roasted legs of lamb? And wedding cake, of course. If so, let those picky souls drag themselves out to eat after the party, she decided.

Gigi had been able to find rental tablecloths that had boughs of flowering pink and white apple blossoms printed on a deeper pink background; the napkins were pale pink, the candles were white, and more clay pots of low white primroses made the simple centerpieces. She'd told her caterer to use forty-eight-inch tables for each group of eight people, and set them up all over the rambling house. Tight tables, as Emily Gatherum had said, gave animation to any group.

Animation. Gigi moaned out loud in an excess of pre-party

410

nerves. Why had she, who knew the sheer terrifying hell of host-essing from the viewpoint of a dispassionate professional, volun-teered to give a party herself? A party for hundreds of people, half of whom had absolutely nothing in common with the other half?

The people Sasha had invited from Scruples Two had never encountered anyone on Vito's list of *Le Tout* Hollywood. No won-der Sasha and her father had never met earlier; the only single guest they knew in common would be Zach. And Josie Speilberg and Burgo, Gigi amended. She could count on Josie and Burgo, both lively talkers, to work to make small bridges across the vast gap between the two groups, but certainly not on Zach, who would, she hoped, have the good taste to make a token appearance and then disappear.

Zach had once told her that the only thing to concern herself with in planning a party was the enjoyment of the guests, that the happiness of the hosts was unimportant because they were nothing more than the producers of an evening.

That had sounded reasonable at the time, but now that she was giving a huge party on her own, and a family wedding recep-tion to boot, the philosophical distance he'd conjured up was im-possible to achieve. On the other hand, the house, much too big for her, was much too small for all the guests, and maybe sheer physical proximity would give the party the *joie de vivre* it needed. Elsa Maxwell, the famed party-giver of the world between the wars, had always insisted on overcrowding as the key to any good party. Gigi prayed fervently for the ghost of Elsa Maxwell to bless her as she jittered with anticipatory "klung." This useful word that Sasha had taught her, even if it couldn't be found in any dictionary, meant a swift rush of shit to the heart.

As Gigi confirmed the twelve valet parkers from Chuck's Parking, and the eight violinists who would play romantic melodies from the largest of her balconies, and the dance band that would alternate with them in the courtyard, she blessed the day that Sasha had negotiated a contract with poor Mr. Jimmy for his repro-ductions of her antique lingerie. After his death, that contract had been taken over by Scruples Two, and her royalties, religiously saved for years, now amounted to a sum she'd never have dreamed she could call her own. It was no longer possible to think of it as a nest egg, unless the nest belonged to a particularly enormous and fertile dinosaur who laid huge eggs in large batches. Even if this party was the expensive disaster she expected it to be, she could afford to pay for it without thinking twice.

Gigi dressed for the party with cold hands that fumbled with every button and almost caused her zipper to jam. At Neiman-Marcus she'd found a chiffon dress of a color she called "waternixie green," a light green that made her think of mermaids disporting themselves mischievously with a school of lusty mermen on the banks of a river in the early springtime. It had a closely cut bodice with tight, concealing sleeves that ended in tiny cuffs at her wrists, and a deeply cut neckline that somehow managed to begin exactly where the pink of her nipples abruptly interrupted the blue-veined whiteness of her breasts. The bodice clasped her torso tightly all the way to her slim waist, where it was secured by a simple chiffon belt. The skirt, made of three layers of chiffon cut on the bias, undulated as she moved, to reveal every curve of her lower body, although its slightly flared hemline gave her the freedom to move easily. It ended a hair above the middle of her knee, at exactly the length that proclaimed that it was late 1984, not a day earlier, not a day later.

When your father marries a woman who is only three years older than you are, Gigi told herself, as she bought the most audaciously daring and provocative dress she'd ever owned, you have a duty to make sure that your new stepmother won't feel that she's been burdened by a stepchild who's too innocent to take care of herself. Or too modest. This dress would be modest only for a woman who believed that her arms were her primary erogenous zone.

Anyway, who'd ever heard of a modest waternixie, Gigi wondered, as she layered her eyelashes with more mascara than usual and stood in front of her full-length mirror looking as poised as she wished she felt. Perhaps it was obvious for a green-eyed girl to wear green, but this was Hollywood, after all, where a subtle effect might be wasted.

This dress had nothing in common, except for the fabric, with the lavender chiffon dress, that dream she'd worn to Sasha's wedding to Josh Hillman, that balletic bridesmaid's dress. Nor, she brooded, forgetting the party for a minute, was she the same person she'd been roughly two and a half years ago. So much had happened to her: she'd pushed herself out of the nest of Scruples Two; she'd made the hard decision, the all-but-unthinkable decision, about her lack of a future with Zach; she'd discovered her first enemy in Victoria Frost, and learned the limits of what she was willing to do for success; she'd had two lovers and been roughly initiated into the dangerous whirlpools of masculine jealousy and possessiveness; she'd begun to develop a knack for inventing twists on existing businesses; she'd even brought herself to buy a grown-up dress instead of putting together her usual bits and pieces. Whatever it all added up to, she'd changed, Gigi realized, and if one of the changes had been like taking a saw and cutting off a limb, it had not been avoidable. Was change ever avoidable, once you'd seen the need for it, she asked herself, as if the mirror could give her an answer.

Pushing aside fruitless philosophical speculation, Gigi turned away from her questioning eyes and stood sideways, inspecting herself critically. Tonight she looked shamelessly sinuous and as unblushingly voluptuous as any essentially slender girl could look, she realized with a rush of pleasure. She'd let her hair grow longer than it had ever been since she came to California. Now it reached between her chin and her shoulders, and like a bright fall of autumnal plumage it ruffled in a winged swaying movement whenever she moved her head. There was no need to add one more thing besides her gilded sandals, Gigi resolved, as she put away her jewelry. This dress had a statement to make, and even a bracelet would dilute that statement of—what, exactly? Of course . . . the perfect hostess: collected, composed, unflappable, welcoming, self-possessed, and adult. Especially . . . adult.

An hour later, with the party in full swing, and dinner still to be served, Gigi was able to relax and move through the crowded rooms with that particularly heady satisfaction that only a triumphant hostess knows—a sense of victory over all the mingled inner fears and self-doubts that hospitality on any grand scale produces;

over the complications of logistics and invitation lists; over whether a party can be carried off as it has been imagined, or whether it will miss in spirit or execution.

This party had been a smash from the minute the first guests arrived. The Scruples Two people, who, like everyone else in Los Angeles, thought of themselves as being in two businesses, their own and show business, were thrilled to meet the Hollywood crowd, who were equally pleased to find a new and eager audience for their sense of their own importance. The guests had all dressed up in their best, unusual in this casual town, but something about the idea of a wedding reception had appealed to their normally defective dress code.

The sense of occasion was almost visibly hanging in the air, as real as the lanterns and the full moon, and Gigi's mood waltzed and eddied and spun to the music as she flew from guest to guest in her gilded sandals. She felt as if the champagne she'd been drinking had lifted her a few inches above the ground. She should give more parties! Yes . . . this could be her First Annual Harvest Moon Ball . . . at Christmas she'd have a Twelfth Night party, just when people were feeling the post–New Year's Eve letdown . . . on April Fool's Day she'd have a masked ball at which everyone had to dress in red . . . she paused for a moment, near the front door, between one group and another.

Her giddy sense of insubstantiality suddenly shattered as Zach appeared, almost filling the doorway with his shoulders. Gigi felt a deep shock, an unmixed shock of pure glad remembrance, as the party disappeared around her. There was a moment in which neither of them did anything but stare at each other. Braced as they both had been for this meeting, nothing had prepared them for the disappearance of the passage of time. As if their year of separation had never existed, they found themselves deep inside the unquestioned middle of a long intimacy.

"Waternixie green," Zach blurted in surprise, startled out of his determined cool. "You never dared to wear it in public."

Gigi gasped, speechless. She had forgotten the color of a costume he'd had dyed especially for Ariel in a production of *The Tempest*, a fabulously effective collection of scraps and straps, so revealing that she'd been too shy to borrow it for a costume party, but not too shy to wear it for him.

414

"It wasn't the color, it was the f-fit," she justified herself, stuttering slightly.

"You've let your hair grow," he said, half-admiring, half-wistful.

"So have you."

"My producer won't give me time for a haircut."

"Why don't you complain to your agent?"

Gigi remembered the times she'd circled him in the bathroom, dodging his kisses, giving him an emergency trim with her manicure scissors when his hair had, as hair does, grown too long overnight.

"Well," Zach said, and stopped.

Without a stage direction, without a line, without a prompter, his mind went blank. She was intolerably lovable, but if he couldn't, at the very least, tell her that, what would be safe to say? If he looked closely into her eyes, it would be worth his life, it would be like taking bare electric wires in his hands.

"Well," Gigi echoed, swaying toward him slightly, wondering frantically what she could say next that wouldn't trigger another memory of their life together. Automatically she thrust her champagne glass at him.

"What should I do with it?" Zach asked.

"Drink it."

"This glass seems to be empty."

"Oh, sorry—here, give it back to me. Why don't you go greet the bride and groom and get a drink?"

"Bride and groom?" He looked at her in confusion. From the minute he'd walked in the door, he'd forgotten the reason he was here in the unbounded sweetness of looking at Gigi again.

"Sasha and Vito," she managed to remember, thinking that she'd never seen Zach confused before, not Zach, who habitually dominated any occasion with his firecracker laugh and his longshoreman's build and his flaming focused will.

"Oh . . . them. Right! I should say hello. That's why I came, isn't it? Where are they?"

"At the head of the stairs, in the living room."

Gigi blushed so deeply that she could see the flood of color reaching her breasts. The head of the stairs was where she had last set eyes on Zach, that was where she had told him to leave.

"I'll find them," Zach said. "You have more guests coming."

The front door opened behind him and Ben Winthrop walked into the hallway. In his purposeful, rapid way he ignored Zach, going straight up to Gigi.

"Hello, my darling," he said, kissing her lightly on the lips. "Sorry I'm late—I couldn't end the meeting a minute sooner. You look enchanting, but if ever a dress cried out for emeralds, this one does. Why didn't you tell me what you were going to wear? I'd have brought them over."

"Ben, this is Zach Nevsky. Zach, Ben Winthrop."

"Nevsky? You must be the brother of the bride," Ben said affably, as they shook hands. "I've heard so much about Sasha from Gigi that I can't believe I haven't met her yet. Or Gigi's father, for that matter," he added with his slow, confident smile. "I suspect her of hiding me from her family. Come on, darling, lead me to the guests of honor so I can finally congratulate them."

Gigi turned and scampered up the staircase, letting the two men follow her in any order they pleased, her only desire to melt away, dissolve, disappear, vanish, hide under the bed. What devil had inspired her to allow Ben to invite himself tonight? At the time it had seemed like a natural way to have him meet Vito and Sasha casually, without making too much of a production out of it, but she'd failed to imagine him and Zach together. Some adult hostess she'd turned out to be!

Maybe, she thought in a panic close to an anxiety attack, all her hostess-pride forgotten, maybe they'd cancel each other out, both so dominating by nature that they wouldn't even notice the other. Why didn't she know any meek men? Someone nice and mild and easygoing? Like Davy Melville . . .

So this, at last, was Mr. Wonderful, Sasha thought, as she greeted Ben with fascination. Yes, sexy as hell, she had to admit, and masterfully self-assured. They talked easily together as her shrewd mind worked busily, appraising him. Although Ben was slightly taller than Vito, there was a specific quality, an aura about him, that instantly recalled several of the noticeably short men she'd known in New York who'd always stood tall on their invisible money. Even if you hadn't known about Ben's wealth, Sasha

416

thought, you could sense it in his stance, in his attractive under-reaching, in his deliberate lack of any overt attempt to charm. He knew he would charm anyway, this intelligent guy with his bookish look, and he was as sure of his welcome as any man could be. In fact, now that she thought about it, wasn't it almost indecent for him to be so cool when he was meeting his beloved's family for the first time? He must be a great fuck. Typically Gigi, not to have mentioned that. She was characteristically unwilling to share dick-trivia, a selfish trait that Sasha deplored.

But, all that aside, as far as Ben Winthrop was concerned, Sasha concluded, a little self-consciousness, a real touch of genuine nervousness, even awkwardness would be in order here, under these delicate circumstances, if only as a tribute to Gigi.

My God, Sasha thought as Zach came up and enveloped her in a huge hug, Ben Winthrop didn't deserve to replace her brother in Gigi's life. He would never love her in the same hopelessly wholehearted way Zach did, because he didn't have as much heart to love with. And Sasha Nevsky Orsini knew a thing or two about hearts, as well as about great fucks, she told herself, as she and Ben continued to chat and, adroitly, she found an opportunity to hint about a ride in his jet.

"Well, of course, I'd be delighted, any time that suits you, but I have an even better idea," Ben said to her. "Why don't you and Vito fly to the party in Venice with Gigi and me, as my guests?"

"Oh, Vito, what do you think? Is there a chance we could go?" Sasha turned to him, full of excitement.

"Well . . . that depends," Vito said slowly, seized by surprise at the unexpected invitation.

"On what?" Sasha implored him. Even if it was a PR junket, a party in Venice!

"We've just wrapped the picture . . . now the editor's making his assembly, that takes a week or so, then Zach has a couple of months for his director's cut . . ."

"Then you'd absolutely be free in ten days," Ben pointed out.

"Theoretically, yes," Vito replied reluctantly, hating to be rushed into any plan he hadn't initiated. But how could he deny Sasha anything she wanted?

"Wonderful! I'll count on it." He turned to Gigi. "Darling,

you'll make all the arrangements, won't you? I think a suite at the Gritti would be best. Then Sasha and Vito could wave at you from across the canal."

Oh, they could, could they, Vito said to himself in deep, well-hidden irritation. He'd be triple-fucked if he'd lean out a hotel window and wave at his daughter lodged in this guy's place. He was a modern father and he'd accepted the fact that his daughter was . . . in all probability . . . chances were . . . not quite, not altogether a virgin . . . but he didn't like to have his nose rubbed in the reality of the details of her private life. Some things shouldn't be brought to the light of day, especially not in public. There was something . . . indelicate . . . about the otherwise smooth Ben Winthrop. Look at the way he kept his arm around Gigi's shoulders, oblivious to her rigidly uptight posture. Winthrop had the speed, nerve, and throwaway elegance of a tap dancer, so why didn't the guy have any respect for body language?

Zach had gone to lean against a couch on the far side of the room, where he was quickly surrounded by a group of friends from past productions. Every minute, he found himself glancing quickly at Vito and Sasha, who still stood at the top of the stairs greeting late arrivals. Gigi and Ben Winthrop were lost to sight in the maze of other rooms. He had planned to be long gone by this time, but now he was one with Othello. Could he leave while Winthrop was here? Could Othello tell Iago to take a hike, he'd never listen to another word? So that green called for emeralds, did it? If ever a color would be destroyed by emeralds it was delicate waternixie green. What a pompous asshole, what an insufferable, self-satisfied, smiling, damned villain!

Finally, under Zach's close observation, Gigi and Ben rejoined Sasha and Vito, standing with their backs to him.

"It's almost time to serve dinner," Gigi told them.

She could feel Ben's hand slipping below her waist until it was planted firmly on her ass. She brushed it away with a small whisking motion that she trusted wouldn't be noticed by her father.

"Sasha, have all your guests arrived?" Gigi asked.

"If they haven't, they're late," Sasha answered, indifferent to the possible latecomers.

"My friends are all accounted for," Vito assured Gigi.

Ben Winthrop, not to be denied, put his hand back on the curve of Gigi's bottom and let it rest there caressingly.

"Stop that," Gigi hissed sideways at him under the babble of the party.

"Stop what?" he asked, cupping the flesh beneath the thin chiffon even more insistently. "I can't resist you in this dress." She *was* irresistible in her delicious, prudish confusion, couldn't she understand what a tribute it was that he teased her?

Zach didn't know that he'd moved across the room in three large steps, until he spun Ben around by the shoulder and punched him hard in the eye. Ben staggered back, immediately recovered his balance, and went for Zach with the concentrated determination of the college boxing champion he'd been.

The two grunting men pummeled each other viciously for moments that were frozen in unreality. Almost no one in the room had ever witnessed a fistfight, except on the screen, and they were in such an elated mood that the sudden explosion of rage seemed part of the evening's excitement. Gigi and Sasha clutched each other, immobilized by sheer astonishment, while Vito stood back in kingly dignity, protecting them with his arm, and watched the fight like a professional referee. Whatever had started it, his money was definitely on Zach, for sheer size and motivation, although Ben had him on form.

Burgo O'Sullivan, veteran of many a barroom brawl, appeared out of the bewildered crowd and, with the help of the Jones brothers, eventually separated the fighters, both of them badly bloodied but still on their feet.

"Oh, Gigi, those jealous thugs have ruined your wonderful party," Sasha wailed.

"Oh, no!" Gigi laughed, mysteriously elated. "They've made it a night to remember."

She picked up a bunch of radishes that was rolling on the floor, stuck it behind her ear, and signaled the caterer to begin to serve dinner. So this, Gigi thought, was what it was like to be Helen of Troy.

19

T his is worse than an arranged marriage," Byron muttered through tense lips as he, Archie, and Victoria waited for the elevator to take them up to Beach Casuals. "I feel as if I'm about to lift the veil from the unknown face of a woman with whom I have to spend the rest of my life—someone my mother picked out because she was wholesome."

"Butch up, By," Archie advised, rearranging the knot in his tie for the tenth time in two minutes. "Look at Victoria, she's as collected as Queen Elizabeth. Terrific suit, Victoria."

"Thank you, Archie. I thought the occasion called for something new."

Victoria Frost smiled thinly at her partners. She was as nervous as they were, as they stood waiting in the bustling lobby of the large Seventh Avenue building, but her professional armor was impeccable. She wore a slim black cashmere suit with the point of a plain white linen pocket handkerchief punctuating the jacket, an otherwise unadorned three-button suit that had cost two thousand dollars. Only a few women in the world would guess what she'd paid for the flawless suit, but no one who looked at her, no matter how casually, would take her for anything less than a woman of sovereign stature and importance.

Her head had never been so regally poised; her classically beautiful features were so composed and her eyes so focused on maintaining their calm that they were as blank as if she had turned into a statue. On her exceptionally lovely earlobes she wore superbly simple black pearl earrings. The perfection of her skin was lent its only touch of life by her meticulously applied bright red lipstick.

It was ridiculous to be this tense, Victoria thought angrily, trying to breathe deeply. This wasn't a pitch, this was a first meeting with a new client.

Harris Reeves, who had decided that he wanted to meet them on an informal basis before they were introduced to the rest of his management, had set this convocation at ten-thirty in the morning for coffee in his office.

Tomorrow they would begin the intense work of getting to know the Beach Casuals people and the culture of the huge company, but this afternoon was empty of engagements, so Victoria had used her free time to make an appointment with Joe Devane of Oak Hill Foods, for she never came to New York for any length of time without paying a call on him.

She'd never make the basic mistake of taking any client for granted, but Archie and Byron had such a long record of doing remarkable work for Oak Hill that seeing Joe was as close to a proforma meeting as you could get in the agency business, Victoria thought, trying to take her mind off the meeting with Harris Reeves by looking forward to a half hour of friendly banter with Joe Devane. He had never expressed anything but satisfaction over the way his accounts were being handled, and his budget for Answer Soups, Lean and Mean Breads, and Thinline Desserts had grown from twenty million to twenty-five million in two years, as market demand increased.

"Victoria, the elevator!" Archie announced suddenly, startling her. She glared at him as they squeezed into the overcrowded express elevator that would take them to the fortieth floor of the building, where Beach Casuals occupied three entire floors. Why had Archie imposed his own tension on her ability to immerse herself in a mood of business-as-usual?

Harris Reeves sported an attitude of vast self-satisfaction, reinforced by his immaculate grooming. If ever she could imagine a man spending longer on getting dressed in the morning than any woman, it was this burnished and buffed little bantam cock with his magnificent head of carefully arranged white hair, Victoria decided, as she smiled at him across a coffee cup. In his first appraising glance she had amortized the cost of her new suit.

Harris Reeves had pale, clever eyes that missed nothing even as he played the host, his secretaries passing silver trays of coffee, tea, and an assortment of coffee cake that they all accepted but put aside. Only a fool or a far richer man than Harris Reeves would actually bite into a piece of cake at this first stage of an important meeting.

A few minutes passed in art talk, inspired by Byron's immediate interest in the three Modiglianis and the two Picassos that adorned the walls of Reeves's handsome office.

"You'll all have to come to my home to see the rest of my collection," he said, pleased at Byron's admiration. "I only keep a few of my particular favorites here. Manufacturing swimwear is merely my way of being able to buy art. My wife and I spend every Saturday afternoon doing the rounds of the galleries and the auction houses, whenever there's anything interesting coming up. And we never miss a big auction in Europe. But tell me, where are the others? I hope their taxi isn't stuck in traffic, it's impossible to get anywhere in this neighborhood."

"What?" Victoria asked.

"Their taxi. This New York law of only three people to a taxi makes getting around more difficult every day. Personally, I always use a car and driver, it pays for itself in the end."

"What others?"

"But I told you on the phone that I wanted you *all* to come to New York, and obviously that included Gigi Orsini and David Melville, the creative team. Surely you understood that."

"Mr. Reeves . . . David Melville hasn't been with us for at least six months. Lisa Levy, a very bright young talent, has been the art director on Indigo Seas ever since he left. When we talked on the phone, I stupidly failed to realize that you'd want her to be here at this early stage of our learning curve. My partners here are our creative directors—Lisa isn't at their level. I'm terribly sorry for the misunderstanding," Victoria said quickly, through dry lips. "I'll call and have her on a plane within a few hours. She'll be with us tomorrow, of course. Again, I apologize, I feel terribly foolish."

"Well, don't," Harris Reeves said heartily. "It comes under the heading of an understandable mistake. I don't usually make phone calls to a new agency myself, as you can imagine, but I was so fed up with our old agency that I just grabbed the phone. My vice-president in charge of advertising would have straightened it all out with you. This little mix-up will make his day, prove I don't know everything. More coffee?"

"No, thank you."

"You didn't leave Gigi Orsini behind too?" Reeves's question was sharp and sudden.

"As a matter of fact—"

"Well now, damn it, that does annoy me. The Indigo Seas ads depended entirely on the copy, on the concept. Those graphics just underline the terrific sell. You should have brought her, damn it. Gigi Orsini created the campaign that made all the difference for Eleonora Colonna and her boys, surely you realize I know that? We're a small community in swimwear, and we watch each other closely. Cole, Gottex, we all try to be constantly aware of what the others are doing. Indigo Seas isn't in our league, but we never ignore them, especially now that they're selling so brilliantly. Gigi Orsini should have been here today! Here, take my phone, and make that call."

"Mr. Reeves, when you gave us your account, you knew that we had Indigo Seas," Victoria said, fighting for reasonableness.

"What does that have to do with anything?"

"We had to resign Indigo Seas, it was a clear case of client conflict."

"What difference does that make to me?"

"When . . . Gigi was told about the conflict . . . she, ah, she left the agency."

"She did what?"

"She quit," Victoria said firmly, feeling the ground open beneath her feet, but determined to present her most tranquil professional face. "Apparently she'd formed a close personal attachment to Eleonora Colonna and the Collins family, and she was upset enough about our having to resign the account to leave Frost Rourke Bernheim."

"Well, get her back, damn it! Wherever she is, pay her double, triple, whatever it takes, but get her back! What I'd like to know is why you bothered to show up here without her. She should be immersed in our business from day one. You've had more than enough time to get her back. This is a very bad beginning!"

"Mr. Reeves," Archie said, "I've been supervising Gigi's copy from the very beginning of her employment with us. I discovered her and brought her into FRB for the express purpose of getting the Indigo Seas account. I can assure you that the quality of the copy for Beach Casuals will be just as good as, if not better than, anything that Gigi ever produced for the Collins brothers."

"I'm not interested in anything 'just as good, if not better'— I'm only interested in using Gigi Orsini's copy for my company. *Nothing else!* I'm a collector and I buy originals, not copies, thank you very much! Why the hell do you think I hired your agency? For the services of you three people, when I don't know anything about you? No, thank you very much! I don't care if you supervised Gigi Orsini twenty-four hours a day, seven days a week, Mr. Rourke, you didn't write her stuff, did you? No, I didn't think so. A woman wrote it, not a man. *Get her back.* There's no point in any further discussion until you do."

He pushed his coffee cup away in an unmistakable gesture of dismissal. Archie and Byron stood up, looking at Victoria. Would she tell Reeves that Gigi had left advertising for good?

"Mr. Reeves, I apologize again," she said, rising gracefully. "We won't call you until Gigi Orsini is back at FRB. I fully appreciate your position. I'm more distressed than I can ever say that we had to disappoint you this morning. This bad beginning, as you rightly call it, will have a fresh start, an excellent one, I promise you that."

"Good-bye, Miss Frost, gentlemen," Harris Reeves said angrily. "My secretary will see you out. I'm telling my ad VP to find out where Gigi Orsini is. I'll give you till the end of the week to get her back. After that, I'll get her myself."

"Jesus, what the fuck are we going to do?" Byron moaned, as they sat huddled together in the back of the taxi they'd finally managed to find. "I wish I could say I've been thrown out of better offices, but I haven't."

"There's only one thing we can do, By," Archie said. "We've got to get Gigi back at any price, isn't that obvious?"

"Archie's right," Victoria agreed. "You two go to the airport this minute, and wait for the next plane. Don't waste time checking out of the hotel, I'll take care of that. Find her and persuade her . . . offer her anything. You'll have a better chance without me. She doesn't like me and I don't like her, but she can write her own ticket. Don't hesitate to make any promise, including a partnership."

"The thing I'm worried about," Archie said heavily, "is that Reeves is going to figure out, if he hasn't already, that he doesn't need us. He could hire Gigi himself, set up his own in-house agency, build it around her, pay her a sky-high salary, and still save a bundle on the agency commission."

"And he's just the guy to do that," Byron added from the depths of his gloom. "Any art collector knows enough to try to buy from the artist in his studio rather than from the dealer—the price is better and they love all that personal contact, makes them feel like patrons, not customers."

"His VP in charge of advertising is going to discourage it," Victoria said. "The guy could easily find himself out of a job if it should ever happen. I refuse to worry about that possibility until you've talked to Gigi. She must have cooled off by now. Ten to one she'll listen to reason."

"Why don't you come back with us today?" Archie asked, panic only half-repressed in his voice. "Even if you don't talk to Gigi, we need you in L.A."

"I have to see Joe Devane this afternoon," she said with composure.

"Can't he wait?" Archie snapped.

"No, Joe hates to have his appointments changed, even by a half hour. Let's not forget that Oak Hills bills twenty-five million, let's not neglect our first account, boys, management can never afford to get sloppy. We're having a fire drill here, Archie, not a fire."

There had been no message from Angus at the hotel, Victoria thought. She wouldn't leave New York until she'd talked to him and found out what had happened with her mother. Nothing, no ninety-million-dollar account that they were bound to hang on to, one way or another, no Harris Reeves, with his teased coif and second-rate Picassos, was going to prevent that.

Victoria waited no more than a minute in the reception room at Oak Hill Foods. It was no less old-fashioned than Joe's own office, but old-fashioned in a reassuring way that impressed everyone with his lack of a need to impress. The events of the morning had been shut out of her mind with her usual firm ability to compartmentalize. Her only interest now was in quickly fulfilling her obligation to Joe and then getting things clear with Angus, even if it meant going to confront him in his office.

"Mr. Devane asked if you'd care to wait in his office," his secretary said, approaching Victoria.

"Isn't he here, Gloria? How are you, by the way?" Victoria asked the woman she'd known for years.

"Fine, thanks, Miss Frost. Mr. Devane's not in, but he'll be along in just a minute. You'll be more comfortable in there," Gloria said, as she ushered her in and closed the door.

Millicent Frost Caldwell sat behind Joe Devane's desk.

"Good, you're right on time," she said evenly, glancing at her jeweled watch. "Sit down, Victoria." She smiled pleasantly and pointed to the chair next to the desk.

"What—why—why are you here?" Victoria stopped inside the door, too shocked to move.

"Joe has kindly let us borrow his office, Victoria. He understands that we're making an attempt at a family reconciliation, and he realizes that it would be difficult to conduct it in privacy at Caldwell and Caldwell."

426

"Family reconciliation? The bloody hell it is!"

"But that's exactly what it is," Angus Caldwell said, stepping out of the deep recess in a window, where Victoria hadn't seen him.

"Angus! Why didn't you leave me a message at the hotel?"

"He didn't leave a message because we wanted to talk to you together, Victoria," her mother answered. "Please sit down."

Victoria felt Angus's hand on her shoulder, guiding her to the chair, and she drew strength from the warmth of his touch. It was going to be all right. If her mother was here, it could only mean that she had resigned herself to a divorce and was going to try to handle it in the way that would cause her the least humiliation. Wouldn't it be best, wouldn't any sensible woman want to take that course, to leave her husband rather than be left by him?

Victoria felt herself grow steady and sure again as she looked her mother over closely, not bothering to hide her cold inspection. The woman still overdressed, she thought with an immediate shiver of physical disdain. The woman still thought that she could compensate for her fifty-three years by wearing a flattering pale pink silk blouse with a high neckline. She still deluded herself that she could distract the critical eye of a much younger husband by the grossly oversized ruby and diamond bird she had pinned to the lapel of her deep violet suit, by the unsuitably heavy ruby and diamond bracelets she wore on her fragile wrists, on which the veins were large and visible. She must spend hours every day working doggedly on her aging muscles, not realizing how dried up she appeared, in spite of her absurdly girlish outline. She had even had her hair freshly set for this encounter, Victoria saw with contempt as she noted the new wrinkles under her mother's eyes.

Victoria looked at Angus, who had seated himself in a chair pulled up and turned slightly sideways, so that she was between him and her mother. She sought his eyes, thinking how often she had deliberately dressed for him in the unadorned black that she wore today, so that he could force himself on her while she was fully clothed, playing at rape and taking her standing up behind a door. Oh, how cunningly she had learned to fight him off, delaying, delaying, so that he was aroused to real belief in her unwillingness, so that she heightened the fainting bliss of her final surrender. If he would only look up, he would know exactly what she was thinking, but he directed his gaze firmly beyond her, to a point over her mother's head, as if he couldn't allow himself really to see the beauty he worshiped until this was all arranged and agreed upon.

"Victoria," Angus said loudly, after clearing his throat, "your mother knows that you and I have been having an affair for five years." Victoria hardly recognized his voice, so hard and harsh that it showed that he would stop for no interruption.

"Millicent knows how you led me into it," Angus continued, like a motor with a voice. "She knows how I lost all my judgment and allowed myself to make love to you, and she knows that this affair has never stopped, even when I tried to get rid of you by sending you to California. She knows how I've given in, time after time, to my sexual obsession with you, to my insanity. She knows exactly how crazily I've behaved, how criminally weak and foolish I was not to resist you when it first started. I told her everything after you phoned me in Southampton."

"But we love each other!" Victoria clung to that certainty in a passion of refusal. "*You want to marry me!* Have you told her that too?"

Angus's inhuman voice continued, his words marching one after the other with a determination that brooked no discussion.

"I thought I loved you, those first few years—" He took a deep breath, and now he directed his gaze toward his wife. "Yes, Millicent, I *was* in love with her, madly in love, so deeply in love that I couldn't think with any clarity at all. But from the time she began to urge me to divorce you, I've feared her—love and fear don't go together."

"Did he tell you I was a virgin when he fucked me?" Victoria shrieked at her mother.

"I always believed there was something unnatural about you, Victoria," Millicent Caldwell said placidly, in her charming voice. "I didn't know that particular touching detail, no, but what difference does it make what form your neurosis took? You would have been far better off spreading your charming long legs for every man you met than keeping yourself a virgin for your stepfather, wouldn't you say?"

Millicent Caldwell's curly blond head was held high on her

short neck, and she spoke with the clarity and imperturbable precision of all her years of uncontested authority. The feminine fussiness of her clothes and jewelry suddenly seemed symbols of her power rather than signs of weakness.

"Stepfather? Don't try to pull that crap on me!" Victoria panted. "You know damn well that I never was Angus's stepdaughter, that nothing happened until I was twenty-seven—what the hell does his being miserably married to you at the time have to do with a love affair between two adults?"

"Oh, Angus," Millicent Caldwell said quietly, with sadness in her voice. "I couldn't truly credit it when you told me that she had no comprehension . . . no comprehension at all—"

"No comprehension of what?" Victoria screamed, twisting her head from one to another, her features set in a hideous grimace of disbelief. "An imaginary relationship? Not even a relationship —you know, don't dare tell me you don't, that 'stepfather' is nothing but a fiction, a convenient word you're trying to use, without the slightest legal or moral justification. For Christ's sake, I was sixteen before I ever laid eyes on Angus!"

"Poor Victoria," her mother said. "Do you imagine that anyone but you and Angus—and I—would believe that there wasn't *anything* sexual between you for eleven whole years? You were such a mature young girl, he was such a lusty man . . . who would believe that the two of you weren't sneaking off behind my back and sleeping with each other for years and years? The only question would be *when* it started and where . . . in New York, in Southampton, in Jamaica, or in the South of France? '*How long did they wait?*' That's the only question people will ask. You two had every opportunity . . . and I was much older than Angus, wasn't I? In fact," she said smiling gently at herself, "I still am."

Millicent Caldwell examined her bracelets briefly. "That's what they'd say, you know, no matter how I insisted that there wasn't one word of truth in it. They'd think I was trying to protect you both, but people will never let me play the saint, even if I wanted to. They'd so much rather believe the worst, don't you understand that by now? A juicy international sex scandal? An incest scandal? Really, Victoria, where's your common sense? The trouble with you is that you don't see things from any point of view but your own. There's not one person I know who wouldn't remember seeing something going on between you and Angus. The telephones would be jammed with divinely gossipy calls between my best friends and my best friends. No one's good-natured or high-minded enough to be cheated out of that satisfaction."

"So they'd talk! So what? Angus, do you give a shit what people say when they'd be totally wrong? Well, do you, for the love of God?" There was the first note of urgent terror in her inextinguishable defiance. As she had listened to her mother's words, so relentlessly logical, so loaded with implacable worldliness, Victoria had finally become aware of the beginning of a change in the air of the room, as if oceans had turned into ice, as if mountains had melted.

"Are you truly mad? Of course I care. What's wrong with caring about the good opinion of everyone you know?" Angus said in a passion of wild obedience to his self-preservation.

"How could that be more important than living your life with her?" Victoria shrilled, pointing at her mother. "Good opinion can't make you happy, good opinion can't make your cock hard, good opinion can't make you come, you fucking bastard. Are you as dried up as she is? When did she cut off your balls?"

"There's nothing to be gained, Victoria, by being abusive," Millicent Caldwell said, sniffing daintily. "It doesn't become you, it doesn't suit your style."

"Do you think I've ever *cared* what you think? Or what your so-called friends think?"

"Ah, but you see, Victoria, *Angus does.* He's just told you that he does. He hasn't explained everything, of course. He hasn't told you that he can't imagine leading the rest of his life as an exile —a dishonored exile—in California, sunny as it may be. He hasn't told you that there are too many deeply important satisfactions for him here in New York, to ever give them up for that little hot shop you've made such a success with, as I never doubted you could."

"*Is that true?*" Victoria stared at Angus and realized that he had no intention of replying to her question. The answer was written clearly on his features, written on that deceptive schoolboy's face. She couldn't see his eyes because they were still turned away from her, locked to her mother in desperate fealty.

"You'll die here, Angus, you'll die of wanting me, you know

430

that, don't you? *Don't you, you pathetic fool? It's the end of you as a man, don't you understand that?*"

"Oh, I doubt that, Victoria," her mother answered with a tinkling laugh. "Angus and I haven't had a sexual relationship since you started with him. I knew he must be seeing someone, and I'd been resigned to it for some time. It simply never crossed my mind that you were that woman. As far as I'm concerned, Angus can satisfy his sexual needs with any woman he chooses, so long as it isn't with anyone in the agency or anyone with whom I'm personally friendly. *Or with you. No, not ever again.*"

She tapped on Joe Devane's desk with her delicate hand. "Angus will be discreet, and I—I won't think about it. There are worse ways to live together, I promise you. I used to be jealous, I used to make silly scenes, but that's a waste of time. What I intend to have, what I *insist* on keeping, is a husband by my side for the rest of my life, a devoted husband and an excellent business partner."

"Devoted? You think he's devoted to you?" Victoria shook her mother off on a breath of contempt and scorn. "Have you any idea how he hates the life he's been forced to live with you? Any idea how he planned and plotted to get away from you?"

"I think the proof that what you say simply isn't true—and correct me if I'm wrong, Angus—is the fact that my husband intends to keep on living exactly the life you say he hates. You have no idea how meaningful and satisfactory it is, especially as you grow older. There is more than one way to be married, but at thirty-two you haven't understood that yet. You called Angus a liar, Victoria, and you were right. He lied to both of us so that he could have it all. You in bed, me at home. But finally, when he had to choose—it was me, Victoria, not you. And he made that choice in no time at all. Am I right, Angus?"

He nodded.

"I think Victoria would like to hear it from your own lips," Millicent Caldwell said with a soft insistence.

"Your mother is right," Angus conceded, without pausing or exhaling, his voice dull and low. Millicent had let him off so easily that he couldn't expect her not to exact some humiliation. She was too intelligent to continue to rub his nose in it—in a few weeks it would be as if it had never happened.

"Say it again," Victoria demanded. "Try to look at me and say you lied, try to say that you want her, not me."

This time his voice was like a hammer, and he looked at her with vicious concentration.

"I lied to you. I lied to Millicent. I don't want you. I want her. I want to keep my life. I will never be alone with you again."

Victoria sat straighter than ever in her chair. Angus had looked at her with hatred. With disgust. With revulsion. His pride had been destroyed, and he blamed her for it. She was now the cause of his shame, and he would make himself forget her as quickly as he could. The pride of a weak man is more dangerous to destroy than the pride of a strong man, because without it, he is nothing. She had never known that till this minute.

"Now, my dear, now that we've gotten past this miserable moment, shall we get on with it?" Millicent Caldwell asked.

"I have nothing to say to you. Thank Joe for the use of his office."

"No, no, don't be hasty, Victoria. We have some business to discuss, don't we, Angus? I never realized until yesterday how Caldwell and Caldwell lost those three Oak Hill accounts. Now *that's* something I cannot forgive, not in a million years. That's something you *may not* do to me. You or anyone else. It's not personal, Victoria, it's a matter of professional pride. Angus and I have proposed to service those accounts gratis for three years, using our best people. Joe, needless to say, was delighted. So you've lost them, Victoria."

"How petty, how horribly cheap of you! You don't need those accounts, they're a drop in the bucket to you, for Christ's sake!"

"Not at all," Millicent observed with a generous smile. "I did it for your benefit, Victoria."

"That's enough," she said, starting to get up from her chair.

"When you come back to Caldwell and Caldwell, you'll be bringing the Oak Hill accounts back with you. The agency world would expect that. It will save your face, my dear, and in your position you'll need to save whatever you can."

"You're insane! Why would I come back? It's the last thing I'd do!"

"Because if you don't, we'll ruin you, Angus and I. We can, you know, and we will. All it would take are a few words in the right ears about our unfortunate, *delusional, paranoid, blackmailing* daughter, and your agency would be finished—and as for you, you'd never have another job offer."

"You're a monster!"

"Sticks and stones, Victoria, sticks and stones." Millicent shook a slender finger at her daughter. "Aren't you a better judge of copy lines than that? I want you where I can keep my eye on you, I want to know where you are every day of your life until you manage to get yourself married, and even then I'll keep my eye on you. As long as I live. When you have as much money as I do, Victoria, that isn't hard to arrange."

"But why?" Victoria cried in anguish. "Why? You've got what you want. Why can't you leave me alone?"

"I have a responsibility to you, Victoria. You're my only child and you've been running wild for years. But there's hope for you yet. What you need is something to keep you steady, something hard and challenging. I'd be remiss if I didn't try to help you. Perhaps you imagine that I neglected you as a child? Heaven knows I did my best, but with children you're damned if you do and you're damned if you don't. Everybody agrees on that. In any case, I partly blame myself for the mess you've made of your life."

"We've decided to send you to the Tokyo office, as manager." Angus pronounced her sentence quietly. His eyes moved toward her for a brief, blackened instant and she saw nothing in them. Nothing at all except a desire to finish this conversation quickly.

Victoria never remembered how, like a fatally wounded animal, she lurched out of that room, but she never forgot hearing her mother's ruthless, petty voice behind her, commenting complacently on her daughter's doom.

"I think this little family problem is behind us, don't you, Angus? Joe *will* be pleased."

20

Nonstop?" Ben said, answering
Sasha's question. "We can do Washington, D.C., to Anchorage
or Brasilia, Moscow to Peking, Melbourne to Guam—"

"So why can't you fly from L.A. to Venice without refueling?"
Sasha asked.

She's been on this plane less than an hour, Gigi thought, and
she's already found something to complain about.

"We can't carry that much fuel," Ben said in surprise. "This
is as big as a private jet gets; it's designed to fly three thousand six
hundred nautical miles with eight passengers and baggage, but
Venice is more than five thousand nautical miles from L.A."

"But there are only four of us," Sasha sighed, with only the
slightest whisper of a hint of criticism. "Shouldn't that make it go
farther?"

"Even if the ship were empty, you could get only two hundred extra miles in an emergency. Tell you what, Sasha, if you're still awake when we get to Frobisher Bay to refuel, you can get out and stretch your legs."

She'd freeze to death at the Iqaluit Airport in the eastern Arctic if she stayed outside for half the hour it took to refuel, which might not be an undesirable incident, Ben thought, not undesirable at all. Even a small case of frostbite would be welcome. The tip of her haughty nose might be improved by turning a shade of gray-white.

Ben Winthrop was accustomed to first-time guests being all but speechlessly impressed by the luxury and size of the plane, with its forty-one-foot cabin. He'd had it custom-designed so that six people could sit in the forward part of the aircraft in deep-cushioned swivel armchairs while, at the same time, two people could sleep on the convertible sofas in the curtained-off compartment at the rear of the plane, but so far Sasha had seemed more amazed by the discovery of the trash compactor and oven in the galley than by anything else about the jet.

"I suppose the crew has their own bathroom," Sasha said with a crystalline queenliness that would have made her mother proud of her.

"Actually, no, they use the one we use."

"Well, it *is* nice and roomy," Sasha replied quickly, leaving such a faint touch of a merely fleeting impression of surprise that absolutely no one could be sure that it had been in her voice.

I hope she never gets mad at *me*, Vito thought, repressing a grin of admiration. Sure, Zach had thrown that first punch, but nobody who punched Sasha's brother, even in self-defense, could ever expect forgiveness.

However, that fistfight, now ten days in the past, hadn't made the slightest difference in Sasha's plans to go to Venice as Ben's guest. One thing, she explained to Vito, had nothing to do with the other. Since Gigi said she didn't have any idea what the fight was about, and Zach refused to tell her what had started it, no one could expect her to give up this experience out of family loyalty. He could live happily, Vito reflected, without an unnecessary jaunt to Venice for a couple of days, even if the flight was only going to take fourteen hours, including the refueling stop, but he'd never disappoint Sasha, who was like a kid about this trip. As soon as

Long Weekend was in the can, he'd take Sasha on a real trip, a honeymoon to remember.

But in any case, this gave him a chance to see more of Ben Winthrop. The fellow, after all, had the clear-cut intention of carrying off his daughter and marrying her, but, for all his experience of human beings, Vito found it hard to get a handle on Ben. He had an attractive surface, no question about that, he seemed to have no noticeable faults besides being overly pleased with himself, downright smug if you will, but generous and madly in love with Gigi. What's more, unlike Curt Arvey, who'd also owned a Gulfstream III before his death, he didn't work the conversation around to the fact that it had cost him close to fifteen million dollars to buy one, plus a yearly fortune in maintenance and salaries.

Yet there was an atmosphere Ben Winthrop carried with him, inside of which he lived and thought and felt, an atmosphere something like a wall and something like a deep mist, that Vito, sensitive as he was to essences, found almost impossible to penetrate. Ben Winthrop was fucking inscrutable. There was something profound and important about him that he didn't reveal—would, Vito suspected, never reveal—and in that he reminded Vito of one or two of the old-time Hollywood studio bosses whose ruthlessness was so natural to them, so subcutaneous, that you didn't know it was there until it had destroyed you. As far as he was concerned, Vito thought, the jury on Winthrop was not only out, but at this particular moment they were hopelessly deadlocked. Not that there was much he could do about it anyway. Gigi would make up her own mind when she saw fit, and he doubted that she'd consult him.

"I hope I've packed the right things," Sasha murmured.

"The official tourist season ended three weeks ago, in mid-October," Gigi said, "and the local gentry make it a point to dress in the most polished and sophisticated European elegance, so you'll stand out like a sore thumb no matter what you wear."

"You've always been a comfort to me, Gigi," Sasha responded with a smile that curled dangerously at the corners of her mouth. "What are you wearing for the keel hauling, or whatever it's called?"

436

"I told you to bring jeans and sweaters, didn't I? Wear them out to Porta Margera. At the shipyard, everybody's going to be issued warm jackets to wear and keep as souvenirs, because it might get chilly while they watch the ceremony. Early November can be tricky in Venice. Then we all go back to the hotels, and change for the party."

"Why do I feel as if I'm going to look like a Munchkin?" Sasha asked suspiciously. "Is Ben going to wear a jacket? Is Vito? Will the *Vogue* travel editor put one on?"

"Only if they want to, Sasha," Gigi said, "It's a voluntary thing, we're not inducting you into the army."

"I suppose they're green, like those awful shiny satin things Celtics fans wear."

"You suppose semi-correctly. They're white with green letters," Gigi replied waspishly. "And yes, the letters do say *Winthrop Emerald* on the back. For a girl who sleeps in a T-shirt that says 'Kennedy Before New Hampshire,' that shouldn't be too hard to understand."

"Used to sleep, Gigi, used to sleep. Now I sleep in a '*Mirrors* Wins Best Picture' T-shirt, I'm proud to say. And I'd like to point out that the Kennedy T-shirt wasn't mine, somebody gave it to me. I cast my first vote for the Libertarian Party candidate, whoever he or she was at the time. Ma insisted on it."

"Isn't your vote supposed to be your own decision?" Ben asked.

"Not with a Ma like mine."

"Why couldn't you tell her you'd voted her way and just do your own thing in the voting booth?" Ben probed.

"She'd know," Sasha said darkly.

More power to Ma, Ben thought, pleased to hear that someone could scare this infuriating friend of Gigi's. Even worse than a best friend—her father's wife. It was going to be an excellent thing for Gigi to be removed by three thousand miles from Sasha's influence, he congratulated himself. He hadn't known what to expect when he met Vito and Sasha, but at least he knew what Vito looked like from magazine and newspaper photographs of him taken over the years of his producing career, and so far the man seemed pleasant enough.

Somehow he'd vaguely expected Sasha, though Jewish, to be a slightly older and far less delectable version of Gigi, rather than a formidably sleek Queen of Sheba with a breathtaking profile and, when she chose, the manners of an offended British duchess. A rude duchess, Ben Winthrop knew from personal experience, could be as quietly rude a woman as any that had emerged in the evolutionary process since the first man made the first knife. Or had it been a first woman?

Her loser hoodlum of a brother would be no problem in the future. He was simply a lout, and had been dealt with as one deals with louts. But what if Sasha took it into her head to invite herself to visit them after he and Gigi were installed in New York? When a California woman has a close friend with a large place in New York, the California friend is notorious for finding excuses to spend at least a few weeks in the spring and the fall in Manhattan, shopping and having to be taken to see the new plays and exhibitions. That would be a problem until he put a stop to it, which he intended to do quickly and efficiently.

He had very different plans for Gigi's time, after they were married, than a continued association with Sasha. He could see, in his mind's eye, precisely the kind of ultimate East Sixties town house they'd buy and redecorate in New York; the sex and number of children they'd have—but not for at least seven or eight years; the carefully selected philanthropic committees to which Gigi would donate breathtaking sums of money and lend her name and time; the small and exquisite parties they'd give, the parties they'd go to and, equally as important a decision—perhaps more important—the parties he would decide they shouldn't attend.

Of course there'd be a real knockabout big old summer house, outside of Edgartown, perhaps, although they'd go to Venice as often as possible. He'd be flexible, Ben told himself, as flexible as she could desire. If there was some other place in Europe where Gigi wanted to set down roots—if, for example, she fancied a Queen Anne manor house with land and horses and gardens not too far from London—why not? Or a chateau on the Loire or a villa in Tuscany? Or all of them—she could have *anything.* Just as long as she realized that he came first, that each of these houses had to have a thoroughly responsible majordomo in residence all year long; as long as she didn't waste any of the time that belonged to him in dealing with the details of upkeep, he could be as flexible as any man on earth.

She was to complement him, as a wife was intended to complement her husband, in the old-fashioned meaning of the word in which she would complete his life and make it perfect. He'd reached an age in which a wife was a necessary fulfillment, in which a wife gave a man a finished totality he could never possess without one.

He simply hadn't felt the need for a wife before, Ben realized. He'd been too busy moving around the country, buying land and building malls, to feel the lack of a home base other than his bachelor place in New York, the chalet in Klosters, and the little palace on the Grand Canal that was the outlet for his feelings for beauty. But something about that weekend he'd spent in Martha's Vineyard with Gigi and his college friends and their children had made him aware of the passage of time.

It was one thing to be the fancy-free and eligible object of their admiration, but quite another to become 'poor old Ben, isn't it a shame that he never got married.' He knew that they were all horribly envious of him in their heart of hearts—how could they escape envy when his personal wealth was proclaimed in *Forbes*'s unutterably vulgar list every year, when his eight hundred million dollars had grown by another hundred million dollars this year, and yet nothing about the way he behaved with them changed, when he remained the Ben Winthrop they thought they knew? They couldn't even accuse him of having the poor taste to display any signs of the nouveau riche. That alone must make them as sick as did the fortune he'd made. Obviously his friends would jump on any excuse to imagine themselves happier than he was, because he'd lagged a bit too long in any stage of the footrace of life. He'd seen it happen many times, seen this sort of self-congratulatory emotional superiority spring up almost overnight, although a man could hold out for years and years, almost indefinitely, as long as he didn't become a recluse, whereas a woman, no matter how rich, would be quickly pitied.

He could never have married one of the Boston girls he grew up with; they were so familiar that they seemed like sisters—cheery, bookish, bossy, non-erotic. He didn't care for any of the multitude of New York girls he'd met; they were, by and large, too formed, too sophisticated, often too neurotic. They had been spoiled by their parents and had acquired too hard a veneer too early in life.

Gigi had been made for him.

Her background was impossible, that went without saying. An Irish musical-comedy dancer for a mother, and a showbiz father of Italian heritage! Fortunately he had background enough for the two of them. His marriage would be one in the eye for ever-critical Boston, one in the eye for his father, who persisted in his disapproval of his way of life, one in the eye for all his smug Winthrop relatives, although the fact that Gigi could boast Billy Winthrop Elliott as her "stepmother," or at least her former legal guardian, provided her with a certain stamp that would soften any edge of genuine disapproval they might feel. His taking of an unconventional bride would seal all his other triumphs as no additional financial success could.

Gigi herself was so winsome, so original, and so charming that she would win them over. Everyone who had known him as a young man would be forced to acknowledge, once again, that, unlike them, he was no pale copy of his ancestors. Gigi was—and it was a large part of her charm that she didn't know it—*distinguished*. The quality of her imagination, put to use in the world of philanthropy, would quickly bring her to the attention of the inner circle of older women who ran New York, and one day she would be an important figure in their ranks, a primary figure. Yes, Gigi was the perfect—not "compromise"—he would never compromise in marriage, but the perfect . . . well . . . for want of a better word . . . the perfect choice.

And, of course, he was in love with her. "Madly" in love? No, he didn't have the desire ever to lose himself in any essentially irrational emotion, he was thankful to say. But as much in love, far more in love, than he had ever believed he could be, now or ever again. *Deeply* in love. He could ask no more than that of life.

No one had yet informed the Adriatic Sea or the lagoons and canals of Venice that the official tourist season was over. The water flickered, dappled and silver, under a celebratory sun in the city that even Dickens had said he was afraid to describe. No filigree of mist had yet flung itself over the dusky ochres of the smaller canals, the miraculous pinks of the Doge's Palace, or the golden grays, beige grays, the plum grays, and mauve-burgundy grays of the marble palaces that lined the Grand Canal.

In the blue air, all sounds seemed to hang suspended overhead except for the ringing of bells and the lapping of water. There was no longer any wisteria in blossom, trailing in loops from window to window; the occasional oleander trees hanging over tall walls, sending tantalizing messages from tiny hidden gardens, were denuded of their pink and white blooms; but that lack was more than made up for by the sense of freedom and space created by the departure of most of the five million tourists who came to Venice each year.

Venice was ripe on the day of their arrival, an autumnal ripeness in a city of stones where there could be no harvest. Thoughts of the *acque alte*, or high tide of November, that often flooded the red and white marble of the Piazza San Marco, seemed impossible. Somehow the rocking, lounging water seemed to croon with a humming readiness, a welcome for the press who were due to deplane tomorrow from their staging point of departure in New York. There had been almost no refusals from the two hundred invited guests. Everyone of major importance who wrote about the booming businesses of commercial real estate and travel in the American media was expected tomorrow, along with groups of Canadian and British journalists. Ben's researchers had discovered that when the French took vacations, rich or poor, they preferred to stay in France, and that the Italians, when they took cruises, did so on Italian-owned ships.

The travel agency with which Gigi had been working had made all the complicated arrangements to fly the press to Venice in first-class comfort. A fleet of four dozen *motoscafi*, with their sleek lines and shining decks, flying white and green flags, had been chartered for their entire visit. Their rooms would be waiting for them at the Gritti, the Danieli, and the Cipriani, filled with flowers, fruit, and buckets of iced champagne, mini-bars unlocked and fully stocked. A handsomely engraved and personalized letter of welcome from Ben Winthrop was placed on each night table, along with the schedule of events, guidebooks, and maps of Venice.

During their first full day the press was free to use the speed-
boats to visit Venice, Murano, the Lido, or Torcello, stopping
whenever they felt hungry at elaborate buffets that would operate
around the clock for the entire duration of the junket, in private
dining rooms set up at all of their three hotels. On the second day
of the junket, after lunch, they would be transported on specially
decorated *vaporetti* from their hotels to the railroad station at the
far end of the Grand Canal, where they would board buses for the
trip across the bridge to the mainland, and from there to Porta
Margera. Once inside the shipyard, more buses would take them
to the three rows of bleachers set up along the drydock itself,
where they would listen to a short speech that Ben would make,
explaining the exchange of coins, and then they'd watch Gigi
make the exchange itself, and see the plate rewelded into the hull
of the *Winthrop Emerald.*

On the trip home, the *vaporetti,* now illuminated with strings
of lights, carrying musicians and waiters with trays of drinks, would
return to the hotels in time for the journalists to dress for the ball
and dinner at the specially decorated Municipal Casino, the Palazzo Grimini, where there would be dancing and gambling until
the last member of the media felt like leaving. During the next two
days the press would be at liberty to enjoy themselves, as they had
been on the first day, with their return flights scheduled for the
morning of the fifth day.

"Three and three-quarter days of whatever pleases their fancy
in Venice, the fastest and most expensive transportation, food,
drink, and only one brief event plus a party to cover—if that
doesn't make them go home happy, what will?" Ben had asked
when Gigi had shown him her plans.

"They're blasé about being well-treated," Gigi worried. "I still
think you should have fifty gondolas available twenty-four hours a
day, flying a green and white flag, so they'd be able to tell which
ones were yours."

Ben had given a negative shake of his head. "It'd mean nego-
tiating for days with the gondoliers' union—even getting a job as
a gondolier means you have to be born to a gondolier in a direct
line going back generations—they're a hundred times worse than
the Teamsters. If members of the press want to take a gondola, let

442

them pay for it themselves, darling—after all, everything else is free."

"I know, but why stop at the gondolas? They represent Venice, they're identified with it as nothing else is."

"As far as I'm concerned, they're a rip-off, and I won't do business with them," he'd said stubbornly.

Gigi had sighed and dropped the matter. There was a blind side to Ben, a totally uncompromising attitude that allowed him to go light-years in any number of extravagant directions yet not bend the slightest in another. It was his way, as they said about Lee Iacocca—or was it Frank Sinatra?—or the highway.

Gigi no longer thought this quality was an example of the oddball, often amusing frugality of the very rich. Billy would have seen at once that visiting Venice on the cuff without free gondolas just . . . *missed*. Not enough to spoil the junket in any important way, but still enough to shadow the experience with a tiny degree of incompleteness. The price demanded by the gondoliers' union, no matter how unfair, wouldn't even be noticed in the vast total that Winthrop Development was spending on the whole elaborate affair.

Ben regulated his life by some system of his own that he lived by, with no exceptions, a system that continued to be an enigma to her. What, for instance, if she'd wanted to break his Rule of One on their first visit to Venice? What if she'd been in the mood to spend a whole afternoon looking at pictures—would he have dragged her bodily out of the Accademia while she begged piteously for just one more little Giorgione?

After the fistfight with Zach at her party, she and Ben, with cautious tact, had managed to tuck the episode away. He'd teased her that she'd dressed like a temptress and behaved like a prude; she'd responded that he was an exhibitionist who'd gotten the black eye that he deserved, and she'd pretended to have forgotten it. But she knew she was right to dislike being groped in public, and she was privately as exultant that Zach had so excessively overreacted in defending her as she was irritated by Ben's behavior.

Her problems with Ben, Gigi frowned, aside from the gondolas, all seemed to be about something relatively minor: his fixation —that was the only word for it—on her ass; that embarrassing night in the Vineyard; his insistence on buying the earrings she hadn't wanted; even their first kiss. He had a way of taking advantage of his position to assert himself, to take possession. *Complete possession.*

It wasn't selfishness in the ordinary sense of the word; it seemed to Gigi that nobody could be as generous, as wildly extravagant, as Ben was when he was in the mood. It was some other quality, some deep internal pattern, something she couldn't manage to give a name to, try as she had since their love affair started.

Granted, it had been wildly romantic, but would every woman have been thrilled to have been skyjacked to Venice, come to think of it? Probably. She was just being inordinately picky, Gigi reproached herself. A man's and a woman's ideas of romantic timing might easily not coincide. Most females would kill for someone who threw emeralds at them and swept them off to magic places and didn't mind showing their loving possessiveness, no matter where or when or who was watching.

The thing was that he didn't possess her. Not yet, anyway.

"I have this problem," Archie said to Byron, as they sat in a bar at two in the afternoon. "I can't decide if this is what it feels like to be drowned, to have slivers of bamboo stuck under my fingernails, or to be burned at the stake."

"Try to be betrayed, to be castrated, to be sodomized, *and* to be robbed at gunpoint of everything you own . . . yeah, I think it's more like that," Byron said, striving for conciseness.

"Are we losing perspective? Are we overreacting, By? After all, we still have our health, we still have our hair, we have our suits and our talent. All we've lost is the fruit of the hardest-working years in our prime of life and our reputations in the business."

"We knew we were taking a risk, Arch."

"You mean we *deserve* this?"

"No, just that it happens."

"Byron, if you get philosophical on me, if you say one mellow, shit-eating, rat-eyed word, I'm going to break every bone in your body with my own hands." Archie croaked with the lack of menace of someone who knew he had only enough strength to lift a glass to his lips.

444

"Gigi in Venice for God knows how long, Miss Vicky in Tokyo forever . . . how many accounts have we lost, Archie? I keep losing count."

"All three of our very own low-cal babies from Oak Hill Foods, Indigo Seas, Beach Casuals, and, now that we've heard from Spider Elliott in Paris, Scruples Two."

"You can't count Indigo Seas," Byron said fretfully. "We resigned them. And that's where the trouble started."

"No, the trouble started when we left Caldwell and Caldwell with that double-dealing ice-queen bitch-goddess, Victoria Frost," Archie pronounced his opinion in small, biting words.

"Should we have foreseen that she'd dash home to mummy and daddy the instant they asked her nicely, without even giving us a word of warning? Was that our big mistake?" Byron wondered.

"I don't know, but she was uncomfortable enough with it to telex from Japan. She didn't even have the guts to phone us before she left and talk to us, while we were trying to hunt up Gigi. At least Gigi had a reason—unprofessional as it was—for leaving, and she didn't take any accounts with her. You can't blame Elliott for pulling the plug when he'd been led to expect to get Gigi back . . . can't even blame that foxy grandpa, Harris Reeves . . . is this what they call white-collar crime?"

"I believe it's known as 'business as usual,' " Byron responded. "Also known as reality."

"In that case, I have an idea," Archie said, running his hands through his black curls and sitting up straighter. "We still have a group of semi-respectable accounts, plus, for the moment at least, The Enchanted Attic and the Winthrop Line. Why don't we go see the Russo boys and suggest a merger? Billy Elliott gave the Russos another chance at Scruples Two, and we'd bring new blood to the account—if we got together with them, we'd make a decent small agency. They're good steady guys, just not as hot as we are—as we were—but then who is? Or should I say *was*?"

"Hmmm. Russo, Russo, Rourke and Bernheim . . . no, I don't like the sound of that," Byron said peevishly.

"If we could make it Russo, Rourke, Russo and Bernheim, would you like it better?"

"I think I could begin to consider Russo, Bernheim, Russo and Rourke. I think I could swallow my pride to that point,"

Byron answered. "At least we don't have to work with Miss Vicky anymore."

"Toss you for who gets to make the phone call," Archie said.

"I'm only a great art director, Arch, you're fair with words, or so they say. You make the call. And wake me when it's settled," Byron said, signaling the waiter. "Another bottle of Evian, please, we're going to hell with ourselves."

The magnificent weather held as the press arrived and checked into their rooms. The next day they disappeared into Venice, drifting invariably into the Piazza San Marco before lunch, after lunch, and during the afternoon.

Gigi had put together a group of the yellow wicker tables at Florian's and surrounded them with chairs. While Ben worked all day with Renzo Montegardini, planning how to speed up the re-fitment of the *Emerald*, she sat at Florian's, accompanied by the entire public-relations department of Winthrop Development. Sooner or later their journalist guests would come by to sit down, say hello, order tea, coffee, mineral water, and every kind of sweet cake, some of them perfectly content not to leave, until their informal party grew until it almost filled the ranks of the outdoor tables of the large café.

One particular business reporter, a *Boston Globe* business writer on the verge of retirement, known as Branch T. Branch, took a particular liking to Gigi, whom he took to be a junior member of the PR department. Diminutive, almost fleshless, and deeply wrinkled, the reporter wore a thin wool shirt, a heavy sweater, and a battered tweed hat, even though the day was fairly hot and the sun was high.

"You can't be too careful here," he told Gigi in his low, confidential rasp. "Know the place well, love it, but wouldn't go out without a sweater for anything in the world. Caught a terrible cold here one beautiful July day, waiting for a *vaporetto*—a breeze off the water, another chill coming up from the canal, three minutes' wait, that's all it took, hung on for weeks. Miasma, my dear, miasma. Death in Venice, that's no joke, happens all the time to tourists. These canals are full of things you don't want to think about. At night, on a dark bridge, don't look behind you, walk briskly, that's my advice. Very little crime here, mostly pickpockets, but lots of ghosts, more than make up for criminals. The real Venetian—a dying breed, only eighty thousand of them left, you know—will tell you that if you're not born here, it's courting your death to stay longer than two weeks. And don't ever get sick in Venice, that's my advice. The doctors here come from the school of cupping and leeches. Got stung by a bee here once, had an allergic reaction, leg blew up three times its size, doctor told me it was impossible because Venice doesn't have any gardens, so how could there be bees? Damn place has hundreds of little window gardens, and what about the flower market at the Rialto, eh?"

"Where are you staying, Mr. Branch?"

"Branchie, call me Branchie. I'm at the Gritti. Don't think I'll take that trip to see that keel ceremony, hate to miss young Winthrop's speech, doing a book on the Winthrops, you know, but why risk coming back by night? Much too cold, much too long a trip for my taste, you should have held it in a more civilized location, that's my advice. Mestre, of all places. Plague center, Mestre."

"But the ship can't be moved out of drydock. Oh, dear, I don't want you to miss it," Gigi cried, feeling the *Boston Globe* coverage slipping away. "If I come to pick you up at the hotel, will you go out on the *vaporetto* with me? It'll be perfectly warm at that time of day. Coming back, I'll arrange a special *motoscafo* at the railroad station just for you. You can sit inside the cabin and close the doors. You'll be perfectly snug, and you'll get back long before the others."

"Good of you. Take you up on it, yes, thanks."

"What's your book on the Winthrops?" Gigi asked curiously.

"Historical study, not your kind of thing, my dear. Been working on it for years. Sort of a hobby with me. Young Winthrop, now he's interesting, he's why I came on this jaunt, normally would have sent my assistant, but young Winthrop, he's blazing his own trail, fascinating business story there, he could have been a Venetian, a merchant prince of the old school."

"I think he would have liked to be," Gigi said, smiling at the fancy. "Is the book finished?"

"Years to go," Branchie said waving a tiny hand. "Retirement project, keeps me young, no illusions on need to publish. Too many books in print already, that's my advice to myself, but I keep my ear to the ground, know what's going on. That's for sure. Keep it to myself, my own material, pride myself on that."

"I'll be at the Gritti tomorrow, Branchie," Gigi promised him, "and I guarantee you won't catch the plague in Mestre."

Later, as Gigi and Ben took Sasha and Vito to La Madonna, an authentically bustling, non-tourist fish restaurant, for dinner, she told him about her special arrangements for Branchie.

"I'm delighted that you talked him into it," Ben said. "The man knows everybody, and he's a force at the paper, he has more influence than you'd imagine to meet him. He enjoys making himself out to be more of an eccentric than he really is, but he's written detailed stories about everything I've done, starting with my first mall. Sometimes I think he knows more about my business than I do. Branchie the Branch, my favorite biographer and hypochondriac—did he tell you about the time he caught his death of cold?"

"Yes, indeed. And the bee sting."

"He held both of them against Venice for years. He carried on a personal vendetta against the city in print, believe it or not, as if they cared, but eventually he couldn't resist coming back. He'll probably wear an overcoat and a couple of scarves tomorrow, so don't laugh when you see him. Actually, it makes perfect sense for you to pick him up, since I'll be out at the shipyard checking the bleachers and the sound system a couple of hours before the press arrives."

"Don't you have PR people for that?" Vito asked.

"A dozen of them. But I like to make sure for myself. I hate surprises."

"I know exactly how you feel. Surprises, even good ones, make producers unhappy, unless they're the reason for them."

"Is this sort of a dry run for the christening of the ship next year?" Sasha asked.

"Very much so," Ben agreed, smiling thoughtfully at the clear picture of that day in the future. "Only next year there will be at least five times as many people; all the local dignitaries, the diplomatic community, visiting celebrities, the crew, the families of all the workmen, everything but a marching band, and there's no reason we can't have that too, from the Mestre high school. The refitting of the two other ships should be well under way by then."

"What are are you going to name them?" Sasha wondered. "The *Diamond*, the *Sapphire?*"

"I may not use the jewel theme again," Ben answered her, "although it's memorable. How about the *Winthrop Gigi* or just the *Graziella Giovanna*? Would you like that, darling?"

Gigi shook her head vaguely, evading the question. "Branchie told me he thinks you could have been a Venetian."

"Does he? All things considered, knowing how the man feels about Venice, it's hard to tell if that's a knock or a compliment. And with Branchie, it's always a toss-up. He knows more than he chooses to say."

The next day Gigi dressed in tennis shoes, black jeans, a black turtleneck, and a black velvet blazer. It wasn't her idea of suitably casual drydock apparel, but Ben had asked her to wear the emerald earrings during the ceremony itself, for good luck, and she couldn't think of anything informal except all black that wouldn't make the addition of enormous emerald drops set in diamonds look plain silly. The earrings and the silver dollar were tucked securely into an inside pocket of her shoulder bag, since Ben hadn't wanted to worry about carrying them around on his inspection tour of the dry dock.

"Sensible girl, wore a warm sweater, warm jacket, took my advice," Branchie noted approvingly as he greeted her.

The Gritti-based journalists were crowded around the tables on the large floating platform, surrounded by ornamental wood railings and decorated with pots of pink geraniums, that lies in front of the Gritti Palace Hotel. The most expensive lunch in Venice is served at this unique restaurant right on top of the Grand Canal, with its striped awning and obliging headwaiters. In the middle of the platform, an aisle leads from the front door of the Gritti to a narrow bridge that descends to a smaller floating landing stage for boats of all kinds. The alfresco entertainment consists of watching the water traffic at close range, with the added bonus of seeing travel-weary arrivals, followed by porters carrying their baggage, make their way through the elegant restaurant, either looking around in bewilderment at the unexpected crowd, or show-ing their familiarity with the process by whisking by as uncon-cernedly as if no one were scrutinizing them.

The special *vaporetto* arrived at the Gritti dock, to a chorus of mock cheering. Almost all of the press would rather have stayed in Venice for the afternoon, but they knew the rules of the junket game, and were cynically resigned to their expected attendance at the ceremony. There was a rush for the best seats in the bow of the *vaporetto*, from which the view was incomparable.

Gigi and Branchie watched the outside deck of the ferryboat fill without impatience, since Branchie had declared his intention of sitting inside, where there would be plenty of room and no drafts. Gigi saw her father and Sasha, both unsmiling in the crush, motioning urgently at her to join them, but she wasn't able to leave Branchie's side, as they were carried along onto the ferry.

Finally the mob thinned and Branchie, followed by Gigi, made his way across the short bridge onto the floating landing stage. Just as he was about to grasp the hand of the crewman who stood at the open railing of the *vaporetto* to help people on board, a sudden movement in the waters of the canal caused the landing stage to lurch and the large ferry to swing slightly sideways, leaving a three-foot gap between dock and boat.

A man with longer legs, a man with better reflexes, a man who didn't obsess about things that were buried in the waters of the Grand Canal, could probably have made the muscular adjustment necessary to leap safely onto the deck.

Branchie did not. He missed the boatman's hand and fell neatly into the canal, his mufflers floating on the surface, while the water closed over his head.

Within seconds the journalist was pulled out of the Grand Canal by Gritti porters while crewmen held the *vaporetto* safely away from the landing stage with long hooks provided for that precise purpose.

"HEPATITIS!" he sputtered as he regained the Gritti, wip-ing his face with the nearest tablecloth, and drying his hair as quickly as he could. "Hepatitis minimum, pleurisy, pneumonia, double pneumonia, nephritis, damn this place, double hell, double hepatitis, A and B, I'll be lucky to get home alive . . . Kate Hep-burn fell into the canal doing a movie, never the same . . . sue the place, sue Ben Winthrop, stupid idea . . . leaving this plague spot as soon as I get dry . . ."

"Branchie, Branchie, drink some brandy," Gigi begged, dancing around him in worry as the *vaporetto* slowly pulled away, bearing Sasha and Vito and a full load of press.

"Drink! *Do you want to kill me?* I shut my mouth tight when I went in, hair's still dripping filthy pig slop into my face, dead cats, dead rats, raw sewage, need good shower, disinfectant, that's the first thing to do! Come on, help me to my room. Call the manager, get antibiotics!" Waving his tiny arms, followed by a trail of Gritti porters and two concierges, Gigi and Branchie regained his room.

Within half an hour Branchie was in bed, thrice scrubbed from head to toe and back again, dried, stuffed full of an assortment of antibiotics and a couple of stiff shots of neat scotch.

"Oh, Branchie, I'll never forgive myself," Gigi cried, full of remorse. "It's all my fault."

"Hell it is, young Winthrop's fault, that drydock ceremony, I said it was a stupid idea in the first place, vainglorious, that's what it is. Hubris. Silver dollar, my ass. Here, give me some more scotch. No ice, for God's sake, ice kills you, made from local water. Alcohol might kill the germs if it gets to them soon enough, so they say, doubt it, worth a try."

Gigi poured him half of a water glass full of scotch and watched anxiously as he swallowed most of it.

"Do you feel any better?" she asked.

"*If* I wake up tomorrow, I'll find out. Another of Winthrop's victims, that's what I am," Branchie said malevolently, "like the Mullers. Should never have come, didn't take my own advice."

Branchie was obviously not going to be a happy drunk, Gigi thought, calculating her chances of getting to the railroad station by speedboat before the *vaporetto*. She still had plenty of time, for the trip down the Grand Canal had been planned to be slow and stately and gala. What did he mean, 'victims,' she thought, adjusting his pillows.

"You know about the Mullers?" Branchie challenged her, slurring his words. "Bet you don't, think you do, but I bet you don't. Nobody does but Mullers and me." He pulled the blankets up to his chin and glared at Gigi.

She looked down at him, giving him challenge for challenge.

"The people who owned Kids' Paradise? I most certainly do. I work with their representative, Jack Taylor."

"He tell you that?" Branchie shot back in a bellicose voice, rising up from the pillows.

"Who? Jack? Tell me what?"

"That he represented the Mullers? Bet he told you they still owned a piece of the business, eh? And you believed him? Hah! Another of Winthrop's victims, that's what you are. Bought the party line, eh, like everyone else? Bet you anything you never met a Muller face to face, my dear. Eh? Am I right?"

"So what if I haven't?" Gigi demanded, "They've all gone to live in Sarasota. What difference does it make? Jack represents the family, and I ought to know since The Enchanted Attic was my idea. I've been working with Jack since then."

"Good idea too. Smart girl, good marketing. Winthrop took over every last store, foreclosed, tough luck for Mullers. Lost everything. Bankrupt. Living in Sarasota because they owned vacation house free and clear, not by choice, believe me. He's a vulture, young Winthrop, picked their bones clean, think I'm going to sneeze."

Gigi hastily threw him a box of tissues. "Ben *foreclosed*? That's nonsense! He *saved* their company."

Branchie grinned at her nastily. "Don't believe me, my dear, why should you? Jack Taylor takes orders from Ben Winthrop, gets paid by him, company man, hundred percent. Normal, don't blame Taylor, doing good job. But Mullers built their business from nothing, Winthrop's first tenants, paid him good rents for fifteen years, he could have left them a tiny slice of pie, that's my opinion. Enough for everybody, but not Winthrop's style to share, he forced them to go bust, their problem, not his. Strictly business, typical Ben Winthrop style. Mullers were victims, can't say they weren't, can you now, eh?"

Gigi felt a thickening of the atmosphere in the room, as if it were getting darker inside but not outside, as if the air, like gas, could be ignited with a spark of electricity.

"Victims?" she repeated, sickened as she made herself say the word again. "Your book's gone to your brain, Branchie. I've never heard anyone say anything against Ben's ethics."

"He covers his tracks. People can't talk about things they

never heard of. 'Successful and fortunate crime is called virtue,' Seneca wrote that, nothing's changed. Worse today. Young Winthrop's my special interest, I'm world's expert on him. Only expert, too. Hah! I keep my ear to ground, watch whatever he does. Follow up, ask questions, get the material. He's the vulture, I'm hawk. Got lines out everywhere, but nobody understands Winthrop like me. Wait till my book's published, you'll see. He's done dozens of tricky land deals, county officials bought off . . . Cleveland, Des Moines, Fort Worth, corruption you'd never imagine, my dear, quick, smooth, almost untraceable unless you know where to look, who to talk to. He's smart, runs tight ship, but I've been on to him from beginning. I know dirty truth, and when I write my book, so will everyone else. He's done it before, he'll do it again. Over and over. When my book exposes him, everybody'll know. Until then I keep his secrets, it's my material, nobody else has it, Ben Winthrop's my beat. Shouldn't be talking to you. Take the Severinis, for instance—give me that glass, my dear, believe this stuff's working."

"What about the Severinis?"

"The same story. Lost their company because of this new cruise line. Other journalists here, do they know that? Of course not. Small family company, the Severinis, nobody gives a damn outside of locals, my dear. And me. Good example of Winthrop's style. They were in trouble anyway. He picked up those engines for what it cost to make them minus giant discount for cash. Last straw for Severinis. Excellent bargain for him, should have been a Venetian himself. Merchant princes they were, never lost a bean. Wasted no time on mercy."

"The engines . . . in Trieste?" Gigi breathed.

"Know a lot for a PR girl, don't you?"

"No, I don't know much . . . I just heard someone mention something about engines from Trieste," Gigi said, probing further, her blood thundering in her ears.

"Three of them, custom-built, Severinis couldn't give them away, don't go into shipbuilding, that's my advice. They took a risk, bad timing, young Winthrop picked them up for much less than cost, Swiss lucky to get anything. Hah! Even the Swiss lost out there. Still, fifty percent of something better than hundred percent of nothing. Severinis had to close down. Finished. Bones picked clean, like Mullers. Old company too, established hundreds of years, employed lots of people. He never gave them a chance. If Winthrop paid honest price, the Severinis might have kept their heads above water, not easy in Venice. Hah! Look at me, half-drowned, hepatitis B. My last visit here, my dear, I've taken the pledge. If I live."

"But . . . but . . . why wouldn't Ben pay full price?" Gigi whispered urgently.

"Told you before. Not Winthrop's style. He's a vulture. Not satisfied until the other guy's finished. Way he does business. Show no mercy. Vulture does what a vulture does. It's his nature, his style, for him it's normal. Never shares a scrap, not a scrap of a scrap. How does any man start with borrowed money and become almost a billionaire in fifteen, sixteen years? It's why he's interesting . . . not like the good gray Winthrops of today. More of an old-style Venetian, maybe even a Borgia. Good for my book. Close the curtains, my dear, I'm going to sleep. Don't worry, I'll cover story, say nice things, not your fault, should never have come to Venice. Remember . . . 'successful crime . . . called . . . virtue' . . . You're not too young to learn . . . useful fact . . ."

By the time Gigi's *motoscafo* brought her to the railroad station, she'd missed all the press buses. She hailed a taxi, bribed the driver to break every law, and found herself entering the shipyard just as the last of the journalists straggled through the gates. She leapt onto the last bus to the drydock and stood on the edge of the bleachers that had been set up above the wide area, the size of three football fields, that was dug down more than a hundred feet into the surface of the shipyard so that its gates could be raised slowly into the sea to allow the ships to float. All three freighters lay there, one of them totally covered in scaffolding.

From the minute she'd run out of Branchie's room, Gigi had accepted the truth about Ben Winthrop. She had finally identified the pattern that had puzzled her for so long, a pattern of which she had seen only fleeting glimpses, hints, edges of edges, shadows on the water, as thin, yet as disconcerting, as the first wisp of a dense fog.

She could easily have cut Branchie short as soon as he mentioned the Mullers; she could have shaken her head at his drunken garrulousness, deafened herself to his self-appointed authority, and left him to recover from his imaginary hepatitis with his scotch and his blankets. However, she had been physically unable to leave the room. She had felt an overpowering need to learn what he knew. She'd encouraged him to spill out details in spite of her ever-increasing revulsion. Even if Ben himself hadn't authenticated Branchie, she still would have known that the facts he'd shot at her were as real as they were befouling. They fit too well with everything that had bothered her about Ben Winthrop.

If she had been truly in love with Ben, she would never have encouraged Branchie, she wouldn't have stayed there gathering information until he fell asleep, she would have brushed him off, become instantly, self-protectively, and willfully deaf to criticism of the beloved, as so many women manage to be about the men they love, and by now Branchie would be forgotten, a small-time hobbyist historian who, by his own admission, would probably never see his unpublishable book in print. A drunk, obsessed, bitter man who envied Ben and should be discounted totally.

Gigi looked around for Vito. She needed to talk to him as never before, although she should be at the base of the drydock, standing on the platform that had been set up for the welder, who was busy with his torch, observed by the other members of the official party: Ben, Erik Hansen, the head of the management team, Renzo Montegardini, the naval architect, Eustace Jones, the hotel manager, Arnsin Olsen, the chief engineer, Per Dahl, the captain, and another man, whom Ben had told her would be the mayor of Mestre. They were surrounded by a large group of press photographers from news services and magazines.

To hell with where she should be. If they were in a hurry to put an American coin in that plate, let someone empty his pockets and find one.

Gigi scanned the crowd. As she did so, she saw Vito and Sasha running toward her.

"Jesus, where've you been?" Sasha gasped.

"It's complicated, it's about Ben, listen—"

"I couldn't believe it when you missed the ferry," Vito said rapidly, taking her by the arms so hard that it hurt. "Gigi, I don't know how far things have gone with you and Winthrop, but there's something I must tell you—I know you're in a rush, but you should know—Zach called just before we left the hotel—"

"What's he done to Zach?" Gigi cried.

"Sometime after the fight at your house, Winthrop had lunch with our loan officer at the bank, he informed him that Zach has a serious cocaine problem, he said that Zach was stoned to the gills when he attacked him without any provocation, and that Zach was zonked during the whole shoot of *Long Weekend*—naturally, the bank called the studio, all hell broke loose—the studio called Zach's agent, the agent called Zach. Zach was probably the last to know, except me."

"I'll kill him!" Sasha raged. "I'll kill him!"

"You won't have to," Gigi said, turning on her heel and heading for the elevator that had been rigged to go from the top to the bottom of the drydock.

As she stalked toward the platform next to the ship, she could see Ben's furious impatience written in his face. Gigi reached the platform and mounted the steps.

"What the hell kept you?" Ben asked roughly, in a low voice so that the others wouldn't hear. "I waited as long as I could. The press is getting restless. Damn it, I thought I was going to have to start without you."

"Go on, make your speech."

"Have you got the silver dollar? The earrings?"

"Yes."

"Put them on."

"Make your speech."

"Not till you put them on."

"Then don't speak. It's up to you."

"Shit! This is no time to be temperamental! Can't you see everybody's waiting?"

"Speak, if you plan to."

Ben turned away from her unrelenting face, picked up the microphone, and delivered the three-minute speech he'd rewritten ten times until it was perfectly smooth, graceful, and full of international compliments, explaining the reason for the replacement of the Italian coin with the American silver dollar, and proclaiming that the refitment of the *Winthrop Emerald*, the first ship of the Winthrop Line, would officially begin as soon as the coins were exchanged.

The welder raised his mask, took the plate he had just removed from the keel, and held it in front of Gigi with a gallant gesture and a smile.

She removed the Italian coin and passed it to Ben. Then she reached into the pocket of her blazer and took out the silver dollar.

"Here is the American silver dollar," Gigi said, taking the microphone from Ben and speaking directly into it. She held the coin up between two fingers so that all the photographers could get a good picture. "As long as it remains in the keel of this ship, this ship is safe from harm." She gave the coin to Ben, who carefully put it into the metal container that was set into the plate.

Again Gigi reached into her pocket, and brought out an emerald earring. She held it high, turning slowly, dangling it from its clip so that everyone could see its clear deep flash, a fragment of extraordinary color in the gray scene of the drydock.

"Here is an emerald. As long as it remains in the keel of this ship, the ship is safe from harm. This emerald is for the Mullers." As Ben watched, frozen by surprise and the presence of the spectators, she placed the earring in the container, reached quickly into her pocket again, and held up the second huge, brilliant earring, rotating it in the flashes of the cameras and in front of the people in the bleachers. "Here is another emerald. As long as it remains in the keel of this ship, this ship is safe from harm. This emerald is for the Severinis." As she placed it in the container, flashbulbs popped all around her and a questioning, curious, buzzing murmur rose from the press as hundreds of journalists asked each other who were the Mullers, who were the Severinis?

"Weld the plate into the keel," Gigi instructed the welder, still using the microphone, as the men around her stood unable to move or speak or react, aware of the hundreds of pairs of eyes on them, eyes of reporters, eyes of photographers. They all watched in disbelief as the brief operation took place and the plate containing the silver dollar and the emeralds was welded into the body of the keel.

"This," Gigi said into the microphone, holding up her hand again, as a silence fell so that everyone could hear her. "This is what a liar and a thief gets when he commits slander. This is for Zach Nevsky." She turned to Ben Winthrop and hit him in the face with every bit of force in her body.

For a brief minute, during which not a sound was heard, Gigi looked full into Ben's eyes. Only after he had looked down to escape the blast of her brutal scorn did she leave the platform and walk across the floor of the drydock and into the elevator that took her back to the top.

"Something tells me it's time to go," Gigi said to Vito and Sasha, who grabbed her as she stepped off the elevator. "Even though the party's just beginning."

21

In the middle of an early-
November afternoon, Zach Nevsky chose to sit in absolute isolation in the front row of the projection room for the screening of
the editor's assembly of *Long Weekend*. This was the first time he
would see his work in one piece, as rough as film could get, put
together from the takes he'd chosen, without sound effects or
music. No matter how raw the assembly was, it contained the
essential material that would become the finished film.

Two minutes after the lights had gone down and the film had
started, the door at the back of the theater opened soundlessly and
Vito Orsini looked in. He nodded at the only other person in the
room, the editor, sitting in the last row where he could communicate with the projectionist. The editor nodded back, in observation
of the etiquette of the screening room, which demands utter silence, and turned his attention back to the screen. A few minutes

later he noticed that Vito was gone, but that a small female figure was sitting in the last seat in the last row on the other side of the room. Incuriously he decided that if the producer had brought her in, she had a right to remain there, and he immediately forgot her existence.

More than two hours later the rough assembly ended and the lights were turned on. Zach got up, trying to stretch some of the tenseness out of his body, and called to the editor, "Thanks, Ed. Well, we've got a lot of work to do. So what else is new? I'll see you tomorrow, bright and early."

The editor left quickly, and for a few minutes Zach paced back and forth in front of the blank screen, deep in thought about what he would do in the editing room, how he would change the pacing of scenes, second by second, often frame by frame, until the picture flowed as he intended it to. Editing was crucial, the pure, delicate, and original work of shaping the finished version toward which he had been aiming throughout the shooting of the picture. Finally, still lost in abstraction, he started up the steps to the door to the theater. As he reached the door, he jumped at the sound of a muffled sob.

"What the hell?" He looked around and spotted Gigi trying to hide behind a crumpled Kleenex, sitting in the inconspicuous seat she had been occupying since the beginning of the screening.

"*You?* Hi, slugger, was it really that bad?"

"Oh," Gigi spoke tremulously through her tears. "It's . . . so silly . . . but I always cry . . . at happy endings."

"Did anything make you smile?"

"That was the hardest part, not laughing out loud, so you wouldn't know I was here. Oh, Zach, all those real people with raging egos, who didn't understand each other at all, blundering around and getting it all wrong before they got it right—they were funny and sad and mean and generous and cynical and innocent— so miserably, wonderfully *human*—and yet it's romantic, so unexpectedly romantic . . . how did you do it?"

"Did I really do it?"

"You *must* know you did," Gigi declared.

"Well . . . let's say that I have the tiniest little glimmer of hope that after I spend a couple of months beating this thing into

460

shape, maybe, just maybe, it'll turn out to be ever so slightly better than I expected." As he spoke, Zach knocked steadily on the wooden armrest of one of the seats.

"Still superstitious, I see," Gigi commented in a scoffing tone, giving her armrest a little rap. Just in case.

"How many Kleenexes did you use?"

Gigi groped around in her lap. "Eight, no . . . nine, counting the last one. But there were three different happy endings," she said reprovingly, "so it only counts for three apiece. I'm not a fountain."

"Oh, you noticed all three, did you? And I thought I'd managed to sneak at least one of them in. Nine, huh? That's something I can probably double in the editing. Maybe . . . just maybe . . . it'll turn out to be a date movie."

"You mean where the girl decides what they're going to see?"

"Right. Of course, you're not the average focus group. Perhaps you just cry easily."

"Don't you remember better than that?" Her gently questioning tone was magically complicated. Many things could have been read into it: nostalgia, reproach, wistfulness, teasing indifference.

"Okay, you don't cry easily," Zach said hastily, afraid to interpret anything she said. "Or rather, you didn't. You could have changed since you've started punching out guys all over the front pages."

"Once, don't exaggerate," Gigi said primly, still thrilled by memory of the physical strength that she hadn't realized she possessed.

"You're lucky that gent didn't hit you back. Of course, it would have made him look even worse, if possible, than he looks now, thanks to those photographers and reporters. Gigi, you saved my reputation, and I still haven't thanked you properly."

"I did get your letter."

"Certain kinds of gratitude can't be covered by the best letter ever written. Thank you, Gigi. You were a . . . total wonder."

"You're welcome. Any time. Tell me, Zach, if I hit you, what would you do?" Gigi asked irrepressibly, putting her wad of Kleenexes into her handbag.

"Hold you down and tickle your ears."

"You know too much," Gigi muttered, blushing. Only Zach knew under what particular circumstances she peed in her pants.

"I think it's cute. Don't worry, I'd never tell anybody. Hey, how about a pizza? Doesn't a possible date movie call for a real pizza?"

"I could eat two. After a bad movie I have to have a chocolate soda, after a good movie I yearn for a pizza, I don't know why, but it never fails. It must be something in my blood chemistry. Maybe I should become a professional movie critic?"

"You'd gain a ton. Let's get out of here."

Zach automatically ordered the pizza with extra pepperoni, extra cheese, extra sauce, and triple anchovies, no green pepper, black olives on the side, two beers. Gigi listened demurely, thinking that some things are never forgotten, pizza preferences high among them.

When it arrived, he carefully completed the imperfect separation of the slices with a knife and handed her a slice, presenting her with its outside edge. Gigi folded the sides of the slice together, took two medium-sized bites out of the inside point, and handed it back to Zach, who ate the rest of it, first giving her another slice. They were so hungry that, except for groans of satisfaction, they didn't speak until they'd finished the pizza and ordered another. Halfway through the second pizza, Gigi stopped.

"I don't think I can eat any more. My mouth wants to but my stomach can't."

"Come on, how can you be finished already? Points, what are points? Now, edges fill you up, they're nourishing, but points . . . there's nothing to them."

She was so small, he fretted, she looked too thin, she needed fattening up. All her mascara had disappeared during the screening and she looked so young—it was criminal to run around looking less than sixteen when you were so adorable that no man could look at you without indecent thoughts. He should speak strictly to her about that, but he didn't dare. She took poorly to criticism, he knew that only too well.

"The points are the juiciest part, that's where all the good stuff clumps up," Gigi explained patiently.

"You never appreciated the edges," Zach said, shaking his head in disapproval.

"You never appreciated the points," Gigi retorted.

"You never even *tried* to like the edges," Zach insisted.

"I refuse to argue with you about something that gets me what I want," Gigi said, "and gets you what you want."

"Okay, but you're wrong," Zach said stubbornly.

"Right."

"Right? You mean you agree that you're wrong?" Zach asked in disbelief.

"No, I don't agree, I just don't think it's worth having this particular discussion ever again." Gigi's eyes were alight with a special kind of mischief that no one who knew her could see without a sinking feeling. Zach, still eating, missed it.

"That leaves us with a big problem," Zach said reluctantly, as he finished the pizza and realized that Gigi hadn't added a single word to her last sentence. "What else are we going to talk about?"

"I was hoping you'd make that decision." Gigi sat back in the booth and folded her arms. The corners of her lips tilted upward in a tiny smile that seemed to promise danger rather than merriment. Her cheeks were flushed in the oval of her face, but her eyelids were now lowered decorously over the cooking-apple-green of her eyes.

"Very clever," he told her. "Low cunning, you gave up on the eternal points-versus-edges debate. And I fell for it."

"Well?" Gigi was gently relentless.

"I don't know," Zach confessed, realizing that for one of the few times in his life he found himself without a ready point of view, an instant attitude, a fully formed judgment about what should happen next.

"Don't you agree that we should talk?" Gigi asked in a small voice that managed to be simultaneously mocking and sweet, with a tart sweetness that left him needing to hear it again so that he could analyze why it was so strangely sweet, why it broke his heart and mended it again, in a breath.

"Of course we should talk. How'd you get into the screening, anyway?"

"My father. Is that what we're going to talk about?"

"Why did you come?"

"Idle curiosity?"

"Nobody sits through over two hours of an editor's rough assembly out of idle curiosity. Nobody sane."

"You're right," Gigi admitted without false hesitation.

"So?"

"I could have been killing time. I could have wanted to sit in the dark and laugh and cry without making any noise so that I almost choked to death. I could have wanted to see you again . . ." She fell silent, considering the infinity of possibilities that could have brought her to the screening room.

"Killing time?" Zach inquired quickly before she found any more reasons.

"No."

"Sitting in the dark?" he forced himself to ask, praying that she hadn't developed a new passion for invisible weeping.

Gigi considered his question thoroughly. Finally, in an indecisive, almost contemplative way, she said, "No, not that, I don't think so, not exactly, anyway."

"The last . . . the last thing you said?"

"I suppose it . . . might possibly . . . have been . . ."

"You wanted to see me." He kept any inflection out of his voice.

"Logic would indicate that, yes."

"How come?" Zach inquired with the utmost he could manage in nonchalance.

"Didn't you want to see me?" Gigi asked.

"You know God damned well I did!"

"Why?" Gigi asked again, all flaming inquiry.

"Because I adore you," he exploded. "Because I worship the ground you walk on, because I'd go through walls of fire for you, because I'd climb mountains of ice for you, because I'd swim oceans for you—because I love you insanely, not that you don't know that! Boy, you're tough!"

"Am I?" Gigi wondered. "I suppose I am, when I'm provoked, but you haven't provoked me recently, have you?"

464

"Recently enough," Zach said roughly.

"Maybe," she said slowly, as if she were inventing each word as she went along. "Maybe—although it's just about impossible to see how it could happen, all things considered, with so many things we don't see eye-to-eye on—maybe I had some . . . silly . . . idea that we could make up our—"

"Gigi, darling—" He moved quickly, trying to extricate himself from his side of the booth and get over to where she sat delicately picking his brain apart and kiss her into seeing reason.

"Stay right there, Zach Nevsky! Keep a table between us," Gigi said in a voice that stopped him immediately. "We've got to lay down some rules or the same thing will happen all over again, and I couldn't go through that twice."

"Gigi, I'm different! This last year I've gone through such unbelievable hell—there's no way I could be the same person I used to be. I've gone over and over the things I did wrong, the way I tried to ride all over you, the terrible things I said—you *can't* believe that I'm incapable of changing!"

"Not incapable . . . no, but fundamentally you're always going to be in love with your work, there'll always be a conflict between it and me. Isn't that the way it is?"

Zach uttered a deep, reluctant sound between a groan and a sigh. He'd do anything within reason, anything beyond reason, to be with Gigi forever, but he wouldn't lie.

"If that's the sticking point," he admitted painfully, "we can't get around it. Without my work, I can't imagine what I'd be. *I am my work.* It's half the joy and meaning in my life. But, Gigi, you're the other half, you're *all* the other half."

Gigi's entire being, her whole mind and her heart, were concentrated on Zach, on his singleminded devotion to his art of directing. Here was a man, she thought, who was largely defined by his talents, a man born to take words off the paper they were written on and turn them into a form of reality that could move audiences; here was a man who believed totally in his power to illuminate and animate the vision of playwrights and scriptwriters, a man who had proven his abilities; a man who would always need to use his gifts. She had come to terms with Zach's identification with his work.

"A man who doesn't care intensely what he does could never

interest me," Gigi said slowly, choosing her words with care. "But, Zach, you can't be so centered on your needs that you don't realize that what I do is exactly as important to me as what you do is to you."

"I do! I would—"

"*Wait.* Don't answer too quickly, Zach. I know that you'd make a valiant attempt to value my work if I made a lot of money at what I did, if I were a success in the eyes of the world. But what if I decided to go to college—I never have, you know—or learn Italian or . . . oh, make my own pickles or play the piano or hybridize roses—what if that was how I wanted to spend my time? How much would you value what I did then?"

"I've had a whole endless year to ask myself exactly those questions. You were right when you called me a liar and a hypocrite when I promised that I'd take your job seriously—I couldn't possibly have given you more than lip service. All I could see was that advertising took you away from me, and I tried to make it sound like something no intelligent person could possibly want to do. That was *contemptible.*"

"It truly was."

He looked at her unflinchingly. "Whatever you choose to do with your life will be as meaningful to me as directing a film. I promise you that with all my heart."

"Then that's one problem settled. One of several." Gigi paused to see what he'd say next.

"Gigi, I could shoot myself for forcing myself on you and then . . . saying that you were asking for rape, that all you wanted was to get my attention."

"That really stank. Even Ben Winthrop wouldn't sink that low."

"I can't say I didn't mean it at the time," Zach said, determined to be honest, "only that I didn't mean it a hundred percent."

"What exact percent did you mean it?" she asked with disarmingly wicked interest.

"Too much. Even one-tenth of one percent was too much. How can I ever apologize?" he beseeched her.

"Forget it, you can't. Just—don't shoot yourself."

466

"Gigi, I know I'm controlling, I'm manipulative, I'm over-bearing, and I'm relentless about getting results."

"You know all that? No kidding? Still . . . you're not *all* bad."

"I'm not?"

"You know yourself a lot better than you used to," Gigi said gravely.

"A year of missing you almost twenty-four hours a day gave me a lot of time to think."

"Why 'almost'?" Gigi demanded.

"Sometimes I fell asleep—after I'd watched *The Way We Were.*"

"*The Way We Were?* Good Lord, I haven't seen that in years," Gigi said in amazement. "Zach, do you think that you'll ever stop being controlling and all those other things?" Gigi asked quietly.

"Not . . . not basically. That's what I am, that's my charac-ter, it's all part of a piece. If I weren't sure of my point of view and didn't need to make it prevail, I'd be doing something different, instead of directing movies. Maybe we'd both be making pickles, maybe we'd build a huge pickle empire together."

"Not bloody likely."

"Yeah, that's going too far. But I promise you one thing absolutely. I will *not* behave like a director when I'm with you."

"Do you truly believe you could be in charge of the universe on the set and then come home and switch all that off?"

"That's exactly what I mean," he said soberly. "I *know* I could. You're not an actor. I'll never again try to talk you into living the way I want you to live. *You own your life.* It's as meaning-ful and important to you as mine is to me. I won't make that mistake again."

Gigi nodded soberly at his words. She could tell how deeply he meant them. "But," she asked intently, "what about all those location trips that take you away for more than half the year?"

"I'd cut down. I can pick and choose my jobs now—so I'd simply stay close to home."

"Or . . . I could come with you, once in a while. We could . . . oh, God . . . we could *compromise*," Gigi sighed, hating to use the horrible word, but realizing it was only fair.

"Compromise?" Zach asked, startled. "You'd really be willing to compromise?"

"Not all the time," Gigi amended hastily, "far from it, but I wouldn't want you to turn down a truly wonderful script you were dying to do because it meant a few months of travel. Now and then, that is."

"How could you get away from your job?"

"I've decided to freelance," Gigi admitted. "Immodest as it sounds, I seem to be outrageously in demand. I'm never going back to a regular job. Whatever it takes to be a team player or a businesswoman, I don't have it. I'll work on my own things—and, oh, Zach—they can be just about anything I want!"

"You mean," Zach ventured, looking at the clear presence of a multitude of possibilities in her eyes, "you could do your work anywhere?"

"Don't get carried away," she remonstrated immediately. "I want a real home, I don't intend to be the female equivalent of the Ancient Mariner or the Flying Dutchman. And—now listen carefully to me, Zach Nevsky—there are two more things that you have to agree on. First, you can't be available to needy actors every night of the week. I'm not prepared to share you on a daily basis with your groupies. It's your own craving to tell people what to do that's the problem. You've got to discipline yourself, cut them down to three nights a week, and throw them out by ten o'clock. I'd like to limit you to two nights a week, but I know you too well, so this is another compromise and I want full and grateful credit for it. *Continuing* credit . . . never take it for granted. And second, Zach Nevsky, if you invite people for dinner, I want to know about it well before they show up, and if they don't know my name I'm throwing them out. Before they eat."

"I agree to everything," he burst out. "I'll sign any document you want, in blood."

"That won't be necessary," Gigi responded, trying to look away from the shape of his demanding, reckless mouth, wringing her hands together to keep from putting them in his. "I trust your word."

"What . . . what . . . name were you planning on using for dinner guests?"

"Gigi," she said, allowing him to look into her eyes and see his destiny flower.

"Gigi Nevsky?" he pleaded, entreaty as strong as passion.

"It seems to have a certain . . . inevitability . . ." Gigi whispered, looking at him helplessly. How had she been able to exist without him for an entire year? The rapture of uncomplicated love was wearing down her defenses.

"May I please come and sit next to you now? *Please?*"

"Oh, yes!" Gigi was prodigal with permission, unconstrained, blissfully released from the hard questions that she'd had to nail down once and for all before she could allow this difficult, miraculous, invasive man to once more take charge of her heart as he had so many years ago. Her first real love and, if truth be told, her only one.

"Darling, I'm taking you home right away," Zach told her exultantly, in instant command of the situation, now that he knew she wouldn't mind. "I love you so much I can't—damn, you left your car at the studio."

"No, I didn't. My father picked me up and dropped me off."

"You just . . . went out, like that, *without* a ride home?" Zach asked in disbelief. Nobody, absolutely nobody who lived in Los Angeles, would do such a wildly impetuous and reckless thing.

"What's so strange about it?" Gigi laughed, with a gesture of noble negligence.

How long, she wondered, was it going to take before it finally sank in that he'd met his match? She had to give him another few weeks to figure it out for once and for all. Men took longer to understand certain things than women did, Gigi thought, so transfigured by love that she was prepared to be amazingly generous.

Zach swept her up in his arms and kissed her lips over and over in front of everybody in the crowded pizza place, provoking a rising storm of cheers, hoots, and whistles. Gigi finally heard them and kicked mildly, in half-hearted protest. Zach finally came to his senses and carried her off to his car. Lying safely cradled against the vast warmth and strength of his chest, she felt so incomprehensibly happy that it was too much to cope with all at once. She turned her mind to details, her head began to spin busily with plans for the wedding, a really small wedding, just Billy and Spider and her father and Sasha and everybody's kids and Josie and Burgo and . . . oh, no!—Ma! She could manage Ma, Gigi told herself firmly. And now Sasha would be her sister-in-law as well as her stepmother. Sasha Nevsky Orsini and Gigi Orsini Nevsky? How on earth had that happened? Gigi dismissed the complications in free and airy jubilation. There were so many better things to think about.